IN THE SHADOW OF THE PEACOCK

'Muna – ' Something in her voice made Muna turn away, as if she was afraid of letting Bianca see her face. Bianca made a sudden decision. 'Listen Muna – Kassim has sent you something. He said to tell you to wear it, and remember the songs and dances of the long nights in Madore.'

A wave of beautiful colour flooded Muna's face, and the years seemed to drop away from her. Bianca saw Muna as she had been when she was sixteen. Youth had returned, and a girl's eyes looked up at Bianca, a young girl in the first flush of love. Bianca took a little packet from the pouch that hung at her waist, and put it into Muna's slim, reaching hands. Muna opened the packet, and a great round emerald, set in pearls on a gold ring, flashed green fire from her cupped hands.

'A unique blend of romance and reality ... I haven't read anything so evocative of India ... the writing is beautiful'

Norah Lofts

In the Shadow of the Peacock

Katharine Gordon

CORONET BOOKS

Hodder and Stoughton

Copyright © 1980 by Katharine Gordon

First published in Great Britain 1980 by
Hodder and Stoughton Limited

Coronet edition 1981
Second impression 1984

British Library C.I.P.

Gordon, Katharine
  In the shadow of the peacock.
  I. Title
823'.9' F

  ISBN 0-340-26521-3

Printed and bound in Great Britain for
Hodder and Stoughton Paperbacks, a
division of Hodder and Stoughton Ltd.,
Mill Road, Dunton Green, Sevenoaks,
Kent (Editorial Office: 47 Bedford
Square, London, WC1 3DP) by
Hunt Barnard Printing Ltd.,
Aylesbury, Bucks.

To Peggie, with love,
from the woman who came
to dinner

I

The evening was bright on the lawns that sloped from the house, the trees throwing long shadows like fingers pointing the way to night, though the sky was still golden and glowing, a rare English summer evening.

Rooks were making restless preparations for the night, settling in the trees near the stables, and rising again, vociferous with the day's doings. Down by the lake, which was hidden from the house by thick shrubs, the water fowl were also preparing for darkness. The air was full of the noise of birds telling of the coming of night in the warm afterglow of sunset.

At the top of the curving drive, the gates of Moxton Park were open, and the lodgekeeper sat at her window, peering between the curtains, listening for the sound of a carriage, ready to run out and curtsey and at the same time get a first glimpse of the occupants of the vehicle.

In the big house Jane Reid stood listening. She stood beside the french windows and watched the drive in front of the house, and could think of nothing but the woman who was going to come up that drive very shortly, the woman who had married her only son.

There was no sound of wheels yet. Only the rooks crying raucously and flapping their night black wings as they settled in the trees behind the stables. The evening was still and golden, a summer evening, warm and gentle.

'This is a splendid time for them to arrive. Look at the roses in this light! Murphy has done very well with them this year.' Her voice was brittle with false cheerfulness. Her husband sighed to himself, and getting up he went over to her and put his one good arm around her.

'You sound as if you would rather he had pulled up the roses by the roots and thrown them on the rubbish heap!'

His wife stood rigid in the circle of his arm.

'As Alan has done, Robert, as Alan has done with his life. Pulled it up by the roots, and thrown it on the rubbish heap.' She looked up at her husband and he saw the tears in her eyes.

'Now, Jane. You promised me when we received Alan's letter that you would welcome our son's bride. There is nothing we can do about this marriage, unless you would like me to make a dramatic gesture and disinherit him.'

To this remark, his wife did react, sharply, and he smiled at her.

'Exactly, my dear. Our only son. He has married, which is perfectly natural, he is bringing his wife home to us, and you are behaving as if you expect a funeral cortège instead of your son and his wife.'

'Robert!'

'Well, you do not look very happy. Come my dear, wipe your eyes, and remember your promise to me. Please?'

Jane leaned her head against his shoulder, and he tightened his arm round her, pulling her close. His other arm was missing, his coat sleeve neatly folded over and pinned. They stood, closely embraced, and the carriage for which they had waited arrived in the end, unnoticed by them.

But the lodgekeeper was rewarded for her vigil. She was the first of all the household to see the bride. The lodgekeeper was a woman of few words, and all she could say afterwards was that she had seen a real beauty, like an angel. When she saw the carriage passing, she bobbed a curtsey, and the young Master waved, and the girl beside him smiled at her. The woman stood staring after the carriage and did not see the wagonette that followed, with its sole passenger and a great deal of luggage. The wagonette was driven with a flourish by Bates, the young second coachman. The carriage, followed by the wagonette, went round a curve in the long drive, and was out

8

of sight, and the lodgekeeper sighed and went to pull the gates shut.

The beauty who had so delighted her was an enchanting Eurasian girl called Muna, newly married to the son of Sir Robert and Lady Reid of Moxton Park, in the county of Kent.

Muna, sitting next to her husband, had not looked at the green country through which they had passed. She had watched her husband's face at this, his homecoming. He is like a child, Muna thought, a child holding a bird in his hand, the bird of his happiness at being home. She had paid no attention to the green lanes of Kent, but now, as the carriage rounded the curve in the drive, she leaned forward and gasped as the house in the distance came into full view, enormous, L-shaped, sprawling its mellowed red bricks over nearly two acres of ground. She was not gasping at the size of the house. It was the rose garden that had taken her breath. A mild summer wind sprang up as they drove by, sending the roses nodding and tossing, spilling their scent on the disturbed air.

'Such roses! The whole air smells of roses. You did not tell me of the roses, Alan.'

'I knew that you would like the rose garden, my love. I kept it as a surprise. Muna, you forgot. You must speak English now, always.'

'Always? You wish me to forget my own language?'

'I do not wish you to forget your own language. I wish you to practise your English, so that English becomes your own language. I have not asked you to forget anything, Muna.'

'I know what I must forget, and I know what I must remember. So much to remember! I must remember that your father and mother were in India during the evil year of the Mutiny, and that they lived near Cawnpore. I must remember that your father lost his arm defending your mother and your sister from mutineers, and that although their servants were loyal and tried to help them, your sister fell ill during their escape, and died from dysentery. I must remember all these terrible things. I think of them often, and I think also that it will be very hard for your mother to take me as a daughter-in-law.'

'Nonsense, she will love you at sight. I know my mother.'

9

'I hope you are right. I hope that she has forgotten all that I must remember about her time in my country.'

'Muna, do not be afraid to meet my parents.'

'I am not afraid, Alan. I hope only that they will find it in their hearts to accept me. They could very easily hate me, just because I come from India. I must bring them many terrible memories.'

'No one could hate you.' Alan lifted her gloved hand to his mouth, kissing the tender flesh that showed in a triangle at her wrist. 'No one could ever hate you, and they will feel sorry for you, because I told them that your father and mother were both killed in front of your eyes. They also know that your father was English.'

'My father was English – you think this will make it easier for your mother, that her only son's wife is the illegitimate child of an English soldier and an Indian woman from the bazaars? Or have you not told them this?'

Alan's silence was her answer.

'Oh, Alan, what have you told them?' Why had she not asked him this before? In a few minutes they would be up at the house. Alan turned to her, frowning.

'I told them the truth. You are the adopted daughter of the Ruler of Lambagh State, your parents were killed by mutineers. They understand that your mother was an Indian lady.'

'But that is not all the truth! Did you tell them that I was a dancing girl, a Temple Dancer? No? Alan, are you ashamed of the person I am?'

'Muna, I love you; I have married you. I have told my parents all that should concern them. We will not discuss this any more.'

'Very well, lord. And I must speak English always?'

'It would be best.'

'Then if I wake suddenly in the night, and call to you in my own tongue, asking for love – will you know what I say?'

Her hand on his arm, her eyes looking into his, Alan felt the familiar sweet fire rising in his body. She was held in his arms, her laughing mouth silenced under his kisses, as the carriage drew up at the terrace steps.

The wagonette, rattling up behind them, sprayed gravel everywhere as the driver pulled the horses to a halt. The driver, Bates, a young man with a noticing, laughing eye, jumped down and went round to open the door, so that his passenger could take his outstretched hand and be assisted down.

Her skirts bunched round her, her hair escaping from her bonnet, Ratni, Muna's Indian servant, stood in the drive looking round her helplessly, her full lower lip caught between her white teeth. Bates looked at her with sympathy; she was as pretty and as plump as a little brown partridge and looked, with her melting black eyes, as if she might burst into tears at any moment.

Jane Reid, alerted by a discreet tap on the drawing-room door, raised her head from her husband's shoulder, and looking out, saw Ratni standing beside the carriage in all her confused disorder.

'Oh Robert! Dear heaven, surely – surely that cannot be her?'

Robert Reid saw the bunchy little creature and his heart sank. Stumbling in what were all too plainly unaccustomed shoes, skirts all anyhow, hair falling down – what a figure the girl cut. And where, in God's name, was his son?

He met his wife's desperate eyes, took her arm, and together they went out of the drawing-room and through the great hall to the front door, where Symes and the footman were waiting for them.

Jane Reid would have behaved well after her promise to her husband, no matter what her daughter-in-law had been like. As it was, she never forgot her first sight of Muna as Alan jumped down and turned to help his wife from the carriage. Like the lodgekeeper, Jane stood on the terrace, enchanted.

Muna did not seem to move like an ordinary woman. She floated down the carriage steps and stood for a second looking up at Jane and Robert, and then, as Jane started down the wide steps from the terrace, Muna came forward to meet her.

Muna. Muna the Beautiful, the Rose of Madore. Transplanted from her native land, wearing clothes that were constricting and strange to her, speaking a language only lately

11

learned, her poise was still perfect. Her beauty, in the gentle evening light, was enhanced, she was breathtaking. Her dark eyes smiling from beneath the brim of her grey silk bonnet, Muna looked with a question in those smiling eyes at her mother-in-law; and Jane forgot everything except that this girl loved Alan so much that she had given up her own country to marry him and come to England. She answered the question in the beautiful eyes by opening her arms and her heart together.

'My dear – you are home at last. Come in,' she said, and led Muna up the steps and into the house.

2

The day began with doves.

Muna woke, in the big four-poster bed, to the sound of their gentle crooning, and saw the pale light of an English dawn filtering in round the drawn curtains.

She remembered other mornings coming with the strident voices of the parrots when the scarlet dawn slashed the sky above the domes and minarets of Madore.

She recalled, against her will, the waking cries of the water birds, the soft sound of lake water lapping against marble steps, the blazing light of sunrise on the snow peaks that walled in the Valley of Lambagh.

But now, here in England, the day began with the voices of doves.

She turned in the bed, throwing out a seeking hand, but the space beside her was empty; Alan had gone. She stretched like a cat and then sat up, pulled the embroidered bell pull that hung beside the bed and, without waiting for the bell to be answered, scrambled out of bed. Naked and magnificent, she went over to the window and dragged the heavy curtains open.

The park lay there in front of her, the grass wet with dew, the trees – strange, different types of trees, unusual to her eyes – only just emerging from the morning mist, so that they looked like the dream skyline of some imagined country, black against the light, branches suspended above mist-hidden trunks. To one side she could see the walls of the stables about which Alan had told her, and the bricked walk that she knew, from his description, led down to the rose garden. She pushed up the sash window and leaned out, sniffing at the morning, filling her lungs with the sweet damp air, trying to smell the roses that had so enchanted her the evening before.

She was so engrossed that she did not hear the door open. There was a startled cry behind her, a gasp of indrawn breath, and the rustle of hurrying, starched skirts. A woman servant, her face scandalised, rushed forward, her skirts sounding like a flock of furious geese, and drew Muna back from the window to throw a velvet robe over her shoulders.

'Ma'am – ! The men are all about the grounds!' And you don't care tuppence, the maid thought as she helped Muna put on the robe. Beautiful you may be, but you're immodest, that's what. Her face was screwed up with disapproval but Muna paid her no attention at all. She tied the sash of the full-skirted dressing gown about her waist and said, 'My girl – Ratni, my servant?'

'I can't say,' I'm sure, Ma'am, she's not been downstairs yet. Sleeping I shouldn't wonder.'

'Fetch her.'

There was a snap of authentic authority in the quiet voice. To her own astonishment, the woman bobbed a curtsey and hurried out. Bessie, unexpectedly raised from under-housemaid to wait on the young master's wife, had fully intended showing an Indian woman where she belonged, letting her see that Bessie knew what was what and was not going to be put upon, or ordered about, by any coloured stranger.

Now, hurrying up the dark stairs to where the servants had their rooms, she wondered how she had got the idea that the young mistress was coloured. Her naked body had been the colour of cream, as fair as any she had seen, not like this brown savage of a maid of hers. Now here was a real dark one. Bessie had taken against Ratni – what a name! Like rats really – Bessie had taken against her from the moment that Bates, the second coachman, had shepherded the girl into the kitchen with a kindly arm round her, and a request to the cook for a cup of tea for the 'poor little creature – proper mazed she is by everything and not speaking much English neither.' His solici-

14

tude for Ratni had ensured that she had an enemy in Bessie. Bessie fancied Bates.

Now she tapped smartly on the door of the small room allocated to the Indian girl and went in without waiting. The girl, fully dressed, was sitting on the floor beside the bed, the blankets and sheets neatly folded and put on top of the pillows.

'Well! Well I never! Get up you silly thing. Whatever are you doing down there, and what have you done to your bed? Well, never mind about that now, you had best hurry. Your Madam wants you. Fine one *she* is. Naked as a fish she was, hanging out of the window for anyone to see. Anyway, she's got a sharp tongue and she wants you. You'd better get down there.'

'Please?'

Ratni had mastered very little English in spite of Muna's efforts to teach her as she learned herself. Now she stared, big-eyed and helpless, at the bustling, fat woman who spoke so fast.

'Oh come on, do – come, you silly heathen, I'll show you. Come with me. You're a proper savage and no mistake.'

Ratni, safely in Muna's room, burst into a flood of protesting Urdu.

'Wait.' Muna turned to Bessie.

'Your name? Bessie, is it? Very well. Now, Bessie, take this my servant, and give her my breakfast to bring to me. I will have coffee and fruit. Then I wish my bath. Show her where the room of the bath is, and speak slowly. She will understand. Ratni – go thou,' Muna broke into Urdu, 'and do as this fat one tells thee, and remember to listen with care, and answer in English. Thou canst do it, and it is needful that thou dost. I cannot keep you here, if you do not learn English. Go.' She finished her speech in English, and with a sweep of her velvet skirts, turned back to the window, leaving Bessie to curtsey herself out of the room, followed by a bewildered Ratni. Outside the door, Bessie rolled her eyes.

'Well, proper duchess you've got there. Bath! Show you where the bath is! Oh, my, what a morning this is going to be. Come on Rats or whatever your name is, you had better get

15

started. *You'll* miss *your* breakfast, that's for sure.'

After a breakfast of coffee, so weak that Muna wrinkled her nose over it, and apricots and peaches that she ate with astonished delight, it was Muna's turn to be confused.

There was the sound of clashing cans outside her room, a knock on the door, and Bessie and Ratni came in, carrying towels and a large, thick sheet. The sheet was spread on the floor and Bessie said, 'Is it all right, Ma'am, if I get Boots in with the bath?'

'Boots? Bath?'

Bessie, with a satisfied smirk, opened the door and a boy in a black calico apron came in, staggering under the unwieldy weight of a large, shining, copper bath. He put it in the centre of the sheet and then made several journeys with buckets of steaming water which he poured into the bath. After his third journey with buckets of hot water, he came in a fourth time with two buckets of cold water. Bessie waved him out, shut the door, poured a bucket of cold water into the bath, tested it with a plump elbow, poured in half the other bucket and stood back, saying, 'Your bath, Ma'am.'

All this time Muna had watched with growing horror. Bath! Was this their idea of a bath? Well, this was not her country, and she did not yet understand all their customs. She threw off her robe and stepped into the copper bath and stood, while Ratni, as confused as her Mistress, attempted to pour water over her with a tooth glass taken from the marble-topped washstand. Under Bessie's amazed eyes, Ratni ladled water over Muna as well as she could with this inadequate container, and then proceeded to bathe Muna 'as if she was a baby', as Bessie confided to her fellow servants below stairs later. 'Just stood there, she did, and let that heathen soap her *all over*. Then, if you please, she wouldn't sit down in the bath. Oh no! Said it was dirty, and must be thrown away, and more clean water brought to pour over her. Carried on something fearful when she found there wasn't any more water. I don't know what we're going to do, I'm sure, because from what I could make out, Madam has a bath twice a day. Boots'll give his notice, I shouldn't wonder. Can't say I blame him.'

16

But Boots was far from giving his notice. He'd never seen anything as beautiful as Muna in her wine-coloured velvet dressing gown, with her black hair cascading over her shoulders, and her big, dark eyes opening on him in astonishment. Her slow voice was as sweet as a blackbird's song. Boots ate his late breakfast in a dream, fully prepared to carry baths up and down stairs every hour of the day for the young Mistress.

Upstairs, the young Mistress was clasped close in the arms of her husband.

'Oh, my love, my beautiful love. You smell of jasmine and roses and sandalwood. Did you miss me when you woke? Did you get your breakfast?'

'Alan! So many questions. I have many to ask too. You smell of the outside, and of something – woodsmoke? Yes, I had breakfast, and the coffee was like the piss of horses, but the peaches were better than any I have tasted. My bath was dreadful. That kind of bath I cannot have again.'

'You must tell my father. *Not* about the coffee or the bath, but about the peaches. They are grown here and he is very proud of them. I will see about the coffee; it can be made as you like it. The bath, I do not know, possibly my mother – we will try – but, my love, you are happy?'

Muna did not know if she was happy or not. She was curious and full of interest in this new life, but happy? She did not know, so ignored the question. She demanded to know when she could go out and see the estate.

'And my horse? My beautiful Jasper? Is he well, and recovered from his voyage? Oh, unfair, you have seen him before I have. Why did you not wait for me, Alan?'

Alan had bought Jasper, a splendid black horse, in Austria; he was a present for Muna, and her most valued possession.

'I think you love that horse more than you love me. He is very well and needs exercise. I did not wait for you this morning, my love, because you were very sound asleep, and I wanted to ride.'

'You should have wakened me, you woke me often enough in the night –'

'You looked so beautiful lying there asleep, and I thought, just possibly you might have been a little fatigued? In any case, my love, you will see your horse, and before you ride you need a habit.'

'Habit?'

'Riding clothes. My mother will take you to the tailor.'

'Riding clothes? Yes, you are right, I certainly could not ride in these clothes. Alan, I hate these dresses and bodices, and petticoats, and tight things.'

'And yet you look so beautiful in them. Be patient, my love, this is how you must dress now. You will soon get used to your new fashions.'

Muna privately thought that having now worn these abominable clothes for nearly six months, she would never get used to them. There was such constriction round her supple, muscular waist that she was afraid to draw a deep breath. Her skirt swung out in a wide, stiff bell, with seven starched petticoats beneath it. She thought of her lovely drifting skirts of silk and muslin that had rested easily on her hips; of the short, close-fitting bodice, the *choli*, that had held her bosom, leaving the whole of her waist free from the upper part of her ribs to below the navel. No use to wear a jewel in her navel now! Even in the cold months in the northern hills of India, her robes of pushmina had been as light and drifting as her summer muslins, and yet so warm. She sighed, and put away the memory of her lovely, easy clothes. There were other things that were more important. Alan was speaking of his mother. They were to go to her.

'You are not now afraid of my mother, Muna?'

'I was never afraid of her, Alan, even when I had not met her. I was afraid that she would hate me.'

'Well, you see, you were wrong. She is longing to talk to you, get to know you.'

Muna was well used to people being anxious to see her. She remembered the cries of 'Muna! Bring Muna to dance for us – where is the Rose of Madore?' when the evenings had been long and late, and the rich men of Madore and other cities had been willing to pay in gold and jewels to see her dance, even for a short time. It had been necessary for them to be rich and powerful indeed if they wished her to dance for them alone, in those small, lushly ornamented private rooms upstairs in the house with the carved balconies, the most famous House in the Street of the Harlots in Madore. But like Madore, those days were far away, and in another country.

Now Muna followed Alan along the dark, cold corridor, where from gold frames, strange white faces peered out at her with supercilious eyes. The corridors in the house all seemed to be lined with pictures of men and women in extraordinary clothes, who all looked frozen, even in this summer weather.

Jane Reid was sitting in the conservatory.

'Muna! My dear child, you look rested. You slept well?'

How they all harped on sleep, as if there was nothing else to do with the night! Muna, who had spent the greater part of the night answering Alan's passionate lovemaking with her own, assured her mother-in-law that she had slept very well. Alan left them together, and Jane said, 'I thought we would sit together here because it is warm, and so many of these plants will remind you of India.'

A kind thought. The conservatory was beautiful, like a large indoor garden. Muna had never seen anything like it in her life. Warm and scented, and full of trees and shrubs and flowers that were totally strange to her. She sat gracefully erect, her full skirts spreading out from the tight waist that was almost handspan size. It was certainly warm in the conservatory, and the pungent smell of the orange trees and the strange tropical flowers was heavy on the steamy air.

Muna thought of the fresh breezes of Lambagh Valley, of the snow that never left the high peaks. Even in Delhi and Lahore the winters had been cold, and there had been the crisp sting of frost in the air. The summers on the plains of the north had burned with oven heat, and sand had lifted and blown around the thorn scrub and the dark neem trees and the mango trees with their dusty leaves. None of the lush vegetation in this house of glass reminded Muna of anything, except the orange trees. There had been groves of orange trees around the city of Madore, making the air sweet when the

19

blossom was thick on the branches.

Here in England it was August, and the sun on the glass roof of the conservatory made the air as hot and steamy as Muna imagined the south of India must be. She mopped surreptitiously at the beads of sweat that were forming on her upper lip and along her hair line, and smiled at her mother-in-law. Jane was pointing out various flowers, showing no signs of feeling the heat. She was delighted with Muna, and pleased to have somewhere so suitable to bring her.

'I want you to have everything as you wish it, my dear. Everything. Tell me if there is anything I can do to make you more comfortable.'

Muna found herself at home with this kind, elegant woman. She smiled into Jane's eyes, and told her exactly what she needed to be comfortable.

'It is the matter of the bath,' said Muna. 'If it would be possible to have a room in which I can have a bath?' She explained about the bathrooms in her own country, and then described the bath she had endured that very morning in Jane's house.

Jane laughed with her, and promised that something would certainly be arranged. She thought of the daily 'all-over sponge bath' in the rose patterned china basin on the washstand; of the weekly bath carried in to the bedrooms. She thought back to her days in India, to the big marble-floored bathrooms that were attached to each bedroom as a matter of course in the rich houses in India. Truly, England did seem a trifle behind India in some of its sanitary arrangements. Even Windsor Castle had troubles; it was well known that parts of it were unusable because of the cesspits and the smells caused by them. At least at Moxton Park, so far, there had been nothing like that.

Something would have to be arranged about a bathroom for Muna. Also Jane did not care for Bessie's behaviour. Bessie could go back to her ordinary duties. Instead, Daisy could look after Muna. Daisy was a big, kind-hearted country girl, untrained but very willing. She would be kind to that frightened little creature, Muna's Indian servant. Deciding to speak to the housekeeper as soon as possible, Jane looked up to see Muna looking at her with a puzzled expression.

'My dear?'

'I do not know how I should address you.'

Jane remembered that Muna's mother had been murdered in front of her eyes when she was a small child. Perhaps it would be difficult for her to use the name Mother.

'Muna, call me what you like. You are my dear daughter now. You have no idea how much I have missed my daughter.'

Jane had tears in her eyes, the shadowy figure of her daughter dead for so long, was suddenly vivid in her memory.

'Mother – the name comes easily and pleasantly to my tongue. I am as your daughter. I shall call you Mother.'

Jane smiled with pleasure through her tears, and both women were silent for a few minutes, surprised at how close they felt to each other. The silence was not an empty silence, for it seemed to Muna that a child was laughing, and calling somewhere nearby. She turned her head, listening, but Jane appeared to have heard nothing. She mopped her eyes with a cambric handkerchief, and stood up, saying, 'Do you think that you are warm enough now to brave the flower room? I would be so grateful if you would help me to arrange the flowers.'

Muna breathed the cooler air outside the conservatory with relief. When she saw the flowers that had been cut and brought in by the gardener, she cried out with pleasure.

'Oh, the roses! I cannot believe them. Smell them, so strong, so heavy! Those crimson roses are as large as my two hands.'

Embowered in flowers, Muna and Jane worked. Muna watched Jane and, declining to put on an old pair of kid gloves to protect her hands, soon achieved similar vases, full of flowers arranged exactly as Jane liked them. When they had finished arranging the flowers, one splendid scarlet bloom was left, and Muna tucked it into the heavy coils of her chignon. Her skilful yet casual action, as she tucked the flower into her hair without looking into a mirror, fascinated Jane.

'Muna, you must have done that all your life. You must have always worn flowers in your hair.'

Muna nodded. 'Always.' She thought of the spiky circles of

21

half-open jasmine buds that she had worn on festival days, when the temple gong boomed continuously and the smoke drifted across the face of the stone Goddess she served, hiding it from the worshippers as Muna swung her full floating skirts in ceremonial dance.

She remembered too the hibiscus flower she had picked in the garden of the Madoremahal to wear in her hair, the day she had gone to help Kassim Khan. Kassim Khan, now the Ruler of Lambagh State, had then been a fugitive, trying to steal a palanquin for Sara, his wife. One memory led to another. Through the mists of time she saw Sakhi Mohammed's eyes watching her, heard his deep voice saying 'I would be glad to find you smiling at me in Paradise', and prayed for his happiness in the Moslem heaven where she could never smile at him.

The heavy scent of the rose in her hair brought her back to the present, and her mother-in-law's worried face. Jane was startled by the tragic look she had seen clouding Muna's beauty.

'Come,' she said, firmly, 'come, Muna. Alan and his father will be taking a glass of wine. We will join them and make plans for a trip to town: you must have a habit. You will hunt?'

'Hunt? Hunt what?'

Jane explained the Hunt to Muna and watched her face change from astonishment to horror.

'With dogs – tearing the animal when it is tired? What is this animal. Fox?'

Jane searched her mind for explanations.

'Well, it is like – it is an animal like the jackal that you used to have in India – the fox is like a jackal but bigger. It is destructive, farmers hate it. It kills chickens.'

'So, it kills chickens. It kills to eat. No, I do not think I wish to hunt. In my country they hunt the tiger. Do I offend you, Mother?'

'My dear child!' Jane, who in her youth had hunted without thought and with enthusiasm, was confused but not offended. She looked at her beautiful daughter-in-law, smiled and said, 'Well, then, there will be no need for a regulation habit. There is a very good man in Charchester – we will go to him.'

'Man? For the clothes of women? This is very interesting, for some men also make clothes for women in my country.'

'Yes. I remember that. *Durzis*, the tailors were called. I used to have one working on our clothes. He was a most industrious man, sat all day on the veranda in Jaspur – ' Jane broke off, the very mention of the name Jaspur brought so much back. Imogene's little dresses being made by that thin, tired-looking man. What had happened to him? He had not come on that last dreadful day, the day when the killing had started in Jaspur. Like her precious daughter, he was probably dead.

'Mother,' said Muna, laying a hand on her arm, 'Mother – if I do not do this Hunt, why do I have special clothes to ride?'

She was relieved to see Jane turn back from whatever picture of the past she was recalling. She did not like to see the expression of sorrow on this kind woman's face.

'Well – it is not easy to ride in ordinary dress – we will have a tailored riding dress made for you.'

'Will it be many days before it is ready?'

'Oh, Muna – you are longing to ride. What do you wear in your own country, because you rode a great deal there, did you not?'

'I wore *salwar* and *khamis*.'

'I see. Well, of course, I do not know what those things are but I see no reason why you should not wear them here.'

'I could, indeed I would, but Alan says I must wear only European dress here. He thinks, I believe, that you and his father would prefer it.'

'What nonsense! I shall enjoy seeing you in your own clothes. Let me see you in this – in this whatever you said – this afternoon, after luncheon. Now, let us go into the library, the men will be having a great talk, I have no doubt. Let us go and disturb them.'

Muna followed her mother-in-law, as someone lost in a strange, dark place will follow a kind guide. She thanked her Goddess in her heart that in, Jane, she had found a friend.

3

Muna's life, from the time she arrived at Moxton Park, was a period which she was never able to measure in terms of days or weeks or months. It was a time by itself, unlike any life she had ever known. This new life, with its people, voices, scenes, and feelings, was something apart, like an island on which she was ship-wrecked. This strange island – on it, her life was a life within a prolonged dream, she accepted everything, no matter what extraordinary things happened. She was not afraid. She woke each morning to find herself back in the dream. The reality of life had been left behind in India. Through this dream world in which she lived, she had to learn to find her way.

After she had been at Moxton Park for two or three days, late in the night as she lay in her bed beside Alan's sleeping body, she felt very far away from everything she knew. That night even Alan was suddenly a stranger. She felt a wave of fear engulf her, and lay trembling in a darkness that was blacker than a starless night. Then, like a comforting whisper, she thought she heard the distant sound of flute and zither and the throb of a hand drum. How odd it sounded here, in this strangely furnished room! But how wonderful! She got up, and quietly, gently, she danced to the music, moving herself into peace and acceptance of this strange waking dream in which she had now to live. Finally the music sounded further away, and seemed only the noise of a wind in the trees, and she slipped back into bed without waking Alan, and slept at last.

She watched Jane as she had watched her teachers in the temple as a child, and learned very quickly. Thus one behaved in the dream world, with pleasing, calm dignity, with order, exacting obedience without raising one's voice. Everything proceeded in the house as if it had been set in its course like the stars in the sky. Muna liked the quiet orderliness of Jane's house. It reminded her of the way the High Priests lived, with their set periods for this or that ceremony, for prayer and meditation, eating and sleeping. She moved into position as Jane's daughter and right hand, as if she had been born for it. Alan was delighted. Just so had he imagined she would be, and he was glad to have been proved right. It was decided that Muna would be called 'Madam Muna', and the servants called her this always.

Muna spent days of exploration through the old house – through spare bedrooms, closed and musty, and a schoolroom with books and papers on which Alan's writing grew from childish roundness to maturity. She went up the wide staircase, up from one high-windowed hall to another, and then found a narrow staircase that went still higher, and ended in a dark landing and the servants' rooms, cold and cluttered with old, unwanted bits of furniture. Down again, to light and space, and Alan's sister's bedroom, kept as it had been when she had slept in it as a small child, before she went out to India and death. Muna fingered the ivory-handled hair brush, laid a tender hand on the small pillows on the frilled, white bed and went quietly out of the room, feeling like an intruder. She found a giant ballroom, with a floor as wide and cold and slippery as a frozen lake, and wondered at the sheeted sofas and chairs round the walls, the covered gilt mirrors, and the small stage at one end, where she supposed the musicians would have sat to play. She lifted the lid of the grand piano, and put her hand on the keys, and fled when the tuneless chords echoed in the empty room; and the eyes of the painted people in the gold frames of the pictures on the walls followed her running figure with cold stares.

Muna could understand nothing about this house. For her, rooms were there to be used, warmed and ornamented, to live in. For her, there were servants' quarters where the servants lived their own lives, outside the main house. For her, there were bathrooms and dressing rooms attached to each bedroom. To her eyes, this great, half-empty house was a mystery. Every day a different unused bedroom was opened, and aired and dusted – for what? For whom? No guests came to sleep in these rooms.

She spoke to Alan about the empty rooms and the big room with its sheeted furniture, questioning him. Alan said, 'It was after they came back – back from India in 1859. My mother closed her life to outsiders. She used to entertain a great deal when she was younger and before my sister died. After that – well, we have never had a Ball here since I left school, and she and my father do not live as they were used. Half her life died with Imogene.'

'Strange – to break her heart for a daughter when she has a son. It is something that your people do. We, our women, we wait for a son. A daughter is good, is beloved – but a son – Ah, that is the crown of a woman's life. It is difficult for your father, this half-closed house. I think it is sad for him.'

'No, I think he prefers it. He has his books, his horses, his fruit trees and the roses you love so much. My mother and my father are very close. I think my father is content.'

It was very strange to Muna but it was part of the dream. She bent her head and entered the dream, unquestioning, unknowing, wondering how long the dream would last. She was sure of only one thing. One day she would wake from this dream, and she was afraid of that day.

For the first week after Muna's arrival, Jane was 'Not at Home' to anyone. She was enthralled with Muna, and showed her relief and delight so plainly, that Muna laughed at her, saying, 'Mother of my husband, I think you thought he was bringing you a *houbshi*.'

'What on earth is a *houbshi*?'

'A black woman.'

'Well, no, I did not. In any case, if she had been as you are, it would not have mattered. But a friend of mine had an Indian daughter-in-law, and she was *terrible*.'

26

'Was? What happened? Did she die of cold?'

'No. The marriage was not a success, and she went back to India with a fat purse, and very glad they were to see the back of her. Oh, Muna, my dear, why did you suggest she died of cold? Are you cold? Why did you not tell me?'

'I am not at all cold. I am very well. This place is no colder than the hill country where I have lived.'

Jane was willing to listen for hours to Muna's descriptions of her part of India, the India of the north, the land of Maharajas and mountains, everlasting snows, rushing rivers, gold and scarlet *howdahs* on great, grey elephants lurching through narrow streets, dancing girls, temples and veiled women living contentedly behind high walls.

'But how did you ever meet Alan, with all those veils and walls and strict rules?'

'I was not a veiled woman,' said Muna, looking at her; then, 'But you know India, Mother – you were there.'

'Yes, but not in the north. Only in the south, and although we met the Raja of Sagpur, a most charming man, and went to his beautiful white palace, we saw very little of the real India as you describe it. Then, of course – ' Jane stopped for a minute, thinking back, 'Then we went to Jaspur, for a short time – ' Against her will, her eyes filled with tears. Muna put her arms round her, and held her tightly.

'Oh, Mother, in a bad hour you went there. You lost your child. My mother and father were killed like the Muslims kill cattle. Now we take each other, you and I. I know I am a poor substitute for the daughter of your heart, the child you will meet again in another life. But you – I can tell you with all my love, I think of you as more than Alan's mother, you are mine as well.'

'You are a dear, good child, my own dear daughter. Alan is a very fortunate man.' Jane blew her nose vigorously, looked into the lovely dark eyes that smiled through tears at her, and said with interest, 'Muna, you are a Christian?'

'I? A Christian? Nay, Mother, indeed I am not. I regret if this gives you pain.'

'No, Muna, it is none of my business. I would not have asked

27

you, but you said just now, with so much conviction, that I would see my child again in heaven.'

'No, Mother. Not in heaven. I know nothing of your heaven. I meant that you and your child are bound to meet each other again on one of your journeys back to earth, in one of your many lives – you do not believe this?'

'I do not think I understand it. You think there are many lives?'

'I do not *think*. I know. Do you think that we walk on this earth only once? No, Mother, we return many times until we have earned our final peace.'

'Muna, I do not think the Vicar would approve of me even *trying* to understand. Do not let us talk any more about life and death. You have tears in your eyes again. We are two very foolish women. The past is gone; instead of mourning it any more, let us go and see the roses.'

'The past is gone.' Her mother-in-law's words echoing in her ears like a knell, Muna followed Jane out into the sunlit rose garden. The past – always she carried Lambagh with her, even in this strange dream country. Always. The glow of sunset, the fall of a leaf, the cry of a bird, and she would be caught back, like a spirit blown on a homing wind, to the valley she loved. Love! At last, Muna thought, bending above the glowing, crimson roses, at last, perhaps, I have found the meaning of love, and what it is. To wake to a memory, to see a place that is beloved not only for itself but because it holds one person. To fall asleep and dream of the country because one must not even dream of the man; this must be love. The fire of the body, the ache of desire so easily satisfied, these things were nothing. Love was the only dream from which one never woke.

After that first week, came the first caller. Muna was showing Jane some of her robes, and was dressed in trousers and over-shirt of cream pushmina, with an open coat, high collared and heavily encrusted with embroidery, cream on cream, when the caller was announced. Lady Addison sent up her card.

'Oh, Muna – come down as you are. You look so beautiful.'

'Are you sure, Mother? Alan, I think, could be annoyed with me. He was very sure that I must wear European dress always.'

'What nonsense. In this house you wear what you like. In any case, Caroline Addison is my dearest friend. We have known each other all our lives. She will be enthralled to see you dressed like this. Those earrings – put those lovely jade earrings on. Ah! Now, come and show yourself off.'

So, it was dressed in the plain dress of a hill girl, with jade in her ears and her black hair in thick plaits, that Muna first appeared before Jane's best friend. Caroline Addison, kissing Jane, widened her eyes.

'Good heavens! Who is this lovely child? Part of Alan's wife's retinue? My dear, she is beautiful, and what a nuisance she is going to be when she grows up! In fact, it appears to me that she could easily be a nuisance immediately. What eyes, and what a figure. All the Mammas for miles around will have to put chains on their sons. Your daughter-in-law must be very beautiful herself if she risks having this one about her.'

'Caro, Caro – for goodness sake! This is Muna, my beautiful daughter – Alan's wife. And, as you obviously have not heard, she speaks perfect English. Muna, come and meet Lady Addison.'

Caroline Addison, seeing the smouldering warning in the dark eyes that looked up at her, smiled disarmingly.

'My dear – welcome, and forgive me. You do not know how young you look, dressed in those beautiful clothes. My tongue always gets me into trouble.'

Muna bowed her head over her hands joined palm to palm in the salutation of her own country, smiling as she did so.

'There is nothing to forgive. If your tongue puts you into trouble, I feel sure it also takes you out of trouble again. I must ask to be excused for appearing before you like this – if my husband's mother had not allowed it, I would have dressed in proper clothing.'

'Proper clothing? But what you have on is delightful. I wish I was dressed in these lovely gentle robes, instead of being tortured by a waist at least six inches smaller than my own. Your English is magnificent. I cannot imagine why we all thought Alan would come back married to a black savage with feathers for clothes, and red paint all over her.'

'Oh, *Caroline*!'

'*Now* what have I said?'

Muna laughed as she had not laughed in a long time.

'I should wear red paint – not all over, but just a round spot here, between my eyebrows to show I am a married woman. But my lord will not allow it.'

' "My lord" – how charming. Alan must be getting very above himself if someone like you constantly refers to him as her lord. Oh, Jane, dear, do stop looking like a disapproving angel and let us sit down. I am longing to hear all about this delightful girl. I hope you are not at home to anyone else?'

'I can very easily be not at home – I will tell Symes.' As Jane spoke, she pulled the bell pull, and when Symes came, she gave her order. Not at home to any more callers that afternoon.

'*Now*,' said Caroline Addison, leaning back with an expectant air, 'now tell me *everything*.'

Laughing, Jane looked at Muna.

'I know not what there is to tell,' said Muna, looking at the elegant figure on the sofa. This woman was powerful – she had the feeling of power and determination all about her. She reminded Muna of many of the Begums and Ranis she had sometimes danced before in her old life. Women who were accustomed to total obedience from everyone with whom they came in contact. But there was also kindness in the sparkling brown eyes, and humour, and it was not possible to resist her charm. It was not with a malicious or unkind curiosity that she was looking at Muna – and Jane, the gentle, sensible Jane, obviously adored her. So, Muna sank down in a drift of soft cream wool before the sofa, and said, 'What shall I tell?' like a village story-teller in India beginning a story.

'Well – first of all, how did you meet Alan, and where?'

The well-rehearsed story of the meeting in Lambagh, the instant romance, the life of a mountain State in the north of India – it was simple to tell, and Caroline listened entranced. Muna wondered what her listeners would make of the truth – that she was a *devadasi*, a Temple Dancer, and one of the most famous harlots in the north, and that Alan had taken her to his bed the first time he saw her dance, and had brought her to his parents as his wife four months later. She did not hesitate in her story, her voice went smoothly on, describing the life of the Palace in Lambagh, the customs of the hill people. Then there was a sudden interruption. A carriage rolled up the drive, a bobbing of raised, frilly parasols in the back.

Caroline made no secret of her instant curiosity. As the footman jumped down from his seat beside the driver, she peered through the window.

'Caro – for heaven's sake, they'll see you.'

Caroline paid no attention.

'It does not matter if they do. You are not at home. My *dear*, you will never guess who Symes is shaking his dignified head at – Mrs. Boothby's man – and there is herself, showing signs of argument. How very ill-bred. But who could argue with Symes! There they go. Very put out, no doubt about it. *And* the beauteous Mary with her, too. New bonnets, I judge. Dear, dear, how unfortunate, or not, as the case may be –'

'Oh, how vexing!'

'Jane! Vexing? To be rid of the Boothbys? I should be singing psalms of thanksgiving if I were you. Have you not suffered agonies of boredom every week for the last four years?'

'Yes, but it would have been better –'

'Better to get it over? Yes, I see what you mean. I am surprised that they came. The bruit is all over the county, so they must have heard. Such courage! Or curiosity, perhaps, to see who snatched the prize. Curiosity, stronger than a broken heart.'

'The girl had no *reason*,' said Jane, in an exasperated voice, 'Alan gave her no reason to imagine –'

'But that kind of girl, with that kind of mother, needs no reason. A compliment is enough, or one dance too many at a Ball. What is the mother's name? Rose? Climbing Rose, I think. She will have helped to feed her stupid little daughter's imaginings.'

During this interlude Muna had been sitting, curled in front of them, her chin on her knees. Now she looked up at the two older women.

'This – Mary? She had hopes of marriage with Alan?'

31

'Sharper than a sword,' said Caroline Addison, admiringly. 'Yes, she had hopes, but she had absolutely no foundation for those hopes.'

'She kept that hope for the four years that Alan was in India? That is a long time. She is very young?'

'No, she is not very young. She is going to miss her market if she does not hurry up. She is twenty-three or four, I believe.'

'Twenty-four? She has twenty-four years?' Muna spoke with genuine horror in her voice, 'Twenty-four years, and no husband. This is terrible. What were her parents thinking about?'

'Her mother is a widow, and has had very little luck with whatever she thought of for her daughter. Mary Boothby had two seasons in London, and came back with an empty net. I think she was too sweetly eager. She frightened the fish. Besides, her mother wanted a title for her. Let me see, wasn't Kerrigan dangling after her at one time?'

'The man was sixty, if he was a day!'

'Well? What of it? He wanted an heir, and then he would have left her in peace. But she had seen Alan again, a grown man by that time, and wouldn't look at Kerrigan, title and all. I do not know if Alan gave her any encouragement or not, but Jane, I should I think warn you that there is bound to be unpleasantness. That little Mary Boothby has a bad mouth and a worse eye, both inherited. If they were mares, I would not buy either of them.'

'Caroline, really! But there is nothing they can do.'

'They can say some very cruel things. Meantime, here is Muna looking at us with horror. Do you think we are being very unkind, Muna?'

'Unkind? No. Women talk thus in my country also. But one thing I do not understand. Why did this girl wait so long, assisted by her mother it seems, if there was no marriage arranged?'

'Because she had set her mind on him. I expect Alan said something complimentary. That would be enough.'

Muna nodded slowly, 'Yes. This kind of girl I know. They make big promises out of a flower thrown by a passing drunk man. Well, then, she can do us no harm. I would not like to have a broken heart, but I do not think that her heart is in this, or her body.'

'No,' said Jane, gentle Jane, suddenly fierce. 'No. her heart is certainly not in it. Only her ring finger. She looked forward to the day when Alan's father died, and she could be Lady Reid and inherit all this if she was married to Alan. I used to feel that she was making lists of all the silver and the pictures every time she came into the house. Horrible girl, with a mouth like a steel trap. Do not talk to me of her throwing Kerrigan over for love of Alan. Kerrigan hasn't a penny.'

'Well!' said Caroline, laughing, 'do you feel better now? How you must have suffered through those visits. I must tell you, though, that the horrible girl does not in fact need to look for money. I gather that is the only asset she has. Now, let us talk of something more pleasant. Muna, how do you manage to sit like that, curled like my little cat? Have you no bones in your body?'

'This is how I always sit. Perhaps my bones are different?'

'Perhaps I wear too many bones in my clothes, quite apart from those that God gave me. How old are you, Muna?'

'I have, I think, eighteen or nineteen years,' said Muna, raising her enormous dark eyes to Caroline.

'You have – I mean, you are eighteen? Or even nineteen? No wonder Mary Boothby seems to have entered the autumn of her years in your opinion!' She looked down at Muna, and suddenly, between the two women, the young girl with so much experience behind her already in her short life, and the older woman of a different world, a friendship was born. They smiled at each other, and Jane sat back with a sigh. All was well. Let Rose Boothby and her acid little daughter do their worst. Caroline Addison had taken to Muna, and nothing in the social world could harm her. Caroline would see to that. Her position in the county and her set in London were both impeccable. Muna would be well launched when she entered society.

4

Caroline was admiring the heavy embroidery on Muna's high collar, when Sir Robert and Alan came into the room.

'May we join you for tea, my dear? Caroline, how do you do – I see you have met our daughter-in-law. Here is her fortunate husband, not very much changed by India, I think.'

'Alan! My dear boy. Come and kiss me, and let me congratulate you on your marriage. You are indeed fortunate.'

Muna, standing, watched Alan talking to Caroline. She had met his look across the room when he first came in, and now waited to see what he would say in due course. Tea had been carried in, and Muna accepted a cup of pale China tea and sipped it with pleasure. This was something she did enjoy in England.

Sir Robert was talking to Caroline now, and Alan was free to cross the room to his wife. His eyes, looking her up and down, were angry.

'Muna.' His voice was quiet. 'Muna. Why are you dressed like this?'

Muna, for reasons of her own, answered him in Urdu.

'Because your mother asked me to dress thus. She desired me to come with her, dressed as I am, to meet her friend. They both say that they prefer this form of dress to the clothes that you would have me bind myself into. You met me dressed in my own form of attire, Alan. Has your heart changed? Smile at me, lord – your mother watches us, and she will be distressed.'

34

But Alan did not smile. He turned away and went back to Caroline and began to talk to her, leaving Muna standing alone.

A little flame of anger rose in Muna's heart. She welcomed it, for apart from the anger, her heart felt very cold. She put down her cup. She was still standing, a little way apart from the others, almost in the big bay window. If she took one step back, the sun would be shining directly on her, and would outline her figure. She waited until she saw Alan look over towards her, and then she spoke quietly, but clearly.

'Mother – may I give myself the pleasure of entertaining you as I have often entertained my friends in India?' Jane was smiling her assent, Alan was crossing the room. She ignored him, and stepped back.

The sun, striking through the window, and through her garments, left nothing hidden. Each movement was as graceful and beautiful as she had been trained to make it. Muna brought all her skill to this dance – the dance of the Temple girls, the dance to arouse the passion of a man.

Johnson, the second footman, coming in with a silver jug of hot water, stood in the doorway, caught in an enchantment he had never known. Robert Reid felt his blood rise and stir, watching the barely moving, curved body, the flick and gesture of hand and neck, bosom and hips. Alan, his anger forgotten, was lost again, his breathing quickened, his heart beating like the unheard drums to which Muna danced.

She sank, like a bird coming to rest on water, down to the floor, head low and arms outstretched to touch, with her hand, Alan's foot.

The others in the room did what they could to collect themselves. Johnson backed out quickly and shut the door. Robert drew a single, deep breath and looked at his wife, who was looking at him. Alan stood staring at Muna, and his desire, and her answer, were plain to see.

Caroline, a small smile on her face, sat as one does at a play, enjoying everything.

Alan took Muna's hand, and with no words, opened the french windows and took her outside, closing the windows behind him.

35

Caroline looked at her host and hostess and began to laugh helplessly.

'Oh, Jane – what a perfect afternoon I have had! Please may I beg another cup of tea? Thank you, Robert. Darling Jane, you look as if you should feel shocked. I trust you are not. That was a very graceful entertainment.'

'Yes, it was, was it not. I am not at all shocked by Muna's dancing, I am shocked by my son's manners. Please forgive him, Caroline, I do not know what came over him – ' Her voice trailed away, she caught Caroline's sparkling look, and both ladies began to laugh.

Robert rescued Caroline's cup from his wife's nerveless hand, and said quietly, 'I feel we have a tigress in our midst. Poor Johnson.'

'Oh, dear me, yes. I thought he was going to faint. I dare not ring for more hot water.' Jane laughed again and Caroline, her tea finished, stood up.

'My dear friends – I must go. But you will dine with us next week? I shall send you a card.'

In the bedroom upstairs, Muna, lying beside Alan on the big bed, said dreamily, 'There was a girl – I did not see her, but I heard of her. Would you have married her had you returned here alone? Her name is Mary.'

'Mary Boothby? Good heavens, no.'

'Could she have any reason to imagine that you might?'

'I suppose – women have great imaginations. Do not, I beg of you, begin to use yours foolishly.'

'Oh, I will not. Indeed I will not.'

'And do not make a show of yourself like that again, or I shall beat you.'

'Make a show? What a strange tongue your English is. I only danced for you. Why do you wish to beat me? Did you not enjoy my dancing, Alan?'

His voice was muffled when he replied, his mouth in her hair. 'You are a witch, Muna – '

'What is that?'

'A woman who practises magic. You enslave me completely.'

Muna arranged herself more closely in his arms and relaxed,

stretching like a little cat. Somewhere a silver gong was struck several times.

'What is that?'

'The dressing bell. We must get up.'

'Now? Does time matter so much, Alan? Time belongs to us. We have a world of time before us – we can make the moon stand still. Do you remember, Alan? We were not slaves of time in India. Kiss me again, Alan – kiss me once more!'

They were late for dinner.

Over the port, when Jane and Muna had left them, Alan's father, studying the ruby lights in his glass, asked, 'Alan – you are happy, are you not?'

'I am – I am indeed. You like her, Father, in spite of all I told you?'

'Perhaps I like her because of all you told me. She is a courageous and beautiful young woman.'

'Courageous?' said Alan slowly, his eyes looking into the past, 'Courageous? Yes. Some Indian women are very courageous.'

'I think your Muna is. It cannot be easy for her, Alan. She is making a place for herself here, and doing it very well. Never take her for granted. One more thing. I appreciate all that you told me. It was good of you, because it was unnecessary. I would not have known.'

'As your only son, father, I felt it right.'

'Yes. Well. But let it be, now. Do not feel it right or necessary to tell your mother. Let the story she knows stand . . . the adopted daughter of the Ruler of Lambagh, the child of an Englishman and an Indian lady. She is a simple woman, your mother, and she loves Muna already, which is wonderful because just before you arrived she was full of terrible doubts and memories – memories of your sister and the Mutiny. Muna's past life would be quite beyond her comprehension, I fear. So leave it now.'

'In point of fact, Sir, it was Muna who insisted that you be told.'

'Yes, said Robert, smiling, 'I said she was a courageous young woman. Now, let us go and join them. Oh, just one more

37

thing before we go. Remember how fortunate you are, and how generously Muna has given you her life. You are inclined to be critical of her, I think. Do not criticise.'

'I do not – I assure you father. But she – well, this afternoon – Father, she must not dance so, nor can she wear those clothes.'

'You cannot stop her dancing, Alan. It is part of her life, like breathing.' Robert stopped speaking, and began to laugh. Alan, taken off guard, first glared at him, was unable to sustain his glare, and laughed too.

'All the same,' he said finally, as they walked through to the drawing-room, 'all the same – imagine if it had been anyone but Aunt Caroline. The Vicar and Lady Charlotte, for instance.'

'Yes. Imagine. But very few people are privileged to see Indian dancing of that style, Alan. The Vicar and his lady would possibly have been fascinated. Come, Alan. Let your wife be her beautiful self. Do not try to change her.'

'No, Father, I will not try to change her.' Alan held the door open for his father, and looked across the room at his beautiful, alien wife. His words sounded sincere, and they were, but he was resolved that the episode of the afternoon must never happen again. It was the English side of his wife that he wished to encourage, he wanted to forget a great deal about India.

Alan had not told his father all his anxieties. He had imagined more than the Vicar and his lady arriving in the middle of one of Muna's dances. His imagination dwelt, in horror, on the possibility of some of his brother officers and their wives coming to call.

It had not occurred to Alan that Muna, brought out of India and her past left behind, could ever be an embarrassment to him. He looked forward to displaying his beautiful wife, visualising her amongst the wives of the Regiment. How she would shine, a moon of beauty with no rivals. There had been no question in his mind that any of her background could possibly be known.

It had been a terrible shock to him one Mess night, to hear two visiting Colonels discussing their period of duty in India.

He had listened idly at first thinking of some of his own adventures, and of how he had met Muna. But as he listened, he grew cold with horror and alarm. One of the seasoned old gentlemen was speaking of other adventures, a gleam in his eyes as he leaned towards his friend.

'Such women! None to touch them anywhere else.'

The other man nodded, smiling.

'No. No other girls like those. Trained to please a man. Never known anything like them – though, come to think of it, there was a little girl in Burma – '

'Ah – I'll wager anything you like to mention that no Burmese girl could come up to a girl I found in a House in Madore. She was like silk in the hand – you know what I mean? I've never been able to forget her. I was not a very young man even then, but by God, she made me forget my years – I was young for her. Still could be. Honey and fire. Now, what did they call her – that's it. The Rose of Madore. Cost a fortune for an evening, but worth every penny. Only a slip of a girl, but I'll never forget her.'

The old man fell silent, looking at his memories, and Alan sat beside him, his glass untouched, and iron resolve forming in his heart.

Muna, in European attire, her hair dressed by his mother's maid, would not, he was certain, be recognised anywhere as the famous dancer and courtesan of the North of India. She must lose her Indian identity completely.

As the first days passed, Alan therefore was not as delighted as he might have been that his mother and his wife agreed so well. Muna appeared to have made strong allies in his parents. The morning after Caroline Addison's visit, Muna rose from their bed when he did, and wearing her trousers and shirt and full, long skirted coat, was ready to ride with him. When he expostulated, she did not argue. She let him go, and then followed him on Jasper. Watching her flying towards him down the tree-shaded ride through the woods, her slender figure balanced as if she was part of the beautiful animal she rode, Alan found nothing to say. She had been measured for a riding dress, but until it was ready, Alan accepted the fact that his wife was going to ride with him every morning, if she so wished, in her national dress.

There were other things too. He found that, increasingly, in the house when the family was alone, Muna wore her own costume. The peacock silks glowed in the candlelight, lent colour to the soft faded chintzes and dark panelling of his mother's drawing-room, blazed in the green garden and among the roses. Muna walked in the rose garden with his father, as he had imagined that she might, but not looking as he had imagined she would. Her supple waist was free, her hair swung and blew over her shoulders in dark profusion.

'Why did we buy all those dresses in Paris, Muna? And the gloves and the bonnets and shoes? You never wear any of them!' he burst out at her one evening, when she came into the drawing-room glowing in gold embroidered brocade, roses bunched at her ears, her hair floating like a black veil.

His mother was there, and said, 'Alan, let her be. Those lovely dresses will be very suitable when we go about. But just now, in her own home, let us have the pleasure of seeing your wife as you first saw her. Why not? Is she not beautiful?'

Muna certainly was beautiful. Even Symes, waiting with portly dignity, dropped wine on the table. Johnson, who had never really recovered from Muna's dance, could not take his eyes from her, and Boots – poor Boots – was lost in a dream of paladins and knights and beautiful, dark eastern princesses. Even the women servants fell under her spell. Cook struggled with Ratni's English so that she could make special delicacies for Muna. Daisy adored looking after her, shook out the beautiful silks, brushed and combed Muna's hair to shining perfection, and regaled the servant's hall with stories of her beauty and charm. Murphy brought her roses, and there was not a groom nor a stable boy who did not worship her.

'Far from giving notice,' said Robert to his lady, 'far from giving notice, as you feared, my dear, they are hanging on her every word. I can hardly get anything done for me, and Boots is so bedazzled as to be virtually useless. He appears to do nothing but carry up cans of water to that room you have transformed into a bathroom for her.'

'Well, and why not?' asked his wife, wide-eyed, and Robert laughed and kissed her.

Now, watching Muna in her gleaming brocade, Alan said, feeling churlish, 'Well – I would like to have seen some of the dresses we chose, that is all.'

The following evening, Muna swept downstairs in a dress that was all oyster satin and lace, with tea roses in the low neckline. Her hair was coiled up on her small head, and pearls hung from her ears and encircled her throat. Alan stood staring at her as she advanced towards him.

'I please you?' she enquired.

'You are perfect, my beautiful wife.'

'So, to please you, I must dress always like this?'

There was something in Muna's look that he did not understand, but before he could answer her question, his parents joined them and in the general exclamations over Muna's appearance, the moment to answer, or question her, passed.

Sitting at dinner that evening, Alan felt completely content. This was how he had dreamed of seeing Muna, at his mother's table, candlelight gleaming on her hair and in her laughing eyes as she lifted her glass to drink. This was how he had longed to see her, softened, gentle, and English, her strangeness all gone.

A moth flew in and blundered about among the candles and the flowers on the table, and rose petals fell without sound. But the moth's wings, whispering against the candles and the silver bowls of roses reminded Alan of something – what? A feeling of terrible unhappiness came to him; he could not imagine why. For a moment he saw only darkness and flickering light, heard only the soft, blurred sound of the moth's wings. Then Symes caught the moth and removed it, and everything was as it had been. But it seemed to Alan that a cold wind had blown the moth into the room, and that night, when they went upstairs, he sent Daisy and Ratni away and helped Muna to undress, taking her clothes from her body, garment by garment, as if he was taking the petals from a flower, until he tossed the last bit of muslin and lace away, and held her naked in his arms, her hair streaming over his shoulder.

41

Deep in the star-shot silences of the night, he whispered against her throat, 'Wear what you like, my love, my love – only stay with me, love me as I love you – '

This time, she did not ask him the question that had troubled her since their first night together at Lambagh – 'What is love?' Instead she held him close, taking him warmly into the comfort of her body, while the night burned itself magnificently away.

In the morning, when she dressed in her soft, free-moving clothes, and rode with him, he made no argument. He never again told her what to wear, and Muna repaid him by only wearing her own costumes within Moxton Park. When they went visiting, or were visited she wore the dresses he had bought for her, and her manner was irreproachable. Jane, watching her controlled face, and modestly downcast eyes on these occasions, saw a completely different Muna, and wondered at her chameleon ability to become, to all appearances, a gentle, innocent English girl. Various members of their circle, who had heard stories of the exotic creature that Alan had brought back with him from India, found nothing to marvel at – just a beautiful, quiet girl, nothing unusual at all, except for her beauty, and were disappointed in their hopes for scandal. The women hissed behind their fans, but they would have hissed at any newcomer who had snapped up an eligible bachelor from among their circle. Muna moved serenely amongst them, and ignored them all, except for according them the gentle civility due to her husband's acquaintances.

5

The months passed swiftly. One day, Muna's trunks at last arrived, and were brought upstairs and unpacked one by one. The smell of sandalwood floated through the house, alien and exotic. Jane was given a length of silver brocade, so thick with embroidery that it could stand by itself, and a rope of pearls that made her gasp.

'But Muna – I cannot take these!'

'The brocade will make you a dress for a Ball – '

'The brocade perhaps. But these pearls! They must be worth a king's ransom.'

Muna shrugged, 'Maybe. I was given them once. I do not wear them, and you look beautiful with pearls. Am I not allowed to give my dearest Mother a gift? You hurt me.'

'Muna, I would not hurt you for the world. I love pearls and these are magnificent.'

'So, they are yours, with all my love. You must wear them. Pearls die without the touch of a body, you know. Wear them in your bed at night if you do not wish to wear them all the time in the day.'

'Yes,' said Jane, dazedly, regarding the gleaming rope, 'Yes, I could do that – '

She wore them in bed that night and Robert, turning to kiss her as he lay beside her in their bed, sat up and stared, affronted. 'What on earth is that – a chastity belt at this late date, my love? For heaven's sake take those things off – I feel as if I was in bed with the whole of a Sultan's harem.'

Jane giggled, and the pearls, removed, slipped forgotten to the floor. Later, Jane said, 'Dearest, I do not wish to sound vulgar, but am I right in supposing that Muna is a very wealthy young woman?'

'Muna is one of the wealthiest young women you have ever met, my love. She has a fortune. She owns a great deal of property in India, some of which she has, I understand, sold, but she has retained enough to bring her in very large rents. She and Alan will never need money, quite apart from what they will inherit from us.'

'But where did it all come from? The Ruler of Lambagh, I suppose, the Raja who adopted her. She has told me a great deal about his family, and of how he finally abdicated in favour of his nephew and left the valley to live in a town called Madore, with his Irish wife – now what was her name? Ah, Bianca, that is her name, the Rani Bianca. She must be a remarkable woman. She taught Muna to speak English and showed her how to wear European dress – it is thanks to her that Muna was so elegant and spoke so well when she arrived here.'

'Muna would be elegant whatever she wore, or did.'

'Yes, indeed – and are we not fortunate that it is so! Of course she is obviously used to great wealth, and good living, being brought up in the luxury of an Indian Raja's court. I expect she lived in a style that we cannot imagine – '

'I expect so. Are we to discuss her wealth, and her jewels and her way of life all night my love, or shall we sleep?'

Robert, knowing all about Muna's background, did not intend to explain to his wife where Muna's money and jewels had come from. He trusted that she would never find out. A street of brothels in several large Indian cities brought in a rich income indeed, and as far as he could discover, Muna owned other monies from the Lambagh States as well. He watched his wife picking up the rope of pearls and dropping them on to her table, and drew her close to him again when she got back into bed.

'Take the pearls, my dearest. But wear them at some other time. They make uneasy bedwear.'

Jane fell happily asleep, pearls forgotten, her head pillowed on her husband's shoulder. But Robert lay awake, seeing the pale gleam of the pearls on the table, and wondering what the future would bring. There would be children. What would they be like, Muna's children, when they were born? Would the dark side of the coin show itself, the rich Indian blood give him a dark grandchild? Would it matter? He remembered his school days, and shuddered at the thought of the torments small boys inflicted on anything they imagined was strange and alien.

Robert, staring at the coiled, gleaming pearls, had a bad night, and woke heavy-eyed, and in his nostrils was the faint delicate smell of another country, the aroma of sandalwood and spices.

That scent never altogether left Muna's bedroom, even after the trunks had all been unpacked, and their treasures of silks and brocades, ivory and jewels put safely away. She had put a small figure of the Goddess she had served and still worshipped in a corner of her room. The figure was so old and darkened with time that it was almost shapeless; only the faintest lines of a dancing woman could be seen in the lump of stone. Muna put a little lamp before the figure, a wick burning in scented oil, and she used to burn a pinch of incense before it, the smoke drifting up and wreathing over the barely discernible face of the Goddess.

Alan, coming into his bedroom, would be instantly reminded, against his will, of a great many things he would rather forget. But it seemed to him that the figure of the Goddess overshadowed the whole room.

'Must we have that figure there?' he asked, after a few weeks. 'It cannot be said to be an object of beauty.'

'It is the Goddess, Alan. I belong to her. I cannot put her away, even for you.'

'Very well. Leave her there then, my love.'

But try as he would, Alan could not grow resigned to the presence of the small, stone figure. He was very conscious of it; it seemed to cast a great shadow, far out of proportion to its size. Muna watched his eyes moving always to the Goddess when he came into the room, and after that she took the figure

45

and put it in another part of the room, where he could not see it so easily, and Alan seemed then to forget all about it.

As Muna settled into her dreaming new life, incorporating into it all the memories of her past, like islands of reality in the dream, so her maid, Ratni, settled down too. Her English improved very quickly, and unlike her mistress, she loved to wear her new fashions. Her black, slanting eyes sparkling above rosy cheeks, she went lightfooted about her duties, her skirts always freshly ironed, her waist accentuated by the broad sash of the starched white aprons she wore.

Bates, the second coachman, was never very far from her. He seemed to have business in the kitchen whenever she was there, and her laugh, heard from a distance, would make him lift his head and listen, no matter what he was doing.

Fat Bessie had not fallen under Muna's spell, and she hated Ratni. She watched her like a snake watching a bird fluttering out of reach.

She had had hopes of Bates. She had put herself out, making sure that he had cups of tea, and great slices of Cook's rich plumcake when he came into the kitchen, and she had some-times been able to catch him outside, pressing her great, fat body against him, snatching at his hand – and he had not always pushed her away. She had never managed to get him into the loft, but once or twice he had kissed her moist, cling-ing mouth, more to be rid of her than anything else, though with the incredible conceit of the selfish and stupid, she had not known this.

Now, Bessie watched Bates with Ratni. Bates did not touch Ratni. He barely spoke to her, but he watched her all the time, like a man bewitched. When Bessie followed him out and pushed herself into his arms, he moved away, saying, 'Oh, for the love of God, Bessie, behave yourself. Let me be.'

Bessie grew thinner, and her little, light eyes moved like quicksilver from one enchanted face to another when Ratni and Bates looked at each other.

It was after Muna had been in England for three months that Bessie, sleepless in the nights, came to her decision.

For two mornings, she did not come down for work, complaining of feeling ill. On the third morning, Cook heard her retching, and waited for her to come from the outhouse.

'Well, my girl? What's this, then? Are you in a condition you shouldn't be in?'

'Don't know what you mean, I'm sure. What condition I am in is my business, isn't it? I'm not a tweeny of twelve, you know, Cook.'

'No, and that's the truth. Great lump of thirty or more, you are, and old enough to know better. Are you trying to tell me you've got put in the family way?'

'I'm not trying to tell you anything. You mind your own business, Cook, and leave me be.'

'My name is Mrs. Dooley, and I'll thank you to remember that. *And* it is my business I'm minding, if I have to do all the vegetables single-handed, and set the table for the servants' hall. Don't you get uppity with me, Bessie. You pull yourself together, or I will have you up to Mrs. Whickers.'

Bessie was late again for two more days, and did practically no work, groaning and retching in the outhouse, and Cook stamped off to Mrs. Whickers the housekeeper. In due course, Bessie was standing in front of Mrs. Whickers, twisting her apron, and trying to squeeze tears out of her cold little eyes.

'Not my fault, Mrs. Whickers. Promised me marriage, Bates did, and if he'd not said about marriage, I'd never have let Albert Bates near me. Been a good girl all my life I have, which Albert Bates could say, *if* he would.'

Mrs. Whickers took the trouble to Jane, who was distressed, but not for Bessie.

'Oh, Mrs. Whickers! Not Bessie and that nice young Bates! I cannot but wish that I had never agreed to her being engaged. Yes, yes, I know she had good references, but I've never liked her, and she is not by any means good enough for Bates. In fact, if he *did* interfere with her in any way, he must have been drunk.'

Mrs. Whickers blinked and blushed, and Jane sighed, and said sadly, 'Well, if he has put her in the family way, he'll have to marry her, I suppose. But I really cannot believe it. I'm going to speak to Sir Robert.'

Robert had a trying interview with Bates, and came to see Jane, finding her arranging flowers with Muna.

'My dear – Bates swears he's never laid a finger on her. All he ever did, when he couldn't avoid it, was kiss her. Tell you what, Jane, I believe him. Another thing – he's in love.'

'Oh, good gracious. More complications. With whom does he think he is in love?'

Robert looked at Muna, where she stood arranging one of her flower pyramids.

'That little girl of Muna's. Ratni.'

'Well! Well, I can understand that. Much more likely than that great, blousey Bessie. Bessie smells so horrible.'

Robert shook his head at his wife, 'Whether Bessie smells or not, she's levelled a pretty serious charge against Bates. What are we going to do? Sack him? He says nothing will make him marry Bessie.

'I entirely agree with him. I think she is lying. I feel much more inclined to sack her. Oh, really, Robert, why do we have to have this annoyance in the house at this particular time?'

Muna looked up from her flowers. 'What is this annoyance? Bates is one of the drivers, and Bessie is that fat woman who was my maid for one day? She is trying to tell you that she is pregnant, and that Bates is the father? This is not possible. No. For one thing, she is not pregnant.'

'How do you know, Muna?'

'I know men and women. That fat one is lying. She is making a long face, and pretending to throw up in the mornings, but she still has her courses of the moon – she has it now. As you say, Mother, she smells, and that is one of the things of which she smells.'

Jane blushed scarlet, and Robert stared, fascinated, at his daughter-in-law. Muna, quite unconscious of the sensation she had caused, continued unperturbed, 'As for Bates – he would not touch that great, fat thing. He greatly desires my Ratni, and she is sick for him too.'

'*Sick* for him? You cannot mean –¹

'No, my dear wife, calm yourself. She does not mean what you fear. She is using a figure of speech which implies that

48

Ratni is also in love with Bates. What an attractive fellow he must be to the fair sex! Well, what do you want me to do? We cannot have all this upset going on. Perhaps both Bessie and Bates had better go.'

'Oh no, Robert, that would be very unfair. Leave it for a day or two. *I will* see Bessie.'

Bessie, summoned to her Mistress's day room, was alarmed to find both Mrs. Whickers and the young mistress there as well. She bobbed a curtsey and stood awkwardly before Jane, while Muna sat, bolt upright, in a chair beside her mother-in-law, her eyes fixed on Bessie.

'Now, Bessie, what is this I hear? You say you are expecting?' Jane's tone was formidable.

Once again, Bessie tried to squeeze out a tear, but failed, and Jane said firmly, 'Do not be ridiculous, Bessie. You are not weeping. In fact, I do not believe you are expecting a child at all. How long do you imagine you have been pregnant?'

'About three months, m'lady,' quavered Bessie.

'Well – how do you know it was Bates?'

'M'lady!' Bessie quivered all over with insulted virtue.

Muna spoke, 'Will you excuse me if I say something, Mother?'

At Jane's nod, Muna turned to Bessie.

'You are not expecting a child. Do not ask me how I know this because you will not like the answer. You are trying to trap a man into marriage, a man whom you have often tried to seduce, and who has always refused you. You are a fool, Bessie, and a liar. This man is not for you.'

Bessie turned a deep shade of scarlet. Her little eyes burned as she turned them on Muna, and in her rage, she forgot all discretion.

'Ho! Isn't he indeed? And what's it got to do with you anyway, you and that black savage of a maid of yours. Going to get up to some of your monkey business are you? I know what you do up there in that smelly room of yours, burning God knows what in front of that filthy image. Don't you try anything with me, Madam; I'll take you to the police, I will. As for Albert Bates, he'd better look out – I'll have the law on him, see if I don't, when the child is born. Nice goings on in what was supposed to be a gentleman's residence till you lot came here with your outlandish customs.'

Mrs. Whicker tried to hustle her out of the room, but she was fairly shouting now, a thread of spittle running out of her mouth.

'No better than what you ought to be, that's what we all think if you want to know – with your body all showing and that black image up there –'

Jane rose to her feet.

'Bessie, that will do.' Her voice was like a knife. 'You are insolent, and I will not have you in my house for another day. You will go upstairs and pack, and the wagonette will take you to the village tomorrow morning. You will have three months' wages, and a reference saying you are a competent under-housemaid. Go away to your room at once. Do not let me see you about the place again, in case I change my mind about your reference. Get out of this room.'

Bessie left in silence, followed by Mrs. Whicker, and Jane, with a deep sigh, turned to Muna and said, 'What an odious creature! I am glad to be rid of her. I am sorry that you have seen such an exhibition. Would you be so good as to ring for Symes. I must have the windows opened.'

'I will open them, Mother.'

Muna crossed to the windows and flung them wide. A wave of fresh garden air poured into the room, and Muna took a long breath of it before she turned back to Jane.

'As this concerns me, through Ratni, I am glad that I was here. You have the attack of a lioness when you are angered. Do not ever be angered with me, Mother!'

'I feel that will be very unlikely, my dear. Now, let us forget that horrible woman, and talk of other things.'

'Would you like to stroll in the garden? There is a rose I want to show you.'

'My dear Muna, what an excellent thought. The roses will be over so soon. Let us go and fill our eyes with them.'

Smiling, Muna followed her mother-in-law out into the afternoon sunlight. They walked among the roses, and Jane was soon calm and good tempered again, though Muna herself felt deeply disturbed. Hatred was a bad and dangerous emotion, and hatred had struck at her this afternoon.

That evening there was a disturbance in the kitchen. Bessie, her packing soon finished, her bag strapped and locked, went boldly down for her supper, to find that Cook had arranged to send it up to her. Ratni was in the kitchen, sewing buttons on to Cook's working aprons when Bessie marched in, and Bates was sitting at the table. Cook, a little flustered, saying, 'Well, Bessie, I didn't think, seeing how things are, that you'd be down, so I have readied you a tray,' pointed to the tray, neatly arranged, which was on the table near where Ratni was doing her sewing.

'I'm not sitting up in a cold bedroom, eating a cold supper to please anyone,' snapped Bessie.

'Well, as you're down, I'll put it on the table with the rest — we're all having a cold supper tonight.'

Bessie interrupted her, '*Just* a minute, *Mrs. Dooley*, if you please. What's that black heathen doing near my food?'

'Now, Bessie, don't talk like that. She's sewing on my buttons for me, that's all she's doing. Don't you start trouble, Bessie Flagg, or I'll send you out. I will not have trouble in my kitchen, and that's final. Sit down and eat your supper.'

'Well, I'm not touching a mouthful of anything *that* one has been near, and *that's* flat, too.'

'Go without, then,' said Bates, raising his eyes to Bessie's face, which slowly flushed scarlet as he added, under his breath, 'You've got enough fat to live on for years, anyway, without eating for a month.'

Bessie turned away from him, and stood lowering over her tray, her great bulk planted firmly in the middle of the kitchen.

'Bates!' called Mrs. Dooley, alarmed. 'You behave yourself too. Don't provoke her. Now, Bessie, give over and sit down, and let us all get on with our suppers. Stop glaring like that, you silly girl. Ratni hasn't done you a mite of harm, you know it. Now sit down.'

Bessie's answer was to pick up her cup of soup and fling the contents full into Ratni's face. Ratni dodged, and the liquid in the cup splashed down, and lay in a puddle on the floor.

51

One of the yard dogs, beloved of Cook, was lying at ease in front of the kitchen fire. He jumped up as the contents of the cup fell beside him and, nothing loth, proceeded to clean up the puddle with an enthusiastic pink tongue.

Bates got up and put his arm round Ratni, who was looking at Bessie in astonishment, scrubbing at her clean apron.

Cook got up very slowly, a figure of controlled rage, and said firmly, 'Very well, Bessie, that will do. Up to your room. I said I won't havè trouble here and I meant it. I'll send you something up so you won't starve – *not* that you deserve it.'

'Did I deserve *that*, do you think?' Bessie pointed, and they all turned to look at the little brown and white dog. He was moving slowly in a circle, his legs stiff. Suddenly, he howled and his body went into a terrible convulsion, his stomach contracted and his back bent like a bow. Twice this dreadful convulsion took him, and then he straightened out, moaning. His legs worked, as if he was trying to run away from his pain, his eyes glazed and he cried again, feebly, and lay still. Bates bent over him, and looked up, his face white.

'He's dead,' he said.

'There!' said Bessie, shrilly. 'There! Thank you, Mrs. Dooley. Don't bother about me. I'm going now. I wouldn't stay here to be murdered for anything. I'll send for my bag, but stop here another minute, I will not.'

The door slammed behind her, and none of them had moved.

Ratni was the first to speak, 'What – I am not understanding what she does?' Her voice was piteous.

'Never you mind, my love. There's something funny here – we should have stopped her going. Here, Cook, I'm going to get the Master. Don't touch anything – I don't like the looks of this.'

'I won't touch anything. What an awful thing – poor little Dash, what an end!'

Bates, wondering to himself what would have happened if that liquid had landed where it was meant to, in Ratni's open eyes, hurried out.

Robert, brought down to the scene of disaster, looked closely at the dog, listened to Bates' description and said, 'It sounds like arsenic – but how did it get into the soup?'

'It's my belief that she put it in herself, hoping it would look as if Ratni had done it. She was standing right over the cup, and none of us could see what she was doing.'

Cook chimed in, 'Yes, you're right, Bates. She could have done anything when she was standing there with her back to us. No one else was near the cup except Ratni here, and she had her hands full of sewing. My word, what an awful thing. Whatever would have happened to poor Ratni if that stuff had got in her eyes?'

Leaving the kitchen buzzing, Robert went back upstairs and told his family what had happened.

'I suppose we'll have to get the police in.'

'Oh no, Robert, do you think so? I feel it might cause terrible trouble, you know what the police are like. After all, only the dog died, poor thing.'

'If Bessie goes to the police herself, Ratni could be under suspicion – she was the only other person who could have put anything into that cup.'

Alan shook his head. 'No one could imagine Ratni doing such a thing.'

'No one here, in this house, Alan. But we know her. A great many other people do not. If Bessie starts spreading stories, it could be very bad for Ratni.'

'I do not think she will dare to go to the police, because I think she did it herself. No, Father, I think Mother is right. Let us leave the whole thing. I doubt if we will hear anything more.'

Robert agreed in the end, but was not happy about the situation. Muna said nothing, and the conversation was changed. The next day, Mrs. Whicker was told to warn the servants to keep quiet about what had happened, and the whole affair was, it appeared, over.

A month later, Ratni was baptised a Christian, and a week after that, Bates and Ratni were married. Ratni wore a white dress, and a white silk bonnet with fur round the edge and a bunch of orange blossom on one side, and looked charming; she moved into Jim Bates's cottage and continued to work at the

Hall, and was ecstatically happy, as was Bates himself. Muna had watched Ratni's astonishing transformation into a church-going wife, and had added this to the rest of the strangeness of the dream world in which she lived. But she rejoiced in Ratni's happiness, and was glad that the girl had so easily learned to live a new life.

Ten miles across country, on the other side of the village, Bessie was re-employed in a large, pretentious house. Bessie's sister worked there, and the Grange was owned by the widowed Mrs. Boothby. Mrs. Boothby, who regrettably gossiped with her servants, was enthralled by Bessie's stories of the goings on at Moxton Park. She told her daughter, and Bessie was promptly elevated to the post of Mary Boothby's personal maid. Mistress and servant had much in common. Mary Boothby got every detail of the daily life of Moxton Park from Bessie – and never tired of hearing the descriptions of Muna's way of life, Muna's clothes, Muna's riches. Soon, here and there, were little anecdotes, as poisonous as little snakes, crawling through conversations in houses unfrequented by Sir Robert and Lady Reid. Anecdotes about their daughter-in-law who, however innocent she appeared, was, it seemed, not quite as she looked. Tales of how she was really a native, of how she allowed the men servants to take liberties with her person, of her strange incantations performed before an idol, of her dangerous, murderous servant, black as the devil with eyes like smouldering coal – the little muttered stories grew and spread. Caroline Addison heard one or two of the stories and, after thought, sent out invitations to a Ball, to which all the county, including the Reid family, was bidden.

Muna, in one of her French creations, fresh and charming, and so beautiful that no woman in the room could compare with her, was a sensation. The Reid family were so obviously happy and proud of her, that the gossips paused and stared. Two foreign Royalties were present, and their Ladies. Muna was presented to them, and behaved as if she had lived thus all her life. The gossips saw, and registered, and were impressed. Mary Boothby, dancing with Lord Kerrigan, heard complimentary comments on the beauty and charm of young Mrs.

Reid, and developed a headache that sent her home early to take to her bed.

Caroline Addison had seldom given a more successful Ball.

'I think,' she said to her husband as they stood at the top of the curving staircase, saying goodnight to the last of their guests, 'I *rather* think that that will hold them for a while.' She wondered if any of the tales had reached Jane's ears. Looking at her friend's contented face, she thought not. But Muna – Caroline wondered about Muna. Muna, saying goodnight, had smiled at her with a look of gratitude in her eyes that seemed excessive for a young woman thanking her hostess for a happy evening. Muna had heard something, Caroline decided, and regretted the fact. She went to bed thinking unrepeatable thoughts about Mary Boothby.

Mary Boothby, telling Bessie of the evening, was rewarded by sympathy, and various suggestions, which she spent some time considering. She was recovered from her sudden malaise two or three days later, and delighted her mother by receiving the attentions of Lord Kerrigan more kindly than she ever had before.

6

When Alan and Muna took their morning rides, Muna found that the climate of the country was changing. They rode beneath trees that flamed with autumn, but there was no warmth in the sun. Then the leaves turned brown and fell, and were swept from the paths and the lawns, and burned. The columns of smoke rose straight into the still air, until the last days of the month, when a wind, colder than any wind that Muna had known in England, blew the smoke into long trails that weaved and clung among the bare branches like torn veils.

She had not wished to ride that morning. Alan, after riding with his father, returned to find her lying, ashen faced against her pillows.

'My love! You are ill?'

'No. At present I am dying, I hope. But, in fact, I am neither dying, nor am I ill, and I am very proud. I carry your son, lord.'

Alan, kneeling beside the bed, pressed his mouth into her hand. Then he asked, 'Have you told my mother?'

'Of course. She brings me something soon, herbs and I think lemons and honey made up into a draught to stop this sickness. I trust it does stop. I do not care to vomit all the time. Your mother says it is a wonderful remedy, and is made by some wise woman who is also a midwife, and who is skilled in the use of herbs.'

'Oh – Bella, the woman who lives on the edge of Grants Meadow. Mother goes to her often, and uses her remedies for everything. She has a reputation – ' Alan was frowning, trying to remember something. When was it that he had seen Mary Boothby riding across Grants Meadow? A week ago, or earlier? Some little, carking thought made him go to Jane, and ask her if she was sure that Muna was pregnant.

'Yes, of course I am sure, my dear boy. She has been for nearly two months, but she wouldn't let me tell you until *she* was sure. Why?'

'Well – ever since that ghastly business with the poison and the dog, I have been worried. You know where Bessie now works, of course?'

Jane nodded, and Alan was not surprised. His mother did not gossip with servants, but she knew every single thing that went on in the village and the surrounding houses. Whatever she knew, she kept to herself, and he supposed that was why people confided in her, and brought her scraps of news, interesting or otherwise.

'Well,' said Alan, 'I saw that little horror Mary Boothby riding away from Grants Meadow the other day. You know what they say about Bella?'

'Yes,' said his mother, calmly, 'I know what they say about Bella – exactly what they say about any woman who lives alone and picks and dries herbs: that she is a witch. I also know that Mary Boothby is consumed with jealousy of Muna, and has been spreading some very horrible stories about her. However, the stories do not matter in the least. Your fears about poison only matter if your conscience is not clear. Is it, Alan?'

'As clear as any man's can be.'

'Alan, tell me what passed between you?'

'Nothing, I swear, of any importance. There was a Ball at the Skermers; she was there. I had met her several times at various soirées and Balls. I danced with her. It was a week or two before I was due to leave for India. I dare say I was sentimental, I seem to remember telling her – oh, something about remembering her lovely eyes when I was far away. You know the kind of thing. I did not see her again before I left. If she chose to build something on to that bit of nonsense – '

'You did not write to her, or send flowers?'

'Certainly not. I tell you, Mother, I never saw her again, until the other night at Aunt Caroline's Ball, and then I only bowed. Not wearing all that well, is she?'

'You have set yourself a rather high standard in women's beauty, Alan. Muna is very lovely. As for that wretched Boothby girl – she stayed away from Town, and spent all her time coming here with her fearful mother. She asked after you tenderly each time she came, she bombarded me with flowers and fruit, thereby mortally offending Murphy. She was so sweet, such an affectionate, daughterly girl, that your father took to fleeing to the library whenever she appeared, leaving me to be bored to distraction and annoyed past bearing, watching the lips drip honey, and the eyes taking a careful inventory of everything she would have if your father and I dropped dead directly she had married you.'

'All that because I said I would remember her eyes?'

'She is an excessively stupid girl. I absolve you of blame, and I do not understand why you should be so worried because she was riding away from Bella's cottage.'

'I suppose it is the association between her and Bessie, and I did not like the look on her face.'

'I never liked the look on her face. Her eyes may be beautiful but her mouth is the mouth of a shrew. How did you know that Bessie was working for her, Alan?'

'Bates told me. He said Ratni was doing an errand in the village, and she saw Bessie walking with her sister, who is housemaid in the Boothby establishment. He's worried for Ratni's sake, of course, to find Bessie still so close. But she doesn't seem to have done anything more about that horrible affair. All the same –'

'Alan, stop stamping about the room, you make me nervous. Go away and find your father, and tell him the good news. Do not worry about Muna. We will not let anything happen to her.'

Alan did not go to his father, he went straight back to his wife and stood looking down at her with a frown. Muna looked at him and caught her breath. 'Alan, you are angry with me.'

'Yes, Muna, I am. Why did you not tell me that you were

having a baby before this? You risked riding with me – you might have lost the child!'

'You have laughed at me, if you remember, these last weeks, saying I was riding like an old lady – going round instead of over, you said; now you know why.'

'But if you had told me!'

'I was afraid.'

'Afraid – of *me*?'

'I was afraid you would not want the child, Alan – '

He kissed her mouth to silence, feeling against his cheeks her tears. 'My dear love – what stupidity is this? But they say women have foolish fancies at this time. Is there anything you long to eat, Muna?'

Muna looked at him in astonishment. 'Eat? Ugh, Alan, do not ask me to eat; let us wait for your mother's drugs. Lord, you are pleased? You do not wish me to – to have the child removed?'

'What in heaven's name – '

Muna's hand on his mouth silenced him. 'There are ways. For your sake and for the sake of your family, I would do it. But you truly wish this child?'

'Of course I want my child – our child! Muna, lie back and stop talking nonsense, be good and do whatever my mother says. You are doubly precious now, if that is possible: and I do not understand how you could imagine I would not want my child. What kind of a monster would I be if that were so? You say it will be a boy – I do not care. I imagine a daughter who looks like you – and I am very content.'

'It is a boy – and, Alan, now I am going to vomit again, I think – '

Alan, with an agonised look, rushed from the room, calling for Daisy.

Meantime Jane, Bella's mixture in a bottle in her hand, found herself more worried than she had admitted to Alan. She took a cup of milk, mixed a little of the potion into it, and, feeling like a murderess, gave a saucerful to one of the stable cats. The cat settled down to drink it with great enjoyment, and waited hopefully for more, while Jane held her breath.

After twenty minutes, the cat lost interest, and walked away. '*There*,' said Jane, chidingly, to herself, and took the bottle in to Muna. Muna, retching miserably, smelled at the glass she was given, and nodded.

'It is the one I know. The same herbs grow in Lambagh, and many other places. I would like to meet your wise woman.'

'So you shall. The cottage is most interesting. She appears to be a woman of some education, but I do not know what her history is. Her remedies are wonderful, far better than anything old Doctor Riley produces.'

Events proved her right. Muna's sickness stopped, she began to eat again, and also to ride, in spite of Jane's disapproval.

'I am only bearing a child, Mother, I am not ill – but I soon will be if I am kept lying on a sofa. This child is of great value to me. Do not think that I will do anything that might harm him.'

With this Jane had to be content, and certainly Muna looked wonderful, vital and glowing with health. She said as much to Muna, and added, regretfully, that she herself missed riding.

'Well, why do you not ride? Ride with me, and then you will be able to see for yourself how careful I am. Why did you stop?'

Jane could not explain. On her return from India she had been too weakened and miserable to wish to do anything. Then her health had improved, but for some reason she had never ridden again. Perhaps the lack of her child's companionship had caused it. Her little girl had ridden with her on a pony that still lived in the stables and cropped the grass in the meadow, but no one rode her now. Jane made a resolution, got out her habit and was inordinately proud that it needed no alteration. Thereafter, she rode daily with Muna, and thoroughly enjoyed it.

Alan, his leave over, rejoined his regiment, stationed in Dover and was, therefore, able to return home very often. He saw Muna's glowing face and burgeoning figure with pride, but questioned the wisdom of her riding. Jane had quite come round to Muna's way of thinking.

'My dear boy, she is riding very gently, and exercise is good for her. I ride with her; she seldom goes out of a walk, and we do not jump five-barred gates as I hear she was used to doing when she rode with you!'

One fine winter's morning, with the sun a red ball in the clear, cold sky, Muna and Jane rode over the fields to see the wise woman. The air was crisp, and so cold that the horses' breath blew in puffs, like smoke, from their nostrils. There was a different kind of smoke rising from the chimney of the little white cottage where the groom, dismounting, rapped with his whip on the door while Jane and Muna waited.

The woman who answered the knocking was tall and gaunt. Her red hair, that must once have flamed, was being overtaken by a tide of white that blended over her head like a net of silver, although she did not seem to be very old. She bowed to Jane, and then looked at Muna. Muna saw that her eyes were a strange, pale green, as clear as mountain water, and certainly not the eyes of an old woman.

'May we come in, Bella? I have brought my daughter-in-law to see you.'

For an answer the woman stood back, and the groom took the horses while Jane and Muna went inside the cottage.

The single room was spotless. A fire leapt and crackled in the hearth, and a cat slept with her kittens in a basket. There were bunches of herbs hanging from the beams, dried to different shades of grey-green. Bella had been working on a mixture. A white china bowl stood on the scrubbed, wooden table and a pestle and mortar were beside it. A kettle, hanging from a hook over the fire, began to sputter and fizzle as they went in. The woman unhooked it and stood it to one side, pulling two chairs forward.

'You will sit, m'lady? And you, Sahiba?' Muna stared at her. '*What* did you call me?'

'Sahiba. Sit, Lady from the northern hills, I know where you have come from, though I have never been to your part of the country. But I have heard of your homeland, and the valley where your heart is.'

Muna sank into a chair as if all the strength had been drained

61

from her, and Jane hurried to bend over her.

'Muna! Dear child, are you well? Bella, give her some water, she is faint. What did you say, you foolish woman?'

'I said nothing, m'lady. Your son's wife is well, but surprised at my knowledge. Sahiba, did they not tell you I have the sight? Also, I lived in India for some years.'

'In the north?'

'Not your north, no. I was in the south, Travancore, and Calcutta and Madras. I went and saw great mountains, from Darjeeling, mountains that rose and fell like the waves of a frozen sea. I was married to a man who went out to work on the railways when they were building them. James Craig his name was.'

'So that is where you learned your herbal skills?'

'No, indeed. My Granny taught me all I know, in my own country, which is also a northern country. I come from up beyond Inverness. We have many skills in my family; but indeed, I learned some of the remedies in India. There was an old hillwoman who was very skilled. But India was an unlucky country for me. My man died of cholera, and I came back here to his home – and here I've been ever since.'

Jane was astonished. 'Bella, it must be years since I first started to visit you – just after you came here to live, in fact, and you told me nothing of your time in India. I only knew that you had been widowed very young.'

'At that time, India was not a place that either of us wished to remember, m'lady.' Bella's reply was brief. She was sitting close to them on a low stool, her hands busy with the small pestle and mortar.

They were all three silent for a few minutes, each one thinking of a different India, Bella's bright eyes watching Muna's face. Then Jane nodded at Muna. 'As you see, Bella, your potion worked.'

'Aye. It is a good mixture that, for settling the morning sickness. I am happy that it cured the Sahiba.' Her strange eyes never left Muna, her hands seemed to work of their own accord, rolling and pounding at some substance. Muna was examining the room. She saw brass bowls of familiar shapes, and many other things that had come from India. With a word of apology to Bella, she got up and began to walk round the little room, touching these remembered articles with loving hands, as if she recognised old friends. She had forgotten the others completely. Jane leaned forward to Bella.

'Bella, tell me – does Miss Boothby come here often?'

'Often enough.'

'Why?'

'Oh for one thing or another. Salve to keep her hands white, powders for her skin, a rinse for her hair that I make from nettles, or drops for her eyes. She comes nearly every week.'

'And her maid?'

'Oh aye, that one. She came all right. Wanting a powder to make a man desire her. I doubt the potion exists that would make that miracle. I told her to shake her head slowly from side to side whenever she was passed a second helping, and to continue to do that for two months, and maybe she'd not need anything else to help her. She went away angry.'

'They still come?'

'Only the Mistress. Never the maid. I know fine why you are asking. It is because of that affair of the poisoning of the dog is it not?'

'Yes.'

'Well, m'lady, don't worry yourself. They'll never get anything harmful from me. Never. If you want to know where that poison came from, look in your garden sheds, or in the stables. There will be stuff there you could poison an army with. Used to get rid of slugs and other pests, or to make poultices with. I know – I make them myself.'

'Do you have poison here, Bella?'

'Aye, I do. I need all kinds of things for my simples, and some of the herbs and powders I use, if not properly mixed, could be deadly, though they're safe enough in the right hands. I have arsenic for putting in creams for the skin, and belladonna for eyedrops, and digitalis from foxgloves for the heart. Too many to tell you of. I don't use the arsenical powders in my salves very often, for I have other things less dangerous. But I have poisons in plenty that I don't let on about. No one will ever get any poison from me m'lady.' Bella stood up, and put her pestle and mortar on the table. 'Mind,' she said slowly, 'that woman Bessie is a bad one – and as for her Mistress – well, I can feel nothing but bitterness and jealousy all round her. A right nasty pair.'

Muna had finished her inspection of the room, and came back to join them. She looked sad, and withdrawn. Bella looked at her and then bent to pick up a basket. There was a busy cheeping and stirring in the basket, and looking into it, Muna saw some little brownish grey chicks shuffling and pushing against each other. She looked a question at Bella, who nodded with a smile.

'I thought that you would recognise them. Peachicks. I had them from Macdonald, the gamekeeper at Cheriton. I'm rearing them.'

'They are so plain now, and so beautiful when they are grown. You have shown me many things from my home today, Bella, and called me Sahiba – do you speak Urdu, Bella?' Muna's voice was the voice of someone asking a favour. But Bella shook her head regretfully. 'No, Sahiba, not properly. I could when I first came back, I had learned a little, but now it has all gone.'

'I am sorry. But perhaps if we spoke together, you would come to remember it?'

'I would try, Sahiba. If it would please you, I would try.'

The two women looked at each other smiling. Jane felt that there was a friendship between them, a thread that pulled them together, something she could not understand between two such different people.

Jane took Muna away soon after, and Bella watched them go, standing at her cottage door, and waving when Muna looked back.

'*Well*,' said Jane, looking sideways at Muna's face. 'Well, what a surprising morning. I had no idea that Bella had been in India. Darling child, you look very pale. Did the visit upset you?'

'Upset. No. It was an amazement. For a little time I felt I had returned to another country. She is a very wise and powerful woman. Those eyes see much.'

'She has a reputation round here, of course. The villagers go to her with all their troubles but, none the less, they say she is a witch. Fifty years ago she would have burned.'

'Burned? What? I do not understand.'

'They would have burned Bella as a witch.'

'You tell me that in England they burn their wise women?'

Muna looked so pale that Jane was glad to get her home and into bed. She went uncomplainingly, and this worried Jane, for Muna had shown no desire to rest as much as Jane felt that she should.

Muna lay in her handsome room, warm under the covers of the big bed. She lay very still, her hands folded over her stomach as if to protect the child within. The fabric of the dream in which she lived trembled and reeled like a curtain in the wind. Memories flooded through, places she had loved, voices, people. Kassim's face, his voice, his hard grip and his manner of love-making that had never left her in any doubt that he found her very desirable – and yet she had known that his love was not for her. He did not think of another woman when he lay in Muna's arms, but Muna had always known that she had no permanent place in his life. Her life was to be different and far from him. The mists of the dream world closed his face away from her again, and Muna slept at last, tears still wet on her face.

It was a month later that Bella walked up to the house with a large covered basket hanging on her arm. She was given a great welcome by Cook, and seated in the big kitchen with a cup of tea and a slice of Cook's famous plum cake, she gave advice on various ailments, from Cook's aching back and swollen ankles to the warts on Boots' stubby fingers. All the time the basket was kept close to her skirts. After a while, cures discussed and a second cup of tea refused, Cook asked what the basket contained.

'Peacocks,' said Bella, 'peacocks for the young Mistress.'

'Peacocks! Well, I never. She'll likely be pleased; they come from India, don't they? Or is it Africa? I can't never remember.'

5   65

'They come from her part of India, and I'm thinking she'll be very pleased. Could I see her? If you would be so good, Cook, and send a message to her Ladyship, I think she'll let me up to have a word with the young Mistress.'

'Of course she will. Thinks the world of you, Bella, 'specially since you put Madam Muna right with that potion, the one that stopped her morning sickness. Here – Boots – run upstairs now, to Mr. Symes, and ask him to tell her Ladyship that Bella is here and asking to see her. She has a present for Madam Muna.'

Muna, presented with the young peacock and his harem, was delighted. Jane had reservations.

'Are you sure they will survive the winter?'

'Aye, they will that. Jessop, the gamekeeper, will rear them for you. They are hardy birds, no more likely to get killed by the cold than chickens or turkeys. They'll be in full plumage by May.'

'I would like to have them,' said Muna, looking down at the little birds.

'Then of course you must have them. Bella, that was a very kind thought.'

Bella was not listening. She was raking Muna with her eyes, studying her face and figure. 'May I speak with you, m'lady?'

Jane saw the look in the pale green eyes fixed on hers. 'Of course; come upstairs, Bella.'

She led the way up to her sitting room, followed by Muna and Bella, who walked with a carriage as erect and graceful as Muna's own.

Once the door was closed, and they were alone, Bella sat down and faced the other two women.

'She's too small, m'lady. See – here, and here? She's as narrow as a child, with very small bones. Also – ' Muna, a lay figure in Bella's hands, was turned and prodded. 'See the muscles in her stomach and waist? That might make it easier, but she's awful narrow across, and this measurement here is just ridiculous. M'lady, you'll need to give me a room and I will move in here a month before she's due. There's no call for that Doctor Riley and his instruments. Eh, he's a terrible bungler.

The man's no better than a murderer when he deals with women in childbirth.'

Muna shuddered, and put a beseeching hand on Jane's arm, 'Oh Mother, not Doctor Riley. I will not allow that man near me. I will be safe with Bella.'

Doctor Riley was a fairly frequent visitor to Moxton Park; he lived alone, and Jane was sorry for him. He was not much respected by anyone, and Sir Robert had several times stated that if he ever took ill, he would prefer to be attended by his head groom. The doctor smelt of a number of things, but the strongest odour about him was that of spirits. Jane could understand Muna's horror of him. It was easy for her to promise that Doctor Riley would not attend on the birth. Bella's remarks about Muna had worried Jane. Perhaps it would be better to take her to London for the confinement. But Muna expressed horror at that suggestion too.

'All I need is Bella, Mother; after all, having a child is a thing of nature, nothing strange is attached to it. Bella will look after me, and do all that is necessary. Please, Mother, let Alan's son be born in his father's own home.'

Bella was installed in a room next to Muna's at the end of March, and brought with her a great nosegay of the first prim-roses that Muna had ever seen, and a feeling of confidence and comfort. Not that Muna gave any impression of being worried or afraid. She moved through the waiting days placidly and happily, with no impatience, and no malaise.

'Not at all like a girl having her first child,' said Jane to her husband. 'No nerves, or hysteria. She is wonderful: and quite convinced that the child will be a boy. I don't know – I hope she is not too disappointed if it is a girl.'

Sir Robert kept his thoughts and feelings to himself, wonder-ing if it had ever occurred to anyone of his family that this coming child could be completely alien in appearance – as much an Indian as Muna's mother must have been. The dark side of the coin. Sir Robert looked at his wife, going happily about the newly-arranged nursery, and prayed fervently.

7

The peacocks were in full plumage and good voice by the first week of May.

'Oh, those *awful* birds,' groaned Jane as they shrieked from the terrace where, proud and elegant, the male stepped before his meek mates, his tail spread in all its many-eyed glory. It was early in the morning, a spring dawn barely streaking the sky, and Jane was just settling herself for sleep again, when Daisy came tapping at her door.

'Bella says, m'lady, that Madam Muna has started her pains.' Jane, slippered and in her peignoir, hurried to Muna's room. Incense burned before the dancing image in the corner. Muna was up and walking, her forehead pearled with sweat. She smiled, however, when Jane came in, and assured her that all was well. 'I am happy that Alan is not here. This is not a time for men,' she said, and then bent double, groaning, as a spasm took her. Jane, advised by Bella, hurried away to dress, and Muna resumed her pacing, while the peacock paraded before his mates on the terrace below.

Muna's labour was hard. It was long, and the pains were not spaced; they did not appear to stop long enough for her to breathe. She bore her pains silently, struggling with them as if she fought a tangible enemy. Jane stayed, holding her hands when Muna could no longer walk, and talking to her, until Muna, speaking in single, bitten-off words, begged her to go. 'I tear your hands raw – see, I have your blood on my fingers. Go away Mother. This I do alone with Bella, and the Goddess. You go and stay with Alan's father. He has many fears, I know. Tell him that all will be well, that he will be pleased with his grandson.'

Jane, helpless, went. Muna lay back when Jane had gone, and gasped for breath. She was very near the edge of exhaustion.

Bella bent over her, smoothing back the heavy hair, dank with sweat. 'Sahiba, do not fight your pains. Make your body loose. Think of the pain as a great wave, and let it carry you with it. If you tighten your body against the pain, it will be very hard. Can you try?'

Muna nodded, and when the next pain came, she tried to let her muscles go loose, and indeed the pain seemed easier.

Bella nodded her approval. 'Now things go better,' she said, 'Now it will not be long.'

There was a pause between the pains, the first rest Muna had had. She said dreamily, 'It is strange to lie here in childbirth. We were never allowed to bear children, you know. The girls who give their lives to the Goddess do not bear children. Sometimes one or another would find a seed growing in her womb, and then a midwife would be called, and the child would be taken. If it was early enough, there were certain herbal brews that brought the courses back. If the woman longed for a child, and hid the fact that she was pregnant until it begun to show, then there were other things that the midwife did, and usually both mother and child died. But I was fortunate. I never felt a child grow in my body until now – Aiee, it starts again, Bella, and this is a very big wave!'

'Let yourself go with it, Sahiba – the child is not far off. Soon you must begin to push.'

It was a very long day. At the last, when the waves of pain were continuous, Bella, after a swift examination, said suddenly, '*Now* girl, scream if you will, and push down with all your might.'

Her face suffused, the cords of her neck standing out, her whole body trembling with strain, Muna flung her head back, and sent a long and terrible cry ringing through the house. As it echoed frighteningly down the long, picture-hung corridors, the peacock on the terrace screamed as if in answer.

Then there was silence, and into the silence came the ragged, uncertain cry, raucous and offended, of the newly-born.

Jane, running, the sound of Muna's cry still in her ears, was halted in the doorway of Muna's room, Bella's hand gently holding her back. Looking into the room, Jane could not believe what she saw. Ratni was crouching in front of the idol, her hand holding a small fan which she waved gently, sending gusts of strong-smelling incense which mixed with the smell of fresh blood. The window was wide open to the sky, and Jane did not know what to do first – close the window and send Ratni out, or rush to the bed where Muna lay. But Bella said firmly, 'Leave her, m'lady. I have not finished cleansing her. She has had a terrible labour. You come and see your grandchild – the Sahiba has borne a son.'

Robert was at Jane's elbow. It would have been most unsuitable to have taken him into Muna's room. So Jane turned obediently, and together they went to Bella's room, where Daisy, her face one great broad smile, was bathing the baby.

Robert let his breath go, in a long sigh. The child was beautiful, and Muna was sleeping peacefully, Bella had said. That last scream from Muna had terrified him, because there had been no sound until then. He had found himself praying desperately, 'Oh, God, never mind the child – just let our daughter be safe,' and then realised how close Muna had come to his heart. Now, everything seemed right. The child was like any other newly-born baby, and Muna was safe. He bent to kiss his wife, and went out to walk in the spring fresh evening, glad that the day was over.

The sun had not set, and the peacock was resplendent on the terrace in the evening light, and as if he knew it, he paraded before Robert, closing and then spreading his tail, like a woman opening and closing a fan. He gave his strange eerie cry, but in this moment of joy, it sounded like a cry of triumph. Robert paused to admire him, and then walked on, and down the steps, and the peace of the green garden, waiting for summer, filled his heart, and rested him as it always did.

They carried the child in to Muna just at sunset, when her

room was full of golden light. They put him into her arms, Bella and Jane, and Jane kissed her, and they left her alone with her son. She woke from her half sleep to find him already nuzzling for her breast, instead of sleeping as the new-born usually do after their struggle to reach the world.

'Ohé, Maharaj! Dil Bahadur! Art thou so hungry after thy journey? Wait, joy of my heart, and I will give thee food.' Muna spoke in her own tongue. It was fitting that the first words she spoke to her son should be in her language. After this she would do Alan's bidding, and speak nothing but English to him. But for this one night she had earned the right to do anything she liked. Now, left alone with her son, for a little time he was all hers.

The child fed, and then slept, one hand starfished against his face. Muna lay, spent, watching her sleeping child, thinking back over the many paths in her life that had brought her to this moment. She looked towards the corner where the little lamp burned in front of the stone figure.

'Oh great One, I praise and adore thee, Protector and Mother of all. Take this, my son, under your hand and keep harm from him as he walks the roads of this new life. Hear me, most honoured One. Let him find his way easily through the years.' Muna spoke aloud, and the child stirred on her breast, flinging back one hand as if to ward off some danger. A breeze seemed to blow through the room, and the flame before the Goddess wavered and flickered, and shadows moved over the face of the image so that the Goddess seemed to change position and smile. Muna heard something – what? No sound, and yet words were there, words like a distant bell a crystal glass tapped by a finger nail could make such a sound. 'He is protected as you are, my daughter.' While Muna was still trying to hear the soundless sound, she fell deeply asleep; the daytime world vanished and she returned to the only realities that she knew, the dreams of times past.

Morning brought her back from the realities of sleep to the dream world of the day. The dream opened to let her son enter. But deep in her heart Muna held the knowledge that among the dream figures around her, this one was different.

This perfect baby was reality. One day he would leave the dream, and she was glad to know this. Both glad, and afraid, for when he left the dream she knew that it would be time for her to awaken.

Meantime, everything about her son delighted her. His ravenous hunger, his roars of rage and his sudden deep sleep when he was fed were enchanting.

'My life, but he has a voice like the Bull of Bashan, this boy,' said Bella carrying the roaring baby to Muna where she lay, ready for him, one swollen veined breast bared. The hungry yells died away with satisfied murmurs. Muna and Bella both looked down at him, lost in the urgent business of nourishment. Together, the three lives in the room made a perfect circle of peace and satisfaction.

Presently, Bella sat down, and Muna looked up from the dark head at her breast, and said, 'Bull of Bashan you called him. What is it?'

'Oh it's some creature in the Bible. There was a story, but I cannot remember more than just the name. But your son is surely the possessor of a voice like a bull.'

'Bashan – is that a God?'

'No, I think it is a country. But I cannot say for sure. It is years since I read my Bible, or went into a church.'

'Bella, the Bible is your Holy Book, is it not?'

'It is that. I would read it, for it is full of good things. But I turned from it years ago, and as for church – the kirk would be fine if it were not for the parsons. They blether away there, and I have better things to do with my time than to sit listening to a man who is no better than I am, telling me what to do with my life.'

'You do no worship, and you do not remember your holy writings?' Muna spoke in utter astonishment. Her religion was part of her life, she lived it and breathed it, and could not have done anything without it. Everything she had ever been taught was stored in her head, could be repeated by her, or chanted, word for word, never to be forgotten. She looked wide-eyed at Bella. 'And yet you are a good woman, Bella, there is goodness all about you, and the strength of goodness.'

'Aye well, that's as may be. I've no doubt I'm a sinner in the eyes of most, living as I do, thinking and speaking as I do – but the thoughts of other folk do not touch me.'

'What do you believe, Bella?'

'Lord's sake, what a question! I cannot answer that in a few words, Sahiba. In short, I believe in love and charity, and I do not mean the handing out of baskets of bread like that stupid besom at the Grange does in the village. No, I mean charity of thought as well as deed. I believe in the power of good, and the power of evil, and in trying to live as best I can without hurting anyone while I am on this world.'

' "The world is a bridge; pass over it, but build no house. He who hopes for an hour, hopes for eternity. The world is but an hour. Spend it in devotion. The rest is unseen." ' Muna's voice was very soft. 'That is a Muslim saying. But to us, the rest is not unseen. We know there are other lives, life upon life, crowding behind us and before us. Do you believe thus, Bella?'

'I know there is something more than this life, but more than that I cannot say. I do not have as much knowledge of other lives as I know you do.'

'But you can see ahead?'

'Aye. I have the sight. Now, that is enough Sahiba, your eyes are heavy with weariness. Rest, or your milk will not flow, and then we shall have a bull on our hands in real truth.'

Jane came in with a great vase of white lilac, scenting the whole room. She leaned worshipfully over her grandson. 'Oh Muna, look at him! Is he not beautiful? And so strong – he's as large as a child of three months already. I cannot imagine how you produced him, he's so huge.'

'Nay, Mother, he is puny. An evil baby, with a bad temper – see how he squints and glowers.' Muna, terrified at this open praise of her child said the most uncomplimentary things she could think of, lest the Gods take her treasure away from her, being jealous.

Bella understood, but Jane stared, amazed. 'Puny? *Squints?* Never, he is perfection. How can you, Muna?'

'He has a terrible temper. He roars like a bull.'

'Well the poor little thing is probably hungry. Are you determined to feed him yourself Muna, because if not, there is a very good, clean girl at the farm who has plenty of milk. She lost her own child three days after it was born, poor thing.'

For the first time in their acquaintance Muna was angry with Jane. Her eyes blazing, she clutched her child to her. 'Let another woman feed my son? *And* one who has the evil eye on her, having lost her own child? Never. He is mine, and my breasts sustain him, no one else shall feed him.'

Looking into the blazing eyes, Jane said gently, 'Muna – of course my dear. Do not be angry with me. I only thought – you had such a prolonged labour, I did not want you to be weakened.'

'To be weakened for his sake is my honour, Mother.'

Muna's rage subsided, leaving her nervous, so that she held her child closely, and would not let Bella take him, although he had fallen asleep.

Outside her door, a distressed Jane listened to Bella.

'Now, m'lady, do not praise the child too much to her face. They believe in India that the gods are jealous of anything too perfect, and take it away. Did you not know that? You frightened her, that was what was wrong.'

Her mind going back, Jane remembered something her ayah had said to her after her little daughter had died: 'She was too beautiful, Memsahib. Too beautiful. The Gods were jealous and have taken her.' The memory brought tears, and pain.

Bella watched her quietly, saying only, 'Now then, m'lady, no need to upset yourself. She'll be fine the next time you see her.'

'Oh Bella, I should have remembered. That was very foolish of me. I forget sometimes that she is not my own child.'

'Aye, well, she's not. She is close to you, but however much you both try, there will always be differences. Love helps you both, so just don't fret.'

Jane was very shaken. It was the first time that she had felt that Muna was alien to her, and it gave her great distress. She was sitting, trying to put her thoughts into order, when Robert came to her, carrying a bunch of beautiful white roses, and laid them in her arms.

He leaned over and kissed her, and said quietly, 'For the most beautiful grandmother in the world – my dearest love.'

He was considerably startled when Jane let his lovely Niphetos roses slip from her lap, and flung herself into his arm in floods of tears.

'My dearest girl – what on earth? I thought to give you pleasure. These are the roses I have been carefully nurturing in the coolest greenhouse for just this occasion. Do you not like them?'

'Oh, I do – indeed I do. Robert I love you!'

'Well, I had always supposed you did my love, but why the tears? Let me dry your eyes, and tell me what is wrong – and please do not step on those roses, I know that once your sight has cleared you will be delighted with them.'

Jane dried her eyes, and said she was over-excited, and duly admired the lovely roses, and then they went together to see Muna and were warmly welcomed, and Jane found that there was no barrier between herself and her loved daughter-in-law. But she never again suggested a wet nurse, and if she admired her grandson, she always finished by saying, 'But however perfect he is, I think he is a perfect nuisance as well,' and she and Muna would exchange conspiratorial smiles over the adored child's head, cheating together the jealous gods.

8

Alan came the following day, beside himself with pride and relief. His mother told him that Muna had had a very difficult labour. He went into her room, full of apprehension, and found her sitting waiting for him, her child in her arms.

She held the baby out to him, smiling. 'See, lord – I bring you a son for your name.'

Over the baby's head he looked into her shadowed eyes, and saw how much she had suffered. 'Muna – my love, are you well?'

'How not, lord? Have I not crowned my life by bearing your son?'

Alan bowed his head over hers, holding her close. 'So long as you are safe.'

'I am safe, and so is he – if he is not crushed to suffocation between us. Alan, do not be worried, I had a baby, not an illness!'

Alan picked his son up and took him to the window, laughing at the crumpled, furious face that glared back at him. When the child raised his voice in hungry yells, Alan hurriedly handed him back, saying, 'Good God, what a noise! What's the matter with him?'

'He is hungry. Come then, my beautiful bull, and feed. Do not roar at your father, he will be angered with you, and rightly.'

Alan sat watching his son being fed, and thought Muna looked frail. She laughed at him, and told him that the only reason she had stayed in bed was that his mother had insisted that she did.

'I am well, Alan. Do not look at me as if I was a spirit. In a few days' time, when your mother is less alarmed, I shall be riding again.'

But this Alan specifically forbade, and threatened to tell his mother if she tried to do any such thing. Bella backed him up, and Muna made hideous faces at them both, saying they were jailors. But secretly she was more tired than she would admit, and was glad to lie in her bed, watching the clouds blowing over the sky in a brisk spring wind, and dreaming within a dream about her son's future.

Later Alan told his father, 'He is to be called after you. Muna wishes it, too. Robert Alan Reid. Is he not a splendid baby?'

His pride was so innocent that his father felt his heart move with love for this son of his, who had obviously never imagined that *his* son could have been anything else but perfect. He ventured to remark on how fortunate they were in the child's appearance. Alan looked at him in complete astonishment.

'But why should my son have been dark-skinned as you suggest? For one thing, Muna's father was English; for another, the people of northern India are very fair. My friend Kassim, the Ruler of Lambagh, is as fair-skinned as I am, with grey eyes. It did not enter my head that Rob could be anything but as he is, a beautiful child. After all, look at his mother!'

Robert agreed, and they drank the child's health in champagne, and Alan forgot the oddity of his father's fears about his grandson.

But as he drank the toast, Robert wondered fleetingly what Muna might have wished to call her son if she had really had the choice. Later, Jane told him that the name 'Robert' had, in fact, been as much Muna's choice as Alan's. 'She said to me, "But of course – what else should he be called? He must have the name of his grandfather".'

Robert wondered what Muna's father had been named, and what blood now ran in the veins of his family: but he kept all his thoughts to himself, and Jane went up to drink champagne

77

with Muna, while her grandson slept in a cradle beside his mother's bed.

The days that passed after Rob's birth were happy and peaceful. Alan returned to his regimental duties, taking a promise from Muna that she would rest.

In fact, as soon as his back was turned, Muna was up and dressed, but she did not do very much because she was unexpectedly weak. She stormed at herself as she was forced to go back to bed, but Jane, helping to undress her, said firmly, 'But of course you are weak. It is not called "labour" for nothing. Just walk before you try to run. You will be as strong as ever very soon, Muna. Another reason why it is important that you rest – you are feeding your child, you know.'

Reminded, Muna was willing to do anything to ensure Rob's food. Rob himself flourished, a perfect baby, seeming to grow larger every day.

A few months later Bella, who had not left Moxton Park since the baby was born, came back from a visit to the village, and asked to speak to Jane privately.

'Mrs. Beaker, in the shop – she asked what the baby was like. Told me she'd heard from someone that he was as black as your hat, a real nigger.'

'*What?*' Jane's astonishment fanned Bella's rage.

'Aye, m'lady. Those were her words. Black, she said. I asked where she got it from, and she said it was common knowledge. All over the village, she said and, furthermore, the gentry know all about it too.'

'The gentry? What gentry?'

'What gentry would you think, m'lady? Mrs. Boothby and her friends. Our beautiful boy – black. *And* not too bright mentally, because he was damaged in the birthing. I know fine where they got *that* bit from. Doctor Riley was fair furious when he was not asked to attend at the birth. And he's a constant visitor to the Grange, playing whist, and getting his free drinks and dinners in return for any scraps of gossip he can take them. Oh, I could take a knife to him, the old –'

'Hush, Bella, Madam Muna must not hear of this. Do not think any more about it. Just leave it to me, and thank you for telling me. We cannot let stories like that go about the place.'

Jane sat and thought deeply. The result of her thinking was a visit to Caroline Addison, who heard her out, and then said, 'Yes, well, I was wondering when you would hear the charming stories. Little rosebud Mary is not giving up so easily, and she is very upset. Kerrigan did not come up to scratch in the end. He ran out at the last fence and she did not get her proposal, and the county is laughing. So the rosebud and her mamma are like a nest of wasps. I think you should have the christening quite soon. In the village church, of course.'

'The christening? Good gracious, yes, of course. What a splendid idea. I shall get my Uncle down to christen Rob. He is Bishop of Knightsford. Thank you, Caroline, I shall count on you to help me.'

Driving home, Jane had a shade of worry at the back of her mind. Muna and the christening. Would she raise any objections to her son being christened? Surely not. But it was Alan's business to find out, not hers.

Alan, home for Saturday and Sunday, was captured on his arrival and after a talk with his mother, went, frowning, to speak to his wife. He found Muna in the conservatory, lying in a long chair. She looked languid, a delicate bloom among all the lush tropical growth of the hothouse, but jumped up with her usual welcoming smile when she saw him.

'Alan! You are welcome. How are you?'

'How are you, my dearest?' Then, without giving her time to answer, he continued, 'I hope you are feeling well, and stronger, for it is time to arrange for Rob to be christened.'

'Christened?'

'Yes, take him to church, and let the parson bless him, and give him his names.'

'He will be a Christian, like Ratni?'

'He will be a Christian like me – and my family.'

'Am I not your family? I am not a Christian, but I am his mother.'

'Muna, you can become a Christian whenever you like. The Vicar is all too anxious to give you instruction.'

'I do not wish to be a Christian. You *know* that I can never be a Christian.'

'Yes, I know. But you know that my son must be a Christian, Muna – you have known that from the time he was born, have you not?'

After a rebellious pause, she nodded. 'Yes. It is seen. But Alan – your God and my Gods are very different. Will your God take my child away, so that in the next world I cannot find him?'

Alan saw her frightened eyes and, perplexed, did not know what to say to her. His wife was a heathen, she worshipped strange Gods, and was a devoted follower of a Goddess whose attributes did not at all appeal to him. But he could not bear to see her worried or frightened, this girl whom he knew to be as brave as a lion.

'My dear love. No one can take your child away from you, in this world or the next. This christening is just a custom. Can you think of it like that?'

Muna's brow cleared. A custom was something she could understand. This odd, dream island she inhabited had many customs she did not understand. This was just another of them.

'Of course, Alan, I understand. Tell me what I must do, and I will do it.'

'Part of the ceremony is that there must be Godfathers and a Godmother. Would you care to ask Aunt Caroline to be the Godmother?'

'Godmother?' Muna wondered what in heaven and earth a Godmother could be, but if Caroline Addison was willing to become one, then whatever it was, it must be good. She nodded her head enthusiastically.

'Yes, Alan, of course. I would like her to be – Godmother?'

So Jane, greatly relieved, wrote to Caroline on Muna's behalf, and wrote to her Uncle, the Bishop, and unpacked from their careful wrappings the family christening robes, and sent out invitations to a luncheon party.

Muna, still in great fear and perplexity, sent for Ratni.

'Ratni – when they made you a Christian, what happened?'

'They spoke words to me, and I repeated words that they had

taught me. This is called in English "The Catechism", and it was necessary for me to know all the words. It is a long prayer, this thing one must learn. Then, on another day, a head priest came from Ryechester, and put his hands on my head, and prayed, and gave me bread, and wine, saying it was the flesh and blood of his God, the Christian God, which I must eat in memory of a feast which the God gave his servants. Now I do this thing every Sunday, early, going fasting to the church, and I am a Christian, and my man is pleased with me, and is happy – that is all.'

'But did anything happen within you? Do you now feel that you have lost or gained something?'

'Nay, Sahiba – how could that be? There is no change in me.'

'But you are a Christian?'

'Yes – my man is pleased, and what pleases him is good to me.' Ratni paused, and said in surprise, 'These white people are strange. Not only does he try to pleasure me in love, but he also does work that he thinks will please me in the house. I have never found a man like to him. Do you not find it so, that these white men try to be close to their women in all ways, even doing women's tasks, carrying goods, cleaning – Munabhen, they are kind men, are they not?'

Muna returned from her thoughts, and looked at Ratni's contented face, her happy eyes. There was no answering contentment in her own heart, but she would not destroy another's happiness. 'Yes, Ratni, this is true. But this Christian faith, I do not understand. I do not wish my son to have a religion that means nothing to him, that does not speak to him in his mind and body and heart.'

'Munabhen, your son is in the hand of your Goddess. Do not fear. As I have taken this religion, to please my man, do you let your son take it, to please yours. There will be change, and no harm. Be at rest Munabhen, let me sing to you, and think no more of this religion, or that. We worship the great One; She will guard us. Now clear your mind, and I will sing you one of the old songs – see, I have my sitar here. It is long since I sang for you, but my man likes me to sing.'

So Muna, her thoughts fretting her like gadflies, sat quietly, and listened as Ratni plucked at the strings of her sitar, and began to sing.

'Love is bitter,' sang Ratni, her eyes glowing with happiness, her fingers plucking sad minor chords that matched the words of her song.

> 'Love is bitter, hearts change –
> Love is bitter, love is lonely.
> I am a bird, lost in the wind
> In the dark wind of your love.
> Ah, how cold is love –'

sang Ratni, with sunlight lying like a burnish on her shining black hair, her fingers sending a sad little river of chords to follow her voice. My heart is breaking, thought Muna, my heart is indeed lost. I cannot listen to this any longer.

'Ratni,' she called through the melancholy cadences of Ratni's song, 'Ratni, stop! I need – I need a glass of tea – my throat is parched.'

Ratni stopped singing at once, and hurried out to get the tea with lemon that Muna loved. But even though she was no longer singing, like an echo blown by the dark wind of love, Muna could still hear the words softly sounding: 'Love is bitter –'

The christening was held on a blue day, with white clouds scudding before a light wind. Muna watched the party set off for the village church: Rob resplendent in silk and lace and ribbons, and blessedly asleep, Jane wearing a bonnet and dress of lilac silk and the pearls that Muna had given her, Alan and one of his brother officers, the only one he had invited, in uniform. She watched the carriage go down the drive, and then went to stand before her Goddess in silent supplication. She was not going into the church. She had steadfastly refused to go near the christening, and Robert Reid had supported her, saying firmly, 'There is no need for her to come. She is still weak after the birth. Let that be reason enough.'

When the service was over, and the party came back,

Caroline Addison came up to the nursery with Rob in her arms.

'He behaved like an angel until he felt the water, and then he roared like a fiend. Here is your son, Muna, ravenous for food. You will come down for luncheon when he is fed?'

'I will,' said Muna, taking her yelling son in his crumpled laces. Then, as Rob's howls subsided, she looked full at Caroline.

'Did they all see him? Are they now satisfied that my son is whole and perfect, and a white child?'

Caroline Addison stared at her. 'You know? Who told you?'

'I know,' said Muna, quietly, looking down at her son, 'I know. First I am a monster, so you display me to the county and save our name – and then my son is a monster, so we have this christening. I think the English are very strange people. But I know some of them are kind and loyal friends. I am glad that Alan and his family have you to save them from the shame that I have brought them.'

'Muna – you brought them no shame! These evil stories are all started by one jealous, disappointed girl. Another thing. Anything I do is done as much for you as it is for anyone else in this family. I count you my dear friend.'

'I know. You are my friend, and to you I owe a great debt. But I am very angry. I, and my son – we are not ashamed of anything.' Muna's tone was sharp, with underlying bitterness in her words.

Caroline answered her swiftly, 'Muna. No one is ashamed of anything about you. Your family love you very much and are very proud to have you in their midst. But, as you say, the English are a very strange people. They are an island race, and they regard anything foreign as suspect. It is to save your son from any unkindness in the future that we have done what we have. Do you understand that? Do not be hurt, or angry, Muna. Remember we all love you. Feed your boy, and come down to us. We are all waiting to drink your health.'

She bent and kissed Muna, and went from the room, unable to bear the pain she saw in Muna's eyes. Going downstairs, she cursed the Boothby family with all the most dreadful curses she could think of, and had to arrange her expression carefully when she entered the room where the others were gathered.

Upstairs, Muna finished feeding Rob, and he was carried off to have his crumpled magnificence renewed. Muna, after changing her dress, assisted by Bella, went down to the waiting guests.

A hush fell over the assembly as she came down the curving staircase into the great hall. Her dress of pale grey floated round her like mist; she had white roses at her breast, and in her dark hair. Muna, the Rose of Madore, had lost none of her power to charm, none of her beauty. She lifted her head and sent a smiling glance to Alan, who came forward to lead her into the room, and the welcome she received was warm and genuine. No one was there who was not a close friend, or a relative of Alan's family.

The ranks opened to include Muna, and for the first time in her life she felt she was a member, and a welcome member, of a big loving family. No matter that it was all part of the dream in which she now lived. She felt the welcome, and was made happy. She had already vowed that, to make a place for her son in this strange world where he would have to live some part of his life, she would do anything. But here and now, she felt nothing hard or difficult in taking her place amongst these people. She belonged, was loved, and secure.

The story of the christening, and of the beautiful child and his much loved mother, went round the village and spread further. For the time being, there would be no credence given to any unkind scandal from any source. The villagers had seen for themselves.

9

After the christening, Jane wished to take Muna more into the social scene.

'We will give some small parties for you, my dear, and I have no doubt there will be many invitations coming. Then, when the season starts, I think you should be presented.'

'Presented?'

'Yes. Presented to the Queen at one of her drawing-rooms. I shall ask Caroline to be your sponsor. I think it is important, my dear.'

But Muna proved unexpectedly obstinate about showing herself off to the county, preparatory to having the final gloss of being presented to the Queen. She declined all invitations, except those that came from Lady Addison, and Jane was forced to make the best of it.

'Perhaps this is the wisest course,' she said to her husband, 'I think that to be presented to the Queen will be better, before she begins to go about. She is still weak and easily tired, I notice.'

Robert thought that his daughter-in-law looked as if she was glowing with health, but did not say so. He sympathised with Muna's desire to keep out of the social limelight, and wondered about the wisdom of presenting Muna to Queen Victoria. A wry smile crossed his face at the very thought. However, Jane seemed to have forgotten her social ambitions for Muna, and life settled down again.

Bella stayed on in Moxton Park as a permanent member of

the staff, only visiting her cottage for two or three hours during the day.

Daisy pushed Rob's pram out into the lanes for short walks, stopping to chat to various acquaintances, the baby lying on a frilled pillow, warmly wrapped in cashmere shawls, with a silk and lace coverlet over all. Daisy wished that they were in London so that she could show him off in the Park; it was dull just having him admired by the villagers. One day, as she was out with his pram, Miss Boothby, on a bay horse, escorted by an elderly gentleman, stopped to peer down into the pram, and asked Daisy who the baby was.

'This is Major Reid's son, Miss – from Moxton Park. Just nine months he is, and cutting another tooth – good as gold with it, he is – ' but the young lady had gone, giving her horse a smart cut with her whip, so that he started off suddenly, spattering mud in all directions, and the elderly gentleman was forced to move his mount aside, being almost unseated in the general turmoil.

'Well!' said Daisy, staring after the flying figures, and when she got back to the house, described the whole adventure to Bella. Thereafter Bella accompanied Daisy on her walks with the pram, but she said nothing to Muna about the episode. The villagers continued to admire the baby whenever they saw him, and all the unkind stories that had been bandied about appeared to have been forgotten.

Muna was seen by very few people, and then only in the very early mornings. A cottager's wife, coming out to let her hens into the orchard, would see her riding by in the lane, bound for the open fields. A ploughman, following his great horses up the furrows, seagulls swooping and screaming behind him, would hear the thunder of hooves and see Muna flashing past, flying over gates and hedges as if she and her horse had wings.

Sometimes she went for more gentle rides with Jane, going as far as Bella's cottage and dismounting to pick bunches of sweet smelling herbs, bringing them back to dry them and make little bags to put among the baby's linen.

When Jane entertained, Muna would be at her elbow, beautifully dressed and obviously in perfect health. When

Alan was at home, she rode with him, wearing a tailored riding dress which fitted her as if it had been poured over her body. She wore it easily, mounting her horse as nimbly as she had when she had worn her own riding clothes. The one garment she refused to wear was a corset. Her splendid muscles stood her in good stead, and there was no need for her to wear creaking horrors of whalebone and buckram to constrict her. Muna's figure was as seductive as it had ever been; she was coming into the full flower of her beauty.

Rob was weaned, and everyone expected that his mother would 'go about' more. But she continued to live her usual secluded life in Moxton Park. One day, Alan asked her if she was not growing bored.

'Bored? What is this "Bored"?'

'Well, dull – do you not feel that you would like to go to some parties?'

'Those terrible gatherings where everyone stares, and the women sit waiting for some man to speak to them, or ask them to dance your strange dances – and there is such a crush at supper time that it is too hot to eat or even breathe? No, I do not wish for that. I am very content here with my family and with you. Do I seem dull to you? Do I not please you, Alan, tell me?'

She pleased him, as always. She set his nights on fire for him, she could still reduce him to breathless impatience by a single glance, a passing touch. Alan asked no more questions, and assured his mother that his wife was perfectly content.

She was, in fact, living very much as she would have lived in her own country, as a wife with a son, living in her husband's parents' house. Had she been married in India, she would not have expected to go anywhere, except possibly to the marriages of relatives, or to visit close friends or relations, and then she would have gone to the women's quarters, to sit and exchange gossip, and tales about her child, and learn a new recipe for some sweetmeat, or a new mixture of oils for her hair. She certainly would not have been expected to go out and about in public, and meet strange men. The only men she would have spoken with would have been her husband and his closest relations – his father and his brothers. So Muna saw nothing strange in living quietly in her mother-in-law's home. It was what she expected to do. Anything else was strange, and she did not enjoy it. The days of meeting many men – and, indeed, only men – were over for her now. She was a respectable married woman, with a son.

Her happiest moments were spent with her son, lying on her big bed, watching him exploring the room, first on all-fours, and then on unsteady feet. His tumbling dark curls, his great, grey eyes, his crowing laugh, enchanted her as much as they did everyone else. Muna spent part of every day alone with him, talking in her own tongue, in spite of her good resolution watching him with adoration, and when he spoke his first words, they were to her, and in Urdu.

Alan was not pleased.

'Muna – please. You will make it very hard for him when he goes to school. He must speak nothing but English. I told you that. English, and nothing else.'

'School? Alan, what do you think of? He is only two years old! There is plenty of time for him to learn English before he has to go to school, surely?'

Alan shook his head, obstinately. 'You have not obeyed me, Muna. He cannot speak a word of English. My son – and he speaks nothing but Urdu.'

'I am your wife – and I could not speak a word of English when you met me. It did not appear to distress you then, Alan.'

Muna turned away, and for the first time since they had married, she walked out of the room and left him fuming, with his son standing between his knees, banging his fists against his father's waistcoat and demanding to be carried – in Urdu.

Muna did not appear for luncheon and later, when Bella was questioned, she said that her Mistress had gone out riding. Jane, who had sensed that all was not well with Alan, went to find him, and ran him to earth in the library with his father.

'What is wrong with Muna?' she demanded.

'Nothing, as far as I know,' said Alan, looking mulish.

'Well, it is not like her to go off for a ride before luncheon, saying nothing to me – and I am worried, if you are not. Have you had a disagreement?'

'No – well, yes, if you must know. I object to my son being unable to speak his own language.'

Jane, at a loss, looked to Robert, who said firmly, 'Alan, you are being ridiculous. Your son will always have two languages. What is the matter with you, boy? You speak Urdu yourself, and you married an Urdu-speaking wife, with an Indian background, as well as Indian blood in her veins. Of course she wants her son to speak her own mother tongue. I told you long ago that you were a very fortunate man to have a wife of such courage and beauty. You said then that you would not try and change her. In my opinion, you have done nothing but try to change her ever since. Now, if I am any judge, you have upset her considerably, and all because a two-year-old child is learning to speak his own mother's language. I do not understand you at all, Alan.'

It was rare, indeed, for Alan to be spoken to in this fashion by his father. He could not explain how deeply important it was to him that his wife should appear to be more English than Indian, that his child should be entirely English in every way. He could not understand his own attitude.

The thought of India, the country he had loved so much, now seemed, in relation to Muna, to both repel and attract him. He adored his wife because she was as she was, part of an exotic time in his life, a beautiful, alien creature. She reminded him of every romantic and exciting thing that had ever happened to him, and yet he longed for her to lose her alien side and become the lovely English girl that she appeared to be when she so chose. At a complete loss, he looked at his parents, and his father took pity on him.

'Lovers' quarrels are soon made up. Go and find her, Alan. I do not suppose she has gone very far. Go and find her and bring her back. Do not worry about your son. He will learn English as easily as he is learning Urdu. Do not, I beg of you, upset our dearest Muna any more.'

Alan rode down the path through the wood and over the fields, and suddenly, in the brilliant light of the afternoon, he saw his wife riding towards him. Her hair flying behind her like a black banner, she was riding her horse hard, taking him over one hedge after another and then settling down in her saddle to a flat gallop over the last field between her and the stone wall that edged that part of the park from the open country.

Alan watched her come in growing horror – she could not mean to take the wall at that speed! It became obvious that she did. He saw her gather the horse for the jump, her slender body leaning forward over the animal's neck; he heard her cry out in Urdu, and then the beast was up, his legs tucked neatly under him and, as if he had been lifted by some power other than his own, he cleared the wall, landed, and was reined in, a hundred yards down the path. Alan, cantering after Muna, could not speak at first when he came up with her. She was sitting, relaxed, in her saddle, ordering her hair, and he saw that she was wearing her own costume and riding astride.

'Muna – my God, you could have been killed!' Muna glanced back at the stone wall.

'Over that? Never. I have taken worse than that going up to the hills, when the going was rough, and the weather bad, and I wanted to reach shelter quickly.'

'And what were you trying to reach today, at such speed?'

'Shelter again, perhaps.'

'I see no rain, or bad weather.'

'It is not only weather one needs shelter from, Alan.'

'What else?'

'Despair.' Her voice was completely flat, and cold.

'Despair? My dearest Muna, what can you mean? I did not intend to distress you. It was only that –'

'Only that nothing of myself – my true self, Alan, not the one you have manufactured – must appear in my son. This I cannot bear. He is my flesh, Alan, as well as yours. If I can have no part in him, then it is better if I go away – or die.'

Facing her, he saw the misery in her eyes, saw that truly, she was in despair.

'Muna – Oh, God, I never meant to hurt you. Muna, listen – ' Her face was remote, her eyes seemed to be looking through him, miles away, she was already gone from him, started on a journey that he was terrified he might not be able to stop. He flung himself off his horse, and going to her, put his hands up and took her from her saddle, gripping her tightly as if he was afraid to let her go.

'Muna! Look at me – please! Muna!' He called to her as if he was calling to someone far away and, as if she was returning from a great distance, her eyes slowly turned and focused on him.

'Oh, Muna – do not leave me! Forgive me, I did not mean to cause you pain. Of course Rob is your child as much as mine – I do not know what made me behave as I did. I think I am always afraid that something – something in your country is pulling you away from me, as if I might lose you – and that would be more than I could bear. Muna, look at me, tell me you forgive me – I love you so terribly.'

'Love?' said Muna, her voice still quiet. 'Love? Oh, Alan, I have never had an answer to my question. What is love? Is it all pain and uncertainty, and strangeness? Alan, tell me, what is love?'

As so often before, he did not answer her. He bent his head to kiss her and then, looking round him, saw a thicket. Taking her up in his arms he carried her into the heart of the leaf-shadowed, bough-covered shelter, and there took her as if it were, for him, the first time – and as always, she accepted his love-making, and increased it with her own – until Alan could no longer hear her sad, questioning voice, 'What is love?' but only the thunderous beating of his own heart.

10

On a day in late spring, a few weeks before Rob's fifth birthday, Muna woke to grey skies and rain spattered window panes. Alan was with his regiment, and there seemed no reason to get out of a warm bed on a morning so dull. In any case, Ratni had not yet brought her morning tea – in fact, she was late.

When Ratni came, she brought not only Muna's glass of lemon tea, but the very smell of spring with her. She carried a garland of flowers, blue hyacinths from the woods, and primroses that Muna had come to know and love. Muna opened her eyes wide at the sight of the flowers.

'Oho – we celebrate something? On such a day, when even the skies weep? Ratni, do you remember how we used to long for rain in the hot season, and sit in the room and lay bets on which cloud would break at last and give us a little rain and coolness? I remember that I lost a gold earring to the Nawab – what was his name? It does not matter. I have forgotten, and you are not even listening to me – Ratni! I was telling you something, but it seems I grow dull in my old age, for you have not heard a word I said.'

'The Rose grows dull? Nay, Munabhen, that is not possible. But I can listen to nothing but my own heart this morning – and my mind is full of words that I would say to you.'

'So! I can see, your eyes are like the eyes of a girl with a new lover. Oh evil Ratni – is Bates no longer the man of your heart?'

'He is the man of my heart, and more. He is the father of my child.'

'Ratni!'

'Yes. After so long, I am at last with child. I waited three months before I dared to think it was true. Now it is almost four months, and he has moved – like a bubble rising in a boiling pot of lentils, I felt him move. I say "He" because I am sure my child is a man child, a servant for your son.'

'Ratni, what joy you bring! On such a morning, to be able to make sunshine with good news. But the flowers – were they a gift from the man of your house?'

'Nay – these are to give honour to the Goddess. See, I have some oil, also, and I will make an extra light for her, and give her my thanks.'

An unaccountable shadow suddenly fell over Muna's spirit, as if the dark clouds outside had invaded her room. She felt cold and distressed, and all her pleasure in Ratni's news seemed to have gone.

'Ratni, wait – '

Ratni, on her way to the corner of the room where the ancient image of the Goddess was enthroned, looked over her shoulder enquiringly.

'Munabhen?'

'Wait, Ratni. You are a Christian. Should you not be giving thanks in your church?'

'I? How? Do you wish me to sing a *raga* there? They would think I was mad. Munabhen, I told you, I only said words without feeling. I go to that cold grey place to please my man and my mother-in-law. I have not taken my allegiance from Her whom I do not name. Like you I was vowed to her, but as a servant, not a dancer. I am still hers, as I am yours. *So* I come to give thanks where it is due. Do you think that the cold God of the Christians understands a woman's longing for a son? He, they tell me, sent his son to die on earth, and did not help him, when his son cried to him – and the son himself, in their holy writings, repudiated his mother, when he was on earth as a man. The Christian God says that we must leave everything for him – husband, child, gold – all to be thrown

93

away, and at the end of life, death, and some strange awakening in the clouds, where there is no more marriage. Nay, this is not for me. I worship the Mother, the Bringer of Life.'

Somewhere a voice seemed to whisper, 'The Bringer of Life, and the Destroyer.' It was like a cold wind blowing through dead leaves, a rustling frightening whisper, gone before Muna could be sure that she had heard the words.

Ratni had lit her little lamp, had laid her flowers before the image, and was now sitting cross-legged, her eyes fixed on the Goddess, her lips moving in prayer. Muna, strangely reluctant, rose and joined her – but it was a stone she looked at, and she was filled with alarm and horror. She had worshipped before many images in many temples. Not all had spoken to her, or filled her with reverence. But her own Goddess, to whom she had given her life willingly – in her shrines, or before her image, there had always been the knowledge that she was in the presence of power. Now Muna sat beside Ratni, who was lost in prayer, and Muna felt nothing. There before her was a stone, old, scarred and almost without features. The smoke of Ratni's scented oil coiled up and covered the stone face, and it was as if the cloud on Muna's spirit had come and veiled her Goddess from her sight.

Ratni noticed nothing amiss, that was obvious. She finished her prayers, got up, and left Muna, her face as radiant as it had been when she had first come into the room. The strange weight on Muna's spirit did not lift. All that day she was lonely, like a child suddenly bereft of its family. She felt cold and sad. Jane was worried about her, and suspected that she was sickening for a summer cold.

Bella looked at her narrowly, and said, 'Sahiba – you feel something evil?' and Muna, for some reason afraid to tell the truth, shook her head and denied it, saying instead, 'I think I must be – how do you say it? – "catching a cold". Strange, as if one ran about, trying to become the owner of a thick nose, and swollen eyelids.' Both Jane and Bella laughed, but Bella was not satisfied with Muna's answer. She sensed that this was a heaviness of the spirit, not the body.

But in the morning, when Muna made her early prayers, all

was well. The power was there, and Muna's prayers were not beating against blankness like birds trapped in a room. The power and the knowledge were there – but no voice answered the questions in her heart. Muna bowed her head over her hands, and left the corner of the room which was her shrine to the Goddess. An answer was not always vouchsafed to a worshipper, and it was enough to feel that her prayers were heard. Muna put her worries away from her, and watched Ratni go about her duties with the sun shining from her face.

On Rob's fifth birthday, the barber came and cut off all his curls. Jane bewailed his shorn head.

'But Mother, in my country it is the custom to shave the boy's head bare. Two years ago he would have been shaven-headed, and only now would his hair be growing.'

'Barbarous!' said Jane, and Robert, hearing, laughed at her and said, 'Oh Jane, what a play on words,' but Jane did not laugh. She took two of the soft black curls, still warm from Rob's head, curls that clung round her fingers with a life of their own, and put them in a locket, which she wore thereafter, constantly.

Rob was delighted with his manly haircut, but deeply disappointed that he did not immediately grow sidewhiskers. He spent the rest of the day marching up and down the halls of the big house, giving himself orders, and coming smartly to the salute whenever he saw his grandfather. His father's fears about his language problems had been quite groundless. He now spoke English and Urdu with equal facility.

Late that night Bates arrived at the back door, frantic with haste, his horse's hooves clattering and sliding on the stable cobbles, so that his coming was heard in the drawing-room. Robert and Jane were already questioning each other as to who could be in such a hurry at that hour, when Symes came to tell them that there was trouble up at Bates's cottage. Ratni had been taken very ill, and Bates had come to ask Bella to return with him. Bella was in bed, and Muna had also retired early, but she heard the knocking on Bella's door, and the voices, and got up at once to see if there was anything amiss with Rob.

She stood with Jane and Robert and Bella and listened to a white faced Bates describing Ratni's symptoms. Before he had finished speaking she had left the room, and when Bella came back dressed, Muna was with her, and no one tried to stop her going. Jane suggested that they should take the pony and trap, but Muna, kissing her, shook her head. 'It is better that we ride, Mother. If we ride, we can go over the fields, and make the journey shorter.'

Robert went out to the terrace, to see the three ride off – Muna first, her horse going at a flat gallop, the other two following. He went back into the drawing-room to Jane.

'I am going to wait until they return my dear, but I think you should go up. They may be very late.'

'I would rather stay with you, Robert. I would not sleep if I went to bed. I wish we had not allowed Muna to go.'

'I saw that it was no earthly good trying to stop her. If I had forbidden her to go, she would have disobeyed me, which would have been most embarrassing for all of us. Bella is very capable, she will look after her. If you are going to sit up with me, will you take a glass of wine, my dear?'

They sat together, drinking their wine and looking into the fire, each quiet with their own troubled thoughts. Jane thought of Muna riding through the night, and wished that Alan could have been with them. Surely he would have been able to prevent her going, or if she had insisted, he would have gone with her.

Robert too was thinking of Muna, but not of her wild ride into the night. He was thinking that Muna must have a special feeling of responsibility for Ratni, who had come so far away from her own country because of Muna, and who was also a link with Muna's past life. He thought of Alan, who lived the life of a bachelor, never taking Muna with him to Dover, although he could have found a house for her there quite easily. Knowing his son, he understood why. In spite of all her charm, and her beauty, Alan was afraid that his regiment might discover something about Muna's past, and despise him. He was unable to accept Muna as she was; he was ashamed of her background. He thought sadly that Muna had guessed this long ago. Muna was lonely, but it was not loneliness that Alan could fill. Her loneliness was of the spirit.

As if their thoughts had met, Jane looked up at him and said, 'Robert, I am so fortunate. Nothing ever seems too hard to bear if you are with me, and you have always been with me when I have needed you, always.'

'I am fortunate too, for I need you with me always, otherwise my life would be empty. You are right Jane. We are two lucky people.' He kissed his wife warmly, and standing up, threw the dregs of his wine into the fire. 'A libation to the Gods for all the kindness they have shown us.'

'Are you becoming like Muna, afraid to tempt fate?'

'No. But you are! I notice that you never praise Rob now without adding that really he is a terrible nuisance –'

'That is because Muna gets so distressed if I say he is a lovely child. Robert! Listen!' Jane went over to the french windows, and opening one, leaned out.

'Are they back, Jane?'

'I thought I heard – yes, I did hear horses. They are back, and it sounds to me as if they have brought Bates back with them.' Robert went out quickly, but Symes had been before him, and Robert saw him taking Bates through the green baize door at the end of the hall. Muna and Bella came in together. In their dark cloaks it seemed that they brought some of the night in with them. Muna went straight into the drawing-room, and stopped as if the lights in the room had blinded her. It was Bella who spoke.

'Ratni is dead.'

Robert's horrified questions, Jane's cry of denial were all swallowed into the silence that Muna had brought with her into the room. For a moment it was as if they were all frozen, fallen out of time into some dark, silent place. Then Jane hurried over to Muna, her pity for the sorrow that she saw on Muna's face taking every other thought from her mind.

'Come my dear child! What a terrible shock you have had. Poor little Ratni, I know how you loved her, indeed we all did. Come my dear, with me, come up to your bed. Try not to think of anything just now. Let it all go until the morning, it will seem better in the morning, my dear child.'

Just so had Robert heard Jane speak to her own daughter when the child had been distressed about something. Jane's voice was full of tenderness and love, and something in the voice, not the words, broke through the wall of cold and darkness that was round Muna, and she closed her eyes and then opened them again to look into Jane's loving face, and allowed herself to be led from the room.

'Thank God for that,' said Bella, 'I never thought I'd get her away from the cottage. Sir Robert, I have something I must tell you. Ratni was murdered.'

'What!'

'Aye. Poisoned, just like that dog. You remember the dog? Well, that was how Ratni died, only it took her longer.'

'Bella, I cannot believe this. Who would want to murder Ratni?'

'The woman who never forgave her for marrying Bates.'

'Bessie? Impossible, Bella. That was all over long ago.'

'There is nothing more vicious than a woman who thinks she has a man and then sees him taken from her by a younger woman. Bessie would not forget in a hurry, and now she's had her revenge. I know. I saw Ratni die. Listen, Sir – ' Half way through her description, Robert covered his face with his hands.

'Please Bella, I have heard enough. How on earth did Bessie get the poison to Ratni? Where did she get it from? No Bella, we have to have a better story to take to the police than mere suspicions about a jealous woman.'

'Giving Ratni the poison was easy enough. I was talking to Bates's old mother, while the Sahiba was with Ratni. Old Mrs. Bates has a good friend up at the Grange. The Cook. And Sir, that Cook is Bessie's sister.'

'Great God! Did she plot with Bessie to poison Ratni? I cannot believe that.'

'You do not have to, Sir. The Cook is a good old woman, not at all like her younger sister. She had been old Mrs. Bates's friend for years, and could never understand why her sister was so unkind about her. She was a simple woman, but a wonderful cook, and latterly, when Ratni was in an interesting condition, and not eating as well as she might, the Grange Cook used to bring down little dishes to tempt her appetite. How simple it must have been for Bessie to drop the poison into one of those little dishes. They were only for Ratni. Not that Bessie would have cared if she had killed the whole family, Bates included. As for where she got the poison, she could have got it in many places. Powdered arsenic is used for putting in creams to whiten the skin – it is put in tinctures for taking down swellings – look in your own stables, Sir, or in the garden sheds. Poison is easy to get. For that matter, she could have gone down and got it out of my cottage, for I have it there.'

'Oh God – what a ghastly business. Well, we'll send for the police in the morning, and set everything going.'

Disasters rushed in ugly procession through Robert's mind. The police enquiries, the story of the dog that died in the kitchen from the same poison, all the old scandals renewed, black magic and devil worship, and wicked foreign women living in Moxton Park – like rubbish blown by a wind, his thoughts were scattered and distraught.

Bella nodded her head as if he had spoken. 'Aye. All that old trouble started up again. Which is what was intended. All those horrible stories would have been retold, and embroidered.'

'*Would* have been? They will be, because this time there is no question of not calling in the police.'

'No. For we have been saved by the most unlikely person. Doctor Riley. Old Mrs. Bates was so distracted about Ratni, that while we were working over the poor lass, she went off and called on Doctor Riley, and brought him back with her. He came just after Ratni had died, examined her, and signed the death certificate, saying she had died of a haemorrhage after miscarrying, the old fool. But it has saved us from needing to get the police. There's only one danger, Sir. Get Bates away as quickly as you can, for he is as sure as I am that Bessie killed Ratni, and he'll swing for her, if we don't watch out. The poor lad is half out of his mind.'

'Poor boy. I'll get him out. Where is he now?'

'Symes took him to the kitchen. With your permission Sir, I'll arrange for him to sleep in the rooms above the stable. His mother has Dolly, the kitchen maid, with her.'

'Thank you Bella, you have thought of everything. I will get Bates away as soon after the funeral as I can. I will send him up to town. As you know, Lady Reid has been anxious to spend a little time in London, so it will be perfectly natural if we go up quite soon. A change of scene will help us all recover from this terrible business – I hope.'

'Yes, Sir,' said Bella, and said goodnight and left him; and he stood looking out into the dark garden, and planning the forthcoming trip to London, as a man will plan an escape from danger.

Upstairs, Jane helped Muna to undress and get into bed. Rob was sleeping in his mother's room, and when Jane suggested moving him back into the night nursery so that Muna should sleep late in the morning, Muna refused, looking so desperate that Jane did not argue, but pulled the curtains close over the window, and went back to tuck Muna in as if she was a child.

'Please try to sleep, Muna. We can do nothing now, dearest, nothing until the morning. Then we will see to everything, it will all be arranged as you would wish it. Promise me you will sleep, Muna?'

Muna gave the impossible promise, and watched her mother-in-law leave with overwhelming relief. As soon as she was alone, she climbed out of bed and going to the window, pulled the curtains wide, and opened the window to the night.

The presence in the room with her was a small and humble one, a girl from the hills, obedient and gentle, who had followed her to a strange land, and found happiness, and was now leaving the life she had loved for the wide unknown of another life. Muna heard her voice clearly, her prayers were like the gentle patter of rain. There was grief in the gentle muttering voice, but acceptance as well. Muna, her body cold, went to prostrate herself before the Goddess, hearing beneath her own prayers the gentle beseeching whisper, the voice of a girl praying that she would find her child waiting for her in the new life ahead. Then, from one moment to another, the voice was still, a little wind moved the curtains, and the room was empty, save for Muna and her son. But as Muna prayed, power came into the room. The lamp before the Goddess flared up, and the wind that blew in the room was strong, and a voice deep in Muna's heart answered her questions. Then the wind was still, the ringing crystal voice that had no sound was gone, and Muna stood up and began to dress swiftly, choosing dark clothes, trousers and loose shirt and over-tunic all in black, and a black cloth for her hair. She listened at her door for a moment, took a last look at Rob, sleeping peacefully, and slipped out and down the stairs.

She went out of the side door, closing it behind her, and into the stables, keeping to the shadows as she crossed the yard. None of the dogs barked – why should they? Here and there a horse whickered softly, but there was nothing to disturb any-one in that. She reached the stable where her horse was already pricking inquisitive ears, and snatching up a bridle, led him out, thanking all her Gods for Robert's penchant for grass paths.

Silently, swiftly, she went down the grass verge of the drive and, skirting the lodge, had at last the open country ahead of her. She swung herself on the horse's saddleless back, and urged him into a quick canter, and from that into a gallop, praying that no rabbit burrow or molehill would destroy her. But then she put all fear away from her. This night she could not fall. This night she was riding under protection. Under the moon-less sky they fled like one shadow, horse and rider, and before an hour had passed, Muna was dismounting in a field near the Grange. She tied her horse to a fence post and went swiftly up to the house; then like an animal of the jungle, she prowled silently round it. Doors and windows were all shut. Muna paused to think, and to pray to her Goddess. A tree stretched a great branch out, brushing the side of the house. It was enough. Muna swarmed up it, and along the first branch, until she reached the first open window; it was for her like walking up stairs. The window slid up easily, Muna put a leg over the sill, and was in.

She found herself in a small hall, and smelled the smell of stale bodies and of sleep. This hall was high up in the house, and the doors were small and low. Muna put her hand to a door, and then turned away. That was wrong. The next door she tried opened to her, and she slipped inside.

The bed was on the far side of the room, and mounded under bed clothes was the body she sought. Muna had never forgotten the smell of Bessie. She waited until her eyes were adjusted to the dimness of the room, and then moved catlike to the bedside, and took off her head cloth. Bessie was lying on her back, and her snoring was very loud. There was a candle and tinder beside the bed. Muna struck a light and lit the candle. Yes. It was Bessie. The light flickered out under a silent breath, and the sound of Bessie's snoring had not wavered. Muna stooped, the head cloth rolled into a rope in her hands, her wrists bent. The cloth whipped out like a snake, Bessie's snores rose to a roaring crescendo, dropped to snuffling snorts, and died away. Muna stood as she was, stooped above the bed for a few more minutes. It was enough. She stood listening, then taking her head cloth, went as quietly as she had come.

She rode home slowly and heard, deep in the sorrow of her heart the soundless voice that, satisfied, praised her. Muna's Goddess had many attributes indeed, and one of them was vengeance.

When she got home she put her horse safely back in his stable, with his bridle hanging on its peg, went back to her room unheard and, stripping off her clothes, made them into a small compact bundle. There would be a way of disposing of them in the morning. She would never wear them again. Until morning came she sat, wrapped in one of her pushmina robes, and watched the night sky, and thought about Ratni, and the soul that was already taking up the burden of a new life. Of Bessie she did not think at all. Her son slept peacefully beside her, while she waited for the morning.

When Daisy came to take Rob to give him his breakfast she found him playing on the floor, and Muna sitting up in bed watching him. He kissed his mother and rushed off to begin a

102

new wonderful day, and Daisy picked up a piece of cloth from the floor.

'There,' she said, 'He's been playing with one of your beautiful embroidered head cloths, Ma'am. Scrumpled it all up, he has.'

'It does not matter. Give it to me, Daisy. It is an old one, in any case. Daisy, I am very thirsty. Could you ask Bella to bring me my tea?' Remembering how Ratni had always brought Muna's tea, Daisy's eyes filled with tears and she hurried out. Muna got up and folded the scarf into the bundle she had already made of her other clothes, and put them all together into a carved chest. By the time her tea came she was back in bed, and Bella was glad to see that although she was very pale and drawn, she looked rested, and had lost the terrible haunted look her face had worn the night before.

As Bella poured the tea into the glass with its silver holder, and added a slice of lemon, Muna said quietly, 'Bella, there is a bundle of clothes in that chest. I do not want them. I think you could dispose of them?'

Bella's face was very pale, but she nodded. 'Aye. I'll get rid of them; now drink your tea, and think no more of the clothes —nor of anything else.'

It was decided that Ratni's funeral would take place the following day. Bates was now staying in a room above the stables, because Robert wanted him near-by in case he lost his head and did anything foolish. His mother would stay with the lodgekeeper until she had recovered from her grief and the shock that Ratni's death had given her. Jane made all these arrangements in a state of shock herself. Robert's story of Ratni having died from drinking poisoned broth had terrified her. She asked no questions, but began to prepare to leave for London sooner than she had expected. She had many wild suspicions, but after looking at Bella's stony face, and seeing Muna grow thin and drawn, she kept all her thoughts to herself. Bates was leaving for London directly after the funeral. Robert had warned Jane to be ready to leave within the following three weeks. He said very little more, and Jane, conferring with the housekeeper about the coming move, found it hard to keep her mind on her lists, and her arrangements.

It was a strange relief when the news came from the Grange. It was brought by Doctor Riley himself, who had come up to speak with Robert about his fee for attending Ratni's dying. Robert gave him the brandy that he had really come for, and he sat, savouring it, and said, as he drank, 'Well – a Doctor has a hard time of it. Two in a night, you may say. Very sad. I was up all night, and no respite all day. Mrs. Boothby took to her bed, and Miss Boothby is keeping the whole house together with difficulty, for the Cook went into strong hysterics, being Bessie's only sister, and is now prostrate with grief.'

'Really?' said Robert, with no idea of what the Doctor could mean.

'Yes. Nasty business. The woman was too fat anyway, and it seems she had a very hearty meal last night, with several glasses of porter. Very cheerful she was. Well, it was a good thing that she was happy, for it was her last meal. It finished her. She died in her sleep.'

'What on earth – are you telling me that the Boothby's maid, Bessie, is dead?'

'Just that, Sir Robert, just that. Apoplexy. Couldn't have known anything about it. Just snuffed out. In the midst of life, we are in death, as it were.'

'Great heavens!' said Robert, and gave the Doctor another brandy, and took one himself. Then, the Doctor sent muzzily on his way, Robert went to find Jane.

At first Jane was inclined to rejoice, at least the wretched woman was dead and so Bates could not get into trouble by killing her, and surely that was a mercy. Bella, however, who was present when Robert told Jane the Doctor's story, looked very distressed.

'Bella what is it? I think it is an excellent thing that the woman died of natural causes, if greed can be called natural. At least we shall have no more trouble with Bates.'

'That Doctor would not know natural causes from a public execution. Let us hope that – ' Bella, looking at Jane's widening eyes, broke off in mid-sentence and turned to Robert. He looked as worried as she did, but they did not speak, and Jane

104

was faced with yet another mystery that she was afraid to think about. She hurried away, glad that there was so much to do that she could not stop to think for very long. But in spite of all the planning and checking that was to be done, her mind would not be quiet, and she longed for the moment when they would leave Moxton Park.

Muna took the news of Bessie's death with no astonishment. She just nodded when Jane told her, and said quietly, 'Well, she was a bad woman, it is good that she is dead. Let us now forget her.'

Jane, surprised at Muna's calm, was only too glad to have no further discussion on the subject.

Just before sunset they buried Ratni. It was a bright evening. Spring had come late, but on this day there was sunshine.

Muna did not go to the funeral. Sitting at home, at her window, she saw the last of the sun, and thought of how Ratni's hair would have gleamed blue-black in that late sunlight, and of her sparkling eyes, brighter than the eyes of the blackbird that sang in the lilac bush below her window. She thought of the river bank where the burning would have taken place, had Ratni died in Madore. It would have been a hot summer evening there, and the smoke from the pyre would have risen straight into the air, like a tower, for there would have been no wind. Here, a spring wind blew in through her open window. The lamp flame, burning before the image of the goddess, flared and quivered. The face of the image looked down, eyeless, dark. Time had defaced the carved features, but as the lamp flared, it seemed to Muna that for a moment the face was clear again; the full lips appeared to move, and then settle into a secret smile, and then a shadow fell across the face and it was blank once more. Muna turned away and looked out at the bare branches of the trees tossing in the wind, a mist of green just beginning to clothe them after their long winter bareness.

Most of the village attended Ratni's funeral – some out of curiosity, but most came to mourn, for Ratni had made many friends. When it was over, Robert himself took Bates back to his cottage, and watched him put his gear into the trap, and saw him off, taking a promise from him that he would stay in

London and not do or say anything foolish. The white-faced young man looked down at his master from the seat in the trap, and nodded.

'I will do nothing, Sir,' he said quietly. 'There does not seem much to do now, except get through my life.' He shook the reins, the pony and trap rattled off down the road, and Robert watched him out of sight and then mounted his horse and began to ride slowly home, passing the churchyard on the way and seeing another grave being readied. Of course Bessie would be buried there the following day, an odd turn of events.

Deep in thoughts which led him nowhere, Robert continued on his way.

II

When Robert got home, he sent a message down to Dover, to his son. Alan arrived three days later, and was closeted in the library with his father. He heard all that his father had to say, and agreed with all his plans. Jane came in, and was told that if possible, Robert would like them all to leave for London the following week.

'I can be ready, Robert. I have already written to Aunt Charlotte. Caroline is going up now too. She will sponsor Muna at one of the Queen's afternoons.'

'Have you told Muna that we are leaving?'

'Yes. She has arranged everything, and Bella will come with us, of course. It will be good for Muna, Alan; this has been a most distressing time for her. A little gaiety and going about will help to keep her mind from unhappy things.'

Alan agreed. He was worried about a number of aspects of this trip to London, but when he heard from his father that his mother was planning to present Muna to the Queen, he was completely horrified and told his father so. Robert listened to all that he had to say, and then sat in thought for some minutes. When he spoke, his remarks did not help Alan at all.

'I see no way out of this, Alan. Muna is as dear to your mother as our own daughter was. I truly believe that she has forgotten that Muna is her daughter-in-law – she thinks of her as her own child. To tell her at this stage that Muna was a famous harlot in India, a dancing girl who dispensed her favours to any man who could pay her price – which was very high, I understand – well, my dear boy, could you tell your mother this? I could not, and I will not allow you to do so. It could very well kill your mother with shock.'

'But Father, she is planning to present Muna – Muna, Father – to the Queen! I just do not believe that such a presentation should take place. And Aunt Caroline is to be her sponsor. If it was ever discovered who Muna was, before she came here – '

'Do you think we would all be sent to the Tower? Come, Alan, I think you are taking this very seriously.'

'It is a very serious matter, Father. If it was discovered, I would certainly have to resign my commission, and I do not think that Aunt Caroline would ever appear at Court again – nor indeed, Great Aunt Sophie! It would bring everything tumbling about our ears,' said Alan desperately, his agitation growing in inverse proportion to his father's calmness. Alan was very much a man of his time, and Robert looked at him astonished, realising what it must have cost him to have brought Muna back as his wife – surely he must love her very deeply.

'Alan, have you ever thought of the backgrounds of some of the people who were, and are, closest to Her Majesty? I do not imagine that their private lives could bear very close scrutiny. There is nothing you can do about this, except take everything as it comes, and do not show that you are worried in any way. After all, look at your wife, boy. Who is going to point a finger at her? Where will any scandal rise? Your regiment? I think you told me that none of them met Muna in India. As far as they know, her background is as you told us – impeccable. If you go about looking hang-dog, you will help to cause conjecture. Stop being so distressed about nothing. Let things take their course.'

Alan returned to Dover to find that his regiment was being transferred to Camberley, and the remove and his duties took several weeks. When he went up to Town, he found the family installed in the town house. Muna appeared to be enjoying her round of dinners and Balls with Caroline and Jane chaperoning her. She looked beautiful and happy, and he learned that she was to be presented at an afternoon drawing-room early in June.

Muna went through the entertainments arranged for her as she had progressed through most of her life in England – moving through yet another aspect of a dream. She wore her beautiful clothes, smiled, danced, and rode in the Park, or went with Jane in the open Landau, as directed.

During these first few weeks, Muna was seen about a great deal, and caused a sensation. So much so that an artist, famous for his paintings of beautiful women, went out of his way to ask if he might paint her portrait. Both Jane and Caroline, consulting together, thought this an excellent idea. Appointments were made, and at Caroline's insistence she, and not Jane, chaperoned Muna, for the man was also known for his love for beautiful women. Caroline was certain that Muna was perfectly capable of dealing with any advances made to her, and was equally certain that Jane would be alarmed into cancelling all the sittings if she thought Muna was liable to be annoyed by a practised seducer.

After the first two sittings, when the artist made charcoal sketches of Muna's head and shoulders, Caroline left them together and went about her own business, collecting Muna at the appointed time when the sitting was over. The man was indeed an artist, and having made his play, and been very firmly put in his place by Muna who showed obviously that she was not interested in his person, and her 'no' meant exactly that, he turned his attention to the portrait, only occasionally bewailing the fact that he could not have a closer association with his subject. He knew exactly how he wished to portray Muna, and here he met with no repulse. She was delighted to comply with his wishes on the subject of the portrait itself.

The finished picture was to be shown at the Royal Academy. Caroline had her first sight of it on the day of the last sitting when the artist displayed his work to her with great pride. Caroline regarded it in silence, then gave unstinting praise. But driving through the London streets, she spoke to Muna.

'Muna, my dear, what possessed you? That picture is utterly

beautiful, but did you not think of what your family's reactions are going to be?'

'No. I see no reason why they should feel distress. That is a portrait of me, myself, as I really am.'

'Yes. But Muna, how will Alan see it?'

'Alan?' said Muna slowly, 'Alan? Surely he will not be distressed. After all – ' Her voice was becoming less certain.

'Alan is going to be very distressed. And worse, so is Jane. Muna, I fear you have been foolish.' Caroline's voice was uncompromising, and Muna looked at her, her face clouded.

'Am I never to be myself – even in a picture?'

'Ah Muna, are you not yourself now, or when you go about with us? You make me feel like a dragon. Do you hate us all so much, that you do not feel you are one of us?'

'You know that I do not hate you – you know how I love my family. Every moment I live is for them. But no, I do not feel as if I am one of you. I dream I am – but a whole life, another country, my very blood, tells me I am not, I am alone.' Muna spoke with passion, and Caroline took her hand. Indeed, this girl was right. She was being apart, her attitudes of mind, her innermost thoughts, must of necessity be totally different. She had, from the time of her arrival in her husband's country, been forced into a mould that must have frequently irked her, always confused her. Yet she had never rebelled, and behaved with incredible patience and obedience.

Caroline tightened her grip on the slender hand she held. 'My dearest Muna – you may be alone, but remember how much you are beloved. I only spoke about the picture because I fear that Jane may be distressed also, but do not worry. We will arrange something.' They spoke of other things, and Jane was told the portrait was beautiful.

She saw it the following day. She admired it extravagantly, and Muna listened to her and said nothing. Jane was still admiring when they were alone together, but asked if it was true that the picture was going on public exhibition. When told that it was, she said she could understand the artist wishing to display such a brilliant work. 'But I could wish, Muna, that you had worn one of your Paris dresses for the picture – or there is the new ball gown.'

'But Mother, you told me that you liked me in the dress of my country – you allowed, no, encouraged me to wear it, even when Alan was angry. Mother, I have displeased you, I am sorry.'

'Muna! Of course I love your country's beautiful dress, and you have not displeased me at all. But this portrait will be displayed before a great many people. I think Alan would have rather seen you depicted as his wife, in one of your beautiful gowns, rather than –'

'Rather than as myself – Muna. I should have worn lace and roses, and my pearl and diamond collar, and been painted as "Young Mrs. Reid", I see. Well, as you all think that my husband will be distressed, then he must not see the picture.'

'Oh Muna, I have hurt you – please do not be upset! Of course Alan must see the portrait, it is perfectly beautiful. I have hurt you because I have explained badly.' There was, thought Jane, no way in which she could explain to Muna that her London Season, and her coming Presentation to the Queen, had been specially arranged to stress her European background.

The artist had painted Muna in her Lambaghi riding dress, with her long black unbound hair hanging in silken luxury over her shoulders, and she certainly did not look English. Firm-limbed and slender, Muna looked out of the picture in all her beauty, but Jane had never noticed before how her long eyes were slightly tilted above her high cheekbones, nor had she realised what a tragic look those dark eyes wore. The colours of the portrait were cream and ivory, the creamy richness of Muna's robes, the ivory of her flesh. The emerald background threw all into prominence, made the whole picture more exotic. This was no European, this beautiful creature. This was a girl from a far country, an enchanting stranger.

Jane, in desperation, went to Robert. He went to see the portrait and admired it very much. But he too thought it was a disaster He told Muna, and to him she listened calmly.

'You must not misunderstand anything, Muna. In fact, you

111

know perfectly well why you have come to London, and why you are going through all this mummery – do you not?' Under his straight look, Muna nodded.

'Yes, of course I know. But I thought – Father, I did not know that this picture would be displayed. It was to be for the house, for you and Mother, and for Alan, and for Rob and his children in due course. Forgive this stupidity of mine. Do not think of it any more. I will arrange it, if you will trust me?' Robert did, implicitly, and his trust was not misplaced. Muna spoke with Lady Addison, and then went with her to see the artist. He was outraged at first, but the size of the fee he was offered overcame his artistic sensibilities. When the portrait went to the Royal Academy, young Mrs. Reid looked out from the canvas, her face serene and beautiful above the lace and cream roses that she wore. Her luxuriant hair was coiled and dressed high in the latest fashion, and she wore a pearl and diamond collar round her ivory throat. Alan was enchanted with the portrait and immediately bought it, and no one asked what had become of the first portrait. In fact, no one mentioned it. Caroline knew of its disposal, and had helped Muna with the careful packing and despatching of the portrait. It was sent to Lambagh.

Muna showed no signs of distress, and assured Jane that of course when they went back to Moxton Park she would wear her own costumes as often as she had done before – but that she quite understood that they were unsuitable for London. Robert watched her heal Jane's wounds, and wondered quietly to himself as to the wounds that Muna herself must have suffered to enable her to be so gentle with another's feelings. His admiration for Muna grew with every day he knew her.

Muna, as always, kept her own counsel. Her face was as controlled and serene as it was in her portrait, and she watched the days go by with the eyes of a dreamer. Rob was part of the secret heart of her life. He would come running into her room when she was changing her clothes for yet another foray into the social scene of London, and perched on her bed would regale her with tales of what he had been doing. He had sailed his boat on a pond in the Park, he had ridden his pony, and, unforgettable, had watched a splendid troop of cavalry ride through the streets. He told her all this in Urdu, which was, like his English, faultless.

He was a sturdy small boy, his features still blurred with babyhood, his dark hair always untidy. Everything he did, everything that happened to him during the day, he brought to Muna like a present. It did not matter what she was doing, there was always time for him. He never went to sleep at night without her final good night embrace, and she was the first person he went to see in the morning as soon as he was dressed. In all the extraordinary aspects of Muna's life, he was her one reality, and through him she kept her hold on things which had seemed forever lost. Sometimes Alan, up in town for a few precious hours with her, would feel an impatience with the amount of time that Muna took from him to spend with Rob. But then the child's transparent pleasure at seeing his father, his shouts of 'Come and watch me riding, Papa, please!' would enchant him into forgetting any momentary jealousy. He would ride with Muna in the Park and wait, watching his son riding his pony, with Bates schooling him; and on the day when Rob sent his pony into a fast canter, lost his seat and fell off, it was Alan who leapt from his horse and ran to him, whilst Muna sat smiling, and only said, 'My son, you must learn to ride properly before you try to ride fast. Get up, and this time do what Bates tells you,' while Alan, still pale with fright over his son's fall, could only marvel at her detachment. As he himself remounted and they moved off, leaving Rob to the ministrations of Bates, Alan said 'I thought you would be frightened.'

'Frightened? Of what? Because Rob fell off his horse? Alan, how many times did you fall before you rode well – and indeed, as I recall, you came off one day when we were riding together at Moxton Park. No, I am not frightened of Rob falling from his horse. There would be something wrong with his riding if he did not fall.'

Alan shook his head at her. 'You are a wonderful woman, my love, and I do not understand you at all.'

'You understood me very well last night, no?'

'This is not the time for us to speak of last night – there is no shelter here for lovers. We will be a scandal, if you continue to speak about last night.'

'That would distress your mother. It is only now a week before I am to go before the Queen. You will be here?'

'Of course. We go to a Ball at Marlborough House that night. I shall be up here for three days.'

'I am glad. Your mother has given me a dress that will please you, I think. It is the colour of cream, and is full of lace, with a long train. I have been told how to pick it up, and put it over my arm, and go from the Presence backwards. I must look at the Queen all the time. This train is to be lined with the darker cream of the roses I carry, and is three yards in length.'

'Are you nervous?'

'How should I be nervous? She is an old lady, and powerful, but I have danced for many old and powerful Maharanis. I do not even have to dance before her – there is no reason to fear.'

Dance before the Queen! Alan shuddered, and rode home beside his wife with all his previous apprehensions rearing terrifying heads.

The great day of Muna's presentation dawned. Jane and Bella dressed Muna, her dress fitting her so closely that it could have been a second skin. Her lovely dark hair was arranged, and three ostrich plumes fixed into the cream tulle veil on her head. Caroline Addison arrived and Muna went slowly down the stairs to the drawing-room. Jane and Caroline both stood silent, looking at her.

'There will not be another there to approach you in beauty, my dear,' said Caroline finally, and it was true. Then they went out to the carriage and joined the long queue of other carriages, all on their way to Buckingham Palace.

Afterwards, Muna could remember very little about the actual presentation. There was a terrible crush in the ante-room, and then she remembered hearing her name called. A small, commanding figure in black, glittering with diamonds, held out an imperious hand to be kissed. Muna performed a beautiful curtsey, kissed the fingers that barely touched her own, and looked up into a tired, sad old face, a face that held more royal authority and knowledge of power than Muna had ever seen in a human face before. Her eyes fixed on the wise eyes that looked at her, Muna backed away, caught her train up over her arm as a page lifted it for her, and left the Presence.

That night, Muna was given the final accolade. The Prince of Wales chose her for his partner in one of the first dances of the evening. During the quadrille, there was time for him to speak with her. He reminded her very much of many rich men she had known in the past. She listened to his compliments, delicately phrased in his guttural voice, looked into the sleepy, experienced eyes and knew that with a responding glance, a certain smile, a few carefully worded phrases, she could join a series of famous ladies who had been favoured by this man, the heir to an Empire. He appeared to be a kind man, and she felt sorry for him. It was hard for a man to wait for his inheritance and for his place in the world. This Prince had been in the ante-room to power for a long time, allowed little authority, treated with contempt, frittering his days away with amusements – a man of integrity and a born ruler, wasting precious years.

But the days when she had been chosen to comfort many such men were over for Muna. She danced and talked charmingly but gave no other sign; her eyes raised to his were innocent of any promise. When the dance ended, an Equerry was waiting to take her back to the gilt and velvet sofa where Caroline sat with Jane and Alan. Muna saw the Prince joined by a magnificent blonde woman who had been sitting near the Princess of Wales. The woman had beautiful skin and eyes, and a proprietary air. She gave the impression of beauty, but her strong jaw and determined manner were not assets. She took the Prince's arm possessively, and Muna looked at the Princess, whose flawless face was smiling and calm above her wide collar of pearls. This seemed a strange Court, where the favourites were openly displayed before all, in the presence of the Royal wife. Muna, watching, thought that the habits of the *Zenana*, where each woman had her appointed place and did not step out of it, were preferable to this odd behaviour.

There were many beautiful and high-born women in the

ballroom; they carried themselves with decorum, but she had heard stories. When the Prince was a guest at various great houses, his hostess would be forewarned. She would be told which lady pleased him and would adjust her bedrooms accordingly, ensuring that His Royal Highness would have easy and private access to the room of the current favourite. The husbands of these favoured women did not appear to object. Muna looked across the room again at the graceful figure of the Princess who would one day be Queen Empress, and felt pity. In India she would still have had rivals, her Royal husband would have enjoyed his pleasures, but his wife would never have been seen in any place where the Court favourites were received. Muna felt that England fell behind the eastern courts and turned away, to find herself being watched in her turn by the Prince, his eyes dwelling on her with obvious pleasure, and presently the Equerry was at her side. His Royal Highness requested. Muna found herself dancing again, the sleepy eyes looking at her with a spark in their depths. She was asked how long she would be in town, and after the dance, was led over and curtsied before the Princess, who smiled her sweet smile and spoke of the afternoon's Court, praising Muna's gown and saying that Her Majesty herself had remarked on Muna's grace and bearing. Muna, making suitable replies, looked at the controlled, beautiful face and admired her very much. She noticed a strange, strained look in the misty violet eyes – a listening look as if the Princess was hearing with her eyes instead of with her ears. After a few minutes Muna curtsied again, once to the Princess, who gave her her hand, once to the Prince, whose eyes met hers with determination. Then she was escorted back to her party and the group around the Royals slowly parted, as, bowing to right and left, the Prince of Wales and his Princess left the Ball together, every woman in the room sinking gracefully to the floor in curtsies that were like the bowing of flowers when a wind passes over them.

Safely in the carriage, Caroline said quietly to Jane, 'She took his eye, of course. Had you thought, Jane dear?'

'No, I had not. Oh dear, now what do we do? It would be unfortunate.'

'Indeed it would. *Most* unfortunate. Particularly as, of course, no offence must be given.'

The two ladies fell silent and Muna, sitting beside a sleepy Alan who was drunk with relief that the presentation had passed without any dire scandal, leaned over to say, 'Mother, you and Lady Caroline are worried because the Prince looked at me and considered me for his harem?'

Alan jolted upright in his corner, Caroline turned a fascinated face, and Jane looked horrified.

'Muna, what on *earth* do you mean?' Alan was staring at his wife.

'Well, what do you imagine? Such a man – Alan, I have seen many princes in India. *They* choose whom they wish, and they are not as powerful as this one.'

'Did he – what did he say?'

'He said nothing the whole world could not hear. But he chose me. What shall I do?'

'You will come straight back to Moxton Park with me. Do not, I pray you, be ridiculous, Muna. What did you imagine we would do?'

'But will this not anger him? Could it imperil your position? In India he could have you imprisoned, and take me.'

'Well, he cannot here. Muna, for heaven's sake, you are upsetting my mother and Aunt Caroline! Of course he cannot have me imprisoned!'

'That is a relief at any rate,' said Caroline Addison, a thread of laughter running through her voice. 'For a moment I thought we were living in the Arabian Nights! Muna is right, of course. His eye certainly lighted on her, and his mind too. I think a strategic withdrawal down to Moxton Park would be in order. Do not worry, Muna, our Princes are not as dangerous as they were. Now had we lived in the days of Henry VIII, Alan would no doubt have finished by being hung, drawn, and quartered.'

'Hung, drawn, quartered? What is this?'

'Never mind, Muna dearest, I do not think I could stand the explanation. Yes, Caroline, we must go back – quite soon, I think.'

'Well, Mother, Muna and I are going down tomorrow. I

117

have some leave and wish to spend it with my wife.' Alan's voice was belligerent. Silence fell in the carriage for the remainder of the journey, while the four inmates pursued their own thoughts. Jane longed for Robert. He had not accompanied them to the Ball, but with Caroline's husband had gone to his club. Jane looked at her daughter-in-law in some dismay. Beauty was not always an asset.

Alan's loving that night was demanding, and he held Muna possessively close to him all night, as if he would guard her against some danger. They left early the next morning, Alan driving in the light curricle.

Caroline, watching them go, said, 'Just in time. I would judge there will be a spate of invitations.'

'Yes. How very awkward –'

'Nonsense. I expected just this. I am sad in a way. It would have been amusing to watch Muna taking London by storm. But Alan would not have been amused. I do not think he would wear a pair of horns with grace.'

'Caroline! Really – you say terrible things.'

'Well, my dear, Royal or not, Edward would have certainly clapped a pair of horns on Alan's head if he could have done so. But Muna – strangely enough, Muna was glad to go.'

'Yes. I was afraid she would be disappointed, missing all the gaiety – but she was positively delighted to go.'

'A strange girl.'

'No – just a girl longing to go home. There is nothing strange about that.'

12

Muna returned to the part of the dream life that she knew best; she rode every morning and Rob accompanied her very often. Bates had thrown himself into the job of teaching Rob everything about horses and riding that he knew, and his knowledge was considerable. He was glad to have something to keep his mind from the things that he still could not think of without pain. Rob was a willing and brilliant pupil. Bates remarked on his skill to Sir Robert.

'It's just as if he was born to it, Sir. A real horseman he is; he seems to be able to talk to the beasts, he can do anything with them. Only got to show him something once, and he's got it perfect; he's a pleasure to teach.'

Rob graduated to a larger pony, and looked after him mostly himself. He did everything Bates showed him, faithful to every detail, hissing through his teeth as he rubbed Munshi down. Robert, watching his grandson, could not believe that the boy was only five. He was tall for his age and very intelligent. Robert began to cast about for a suitable place for Rob to continue his education for, other than horsemanship, he did not appear to be learning very much.

It was decided that he would go to the Vicarage every day and share the tutor who taught the Vicar's two sons. The arrangement worked well, and Rob settled into the life with great contentment. Now he not only had his mother and father, an adoring grandmother and a grandfather whom he respected very greatly, his much loved Bates and Munshi; but he also had two friends of his own age – Guy and James Munnings – and a whole world of things to learn and to ask questions about. Rob's life stretched ahead of him like a wonderful new universe, filled with places to explore and people to love; he was an extremely happy small boy.

The summer went on, one warm day after another; it seemed that there had never been a more perfect summer. Cloudless skies, gentle winds to make days cooler that otherwise might have been almost too warm, and an occasional rainstorm, always at night, so that everything was washed and clean and sparkling with fresh green by morning. The roses were magnificent, and the whole summer garden smelled of their perfection. Muna spent hours sitting in the garden, absorbing the sun and the smell of the roses, and Jane would join her. The two women grew even closer until Robert, watching them, felt that Jane had completely forgotten that Muna was her son's wife, not in fact her own daughter.

Autumn came, a gentle autumn, with still sunny days, with the leaves on the trees turning magnificent colours and staying on the trees because there was no wind to blow them off. Harvest was over and the orchards had been cleared and the apples laid in neat rows in the cellar, except for those that were taken for cider. One perfect day followed another and it seemed that there was going to be no winter, it was so calm and warm.

But winter was waiting, just round the corner of the year.

One evening, Jane and Muna and Robert sat late on the terrace, watching a great, lop-sided orange moon rise above the trees. The light was extraordinary, as if they looked at the lawns and the bushes by the light of a fire – everything seemed to be bronze and copper and the stretch of lawn was like a golden pool, flat, unpolished gold with no reflections in it. Muna looked at the strange burning moon and shivered.

'In India we would expect an earthquake – or a bad wind. This is a very strange moon, so full of fire. Look how the trees burn in its light, as if they had been painted in flame.'

'It is the turn of the moon – there will be a thunderstorm, I expect, Muna, not an earthquake. This will be the last night

120

that we will sit out here, I think, for the rest of the year. That moon brings us winter. Let us all go in. The wind is rising, and it has a bite in it. Tomorrow no doubt we shall need a fire.'

As they walked towards the house, the wind blew more strongly, and Muna heard the rattle of dry leaves beginning to fall. The beautiful months were over and winter was beginning. She went straight to Rob's room to make sure he was properly covered and took one of her Lambaghi quilts to put over him. In the light of the candle she carried she looked down at her son, so surrendered to sleep that he did not feel her tucking the quilt round him, nor stir when she bent and kissed him. How she loved him! Her heart seemed to crack with love as she watched him. When she went back to her own room the first thing she did was to pray before the Goddess, begging for health and strength and protection for her son.

'Let all danger come to me, not to him! I offer myself again, with joy, take my life for his,' prayed Muna, and heard from long ago the old vow, 'My life for yours, now and always.' The words seemed to echo in her head long after she had undressed and gone to bed. The moon was orange and had a strange coppery glow. Muna lay looking at it through her window, and listening to the wind, until at last she fell asleep.

Alan came home for a long week-end a month later. Running upstairs, eager to see Muna, he found her in her room, alone, sitting close to the window, looking out at the winter bare trees and the grey skies where the rooks wheeled and cried, blown by a rough gusty wind. He stood, arrested, in the doorway, looking at her. Coming on her suddenly he was always struck by her astounding beauty, but now he noticed something else. She looked very small and young, and very sad. Everything he had been going to tell her went out of his head. He was across the room in two strides and had pulled her up into his arms.

'My dear love, what is it? You look so unhappy!'

Muna did not ask him, as she would have liked to do, 'What is happiness?' because she did not think that there was an answer to that question. But she rested in his arms, her head on his shoulder and admitted to homesickness.

'Oh, Muna, and I thought you had settled here so well — what has made you homesick?'

He followed her gaze back to the window, saw the blowing, grey landscape, and said, 'But Muna, you have winter in India too.'

Muna nodded. 'Yes, we have winter. But it is a coloured winter, with all the land wearing the change of season like a different robe. There is sunshine, and sparkling snow on the mountains; and on the plains, although there is no snow, there are blue skies and in the evenings, the sunsets turn the evenings into jewels, even the dust clouds that the cattle raise on the plain outside Madore used to look like gold dust, and the smoke from the fires was blue. The women, as it got colder, would wrap themselves in scarlet and yellow and pink shawls — Oh Alan, I long for colour! It is all grey here, so terribly grey! Even my dress is grey.' Muna pulled at her silk dress, the colour of a grey pearl, a dress that Alan admired.

'But do not wear the dress, dearest, if it makes you unhappy.'

'But you like it.'

Muna was weeping suddenly, and Alan was astonished. He could not remember ever seeing her weep with such abandon. He held her shaking body in his arms and looked at her tear-streaked face.

'Oh Muna, it is more than just the weather, surely!'

'I told you, Alan, it is homesickness.'

'No. More than that too. What is it, Muna?'

Muna looked up at him in despair. How could she tell him what she felt? In the end, her words tumbled out in her own language, and Alan, unpractised, only understood about half of what she said, and could not make much sense of that. As usual, when confused and worried he grew angry.

'Muna, are you trying to tell me that my family have not made you welcome?'

'How could I tell you that? You know that they are like my own parents. I love and honour them as I would have loved and honoured my own father and mother. My grief has nothing to do with them. How can I tell you? You cannot understand, and

I – I find that your language does not always speak the right words for me.'

'Try, Muna. I am listening.'

'It is this, then. It is that nothing that I do makes me awake. I dream, always; it appears that I live in a dream here; and yet, although I try to wake, I am at the same time afraid to waken.'

'You are right, I do *not* understand you. What do you mean, you dream? You are awake, here in my arms – is this a dream, or this?'

'Oh Alan, you kiss me with such force, it is as if you are angered with me; I cannot make it clear to you – I cannot.'

'Well, go on – I still listen, even if I don't understand.'

'Nothing that I do seems real, and in this dream, evil things happen to everyone I love. I grow fearful for you all, lest Fate should harm you through me. Your country rejects me, Alan, not your family.'

'To me you are talking nonsense, Muna.'

'Yes. I know. You see, you do not understand.'

'But I listen. Go on telling me.'

'Well then, think, and remember. Your parents have had pain through gossip about me. I heard such gossip in my own country. The enclosed *zenana* world loves to spin tales, and whisper of this and that, and also much gossip comes into those houses that you do not like me to speak of now. I have gossiped and laughed at the gossip myself, in *those* days. But here it is as if they used their tongues as daggers, to kill. Gossip killed Ratni just as surely as the poison did. I fear. I fear where the serpent of fate will strike next. My karma is bad, I think, in this country. I carry ill fortune for those I love.'

Involuntarily, Alan looked over to the image in the corner of the room, and Muna saw his expression.

'You must take that thought from your head, lord. *She* has guarded us all – even though I broke my vows and left my country, crossing the black waters to come with you. She has never left me; I can never leave her. So perhaps the night when you followed me to the lake shore in Lambagh – perhaps it would have been better if I had not listened to you on that silver night.'

123

'Better for you?'

'Ah no, that I can never say, with our son growing like a young tree before my eyes — may it be spoken in a good hour. No. Better for you and for your family. I have brought you nothing but grief.'

'You brought me the son you are so proud of — and the delight of your company. You gave my mother back her daughter, and my father loves you. How can you reward all this love by saying it would have been better if we had never met? By feeling that you live in a dream — or is it a nightmare, Muna, that you hate life here so much?' Alan's voice was hurt and angry. It now appeared to him that the only thing that Muna cared about was her son. Muna saw the anger and jealousy in his eyes, and put her hands over her face, weeping again.

'Now see, Alan, I have caused you pain, but only because you do not understand.'

'But I listened, and all I heard was that except for Rob, you wish that you had never met me!'

Muna lifted her swollen eyes and stared at him in horror. 'Now I see the measure of your comprehension, Alan. I cannot tell you, I cannot explain, for all I do is distress you!' Another spasm of weeping took her, and Alan held her in his arms, now trying to comfort her, drying her tears with his lips, kissing her wet cheeks and eyelids.

'Alan, forgive me. I have been stupid. Now you are drinking my grief.'

'I would drink all your grief, my love, until there was no sorrow left in this world for you to bear.'

'Would you, Alan? Take all my griefs upon your head? Then we should be a very happy couple, for I would do the same for you. But I am not unhappy, only stupid. How can I waste my time weeping like this, for nothing, when I have all that I would wish here? And may the Gods not be jealous of me when I say all that any woman could wish — a husband, a son, and loving parents. Forgive me, Alan, and forget all my foolishness.'

Alan kissed her again, and looked down at her lovely face,

blurred with weeping, and was suddenly confronted with a great many decisions that he had put at the back of his mind, not wishing to think of them at all. Now he knew that the time had come to make a decision, and this to him was difficult and distasteful.

Several times during their years in England he had wondered if he should send Muna back to Madore. Well endowed as she was, even without any help from him, she would be a woman of wealth wherever she went. But that thought had only come into his mind when he realised that her past life could not be wiped away as if it had never been. When he heard officers from Indian units discussing their exploits among the harlots and dancing girls of northern India, of the skills and beauties of these girls, Alan had cringed and determined to send Muna away from him – until he saw her again, and held her in his arms, and knew that he could not live without her. He had admired unstintingly the manner in which she had fitted into his family's way of life; he was delighted that his parents loved her so much. When Rob was born Alan was proud and happy, until he heard his son speaking his mother's tongue like a native, before he could speak a word of English. Then again he had the thought that Muna should go – because Rob was *his* son, and would one day inherit all that Alan's family owned and represented. His only son had to be an Englishman in every way. There must be no taint or strangeness in him.

But he could not bring himself to send his wife away, for life without her was a terrible thought, a frightening thought, an impossibility. Therefore there was only one thing to do. It would be hard for him, but it was necessary. He did not believe in all this clap-trap about Fate and ill-luck; but one thing was certain. He could not have gossip about Muna, the mother of his son, because it could harm Rob in the future. As he could not bear to send Muna away, then he must leave England himself, taking her with him.

He said nothing to any of his family. On the evening of their talk together, Muna took off her grey dress, and bathed, and dressed herself in crimson velvet with a deep neckline, and put rubies in her ears and round her throat, and sat glowing in the firelight in the drawing-room that night, the wine in her glass matching the colour of her dress. Alan imagined that he could see the red wine burning through the white skin of her throat when she drank. He could not look away from her, and when they went up to their room, she sent Daisy away and he watched her undress, and stopped her taking off the jewels.

'I want to see you wearing them – and only them, Muna.'

So Muna disrobed and stood before him in nothing but her beauty and the rubies, and seeing the look on his face, she danced for him; a quiet, scarcely moving, creamy figure, with jewels scarlet at her throat and ears and wrists. Alan watched until her dance was finished, and then took her in his arms and snuffed the candles until there was only one left beside the bed, and that one burned down to nothing, unregarded, long before they slept.

On Sunday Alan went to church with his parents, taking Rob with him. Muna had never stopped him taking Rob to church. It was part of their life, that their child should accompany his father to his place of worship. In fact she never interferred in any way with Rob's upbringing. His schooling, his behaviour, all this belonged to her husband and his mother and father. Muna was his mother, and ensured that he knew himself beloved and secure. She was his private haven, his dream – as he was her reality. She took it for granted that he was being brought up as a Christian, but it did not any longer distress her. Her knowledge of his safety, and of the powers that guarded him, was certain. Both Jane and Robert admired her detachment very much and were grateful that she did not insist that her child was brought up as a caste Hindu. Robert was not sure where, in the Indian caste hierarchy, Temple dancers would stand, but would not have been surprised to hear that they were high caste people. Muna certainly showed no signs of being low caste in any way. Everything about her spoke of birth and breeding, not least the manner in which she wished her son to be brought up as his father before him.

Driving back from the service in the cold village church, Jane said as much to Alan. 'We are so happy in our lives together, Alan. Do you know, it is seven years since you came back with Muna, and they have been perfect years. We love her dearly, and cannot imagine anyone more delightful. You are a most fortunate man.'

'And yet you were very upset when we married.' Alan was riding in the coach alone with his mother, Rob and his grandfather having chosen to ride home through the fields.

'Who told you that?'

'Well, is it not true?'

'Yes, but I did not know what Muna would be like. I could only remember Emily Sawdon and her truly terrible daughter-in-law. But Muna – my dear Alan, she is like my own child, I do not know what I would do without her.'

Alan was silent, looking out at the fields and the bare trees, but his mother did not notice his silence; she talked happily on, while Alan looked out at the grey country, hard held in the grip of winter.

He went back to his regiment, had an interview with his Colonel, and three weeks later came to Moxton Park and took his father into the library to talk with him alone. He told his father that he had agreed to go back to India, to do an attachment to a native regiment. He would command the regiment as Lieutenant Colonel. He had taken leave, and would travel out with Muna by Italian Line from Trieste. Rob would not be accompanying them. Robert heard him out, and when Alan had said all that he had to say, and had fallen silent, watching for his father's reactions, he was astonished to hear Robert's first words.

'I think you are doing a very sensible thing, Alan.'

Alan released his breath in a long sigh. 'Well! I am delighted to hear you say so, Sir, but would be interested to hear why you think this. I expected a terrible argument.'

'The thought of losing both you and Muna is a sad one, but I think you are right to go. As you say, I think Muna is home-sick, and it will be good for her to see her own country again. You certainly could not take Rob. He will be going to school shortly, so there would have been a parting in any case. I dread the scene we will face with your mother. How long will you be away?'

His wise eyes looked into Alan's troubled face as his son answered slowly, 'Oh, three or four years is usual for these attachments,' and he knew in his heart that Alan was lying, and that he intended to stay away for much longer than he said. Alan turned away from his father's eyes.

'I am afraid you will both miss Rob,' said his father quietly.

Alan could not face what the parting from Rob would mean to Muna, so he put it from his mind quickly. 'Yes – yes indeed. But Rob will be all right with you, and with his grandmother. Children are resilient creatures, are they not? I expect he will have recovered his spirits by the time we have crossed to Trieste. Then there will be letters. He will enjoy hearing about our journeying.'

His father was silent, and Alan could not look at him. With lowered head he said, 'Do you think Rob will be very unhappy? I remember how I felt when you and my mother went to India. It was the end of the world. But I recovered. It did me no harm, did it? Rob will be like me, don't you agree, Father?'

He looked up then, straight into his father's eyes, pleading to be told that all would be well with his son. Robert could not let him beg for comfort, because he knew how hard it had been for Alan to come to this decision. If Rob was to be brought up to forget his mother's native land, then his mother must go away.

Poor Muna! He could think of nothing that would comfort her when the time came for her to be told. But he comforted Alan by saying that, indeed, children were resilient: 'I am sure he will get over your departure very quickly. Alan, you have made your decision. Comfort yourself by remembering how many children have parents abroad and some of them are not as fortunate as Rob. He at least has us, and a home that he loves.'

And Muna was the pivot of that home, and of Rob's life. Alan and his father sat in silence.

Then Robert said quietly, 'I will tell your mother tonight, Alan. You leave that to me; you will have enough to do breaking the news to Muna.'

That night, Muna sent Daisy away as she often did when

Alan was at home. She undressed slowly, knowing that he was watching her, knowing what gave him pleasure. He held his arms out to her and when she was close within his grasp, he pressed her head into his shoulder and said quietly, 'Muna, do you love me?'

'Lord?'

'I asked if you loved me. I have a hard thing to say to you. I do not think you will be able to listen to me unless you love me.'

'Alan – you know that I answer you always with a question.'

'Yes, I know. Do not ask me now. I am going to ask you a question instead. Muna, I return to India. Will you come with me?'

He saw the incredulous joy on her face, and watched it fade. She glanced towards the corner of the room where the Goddess had her place and then looked back at him.

'Where you wish me to go, I go, lord. You know that.'

'Rob stays here.' He said it brutally, because he could say it no other way. He saw her face as if a veil of darkness had dropped over it, hiding everything from him but the mere mask of her beauty. She moved gently out of his arms, and stood a little away from him, in distance nothing, but he had the feeling that ages separated them, that she had gone away from him completely. As once before, he called out to her, loudly, 'Muna!' and after a terrible moment, when she did not seem to hear, she turned and said, 'Lord?'

'Muna, you know that I would not do this, if I did not have to.'

'It is seen, Alan. I will not disobey you, but it takes a little time to absorb the blow. I do not think only of myself. How will we tell him, Alan? I cannot. I am not able to go to my son and say that I leave him alone in a strange country.'

'Muna! What strange country? You forget. This is the country of his birth, this is not strange to him! He knows no other country. He is at home here.'

Muna stood looking at him, but she did not see him. She was looking at the days of her life with her son, hearing his voice asking her countless questions, hearing her own voice answering him, making pictures for him, filling in every minute detail that she could. She heard herself and her son, and saw the pictures that she had built for him from words. There was no part of her country that was not known to him; he had lived there through her, and had been at home. Her wide, dark eyes closed for a moment, and the blow that Alan had dealt her travelled from her heart to her mind, and she was appalled at the suffering that lay ahead of her and the pain she would have to give the boy.

As she stood there, behind the darkness of her closed eyes, into her desperate thoughts came the voice that was felt more than heard, 'Be still, my daughter. This, too, is part of your road. You travel with my hand on your shoulder. Do not fear for yourself or your child. The road is a long one, but remember, you chose it yourself. Be still, and set your feet firmly on your chosen path.'

Alan saw her open her eyes and look dazedly across the room. She looked like a woman who had been suddenly roused from sleep, and he ached for the sorrow he saw on her face. He took her up into his arms, and carried her to the bed, and gave her the only comfort he knew, and so comforted himself, and fell asleep.

Muna lay beside him, and above his even breathing she seemed to hear something breaking, cracking – and knew what it was.

She had always feared the day when she would waken from the dream in which she lived. Now it seemed to her that there were great cracks in the dream and she was afraid of what she might see through those cracks.

13

Alan woke at his usual hour in the morning, and found Muna gone.

This had never happened before. She had always been there when he woke, and he was conscious of the strangeness of being in the room without her, a room where everything spoke of her; the faint scent of sandalwood, the little silver boxes in which she kept her cosmetics, her peignoir and nightrobe tossed across a chair. So she had dressed. He imagined her dressing, making no noise so as not to waken him, and then knew it would not have been like that at all. Muna would have gone out of the room and dressed in her bathroom. Then she must have come back and put her nightrobe on the chair, and slipped out again. It was only just after sunrise; he saw the cold light of the winter sun striking in through the window – they had forgotten to close the curtains the night before. His thoughts came together from their sleepy wanderings, and he remembered the night before, and got out of bed quickly. Where could Muna be? He was full of fear suddenly, and went to the bedroom door and looked down the passage to Rob's room. The door was open.

Alan dressed quickly and went out to the stables. Yes, Madam Muna had gone out early and Master Rob had gone with her. They had gone over the fields towards Ballnet Woods – a favourite ride of Rob's, as Alan knew. He was debating whether to take his horse and follow them, when his father came out and called to him.

He joined his father on the terrace, and Robert said quietly, 'Alan, let them be. Muna has a hard thing to do this morning, leave her alone to do it her way. It will, you can be assured, be done well, and will be easier for the boy if he hears it from his mother first.'

Muna rode with her son beneath trees so transparent with winter that they seemed to be blowing like smoke across the sky as the wind flung itself at their branches. Rob was like the wind, rushing ahead, his pony capering with an excitement caught from his rider, and then tearing back to his mother, crying, 'Hurry, hurry – you ride slowly today, my Mother. I wish to show you how Munshi jumps, and there is only one good place, just one place where I can show you – where the big tree came down in the last gale. Munshi jumps that like a bird flying, and I have only fallen twice. Please hurry, it will be time to go back to breakfast, and I want you to see me jump first.'

Rob was off again, tearing ahead, looking back over his shoulder to see if his mother's horse had broken into a canter. This was the kind of day he loved best. An exciting day, beginning superbly, with his mother waking him so early that he was able to see the sun come up behind the trees like a great orange, a winter sun with no warmth in it. He and his mother had crept out of the house like thieves, and had saddled their own horses. Now, Rob riding alone with his beloved mother bounded in his saddle with sheer delight, and his pony bounded under him, and Muna followed her joyful son with tears blinding her, so that she had to ride slowly, and indeed had no heart to do anything else.

They reached the great fallen tree and Rob, shouting wildly, put his pony at it; and Munshi cleared it easily, as Rob had said, flying over like a bird. Transported, Rob turned the pony and took the jump from the other side. Once again, Munshi took it cleanly, but this time Rob did not accompany his pony. He came off hard, and sat for a minute, stunned, while Munshi cantered off, swishing his tail and giving little jumps, as if in derision. Muna dismounted, and went over to her son.

'Rob – are you hurt? That was a hard fall. Let me help you up.' She leaned down, and took his hand and pulled him to his feet. Munshi had stopped, and was standing looking back at them, and Rob would have gone after him, but Muna stopped him.

'Wait, Rob. Are you warm enough to sit here with me for a few minutes? It is sheltered here – we can sit on the tree that defeated you.'

Muna had learned many arts to please men. Had she been an ugly woman she would, with her training, have been able to charm any man. Had she been untaught, and had had only her beauty, she would have taken men's eyes and their thoughts forever. Trained and groomed in mind and body, beautiful and full of natural charm, Muna was irresistible. No man had ever attempted to resist her, and had all her life been able to charm a man out of boredom, rage, or misery. Muna, the Rose of Madore, seated herself on a damp tree trunk, in a wood that was winter bare; she looked at her man-child, and called on every skill she could think of, and knew that they were, for once, going to be of little help to her. Rob was rubbing his shoulder ruefully.

'Does it hurt you very much?' she asked him.

With bravado, belied by his wincing as he touched it, he assured her that it did not.

'That is good,' said Muna, 'I am glad your body is without pain. For, my son, I am now going to hurt your spirit very much, and I can give you no physic for the pain I am going to inflict.'

While he stared at her, uncomprehendingly, Muna told him, flatly and as suddenly as Alan had told her the night before, and with her feelings in rags she watched him go pale and bite his lips under her words. When she had finished he was silent, looking at her with shocked eyes, and she took his hands and said quietly, 'Rob, I have dealt you the first of many blows that life holds for you. Mine had to be the hand that held a knife to let some of your faith in the perfection of the world bleed away from you. My son, you hold back tears. Let them go. Weep with me, for my heart is broken at the thought of being without you. The English say that a man does not weep. In our country, we know the value of tears, the ease they

133

bring. Weep with me, my son, or our hearts will burst.'

Then Rob cast himself into her arms, and his sobs shook both their bodies, so that he thought his mother wept with him. But Muna held her son in her arms, listening to his crying, and stared out over his head at the bare trees, and the winter cold seemed to have frozen her whole body; she had no tears to shed.

Rob was only a little boy. When he had cried, he felt better. There were questions to ask, the pony to catch, the ride home, and a splendid breakfast waiting with his father and his grandfather to share it with him. Alan saw his son's swollen eyes, and Muna's frozen, white face, and was glad he had taken his father's advice. Whatever she had said to Rob, he had taken it well, and, putting away a hearty breakfast, was as full of chatter and urgent questions about his parents' coming journey as Alan had imagined he might be.

Muna went quietly upstairs, took her morning bath and dressed herself slowly; drank her coffee, and kept her mind completely blank. She went out with Jane in the carriage to do some shopping that Jane deemed necessary, buying various things to make the travelling less arduous. Jane did not speak of the coming separation; she could not. Driving home from the market town where she had tried in vain to buy a water filter and a cabin trunk, she took Muna's hand and held it tightly in hers; and Muna lifted the kind and loving hand that held hers so firmly, and laid it to her forehead as she would have done in her own country, and they drove on unspeaking.

When they got back to Moxton Park, Muna sent for Bella. Her first remark when Bella came in was a strange one.

'Bella. How old are you?'

'How old? Well, Sahiba, I know I look very old. But I was married and widowed by the time I was eighteen. I am now thirty-three years old. Why do you ask?'

'You are still a young woman. Bella, will you come with me to India, or do you wish to spend the rest of your days here?'

'It never entered my head that I would not be coming with you, Sahiba.'

'Even though India was a place of unhappiness for you?'

'Even so – I will come with you. You need me, Sahiba.'

'And Rob?'

'If Rob can do without you, Sahiba, he will do very well without me. No. From the beginning of this, I knew that I would go with you.'

Muna smiled at her, and took her hand. 'I do not know what I would have done if you had said anything different Bella.'

The remaining days of their time in England seemed to rush by. They were not going alone. A friend of Alan's was going with them; Captain Richard Sunderland, going on detachment to the same regiment.

Muna took very little interest in the packing, but she herself put the figure of the Goddess into a small sandalwood box, and saw it securely packed away inside another box. Otherwise she left all the deciding of what should go and what should stay to Bella. She herself spent as much time as she could with Jane and with her son.

The packing was finished. Alan and Muna rode with Rob over the fields, but they did not go to Ballnet Woods. Rob seemed to have lost his liking for that particular ride. They went into their own woods instead, and Alan admired Rob's riding, and watched Munshi leap a hedge and ditch perfectly, and congratulated Rob, saying, 'You will be riding Jankers before we come back – think of that,' and Rob said, 'Jankers? The new horse? Will I really? That will be wonderful!' and Muna said nothing at all, looking round her at the fields and woodlands as if she had never seen them before.

The last days coalesced, it seemed, into one long day. Caroline Addison came to say goodbye, and whispered to Muna. 'Do not worry, Muna – he is my godson, and I love him dearly. With me, and with your mother-in-law, I promise you that he will have all the love he can need until your return.'

And I? cried Muna's heart, what shall I have instead of his love and his presence? As if she had heard the question, Caroline said, 'At least you will be glad to see your own country again, will you not, Muna?' and then wondered what she had said, for Muna turned such empty, tragic eyes to her.

Her own country! She had only learned three days before

where Alan was to be stationed. Muna had listened with blank disbelief when Alan had told her where they were going to live. They were joining a company of Jackson's Horse, stationed in Sagpur.

Sagpur was far down in the south of India, in the steamy, hot south, where Muna had never been. It was as far from her own part of India in distance and custom as it could be. It was ruled by the son of Hardyal, an old and bitter enemy of the Ruler of Lambagh. Hardyal was dead, and Muna knew a great deal about his death. Because his son was under age, his mother was Regent. In no way could she be considered to be friendly towards anyone with any connections with Lambagh. It was possible that she did not know anything about Muna, or her marriage to an Englishman. Possible, but not probable. Muna spoke alone to Alan.

'Alan we cannot go there! We will be in great danger. Have you forgotten Hardyal, and the trouble in Madore?'

'Hardyal? No, of course not. How could I? But that has nothing to do with us going to the south. For one thing, Hardyal is dead.'

With astonishment, Muna realised that he did not know, or had not remembered that Hardyal's title had been Raja of Sagpur.

She was silent, and Alan said, 'Come, dearest, I know it is not a part of the country that you know, but there will be time and enough to visit the north – and it will be interesting to see another part of India, will it not?'

She could only agree, and say no more. There seemed little point in alarming him. Perhaps his lack of knowledge would keep him safe. Her own danger she discounted. What would happen, would happen. Muna, for the first time since she had heard the news of their departure, thanked the Goddess that Rob was being left behind.

The day they were to start on their journey was one of those strange, calm days, frost-held, still, and silent, with a sun so pale that its rays seemed to be white, in a sky of blank, cold blue. Jane did not come out on to the terrace to see them go. She could not. All the servants were there, and Rob and his grandfather were going as far as the coast with them. Muna said goodbye to the servants, and as she spoke to Boots, a great sob broke from him and he wept, his tears streaking his red face. It was too much. Muna turned away, with a general wave to the others, and was assisted into the coach, and sat quietly with Rob beside her, Alan and his father opposite.

Rob talked busily all the way to Dover. He pointed out places of interest to Muna, talked about how soon he would be allowed to ride Jankers, and about when he was going to school. He asked questions about the size of the Channel boat, and the distance from England to Trieste. His voice, young and eager, filled the silent coach – and under the fur rug he held Muna's hand in a convulsive grip, and pressed against her, so that she felt his heart beating against her arm, like the heart of a frightened animal.

He was quiet when they reached Dover. Their baggage was on board. Muna was held in Robert's arms for a moment, then stepped aside while Alan embraced his father. Her eyes met the tormented eyes of her son, and she looked deeply into them until the torment eased and he was able to smile, and kiss her, and say, steadily, 'Goodbye, my Mother – I will wait for you,' in Urdu, and added in English, 'I will write to you – please write me many letters.'

And then she turned away and began to mount the gangway up the side of the steamer, while Alan held his son in his arms, said goodbye, and then followed her up. Muna did not stay on deck. She looked down once to see Rob standing, very small beside his grandfather; then she went below to her cabin, where Bella waited for her, and removed her bonnet. She spent most of the rough, jolting voyage to Trieste sitting crosslegged on her bunk, her face quite calm, tears pouring, unchecked, down her cheeks. Bella said nothing. She sat on the other side of the cabin and waited until Alan came down to tell Muna that supper was served in the Captain's saloon. But it was several days before Muna mounted to the deck to join Alan. The sea stretched grey and endless behind and in front of the boat. Muna did not glance back. The parting was behind her, now there was time to live through before she saw her son again.

Time was kind, and lost itself in the monotony of the voyage.

There were breaks in the long days and nights of travel. They transhipped at Trieste, moving from the discomforts of a small ship into the comparative luxury of a larger vessel, and a cabin furnished, apart from the barest necessities, with their own furniture and linen. The arrangements were not entirely to Alan's liking. He shared a cabin with Richard, as the only alternative would have been for Bella to travel with the deck passengers, sleeping in the hold in unspeakable conditions. This Muna would not have, and so Bella shared the larger cabin with Muna, though as both cabins were almost identical it made little difference from the point of view of comfort. After the first three days Bella ceased to protest, for it was obvious to her that Muna was, in her grief over leaving her son behind, glad of the opportunity to sleep alone, away from Alan.

Shipboard friendships and conversations were limited. There were only six other passengers, and only one of them was a woman. Bella was Muna's companion more than her servant and many past secrets were shared between them during the long voyage. Both women were good sailors. When the sea became mountainous, and the ship rolled abominably, it was for them merely a stimulant, a break in the boredom. Wet table-cloths and fiddles, narrow wooden partitions, appeared on the tables in the saloon to hold the plates steady, and as the ship heaved and rolled, first one row of portholes and then slowly, sickeningly the row on the opposite side of the saloon, filled with a view of foaming grey water. It made no difference to Muna or Bella, but the third female passenger was not so fortunate. Muna and Bella nursed her through the early nausea of pregnancy, aggravated by terrible seasickness. She clung to them, declaring that without them she would die. Her husband was going back to his post as Collector of Nassinjan in the Central Provinces. This was Amelia Wellings's first journey from her parents' home in a country rectory. Bella shook her head over her, saying privately to Muna that she doubted the girl would carry her child to full term. Muna shrugged.

'It is probable that she will not. If she does – well, they are going to be stationed in a terrible climate. If she bears the child, she will be lucky to rear it. Poor Amelia – if she knew that of the two women with whom she has made such firm friends one is a half-caste dancing girl – '

' – and the other a Scots servant, frequently suspected of witchcraft?'

'Eh, but she'd have a terrible turn,' finished Bella.

Muna nodded, but did not smile. She did everything with only half her mind, her thoughts looking backwards always. Night found her sleepless, and when the sea became an extension of the sky, and lay blue and glassy under the hot sun, she would imagine the ship's wake to be a road, that led back to her son, and longed to set her feet upon it.

Suddenly the voyage was over. One night the stars seemed more numerous, and low on the horizon. There was a strange smell, compounded of spice and decaying fish. In the scarlet-streaked dawn, towers and palms broke the horizon.

By midday the ship moved majestically into Bombay harbour and dropped anchor.

14

Looking across at the quay, Muna saw a pattern of colour, shifting, changing, a kaleidoscope. The voices were a solid background of sound, they were too far away to pick out one face, or hear one voice among so many.

And yet, her heart beating fast, she searched the coloured mass, as if she would be able to see beloved faces there. There were many small boats milling about at the bottom of the gangway, and people were coming aboard. Muna felt dizzy, and the deck was not solid under her feet. She saw, coming up towards her, Ayub Khan, and Kullunder Khan, Alan's old bearer. It was a dream – or an awakening. She could not speak, and Alan looked at her with anxiety. Surely Muna was not going to be unwell now, at the end of the voyage, just when things were going to become busy for him? He would have a great deal to see about when he got settled ashore. He took Muna's arm. 'What is it, my dear? Do you wish to move into the shade? Are you faint?'

'No, no Alan, I am well. It is only surprise. Look who is coming towards us!' Then as Alan stared, saying nothing, she was afraid he had forgotten, and prompted him, saying, 'Ayub Khan – and your bearer, Kullunder Khan!'

'Yes – yes, I see. Salaam Ayub Khan, how are you? And you, you old rogue, Kullunder Khan! Well, well. The baggage is all down in the cabin, Ayub Khan – will you see to it?'

Muna looked up at the big smiling man before her, and longed to throw herself into his arms and weep away all the strangeness of the life she had been living. But looking at Alan's face, she knew that she could not. She said in Urdu, 'Greetings, my brothers – your health is good, and mine is better because I see you,' and Ayub Khan salaamed low and said, 'Our hearts are made joyful by seeing you, as always. Greetings, oh mother of a fine son – we will speak later.' Ayub Khan had turned and was gone before Alan could ask what he was saying.

Alan was frowning, and Muna wondered if he had a headache; the heat from the land was like a solid smothering blanket. But it was not a headache that made Alan frown, and in her heart Muna knew it. Surely he was not going to object to her speaking her own language in India! It had been different at Moxton Park, she understood that he wanted her to be as English as possible.

Moxton Park! Her eyes blurred suddenly with tears, and her stern resolve not to look back broke. What was Rob doing, where was he? She sent her mind hunting down the days and nights of time, through the miles to find him, but her concentration was destroyed by the sounds and smells and voices all round her. She received a broken impression of a small figure, and then for a moment Rob's eyes seemed to look straight into hers, puzzled eyes, questioning; then she could see nothing, the picture was gone, and Bella was beside her.

'There are men, Sahiba, trying to take the luggage. My Urdu is all gone from me, I cannot understand a word they say.'

'It is all right Bella, they are our people from Lambagh. They have come to get the baggage ashore.' Bella hurried back to the cabin, and Muna looked back at the shore.

She turned at Alan's touch on her arm. 'The baggage is going down to one of the small boats. Ayub Khan is seeing to it, and we are to follow in another boat. No customs troubles or any other kind of trouble for us! Kassim has arranged everything, we are being treated like the Royal Family. There is a house all ready for us.'

'Kassim – l' Muna caught her breath. 'Kassim Khan? Is he here?'

'No, no – but he has made all the arrangements for us.'

'How did he know we were coming?'

'Because I wrote to him, of course. Surely you wrote to the Begum? They will have thought it most uncivil if you did not. They are expecting us to pay them a visit in the Valley as soon as possible. Ayub brought me a letter, and here is one for you. I cannot imagine when we will be able to go to Lambagh, there is so much to do, and of course I do not get leave for some time.'

We will never go, thought Muna in her heart, never. She recognised the delicate, pointed writing of Bianca on the folded paper Alan gave her, the writing that it had taken Muna so long to learn to read. The very sight of it was like a calming hand laid on hers. She tucked the paper away to read when they got to the house that had been arranged for them.

'This house – do you know where it is?'

'House! A Palace probably. It belongs to a kinsman of the Lambagh Rulers. A man called Uzbeg Khan. Do you remember him by any chance?'

Muna remembered Uzbeg very well, but Alan was frowning again, so she said nothing. Alan would not care to hear of nights spent in Lambagh, where the Nawab had paid highly to have her dance for him, and later had paid even more money to enjoy her company in the long summer nights of those days before she had become Mrs. Reid. So she shook her head, and relegated the handsome Uzbeg to the limbo of a great many other purposefully forgotten people and incidents.

'Well, it is his Palace we have. I think, when you are ready my dear, we could go down to the boat that will take us ashore. Is Bella here?'

Bella had been standing in the shade of an awning. 'Aye, here I am. That great giant of a man who speaks in gibberish has taken all the luggage, even the hand luggage. No doubt it will all be well, but he had a wicked glint in his eye.' Bella had bright spots of colour on her cheek bones, and her green eyes looked angry.

'Bella I promise you that all the baggage is safe. That was a dear friend, that giant – his name is Ayub Khan, and you will become very fond of him. He is a wonderful man.'

'Will I now? – well, we'll see.'

'When you have finished discussing Ayub Khan, my dear – ' Alan's impatience was not disguised. Muna looked round the deck. It was as if, suddenly, the ship was home, and she did not want to leave.

'Muna – are you ready? Richard has already gone, and is waiting on the quay, being consumed by heat, poor fellow.'

There was nothing more to delay them. Muna went down the gangway, parasol tilted elegantly, to where her childhood waited for her, with outstretched arms and bright loving eyes.

'Heh! A memsahib, a ladysahib, we have with us! Nay, Ladysahib, you should not weep. No one so beautiful should weep.' Goki, clasping Muna in her arms, was not weeping herself. She held Muna away from her, looking with keen searching eyes into the beautiful face of the woman who had matured and grown into full flowering since Goki had last seen her.

'My child, you have been blessed with great beauty,' said Goki slowly, 'Great beauty. And happiness?'

Muna, looking into the bright old eyes, made no answer.

'Happiness?' murmured Goki, on a questioning note, and was silent, searching Muna's face. They stood, islanded together in silence, while the chattering jostling crowds swirled about them. Isolated from the clamour by all the memories of the past that each evoked in the other, they heard and saw nothing; they could have been alone in a field or on a beach, instead of being surrounded by many people.

Presently Muna spoke, 'Goki – is all well with you?'

'What else? With my child returned to me at last, I am very well.'

Goki saw the question forming in the lovely, wistful eyes in front of her. With sudden clarity, she remembered another question she had been asked, another pair of beautiful eyes staring up into hers, with hope and happiness in them: Bianca, asking about Sher Khan. But there was no hope or expectation of happiness in Muna's eyes – only the question, and an expression Goki could not fathom. Was it fear? She answered before the question was put into words.

143

'Nay Muna, we come alone, Ayub Khan, Kullunder Khan and myself, and the men that Kassim sent from his own bodyguard. We have brought furniture, cushions, hangings, and carpets for you – you will see. And many messages. But we are alone.'

Muna's indrawn breath was barely perceptible, a sigh as light as the movement of a moth's wings. 'I see. Goki – '

Whatever she was going to say was interrupted. Amelia Wellings came up, one white kid gloved hand extended.

'Gloves on the hand, in such heat! This one is going to die before she has been in this country a week. Eh, these white mems – poor creatures.' Goki's comment was fortunately not understood by Amelia.

'Dear Mrs. Reid, we are just going. I would like to say goodbye, and thank you for your kindness and understanding on this terrible voyage we have just endured. If you should find yourself in Nassinjan, or nearby, do not forget there will be a welcome for you – ' Under Goki's close scrutiny, her words died away. She looked at the old woman in her white robes, and then at Muna's tear-stained cheeks. 'Your old servant come to welcome you? How charming – how touching. Such faithful love these native servants have. I was told I would find them to be like this.'

Poor Amelia. Muna had an overwhelming desire to say, 'This is not a servant, this is one of the dearest and most beloved people in my life, closer to me than the mother I can only just remember,' but she knew what surprise and discomfort she would cause. So she contented herself by saying a warm goodbye to the bride, and watched her go away, wondering how long she would manage to keep her illusions about life as a memsahib in a small isolated station, where she would be bitterly lonely for most of her time. Poor Amelia, with her beautiful white kid gloves. Meantime Amelia, on her part, was thinking that the charming Mrs. Reid was really too emotional – imagine weeping in front of a native crowd! Poor Mrs. Reid, so beautiful and yet, as her husband had said, there was something a little strange about her. But so kind.

Meantime, Alan had come up and, greeting Goki, was

shepherding them both out of the customs shed into the blazing steaming heat of a Bombay morning. Bella was already seated in one Victoria, with luggage heaped about her, and Ayub Khan up beside the driver. Goki, looking at Bella, smiled.

'That is your white servant, Muna?'

'She is my friend and my servant. She is wise, Goki, and has the power of seeing. She comes from the north also, but it is called Scotland. She says she is a highland woman.'

'Can she speak our tongue?'

'Not a word of Lambaghi. A little Urdu. But she will learn.'

'It is well.'

Goki climbed nimbly up to seat herself beside Bella, and the two women exchanged smiles and nods. Ayub spoke to the driver, and the Victoria creaked into movement, followed by the superior model in which Alan and Muna sat, with Richard facing them.

Muna looked out at the alien Bombay streets, with the hurrying crowds of men in their loin cloths, and round black hats, and the pale aristocratic-looking Parsis in high buttoning long coats and shiny blacks hats, who moved so languidly amongst all the bustle around them that they reminded her of festival days, when the painted Gods were taken in procession to the temples. These men might have been those Gods, except that they were so thin, so delicate looking, like ivory models of the Gods. She longed to see the crowds of brightly-dressed, laughing people of her own north. This place with its steaming heat and heavy smells did not seem like India to her. The air was foetid – the sour smell of poverty, of drains and sewage, of curry stuffs and spices and charcoal fires choked her. Then, as they passed the street of the flower sellers, marigolds and frangipani and champak blossom added their heavy scents to everything else. It was terribly hot. At last the Victoria turned up Malabar Hill, and they began to climb into fresher air.

The place where they were to stay was a perfect small Palace, a replica in miniature of its owner's residence in his own home State. It stood back from the road behind a high wall. There were green, tended lawns, and a series of small rectangular pools, terraced, so that water fell from one pool to another, and the air was full of the sound of falling waters. The largest pool on the highest terrace had a fountain at each corner, and water lilies lay on the dimpled surface of the water, gleaming white and delicate, as fresh as newly fallen snow.

The drive swept up and round, and under the arched porch. *Syces* ran out to the horses' heads, and two men servants in scarlet and white livery came forward to open the door of the Victoria. Alan stepped out first, followed by Richard, who turned to give his hand to Muna and help her down. They followed the bowing servants up the steps, through an arched entrance and into a central court, where another fountain made a cool splashing, and trees grew, throwing deep shade over lawns and flower beds. The air was cool and fresh, and an open arch ahead of them framed a view of Bombay and the Indian Ocean beyond. As they moved, following the servant who was guiding them, a flight of white pigeons rose into the air, their wings making a clap of sound in the quiet court. Muna suddenly remembered waking on her first morning in Moxton Park to the sound of doves. Time made a circle: it seemed only yesterday that she had been a bride waking in an English house, her past life forgotten. Now, with the clap and whirr of the pigeons' wings, she felt the old life reach out a hand, and pluck at her mind, and was glad when Alan spoke to her, bringing her back to his side.

Later, she lay on the day bed in her room, watching Goki unpack what she would need for a stay of two or three weeks, for it was not certain when they would set off for Sagpur. They would go by rail for the first part of the journey, as far as Orangapura, and from there they would travel the roads down to the southern coast, and the State of Sagpur.

Goki worked steadily as Muna watched. She was a very old woman now. Her whole body, her hands, her lined face, seemed transparent, like a skeleton leaf in late autumn. Only her eyes were young. Age could not touch them. They shone with interest and unquenched vitality as she admired all Muna's clothes, shaking out the full-skirted dresses and the many frilled, lace-edged undergarments.

'I remember when the Begum Bianca wore clothes like this

146

– and her mother. Bianca hated these clothes; she used to take them off whenever she could, and wear a *sari*, or our dress, but it was not easy for her while she was with her mother, who wished her to be always in European clothes. Poor lady – she did not like our country.'

'But the Begum did.'

'How not? She had never been anywhere else, and from the time she fell in love with Sher Khan, there was nowhere else she could imagine, even Paradise held nothing for her like our Valley.'

'Paradise? The Valley is all the Paradise that I would need. But I remember the Begum Bianca giving me many of her clothes, and teaching me how to wear them. I too hate them. In fact – ' Muna paused, staring down at her spreading silk skirts, 'Goki, take out two of my own costumes – the trousers, and the shirt and tunic, and the head cloth – and for now, give me a *sari*. A plain Benarese muslin *sari*, and a *choli*. I am too hot to wear these things.'

Goki looked at her with raised eyebrows. 'And the Major Sahib? Will he be pleased?'

'No. But he will not scold me. He will see that the *sari* is more suitable for this climate, and if he wishes I can dress in European dress should we go out. And Goki – he is now a Colonel Sahib.'

With no more said, the *sari* was unpacked, the scent of sandalwood and attar of roses blowing from its light folds. Muna bathed, had her hair brushed and plaited by Goki's trembling but still skilled hands, and dressed in the floating muslin *sari* and a matching *choli*, she put her feet into little heel-less slippers, and went out to find her husband.

Shortly afterwards Bella came into the room and saw Goki looking at the tumbled trunks and cases with an expression of worry and dismay on her face. There was nothing to explain her distress, and as neither of them could communicate in words, they merely looked at each other, Bella with a question in her eyes. Goki shook her head slowly from side to side, and said in answer to the question that was unspoken, 'She is worried and restless and homesick; this is not her country, but she knows she is within reach of it now, she can almost smell the hills and the scents of the Valley, and she yearns for the place that she seems still to see as home. What did you do to her across the black water, that she is still so lost – and where is her son?'

Bella was then faced with a question she could not understand. The two women looked at each other across the disordered room, and Goki spread her hands. Bella spoke, 'Eh – you'll need to teach me your language, old woman, for I cannot go on without knowing what you are saying; it looks to me as if you have more sense than most. The Tower of Babel was a terrible disaster for the world, and if you could understand me, we'd both be a lot happier.'

They smiled at each other, and began without further useless words to set the room to rights.

Later, Bella walked down a long colonnade, shaded by sprays of bougainvillaea, purple and scarlet against the brilliant glare in the court, where the sun, reflecting in the fountain's spray, flung flashes of blinding light in patterns on the walls and on the white marble floor. She stopped at a door where the man Ayub Khan lounged, his curved sword loose at his side, his eyes crinkling into a smile as he looked down at her.

'Oh woman of the green eyes and the red and silver hair, where go you?'

Bella found that she could not outstare the laughing eyes of this impudent giant, and was annoyed to feel herself blushing under his gaze.

'A woman who blushes like a virgin girl – Wah! You are a jewel of great price. Where do you go, oh green eyes?'

Another question in the tone of voice, in words she could not understand. Bella tried to keep her usual composure, and said firmly, 'Where is the Lady?'

He looked at her, smiling and shaking his head. 'Your voice is like the sound of a bell – but your words are not understood.'

This language they speak! Bella was rapidly becoming angry in her frustration.

'The Lady,' she said on a rising note, with a flash of the green eyes that Ayub was admiring, 'The Lady – the Sahiba –

Muna – Oh, for heaven's sake man, stop grinning at me before I lay my hand on your face. I wish to see Muna; that should be plain enough!'

'Munabhen? Aha, now I understand. Come, green eyes, she is here.' He turned and pulled the door open, and she went past him, very conscious of his eyes watching her.

Muna was sitting amongst a pile of cushions on a marble seat in the window of the room. Bella's eyes widened at what she saw. She was used to Muna's national dress and the gauzes and brilliant silks she had worn when she wished to in Moxton Park. But somehow, this was different. Gone were the spreading silk skirts, the tight waist, the heavy coiled chignon. Muna had shed her European clothes, and with them had shed years. In the setting of the big cool room her native dress looked different; Muna was at home. She looked like a girl, a small, beautifully formed girl, with a long black plait snaking over her shoulder, and a pale green *sari* draping her curves, hiding and revealing, as if she was robed in water. Her slender fingers held a crimson rose, and her eyes, wide and watchful, looked at Bella with surprise. Bella realised that she had been expecting Alan, and that she was afraid that her husband would not care for her change of clothing.

'You look as if you belong here in this palace, Sahiba – as if you have never lived anywhere else in your life. Is it wonderful for you to be back with your own people, and in your own country?'

Muna laughed. 'Bella, when you were living in Moxton Park, were you in your own country, and amongst your own people?'

'Sahiba, you know fine that I come from Scotland, and the far north of Scotland at that. What do you mean?'

'I mean that as far as your country and people were from Moxton Park, so far is my country from here. I am fortunate in that there are some of my own people with me but otherwise, I am as much an exile here as I was in England. And it is very hot.'

'It is that. I was thinking – would it be permissible for me to wear the local dress? For I shall die in these skirts, I tell you that.'

149

'There is no reason why you should not wear anything you wish, Bella.'

'Then I shall try and make that old woman of yours understand what I want. I wish I could speak the language, Sahiba – for more reasons than one. Is Ayub Khan, the man at the door, one of your people?'

'He is indeed.'

'He – I would like fine to take the smile off his face!'

'Bella, you have been enraged ever since you first saw him! Poor Ayub! There are many women who would fall out of a high window to catch his eye!'

'Well, I am not one of them.'

'So it would seem. Tell me, did you learn no language when you were out here last? Did you only learn the language of the south? You called me Sahiba, which is a name from the north, when I first met you.'

'Oh, I learned a good deal of Urdu, but your people speak some tongue I do not understand at all. If anything, it sounds more like the Gaelic than anything I have heard for a long time – but I cannot get a word of it.'

'It is our hill patois. But Bella, we all speak Urdu – it is our second language, you should know that – you heard me speak often to Rob! But do not use our tongue to berate Ayub, I beg of you. He is as my brother, we have taken and conquered many dangers together, Ayub and I. He is a very brave man, and I love him dearly.'

'Well, maybe when I can speak with him we won't get up against each other as we do now. He was sent from the Valley with the old woman Goki and the others by the Ruler, you said. Will they stay with us?'

'Yes. They travel with us as far as Orangapura, and then Goki and two men go back to the Valley, and the others stay with us as long as we remain in the south. It is – there are dangers down there for us, and Kassim Khan remembered. At least we will have some about us that we can trust.'

Bella looked at her with a question, but Muna was staring at nothing, and Bella changed her mind, and asked no question.

Instead she said she had never seen anything like the things that had come from Lambagh.

'I have not opened anything, it would take so long – but there must be a room full of packages and bundles.' Then, her curiosity overcoming her, she asked her question. 'Will we be visiting the Valley?'

'No. There is no time.' Muna turned her head, and looked out at the sparkling fountain. 'My lord has to be in Sagpur by the end of this month. It would take many days' travelling to reach the Valley from here.'

'I am disappointed. I would like fine to see the Valley. Maybe when we are settled, we could go up?'

For some reason Bella felt a great desire to see where all these people lived; but Muna, whose face normally glowed with pleasure when the Valley was mentioned, made no reply. She looked away again, and the sun on the fountain's spray threw diamonds of light and shadow on her face, so that it was impossible to see her expression.

Looking down into the court, Bella saw Alan and Richard coming through the arch. Muna spoke at once.

'Bella, find the man, Kullunder Khan, and ask him to bring cold drinks – they will be very hot and thirsty. Then I think you had better pack away all my dresses. I have decided I shall not wear them for some time.'

Bella looked with raised eyebrows at the small, green-robed figure, and then went out without saying anything. There was something about Muna that did not encourage speech at that moment.

Ayub Khan, still leaning with crossed arms against the wall outside, favoured her with a broad smile. 'Ho – the green eyed leopardess. Never have I see eyes like yours. They make a man think of snow water and secret fern-grown caves – and the green flame that lies in the heart of a fire.'

Bella stopped and looked up at him. Her Urdu was suddenly fluent. 'Why do you not speak to me in Urdu, which I can understand?'

'Wah! She speaks! My green-eyed leopardess speaks! Nay, do not look at me with anger, I speak with no intent to distress

151

you. Why, if you speak Urdu, did you not speak before?'

'Because I did not know you could speak Urdu – and I did not know how much I could remember. You spoke some other languages always.'

'I spoke my own tongue, green eyes. But now we can speak with ease. You use Urdu well – the words fall from those lips with beauty. Let us speak often.'

'I have no time for speech now. I have to find Kullunder Khan – give him some orders – and then I have other work – '

'As for Kullunder Khan, you do not need to do anything. See, here he comes with wine on a tray – Simkin and ice. He knows, he remembers what his master likes on a hot day. Your other work – well, it does not matter if we cannot speak now, we will have time on the journey.'

Bella, preparing to hurry away, stopped and looked up at him, surprised to find how tall he was. 'Do you come with us all the way?'

'Oh, those eyes! Indeed I come with you. Go away, my green-eyed leopardess, before I forget my duty.'

Bella turned away, furious, and heard his deep chuckle as she swung down the colonnade, stepping through the bars of shadow and feeling the cool breath of the breeze blowing over the fountain on to her hot cheeks.

She found Goki still at work in the big dressing room that opened off the room that had been made ready for Muna. As if she had already received the order, Goki was putting away Muna's European clothes, shaking them, folding them, and laying them carefully in two great carved chests. The smell of sandalwood was strong in the room.

'Goki – you speak Urdu?'

Goki's face creased into innumerable wrinkles as she smiled. 'I? Of course I do. It is our second language. How is it that you speak it so well? Why did you not speak before? We have been nodding and waving our hands at each other like two mutes in a boat. Well, then, now we can talk. Tell me – did Munabhen say anything about her clothes? She did? Then I was right. I knew she would not wear them here. So. We put them away. The Begum Bianca has sent many *saris*, and other clothes.'

'I do not think the Sahiba intends to wear her European dress for a long time.'

' "The Sahiba",' said Goki, 'Munabhen, the Rose of Madore. I can see that like me, you love her. She is as *my* child. Tell me – tell me of the boy?'

The bright old eyes sparkled as Bella described, as well as she could, Rob's looks, and his way of life.

'Wah! He is a true son of the north. Rides well, you say? Aiee, I wish that I could see him. It is hard for him to be left without parents. Hard and cruel.'

'Hard and cruel for the Sahiba. At least he has his father's parents, and you can believe me, Goki, they worship him.'

'That is as it should be. But Muna – yes. She has had her cup of grief filled many times in this life, and has drunk it without complaint. Well, these eyes have seen her again, which has crowned my life – and also I have seen her strength. But so many years, so many changes –'

Goki stood, holding one of Muna's dresses, staring at Bella with eyes that saw past Bella, and far away. Whatever she saw, the old woman's face was very sad. Bella moved towards her, and Goki turned as if she was waking from a dream, saying, 'Ay – I grow old, muttering like a crazy woman. See, here are the cottons and muslins that our Muna will wear in this heat. I will not open the silks.'

'You do not come with us all the way, the Sahiba says.'

'No. Part of the way. I come as far as Orangapura, where the road to the north branches off. There I will leave her to you, and go – I shall go home.'

'Is it far, your home?'

Goki's smile was very sweet. 'Nay green eyes – not so very far. I shall be in sight of it, from the time I say goodbye to the Rose.'

'You sound as if you long to go.'

'It is time. I shall rest and perhaps sleep while you are still wandering.'

She turned from Bella, and went on folding and putting away the rich clothes that had come with Muna from across the sea, and Bella stood with her hands hanging idle and watched

153

her, pondering words she did not altogether understand.

Soon the room was orderly, everything put away, and Bella and Goki shut the door, and went out together to sit in the shade beside the fountain until Muna should need them. Friendship had grown between them with speed, as if, thought Bella sadly, there was some need for haste.

15

They stayed in Bombay in the beautiful little Palace longer than they had expected. Muna rested, and Alan and Richard completed various arrangements, coming back hot and tired to the marble rooms where the sound of falling water gave at least the illusion of coolness. In the evenings, when the breeze rose, it was cool at last and the men would join Muna on the open, marble dais above the fountain, and sit looking out over the lights of the city, sipping their drinks and slowly forgetting the frustrations and the heat of the day.

How Muna spent her days, Alan did not know and was too preoccupied to ask. She was relieved that he seemed to take it for granted that she would dress for coolness, that she wished for rest and quiet. There were no remarks made about her dress and there were no social occasions. They went, sometimes, for drives in their host's carriage, going down the hill and over the rough roads to the beaches, where they would stop and, getting out, walk, Muna's muslin blowing behind her, as white and light as the spray that crested the waves.

She was very quiet these days, though her smile was as ready and as warm as ever. She spent hours alone in the big room overlooking the fountain, and she kept her thoughts to herself. Whenever Alan came home she was waiting for him, beautiful and welcoming, ensuring that everything was ready for him, that his bath and fresh clothing were laid out – though really it was not necessary for her to give any orders. The servants were trained to perfection but, nonetheless, she was always there making certain that everything was done just as he liked it. Bella and Goki both watched her, and as she ministered to Alan, so they tried to keep everything as she wished, guarding her privacy, letting her rest; and always Ayub stood by her door, his sleepy, smiling eyes more watchful than they appeared. The great sword that was so negligently slung at his belt was not an ornament.

Bella went with cool grace about the halls and verandas of the Palace, dressed in clothes procured for her by Goki. She wore the loose *kurta*, shirt, and *salwar*, trousers, of the Punjabi woman, a light muslin scarf draped over her shoulders more often than over her head. Every time she passed Ayub he would say something, or roll his eyes and place a hand on his great chest over his heart. Bella seldom entered Muna's room without a high flush on her cheeks and a sparkle of anger in her eyes – or was it anger? Muna smiled to herself, and Bella was happy then because it seemed to her that Muna did not smile very often these days. She spoke to Goki about Muna, and the old woman nodded, her mouth twisting wryly as if she had tasted something bitter.

'She is resting her heart after much sorrow. It is a strong heart, but even a strong heart can crack. All we can do is to be sure that she has time in which to rest. There are people in the city here who knew her well in the old days. If a whisper escaped that she was here, the Palace would be full of her admirers.'

'So that is why she goes veiled when she goes out.'

'You mean when she goes to eat the air with the Colonel Sahib? I wonder that he is so patient about her wearing her own costume.'

'Perhaps he knows that she would be recognised. No, I meant that she is veiled when she goes to the Temple on the hill.'

'In the name of the Bringer of Life! She goes alone?'

'Nay, Ayub is always one step behind her. She goes directly the Colonel has left in the morning and, as you know, he goes soon after dawn.'

'Aiee – I grow old, that this should happen and I not know.

From this day on, I will go with her.'

'There is no need, Goki. I go. No harm will come to her with me beside her – if you go, might you not be recognised?'

'That is true. So – you go. What does she do, at the Temple?'

'She first buys garlands from the flower sellers, then she goes to an inner shrine – where Ayub and I cannot go – but the priests seem to know her. She is there for perhaps ten minutes, and then comes out and we return. She always goes on foot.'

Bella was quiet for a minute, then she said in a voice of sad amazement, 'Goki – she weeps. She weeps as she comes away.'

Goki turned her face aside and drew her head cloth over her eyes. 'My poor Muna. This life is cruel to her. But, as I said, she is strong-hearted. Do not be worried – she will grow calm again. I am glad you go with her wherever she goes. My time is over, I have reached the summit of my years and all I can do for her now is think of her with love. She needs someone like you, and the Goddess, seeing her need, has sent you. But one thing – I think it well if Ayub takes Kullunder Khan with him. I will tell him. We are not in our own place – and even friends can be enemies. There is many a rich man living in this city who would give half his fortune to have the Rose of Madore to ornament his house.'

Bella had reason to remember the old woman's words two or three days later.

It was very early. Parrots and crows were still filling the air with their strident voices, rejoicing in the new morning, when Muna stopped at her usual flower seller near the Temple steps. She was buying long strings of heavily scented frangipani, and garlands of pink roses, sparkling with silver tinsel, when a wind from the morning-bright sea lifted her veil and blew it aside, leaving her face in clear view. A man, buying garlands from the next flower seller, looked over at her and although she put her hand up and caught at her veil instantly, it was too late. The man dropped the garland he was choosing and was at her side in two steps.

'By the Gods – Muna – Muna, it is you – it could be no one else. Where have you been these many years, Rose of all hearts? Where do you dance now?'

Ayub Khan and Kullunder Khan closed in on the pair; Bella, her own veil over her red hair and half hiding her face, took the garlands Muna handed her, and Muna said, 'You do me no honour, Sir, accosting me here. I come to pray at the Temple. You bring shame on me in front of my servants.'

'But, Muna! I bring shame? I did not bring you shame when you danced for me and my guests at the Dhussera Festival in Madore! I remember filling your veil with gold – and your goblet with rubies – and I would again for another such night as we spent then! Only tell me where I may find you – I do not mean to insult you. You have walked through my dreams every night since then and I am sick of waking to empty arms. Where may I find you, Rose of delight?'

'The Rose is dead, friend – withered on the branch. There are other, fresher flowers. Ask no more for Muna, for she is gone – as I go now. Farewell.'

As she spoke, Muna was moving. With an adroit turn and a few swift steps she was hidden among the crowds going into the Temple, where even Bella could not distinguish which of the white-veiled worshippers was Muna. With a curse, the man turned to follow her and found his way barred by Ayub's drawn sword. Kullunder Khan dagger in hand, stood watchful-eyed beside him.

'You heard her, heaven born. The Rose is gone. Ask no more for Muna. Forget her. What is past, is past.'

The man stared, looking past Ayub at the teeming crowds on the Temple steps and, saying nothing, turned away, and was gone.

Bella drew a long breath of relief, but Ayub shook his head at her. 'Not so, green eyes. You shed your worry too quickly. That man is dangerous. Did you not see his eyes? He is a man enchanted. We must try and persuade Munabhen to leave her worship – and we must be watchful as we return. We will be followed, I make no doubt. I think it better if we ride a little. In Allah's name, I hope Munabhen returns swiftly.'

Almost on his words, Muna was with them. Kullunder Khan had called up two carriages. Muna climbed into the first one and, before Bella could follow her, Kullunder Khan stepped back from speaking to the driver and, to Bella's astonishment, climbed into the carriage beside Muna and the vehicle rattled off, leaving her standing beside Ayub Khan.

'Green eyes – you go in this Victoria, with the hood up. I sit up in front and by this time, his men will have come and will follow us – I am known, and they cannot see you. We will ride about for a little. Ah, to be able to sit in the privacy of the carriage and gaze into those eyes – perhaps I may be able to on another more fortunate day.'

Bella sat in the closed Victoria, sweltering in the heat, while they rode around the streets of Bombay, keeping to the populated parts, passing shops, and banks, and the high-walled garden of an English club – and all the time Bella worried, wondering if Ayub's strategy had not been too simple. Supposing Muna was already in the house of her admirer, captured as soon as she had driven away from the Temple.

At last she felt the Victoria turn on to the dirt road that climbed up to the Palace and, shortly after that, the carriage stopped and Ayub opened the door. Conscious of sweat-drenched clothes, and hair so wet that it clung to her neck and temples, Bella climbed down the steps.

'All is well –'

Bella turned, weak with relief, to see Kullunder Khan standing beside the gate guard who was opening the gate.

'We got back and there was no one. But I do not think we go to the Temple again.'

'No, indeed – Ah, green eyes, you have suffered in that sweat box. But in a good cause. Come – I will tell the bath coolie to draw you a cool bath.'

'I must see the Sahiba first.'

Muna was in her usual place in the window. 'Oh, Bella, I was distressed for you – were you followed?'

'No – at least I do not think so, Ayub did not say so. I was very worried, Sahiba. Ayub says he thinks that we should go no more to the Temple now. It is too dangerous.'

'I was foolish. But it will not be long now before we leave. Do not worry, Bella. Go and change, you must be in great discomfort.'

Goki was waiting for Bella, and helped her to change.

'Who was it?'

'Goki, *I* do not know! He was richly dressed, with a scarlet turban and his shirt-buttons were jewels. He spoke of Madore, and of filling the Sahiba's cup with rubies.'

'Well, many men have done that. It could be the Nawab of Subbar or the Raja of Dhil – but the Raja would not be buying flowers himself, so it is more likely the Nawab. Muna will know, or Ayub. Certainly Ayub would know if it was Subbar.'

'She did not tell me who the man was. She says she will not go to the Temple again.'

'Good. She was very foolish but, empty-hearted, where could she go, but to her Goddess? There, Bellapyari, you are fresh and cool again. It is a rest to my heart, knowing you are with her. As for Ayub –'

'What of Ayub?'

'Eh, what a flash in the eyes! What did I say? Do not be angry with me. I am an old woman but I see much. Ayub Khan is a good man, Bella.'

'So?'

'So – and unmarried also. He is a brave man. He has his eyes fixed on you.'

'Well, that I cannot help, Goki.'

'No. Well, I have spoken. I trust you are not angry with me?'

'Goki, we are friends. But I have no man in my mind.'

'No. Maybe not. But time passes and discloses. Things are written for us, and we do not know what they are. And yet Muna says you have the sight.'

'Not for myself.'

'Then look into Ayub's eyes, and see his future – no? Aiee, a blush like a girl. Nay, Bella, do not be angry with me. I am old and foolish.'

'Old maybe, but not foolish, Goki. Now we must keep the Sahiba under our eyes for I do not think that man will be satisfied until he has found her.'

Bella wondered if she should speak to Alan, and decided against it. There would be no need if Muna had decided to forego her worship at the Temple. Bella did not think that the Nawab or Raja, whichever he was, would force entry into the Palace itself.

Two mornings later, just after dawn, while the sky was loud with the shrieks of the bright-coloured Indian birds, Bella stepped from her room, cool and rested after her night's sleep. She wore her hill-woman's costume which she found very comfortable. Her hair was loose, she had not coiled it up, so she wore her *chadar* over her head. Bella's walk was one of her chief attributes. She was not a beauty, she was too thin both in body and face, but her green eyes and her walk made her almost beautiful and quite unforgettable. Now, slender, erect, moving like a dancer, she went down to the gate where there was a great bush covered with small, heavily scented white flowers. Muna loved them, and Bella would pick them while the night dew was still on them and take them to Goki, who threaded them on cotton for Muna to twist in her hair.

The bush was heavy with blossom, and Bella began to pick them, the scent rising round her as she picked. She saw that the gate was open, but it was not a matter for worry – the gate was guarded by two of the Palace men, and although they were not in sight, she knew they were there for she could hear them speaking; sibilant, lowered voices, unusual in a country where everyone seemed to shout, even if they were only a few yards apart. These men were speaking so low that their voices sounded conspiratorial. Suddenly alerted, Bella turned to call – and was, in the act of turning, enveloped in a cloth that covered her from head to foot, while a hand was placed firmly over her mouth. Kicking and struggling, she was carried away. Fight as she would, she could not get free. She was lifted up and into something, banging her head painfully in the process. The man who had his hand on her mouth shifted his grip and Bella immediately sank her teeth into his flesh. His reply was an oath in a language which was not Urdu, and then a knife was pressed hard enough on her throat to cut her flesh.

'Now, Bitch-woman – cry out, and Rose or no Rose, I cut your throat. Drive on, Sethoo.'

The man's Urdu was not good, but Bella understood. So they

thought they had captured Muna! Well, thought Bella, grimly, they, whoever they were, were in for a bitter disappointment. A cold thought crossed her mind – what would their master do when he found they had the wrong woman? Bella tightened her lips and put the thought out of her mind.

It was a long, hot drive before the vehicle drew up, and Bella, still wrapped in smothering folds of cotton, was lifted up, carried into a building and up some stairs, and thrust, ungently, into a room.

'There, Bitch – wait on your lord's pleasure – and bite your own hands for all I care!'

The door banged, she heard bolts shoot home, and knew herself alone. She struggled out of the cloth and found she was imprisoned in a small, white-washed room, a bath room. There was a big earthenware jar of water and a dipper beside it. Bella was thirsty, but she did not drink the water. Instead, she removed her clothes and poured the water over her body, getting some relief that way. She dried herself on her *chadar* and then, re-dressed in her crumpled trousers and shirt, sat by the small window to await events. She could see the corner of a green lawn, and beyond it a white wall, surmounted by a jagged ridge of broken glass and iron. This was obviously a well-guarded place, the Palace of Muna's old friend, no doubt. The room was very small, and Bella felt another shiver of fear. If Muna, who was important to the employer of the men who had kidnapped her, could be put in such a place, what would he do when he found her instead – the wrong woman?

She tried to think of other things, and found Ayub filling her mind. His flashing smile, his deep voice, and his great, broad body. Suddenly she felt comforted. He would not rest, she felt sure, until he found her. She knew, in her mind, that she was being foolish – the corner of the wall that she could see looked very high. How many guards were on the gate, alerted and ready? After such an episode, there would be many. But, none-theless, her foolish heart refused to lose hope, and she kept the thought of Ayub and his strength and reliability before the eyes of her spirit all that day.

Shadows were long on the corner of the green grass that she

could see from her little window, and her prison was growing dark when she heard voices and footsteps – hasty footsteps, the sound of men in a hurry. Bella stood, and tried to order her crumpled clothes. Whatever was to happen, her fate was approaching now.

When the door was flung open, and the lamps were carried in ahead of the tall man whom she remembered from the sunny morning outside the Temple, she was standing, facing the door, her back against the further wall.

'Muna – what can I say to you? You will never forgive me. By no order of mine were you put in such a prison. I have but now returned from Goa and was told with pride, can you imagine the foolishness, that they had brought you, and that you were prisoned here, to await my pleasure. They are louts and fools – '

He broke off, staring. Then he said suddenly, 'Hold the lamp higher!'

In the ensuing silence, while he stared at her, Bella was very conscious of the contrast she would present to a man who was expecting Muna's beauty.

'Louts, and fools – and worse than fools,' said the tall man slowly. 'Rungi Das – you have brought the wrong woman. Who are you?'

'I am Muna's servant.'

'Not the Rose – but close to her! Of what race are you, for your Urdu is good? Are you from the northern valleys?'

'Yes – but not your northern valleys. I come from a country called Scotland, from the far north – ' Bella had a sudden pang of homesickness, remembering the purple headlands, and the thrashing grey seas, and the mists that had pearled down from the mountain peaks of her own far land. Her eyes filled with tears, and she caught her lip between her teeth and, furious at such a moment of weakness, glared at the man before her. He stepped closer and, tall as she was, Bella had to look up at him.

'So – a cornered leopardess, a northerner from another country – and after all, perhaps the evening is not lost. Why do you allow yourself to hide beauty under such clothes? Is Muna poor now, that her servant goes dressed thus? Peera, take her to the women, and, whoever you are, I say again – I would put no woman in such a prison. I will make my apologies more suitably later, woman from the north.'

Bella did not struggle. There were too many hands holding her. She was carried down winding passage-ways, her captors eventually stopping outside a heavy door which opened on a courtyard, where the sound of women's voices was like the sound of millions of caged birds – a constant chatter, louder than the water that fell in sunshot sprays from several fountains.

16

The courtyard, tree-shadowed, flower-embroidered, was full of women. They lay in the shade, talking, dressing each other's hair, painting each other's faces. Their robes rivalled the blooms that made a Persian carpet of the edges of the pools, were as light as the spray of the fountains that made a background noise to the sweet, high voices and laughter of the women – and of the many children that ran, naked and free, about the lawns.

It was the end of a long, hot day. The cool breezes of the evening had begun to release the scents of flowers and the blossoms on the creepers. Serving women, more soberly dressed than the others, were carrying trays of lime drinks, of sherbets and iced water, the ice tinkling against the silver goblets. Birds shrieked their evening excitements, but their voices did not form disharmony. They were swallowed up in the sounds of happiness and contentment that filled the court.

'Perhaps I have died, and come to Paradise,' thought Bella, foodless all the long day – and she swayed on her feet.

The men did not enter the courtyard with her. They shouted, and then stepped back, and two or three of the serving women in their cotton garments came forward, and took Bella's arms, urging her forward gently. The breeze of the evening lifed her veil – her red, dishevelled head, with its silver streaks was bare, and her white face. Slowly, silence settled over the court.

A single voice broke it.

'But the woman is white!' said the voice, and the women

began to crowd round, the faces bright with interest and curiosity. Here was a splendid end to a long and boring day. Only the children took no interest, running about among the flowers and in and out of the fountains' spray, their voices louder than the birds going home to their roosting places. Bella stood, confronting the silken, laughing crowd, and saw that there was not one face that held animosity. Only intense wonder. A woman, more richly dressed than the others, spoke to her.

'You speak our tongue, green eyes?'

The green eyes closed for a moment against that address. Then Bella said, her voice huskier than usual, 'I do. Not well, but I understand.'

'How do you come to be here?'

'I was taken from my Mistress's house this morning. Three men took me, having overpowered the durwan at the gate.'

'Wah! You must indeed have taken our lord's eye, if he goes to such lengths. This is not his State – let us hope your people do not come with soldiers to get you back.'

'He took me by mistake – or the men did. I think your – the man of your house wished to take my Mistress.'

'Who is she?'

'Muna.'

'*Muna* – Muna, the Rose? She is here?'

'Yes. For a few days.'

'And they brought you back to him instead –'

The woman's face crumpled into a wide smile, and the others, near enough to hear, were laughing. The older woman said gently, 'We do not mock you, green eyes – but to think to have Muna in your grasp, and find another woman, would be enough to drive any man mad. Muna is alone, she is the Rose of desire. I have heard nothing of her for many years – I thought she had gone to Lambagh, and left pleasure behind her for ever. Some said she had shaved her head and become a beggar.'

'Not so. She is married.'

'Now you mock me.'

166

'I do not. She is married to my Master, an Englishman, and has a son.'

'This is a matter for long explanations. I see we will have a pleasant time while you are with us. But I must not delay you now. Go with the women.'

'Where – where do they take me?'

'To make you ready for my lord's pleasure – where else? But we will hear your story when you return. Go now, in case he is in a hurry.'

She turned away, leaving Bella to be led away by the serving women, her mind full of a variety of anxieties.

Three hours later, the sudden Indian night had fallen. But the court of the women was well lighted, each fountain ringed with little oil lamps that reflected back from the water, and also with larger lamps hanging in wall sconces. Light flung upwards on to the leaves of the trees, and painted the flowers in different, milder colours from their daytime brilliance.

The light reflected too on a bejewelled Bella. Bella had been stripped naked, massaged with oils and scents, bathed and rubbed clean of oil, and then massaged again; her hair had been washed, and combed to gleaming perfection, sleeked with perfumed oil, and coiled on her head, the red and silver strands twisted with chains of diamonds and jade. Her eyes had been outlined in kohl, so that they burned from her white face like the diamonds they had hung in her ears and round her throat in an effort to hide the little wound the man had inflicted on her when he captured her. Dressed in silk so fine that it lifted with every movement she made, swirling round her like pale green water, Bella stood before the women in the courtyard, and they crowded round her, all paying her compliments, admiring the jewels and the finished result of the maids' handiwork.

'Ah, indeed you will please him – you have the strangeness of some unknown flower, you are different – there has never been one like you here, green eyes. Ice and fire – Ah yes, he will be very pleased. Go laughing, green eyes, and find pleasure where you give it.'

There was neither envy nor jealousy in any of the voices. They all wished her well, sending her off to the honour of their lord's bed. Bella, whose heart was beating uncomfortably fast, wondered what it would be like to live like this, in this happy, flower-filled place, guarded and always in company, whiling away the hours, waiting for the honour of a summons. Going by the number of children that she had seen, none of the women had been neglected, and she saw no discontented faces. She decided, firmly, that there might have been worse fates.

There was a clattering outside the door. Laughing, the women surrounded her, as women surround a bride, and began to half lead, half push her towards the doors. Their voices, calling out their good wishes, faded behind her; the door slammed shut on the twinkling lights of the courtyard, and Bella stood, her head up, her stoic composure belying the desperate fluttering of her heart.

Her captors of the morning were not among the men who waited for her. These were well dressed senior servants. They laid no hand on her. Surrounded, she moved down the twisting corridor that she remembered, up a marble staircase to a higher level, and through a door into another courtyard. There were no fountains here. Three terraced pools dripped water over slopes lit from beneath. On the highest level the Nawab was sitting, a bowl of fruit on a low table before him, a silver goblet in his hand. The men about Bella went away, and she was left, standing at the foot of the steps that led up to the dais where the Nawab sat.

It was very quiet in the courtyard. Only the sound of the dripping, splashing water broke the silence. The Nawab looked down at her, where she stood, her light silks blowing about her, and then he stood up and walked slowly down to join her.

He stood before her, looking at her, and then raised his goblet and drank, bowing his head to her as he did so.

'Yes. I was right. My taste does not fail me. You did yourself no justice, green eyes – now I see you for what you are. An exotic, a stranger – what could be more enticing? Come. Come up and let me hear what that bitter, sweetly-shaped mouth will say to me. What sorrows shaped your mouth so, green eyes?'

'My own.'

He led her up the steps, and to the cushions and rugs of the dais, saying, as he sat down, 'You mean I must not pry? Secret sorrows? Ah well, as we know each other better, we will talk more openly. Sit, green eyes, do not stand over me like a leopardess over her prey. Sit.'

Bella sat, dropping down as far from him as she could, and attempting to sit upright in spite of the invitation of the many cushions and the exhaustion of the day. He regarded her with surprise.

'Will you sit thus for long, green eyes? For I could not. You must be a very strong woman, to sit bolt upright – are you not tired?'

'Very.'

'Well, then, lie back – see, here are cushions, let me pile them. There, is that not better? Green eyes, I think you should drink some wine.'

Bella took the goblet he gave her, and sipped from it, and felt it run through her veins like fire, giving her courage. She turned to look at the man beside her and found he was smiling at her.

'I would not have believed it. A miracle indeed. You come to my Palace, tousled and looking like an old, white fowl, and now, see, here you sit, bearing yourself like a queen, drinking my best wine as if you disdained it, your eyes brighter than the diamonds they have put on you. How do you feel?'

'Frightened,' said Bella.

'Frightened? Who has frightened you?'

'No person. Just – the happenings of today.'

'Ah – yes. That man is a fool. But he thought that he was taking Muna.'

'You mean Muna would not have been frightened – being grasped, and wrapped like a bundle in vile-smelling cloth, and having her throat cut – you think Muna would have enjoyed that?'

'Muna would have laughed – she was used in the old days to keeping a guard against such happenings. But I regret that the cloth they muffled you in smelt vile. And what is this about a cut on your throat? Let me see.'

He leaned towards her, one hand outstretched, and Bella started away from him, putting out her own hand to ward him off.

He sat back at once, and looked at her. 'Gently, gently, leopardess – I only wanted to see your wound. Have some more wine. It will calm you – drink it, and lose fear.'

'Is it drugged?'

'Drugged? Indeed, green eyes, you do me *great* honour. I do not yet have to drug my women. Did those in the *bibikhana* seem so unhappy to you?'

'No,' said Bella, and drank with a long, thirsty swallow.

'You do not use speech very much, stranger, do you?'

'No.'

'I see that we will have to speak in other ways. Give me your hand, green eyes – no, give it me. I only ask to hold it.'

He held his own hand out with a disarming smile of such charm that Bella found she could not withstand it, and put her hand in his. He looked down at it.

'As fine as an ivory carving. Your feet are the same – beautiful, undeformed, a pleasure to the eye. Most women of your race have deformed feet, because of the shoes they wear, but you have the feet to match these hands – long and slim, and made for kisses.'

He bent above the hand he held, pressed his lips into her palm. She felt his mouth move against her flesh, and a quiver started somewhere deep within her, a warmth, like the warmth of the wine. When he looked up at her, he was smiling.

'So, green eyes – we do better. I wish we could for once forego preliminaries and take each other swiftly. Until I have known your body, I will never get to know your mind. But I can see that you are as stiff as a beautiful statue. Let me love you, ice woman, and melt the hardness you have built around you, the ice that has carved your mouth into such a shape. What is it like when you smile? I will see that too – later. Take some more wine – give me your goblet, let me fill it for you.'

'I am hungry,' said Bella, who did not trust the wild fire that the wine was rousing in her, nor the weakness that his words seemed to be spinning like a net to trap her mind.

'Hungry? So am I. But not for food. Green eyes, we will eat later, not now. Now is not the time for food. Drink your wine, and I will take you down paths and to orchards where we will pick and eat fruit that will feed a hunger that you do not know you have – ah, those eyes –'

Bella looked over her goblet, into his eyes from which all laughter had died. Her heart was beating somewhere strange, her whole body felt loose and boneless. The Nawab, with a smile that held no humour, bent towards her, and while her mind cried, 'Back – move back,' her traitor body was doing its best to bend to meet the arms he was holding out.

The noise and outburst at the door was like a blow between the eyes. Bella staggered under it, as if she had indeed been hit. The quiet courtyard was full of men, men who ran, and shouted, and clashed swords, and cried out in pain. The Nawab sprang to his feet, a dagger in his hand and, with a great leap was down amongst the mêlée, shouting like a madman – and as he shouted, slowly the fighting stopped – and men stood, in strange attitudes as if the Nawab's shout had turned them to stone, statues of men in rage and battle. Then the Nawab called out again, and brought them back to life, and they straightened and stood, weapons in hand, in the lamp-lit courtyard, where the water splashed on, tinkling over the lighted falls, unregarded.

'What is this – are we at war with some country? Mhanbir, can you tell me what this is about, what has happened that you break into my court like hooligans?'

'We did not break in, lord. These – these are the Dancer's men. They broke in – and we defended you.'

'I see – the Dancer's men. And why are you here? The Dancer is not here – so why?'

Bella, standing forgotten amongst the tumbled cushions, saw who was down there, turbanless, his thick, greying hair tossed like a boy's above his furious, snarling face.

'You ask why we are here! *You* ask! I ask you why that woman is here. That white woman, who serves my Mistress – did she walk here of her own will? Tell me, oh Nawab of great wealth, who has to go about the streets stealing women. Are

171

you no longer potent, that you must steal women for your pleasure, because they will not come for the asking?'

'Well – you are in great rage, Ayub Khan! Very great rage, so, in memory of old days, I will ignore the insults you level at me. You came too soon, or perhaps I could have proved to you that my potency is not diminished in any way.'

It was then that Bella moved. Like a streak of green, she went down the steps, her feet barely touching them, bruising herself on the marble balustrade, falling almost headlong against Ayub's sword arm as it rose. The Nawab had made no move – his dagger was in his hand but he did not raise it – he stood confronting the naked rage in the face of the big man, on whose arm Bella, in her silks and jewels, hung like a gorgeous, dishevelled flower. As Ayub fought to throw her off, and she hung on with gritted teeth, there was the sound of rending, and a piece of her almond silk fluttered away like a wounded bird. Ayub, wrenching at Bella's hands, swearing vilely, hurt her – but bruised, shaken and with bleeding hands, she clung, crying out wordlessly – and to her relief Kullunder Khan appeared at her side, and added his weight to hers – and eventually Ayub, breathing deeply, was still, and his arm no longer strained against her, his sword hung, quietly, in his flaccid grip.

'Very well,' he said, breathlessly; 'very well, Pakodi – as you have touched her heart, I will leave you now. But, oh man of great riches – keep from my path. Do not speak to me of old friendships, for if I meet you, alone, and she is not with you, so surely as I live, I will kill you like the rat I think you.'

The Nawab's shoulders rose in a splendid shrug. 'My dear old friend, I think you have run about in the sun too long. Had I known that this green-eyed one was your woman, would I have touched her? How long have you known me? Twenty, thirty years, since we fought side by side in the old Ruler's wars – and did you ever see me take a woman who belonged to another man? Never. Tell me now, looking into my eyes, with your hand on your sword. Tell me.'

He waited, and Ayub's breathing slowed, and he said finally, 'Never. But there is always the one woman, the one who takes the eye and the mind, the liver and the stomach, and the blood and heart, as well as the desire of the loins. There is always the one woman.'

The Nawab looked at Bella, white-faced, dishevelled, her red and silver hair tangled with diamonds, her silks torn, her green eyes blazing, her age and her hard life showing in her face, and nodded.

'Ay – there is always, as you say, the one woman. A bone, a finely carven bone, with burning hair and eyes of clear water – and a spirit of fire and ice – is this your dream, oh Ayub? I thought you were a man of the flesh, a man for comfort and curves – when did the fire and the arrow strike you? I see it struck you hard.'

'That is my affair. What passed between you?'

'More important, what was about to pass between us? Who knows. Perhaps I would have discovered a mind in a body at last – but you, my friend, came at a most untimely moment. So far, all that has passed between us has been a great deal of my best wine, and some very few words. She says little, your leopardess.'

'I belong to no man!'

Bella was tired, hungry, and more than a little drunk. She had been shaken on Ayub's arm like a torn rag, and she had found her feelings disturbed in a way she had not imagined possible. She said as much, venomously, and added, 'And when you have quite finished, I wish to go home. Now.'

As she spoke, she began to tear at the Nawab's diamonds, trying to get them disentangled from her hair and bringing it down on her shoulders in a silver-streaked red mane, in her efforts. The Nawab put out his hand, and closed it over hers.

'Cease, stranger – those diamonds are yours. I regret that your silks were torn by my old friend here – he was ever a man of swift movement. I thank you for my life, green eyes – he would have certainly split my skull. But it shall be my pleasure to replace your silks in due course. Now, Ayub. Let us leave this place into which you have brought the spirit of dissension, and go elsewhere. I wish you to see the fate that overtakes those who make errors of great magnitude, before you take your fire and ivory away for ever. Come with me.'

173

He walked ahead of them, and Bella, after raking Ayub with one furious glare, stalked after him. Ayub, his turban retrieved, followed them with Kullunder Khan whose face was a curious study in expressions. The Nawab's armed guards were standing outside, their confusion very obvious. The Nawab ignored them, and led on, down two levels, and into a wide, closed courtyard, which contained no fountains or pools, or trees. There were flaring torches, and they showed, with pitiless clarity, what was the central point in the court. A stone pillar stood there, and spread-eagled around it, as if he embraced it in love, was a man that Bella recognised. He was the man who had held her that morning, the man whose hand she had bitten. The pain of that bite must have been long forgotten, for his back was a bleeding criss-cross of striped flesh, and the man who had thrashed him was still standing there, holding the lash, which gleamed wetly in the red flare of the torches.

Bella turned away, sick to her stomach, but the Nawab stood looking, as if at some interesting curiosity.

'How many has he had?' he asked. His tone was casual, his gaze clinical.

'Thirty strokes, Protector of the Poor.'

The Nawab turned to Ayub. 'Well – enough, my friend – or do you want to see punishment done? He is the man who took your woman, in mistake for Muna. So. What? Enough, or shall we kill him?'

Ayub Khan looked, and spat, and said roughly, 'Enough. I do not kill men thus – nor did you in the old days. We killed by the sword, cleanly.'

'Oh yes, indeed. You can still kill him by the sword if you wish.'

'I said, enough. He was the instrument. It was you who would have done the harm.'

'Are you saying you wish to kill me by the sword, Ayub?' The Nawab appeared to be laughing, but the light in the courtyard flared and flickered so that it was hard to see his expression. Bella, cold sweat on her forehead and crawling on her body, looked at Ayub and at the ring of the Nawab's men, who

174

seemed to have appeared from nowhere, with drawn swords in their hands.

Ayub's hand went to his sword, and the Nawab said suddenly, 'As you said, Ayub Khan – enough. Take your woman, the one woman, and go. Tell me, what would you have done if it had been Muna that I took?'

Ayub did not answer. He looked at the Nawab, sheathed his sword, and turned to Bella. 'You are ready?'

Bella drew her torn silk around her and walked away from the courtyard where the smell of fresh blood was strong, into the corridor and, at last, out to the drive, where the Nawab stood before her, and said quietly, 'Farewell, green eyes. I am foolish enough to imagine that had the interruption been a little later, I might have found something with you that we would have both enjoyed – the final friendship. Go, lovely stranger, and do not disguise yourself as a hen any more – things of beauty are for admiration.'

His teeth showed in a smile that made Bella suddenly understand why his women looked so contented.

Then, with a salute to Ayub, half mocking, half friendly, the Nawab went back into his Palace – and there was only Ayub Khan, and Kullunder Khan, and the empty street, at one end of which hung, like a lantern, the late rising moon.

17

Her rescuers had a carriage waiting, an open Victoria. Kullunder Khan climbed up beside the driver, and Bella and Ayub sat opposite each other.

The streets were still brightly lit. Bella had no notion what time it could be. She drew her veil over her head and sat back, looking over at Ayub, to see his face set and angry. As he saw her looking at him, he spoke.

'Wah! Bejewelled, painted, dressed and scented for a rich man's pleasure!' His voice was full of contempt, and Bella's temper flared.

'How do you dare to speak thus to me! Do you think I ran through streets to his house this morning of my own will? As for you – you allowed him to think I was your property – your mistress!'

'To save you, I told him you were my woman. Would you rather have been his mistress?'

'I am no one's mistress. And, if you are interested, Ayub Khan, his women are happy and contented, and live in luxury. There could be worse fates than to live in a garden full of flowers with a kind man.'

'What foolishness is this?' Ayub's eyes were furious, he spat his words at her. 'Are you telling me that you would be happy to live like that, being chosen, as a man chooses a coat to wear, or a pair of shoes, from among twenty or so other women?'

'Fourteen,' said Bella.

'Fourteen – so, one for every day of half the month. Then he starts again.'

He peered at Bella as the carriage passed from one light to another, and shadows moved over her face, making it hard for him to see her expression.

'Or did you think you might be different – chosen more often perhaps?'

'You, Ayub, you yourself said, "There is always the one woman." '

'Yes, I know what I said in anger. But let me tell you, that man has no heart. He only has a rapacious body. You would have pleased him for how long? He likes new things, new places, new people. How long before his choice began to fall on you once a week instead of every day – then perhaps every two weeks, if you were fortunate? You are not young. So, very soon it would have been long days in the garden, braiding your red hair to hide the silver, and dressing, and hoping, and then the long nights, alone – and finally, helping the other forgotten ones to look after the children of more fortunate younger women. How long – green eyes? Allah! He took from me even your name.'

Ayub's voice had a sudden note of pain in it. But Bella did not hear it. She only heard, echoing in her ears, his voice saying, 'You are not young'; so she spoke flatly, her voice bitter.

'I saw no unhappiness among his women. As for him taking my name from you, well, my name is Bella – and if he called me "green eyes" it was for a good reason. My eyes, ageing as they are, are still green.'

There was silence for a while as they bumped through the streets.

Then Bella said, restless under Ayub's glare, 'You appear to know the Nawab very well? He is your friend it seems.'

'He was my friend. We knew each other well in youth. He then had no expectations of an inheritance. There were several lines between him and his father's State. So, like me, he used his sword to earn his bread and his place in the world. He took service with my Ruler.'

For a moment, Ayub's voice sounded less angry. 'Pakodi of

Subbar is a brave fighter. A brave man. I remember – '

He paused, thinking, and Bella waited, and finally recalled him by saying, 'You remember – what?'

It was a mistake. Ayub snapped at her, angry again.

'I remember a number of things, and one of them is the picture of you, sitting like a drunken harlot, covered with jewellery. Was it earned, green eyes? I find it hard to say that name now.'

'Then do not trouble yourself to say it,' flashed Bella, 'because I have no intention of further speech with you – you – oh, you great *bear*.'

'No doubt you prefer your men to be thin also. It is understood.'

'And you? I heard what you prefer. Fat women with bodies like mattresses. Do not speak to me.'

'Thank you. I will not. I will merely continue to do my duty, risk my life to rescue some idiot women who put themselves in danger, and I shall expect no thanks.'

Ayub folded his arms and looked away at the streets through which they passed. Bella looked up at the sky, and through eyes full of angry tears, watched the stars blurr and tangle together as if they were swinging in a mad dance like her mind.

There were different men at the gate, and more of them. Goki was sitting on a bench, and as the gate swung open and Bella came through, she hurried forward to take her hands.

'You are safe? Unharmed?'

Before Bella could answer, Ayub said, 'Safe? Unharmed? Look at her – hung with diamonds and dressed like a king's favourite. Scented like a whole covey of houris. How else should she be but safe and unharmed?'

He stamped past, saying over his shoulder, 'You are to go to Munabhen. She has been sick with distress for you all day.'

Goki shook her head at Bella, standing in her shimmering silks in the lamp-lit porch. 'Not only Muna has been distressed – Ayub was like a man driven mad.'

'You do not surprise me – he still is. What is the matter with him? I did not go of my will into captivity.'

'Captivity? Of course you did not. But you are arrayed in

178

great splendour, and Ayub knows Pakodi well – as no doubt you now know.'

'Yes. Well, I cannot help that. I was imprisoned through no fault of mine by one of Ayub's disreputable friends. Now I must go to the Sahiba.'

She went away and left Goki to shake her head knowingly at Kullunder Khan, who had just come in, having dismissed the carriage. Goki said firmly, 'Come you, come and tell me everything. You at least do not appear to be either drunk or mad. What happened this evening to make Ayub return with red eyes of fire? I die of curiosity.'

Bella found Ayub at his usual post outside Muna's door. He looked away from her. She, for her part, behaved as if he were part of the furnishings of the hall. As she opened the door, Muna was there, pulling her in, grasping at her as if she could not believe she was real.

'Oh, *Bella*! Is all well with you?'

'I think if one more person asks me that I shall begin to scream. I am very hungry, I am very tired, I am very angry. I have been, during this long day, very frightened. But I was not raped or otherwise attacked.'

Muna dropped her hands and stood back, her face wiped clean of all expression but relief. 'Then thanks be to the Goddess – for you are fortunate. You have spent many hours in the hands of Pakodi and everyone – '

'Yes. I know. Everyone *knows* Pakodi and no one believes I have returned as I went.'

Muna raised her eyebrows as Bella's veil slipped back, revealing her tangled hair, with diamonds still strung across the thick red and silver coils.

Muna shook her head in amazement. 'Well, it is seen that you fought hard for your virtue, my poor Bella. Your silks are torn, your hair so disarranged – '

'I fought for nothing. I did *not* fight. Ayub did this.'

'Ayub? Ayub Khan! What in the name of all heaven was Ayub doing that caused such disorder? Bella, stop pulling at your silks. Sit down and tell me what happened.'

Bella sat down on the cushions opposite Muna and began to

tell her story. The wine she had drunk was still working in her, and the story came out in confused phrases and broken sentences. Muna narrowed her eyes and leaned forward.

'So – you were dressed and adorned for Pakodi, and then taken to him and he gave you wine. I see. Bella, have you eaten?'

'No.'

'Tsk – what foolishness! Wait!' Muna went to the door and called, and gave swift orders and came back. She sat down again. Bella, having seen Ayub's face through the open door, was trying with tipsy dignity to straighten her hair and her clothing. Under Muna's quizzical gaze she suddenly smiled, the smile turned into a laugh, and when the bearer came in with a tray of food, the two women were still laughing helplessly.

Ayub heard the sound of their laughter, and his frown grew dark. He decided that he would ask to return to Lambagh with Goki's party. Abdul Vakil could stay instead. Ayub wanted, he thought, nothing more to do with that green-eyed wanton laughing at him with Muna. He recalled his horror when he had discovered that she had been kidnapped, his wild searches and final discovery of the house, the undignified skirmish in the garden, with his turban being knocked from his head in front of all. He saw again Bella, gorgeous, gleaming in the shadows of the garden, her eyes glowing as she leaned towards Pakodi. The rage in his heart turned to pain, and he moved restlessly. His green-eyed leopardess was as ordinary as any other woman – rich clothes and jewels could buy her, and he had thought her so different. The pain in his mind grew unbearable as he remembered Bella moving light-footed about the Palace in the plain cotton clothes of a Lambaghi woman, her flame and silver hair pulled away from her face, her pale eyes clear and disdainful. He compared that Bella with the exotic woman in Pakodi's garden – almost in Pakodi's arms – and felt himself sicken with disappointment.

The door opened behind him, and he knew who had opened it. The scent that they had put on her was strong, but he would have known in any case. The slender, erect woman walked away from him without a glance, her green eyes turned towards

180

the garden, the silks she wore making a whispering sound, a sound that was calculated to attract a man's attention. Her hair fell tangled down her back, the diamonds still twisted in it, sparkling as if drops of water lay among the silver-streaked coils. She did not look back. She walked swiftly, and was gone. Only the breath of her scent remained, like the whisper of her silks.

A great sigh broke from Ayub as he looked down the long empty colonnade. There had been so many women. Now, he knew, there was only the one.

He heard Muna calling him, and opened the door.

'Munabhen – you called?'

'Yes. Oh, Ayub, what a long face. Tell me something?'

'Ask what you will.'

'Ayub, have you ever spent a day, afraid and alone, having been roughly handled and thrown into a small, airless prison? Then, as you wonder what your fate will be, when evening comes you are splendidly robed, and given a great deal of wine, strong wine, with perhaps a pinch of a special powder in it. Has such a thing ever happened to you?'

'It has not.'

'So. Let us suppose you have been forced to fast all day, and then, still fasting, have drunk deeply and quickly, because of great thirst. What would happen?'

'I would become drunken.'

'Exactly so. Do you know why I ask you these questions?'

'I can think of a reason.'

'Then, Ayub, put away this anger which is making you look like a mad bull.'

'Mad bull! *She* said I was a bear.'

'She was likely right.'

'Muna, she was all but in his arms! Painted and scented, and oiled like – like – ' Ayub stammered into silence.

'Like I used to be? Like a dancer? Yes, that is how a man likes to be made aware if his flesh is satiated. But why are you so angry? You saved her.'

'Much thanks I got.'

'She had drunk much wine. She had seen herself trans-

181

formed into a beauty, and Pakodi had shown he was attracted. Therefore – perhaps she did not wish to be saved!'

'No, by Allah. She would have been happy to stay and become one of his women.'

'Do you know what her life has been, Ayub? Her husband was sick and died when she was young. Since then she has lived with empty arms, seeing no admiration in a man's eyes, no desire burn for her. But in that garden, she saw admiration and desire in Pakodi's eyes. Do you blame her if she longed to taste the sweetness of lying with a desirous man again? She is not a girl, Ayub, to be frightened by passion. She is a woman. Do not be angry because she showed that she was not too old for love. Perhaps there is a lesson there? Go away, and stop glowering – you will crack all my mirrors with that face. Go, and think of what I have said – and, Ayub you have my thanks, thanks from my heart for saving my dear Bella. You will have hers, too.'

Ayub salaamed and retreated, and took up his post until Abdul Vakil came to relieve him. Then he went in search of Goki. When he found her, in the flower garden where the fountains splashed and pattered, he asked, 'Where is she?'

'Who?'

'Old woman, do not try me. Answer!'

'Dear me – such a fierce man you have become in your old age! She sleeps, poor woman, where else would she be?'

Ayub sat down on the rim of the fountain and Goki turned her bright old eyes on his face. Her voice was kind when she next spoke.

'Ay – Ayub. So you have been defeated at last. The sweet fruit that you cannot eat, the flower you cannot pick – is that it?'

'No. The leopardess I cannot tame.'

'Ayub, give it time. The fiercest beast will come to your hand and lie at your side in peace. Just give the gift of time and patience, as well as love.'

'I am not a boy.'

'No. And she is not a girl. Are you not fortunate, to come to

182

love when it is not only fire and fury but friendship and pleasure as well?'

'Huh – at present it is fire and fury.'

'I who am old – I can remember love. The memory of love does not leave the old. It warms me still to recall my lover, and his joy in me, and the joy and security of mind he gave me. Heed me, Ayub. I know of love. You remember my Master, even though you were only a stripling when he was killed in the Madoremahal.'

'Old one, how should I forget? My father died at his side. You tell me to wait – what else can I do? This woman of another race does not even think of love when she looks at me.'

'I still say wait. Wait as the huntsman waits, chain in hand, for the unleashed leopardess to kill her prey and return to his side. As for thinking of love – well, I have seen her eyes when she looks at you. Be patient.'

Ayub gave a sigh that turned into a jaw-cracking yawn.

'Go now and sleep, Ayub. Your eyes are closing. Go and sleep – and mayhap, dream – and, waking, find a new and better day.'

Alan was not told all the story of Bella's adventure, nor the reason for the extra guards and the padlocked gates, which had to be unlocked and opened instead of standing wide open as they had previously. In any case, he was too busy to notice very much of the happenings in the Palace.

Ayub, his sword in his hand, was standing at Muna's door the next day when he saw Bella coming towards him, and braced himself for a cold, unseeing stare, disdainful turning away. Instead Bella stopped in front of him.

'Ayub.'

'Green eyes?'

'Ayub Khan. Yesterday you took a great risk for me, and I was ungrateful. I wish you to know that wine had my tongue and I did not speak or think as I should have done. I am grateful. I would, I think you know, have killed myself in shame if I had become – if he had taken – ' Her words petered into silence under his look.

'Nay, you would never take your life, green eyes. But you might have died trying to take his.'

'Perhaps. But let me say my thanks to you. I thank you from my heart.'

The clear eyes looked into Ayub's eyes and as they looked, the tide of colour that he loved to see rose to her face.

'Ah, green eyes! That you look at me thus is enough. You broke my heart when you would not look at me except as a trapped animal looks at her captor.'

'I broke your heart? Big words. Oh, Ayub of many conquests. You were very rude to me.'

'That is not so. If you think back. Can you remember what I said to Pakodi? Think!'

'I can remember.' The blush grew deeper.

'Then you cannot say I was rude. To be the one rare woman –'

'Oh, those words. You said kind words to save me. But I recall something else you said.'

She was wearing her plain white cotton trousers and shirt, and the white veil fell round her shoulders. Her beautiful high-arched feet, as long and slender as her hands, were bare; her hair was drawn back from her thin face, blanched, ivory coloured, as her blush receded. Only her silver-streaked red hair and her pale eyes had any colour. There was no paint on the wide, straight-lipped mouth today. Ayub, looking into the strange, thin face with its steady eyes found his breath short.

'What did I say?'

'Words I shall never forget. You said, "You are not young." I think those are words no woman can hear without pain.'

'Ach. Words said in anger. I saw you, as it seemed, almost in a libertine's grip – why should such words, spoken in great rage, hurt you?'

Ayub saw the real sorrow on her face and had a strong desire either to kill himself by falling on his sword, or better, to pull her into his arms and take her in love there and then, so that he would see her face burn with passion instead. But she was speaking.

'Because women never know that their youth has gone until

184

a man tells them. I know now. My girlhood is long, long behind me.'

'I would die before I hurt you.'

The words were spoken so low, Bella was not sure she had heard him. Then he said, 'Well. So you are not a girl. Do you truly wish you were?'

'To be young – all the dreams and hopes that you knew were going to come true. The knowledge that you would live for ever, young, beautiful and strong. Other people grew old – but you would never change. Every new day was something wonderful. Yes. I would like all that again.'

'You have all that still. You move with ease, you eat with appetite, you never grow tired – and you have more, much more than that girl you envy, that girl you used to be.'

'I do? What do I have?'

'You have a timeless beauty, burned down to the bones so it can never change. You have the courage of experience and knowledge. You have memories – and you have the same green eyes of that girl, but you see more clearly. You have other things, of which I will tell you when the time is right.'

'Ayub, you make rich amends for your harsh words. You have a tongue dipped in honey. Again, take my thanks for yesterday. Are we friends now?'

'If friendship is what you wish, my green-eyed leopardess, then you have it.'

'If friendship is what I wish – what do you mean?'

'Do you tempt me, green eyes? Shall I tell you of other things that can come from friendship? There is no friendship between men and women.'

'No? Then what?'

'I will tell you another time. When you are ready to listen to me.'

She had smiled and pushed Muna's door open, and left him.

They took up their old relationship and life returned to normal; while Ayub watched and waited, wondering what chains he could forge to bind this hunting leopardess to him for ever.

Within a week from Bella's adventure, they were packing.

Richard went ahead with three of the sepoys from the regiment, taking the train to Salkot where he made arrangements for carriers and carts, and riding horses, and a carriage. Alan and Muna and a retinue of people, and a great deal of baggage, followed a week later.

'This is like a caravanserai setting off in the days of the Grand Turk,' complained Alan as he watched the baggage being loaded under Kullunder Khan's watchful eyes, saw Goki arranging Muna's couch with cushions and rugs, saw a galvanised iron container full of ice in which champagne bottles nestled to keep cool.

'We will be leaving this train in four days' time. Goki is behaving as if we are taking up residence in it for the next four years.'

'Alan. It would have been better had you gone with Richard and left me to follow with the baggage.'

'I would not allow you to travel alone, my love.'

'But I would not be alone! There is Bella and Goki, and Ayub Khan and his men –'

'And heaven knows how many others. But, Muna, do you think I have not known of the risks you run if you are seen – particularly since you have discarded European dress? I am not a fool. I would certainly not allow you to travel the length of India without me.'

He looked stern and tired and irritated. Muna knew that he would rather have gone to Salkot with Richard, free and unencumbered.

She took his hand and, smiling, said, 'Alan, you are very good. I am sorry if you wish me to wear European dress. It was so *hot* –'

'I know, my dear. Of course I would not ask you to be uncomfortable. Think nothing of it. But now, before Goki begins to arrange flowers in there, will you be pleased to get in, my dear. The guard is anxious that we leave approximately on time, and I think we are now half-an-hour late.'

Alan and Muna travelled in a compartment, so transformed.

186

by Goki and Bella that it could have been a small room. There was a bathroom opening from it and the windows were guarded by two separate blinds, one of glass, and one of wood, slatted so that privacy was ensured but air could enter when the glass window was open. Muna settled herself amongst her cushions, Alan nodded to the guard, and all along the train passengers hurried to scramble into crowded compartments. The train shuddered into movement, gathered speed, and Bombay and all its dramas receded into the past.

Bella and Goki shared a small, two-berthed compartment next to their employers. Ayub Khan and his men, together with Kullunder Khan and the house servants – the cook and his *masalchi* and the two senior bearers – were all in a large compartment next door. The sweeper, who was, of course, untouchable, travelled with his wife and his two children in a compartment with others of his caste. A very full complement of servants had come down from Lambagh. Kassim had been determined that Muna, going to Sagpur, should have her own people round her.

At every stop, Ayub Khan and some of his men would take up position outside Alan's compartment. Fruit and food in stacked tin containers was handed in. Sunset came and sudden darkness, and lanterns glowed along the train; and Bella, at the next stop, came in to Muna and helped her undress and put on a loose robe, and arranged her bed for the night, while Alan lowered the wooden, slatted window blinds. Then Bella returned to her own carriage to find Goki had arranged her bed for her, and Ayub had handed in a great dish of fruit – oranges and bananas, and a round basket of sweet grapes from Kabul, pale green and as large as pigeon's eggs.

Alan, alone with Muna in the rattling privacy of their compartment, poured iced wine for them both and, drinking his, said with a relaxed sigh, 'Oh, it is good to be with you alone. This reminds me of something. Do you remember our journey down from Madore?'

'I do. I remember how the shadows ran along beside the train and how quickly the hills fell behind us.'

'I only remember the moon shining on your face and turning

187

it to silver. Come to bed, my love, and let us remember together.'

Long after Alan had fallen asleep, Muna, held closely at his side, lay listening to the sounds of the rattling train. At first, the noise was like stones being shaken in a great iron bowl. Then, the noise began to make patterns of sound, words that she could hear. 'My Mother – Mother!' said the train, in a boy's voice, and Muna lay listening, and seeing a face she loved.

18

The days rattled away, and the train brought them at last to
Salkot station, and Richard waiting on the bare, dusty platform.

The baggage was distributed among the carriers that
Richard had engaged, and the cavalcade set off along the wide,
tree-shaded road, soft underfoot with dust as thick and white
as cream, dust that rose in puffs and clouds with every step
their horses took, with every turn of the carriage wheels.

Their group formed only a small part of the traffic on this,
the main road of India. An entire world travelled with them,
the many-sided, many-coloured world of Asia. Each unit complete within itself, hurrying or dawdling, depending on the
nature of the travellers or their business, they all made their
unheeded way down the Grand Trunk Road.

Muna rode with Alan and Richard, her face and hair veiled
against the penetrating dust that matched her creamy robes.
She left the carriage for Goki, insisting with truth that she preferred to ride. They camped each night at sunset, arriving at a
planned camping site to find their tents pitched, food cooking,
and water heated for much needed baths. Richard had made his
arrangements well, sending relays of men ahead, so that the
party never arrived, tired and dusty, to anything but comfort.

They broke camp each day at dawn, starting while the dust
was still damp enough after the night's fall of dew to lie, so
that they could ride for a while free of its white smothering.

Alan rode with memories of bygone journeys on this road.

One morning when they set off, they met a camel caravan,

the camels walking in a long train, nose to tail, supercilious droop-eyed heads bobbing, feet silent in the thick dust of the road. Their drivers were tall hawk-faced men in black clothes, their faces muffled because of the dust, nothing showing but their fierce pale eyes. Alan recalled the camel caravan he had once seen passing on an evening outside Madore city, and also recalled all that had happened afterwards. He looked at Muna, but like the camel drivers her face was veiled, and her eyes told him nothing. On another day, they overtook several gaily caparisoned bullock carts, with women's voices spilling shrilly from behind close-drawn curtains. Ayub's men grinned knowingly, and one or two shouted bawdy comments, and were rewarded with screams of delighted laughter, and the curtains parted to show lightly veiled, painted faces, smiling invitation. Ayub barked orders, and Alan was glad of Muna's thick veil. These women could, by some not so strange coincidence, have come from the Street of the Harlots in Madore, and Muna was not forgotten in these parts. He knew that the men of the escort from Lambagh looked at her with longing admiration, and much as he objected within himself, there was nothing he could do – Muna was Muna, and would never be anything but the famous Rose of Madore to the men and women of the cities in the north. He hastened his horse's pace, and rode beside his wife as if his presence could drive the past away. For the first time it came to him that this road of memory and nostalgia could speak to Muna of many things too, and he burned with jealousy.

But Muna saw nothing of the road. Goki filled her thoughts. Day after day, as the journey continued, Goki seemed to fade. She was not ill. Her black eyes sparkled as brightly, her voice was as firm as always; only her body was small and frail.

Bella sat in the carriage with Goki very often, and listened to everything she said, listened closely, as if she was storing Goki's words away, as one puts precious things away to take out and examine later, or make use of in time of need.

Bella spent a great deal of time with Goki. But Muna, who loved the old woman so much, kept away, and Goki did not ask for her. Muna rode with Alan, and her thoughts were the only part of her that was with the old woman, all the long day. But at night Muna would go and sink down beside Goki where she lay on folded quilts in her tent. They would speak very little, but would sit together, and then Muna would get up, and with a few words of farewell, go away. The men round the fires saw her go, unveiled and silent, and would exchange glances. The Rose of Madore was as beautiful as ever, as much a heart-taker, a dream-giver as she had always been. But when she came from Goki's tent, she had a look on her face that forbade salutations.

They came to Orangapura, where Goki and Abdul Vakil and two of the men of the escort were to take the road that went up towards Madore, and then on and up and through the high passes to the Valley of Lambagh.

That night they camped earlier than usual, and Muna, after her bath, went straight to Goki's tent.

Ayub Khan stopped Bella on her way to see Goki. 'Later tonight, green eyes. Leave them. Tonight they will wish to speak of many things. It is for the last time.'

'What do you mean?'

'Tomorrow Goki leaves us, and goes home.'

'So? That does not mean that we will not see her again, surely?'

'Ah, green eyes, why do you pretend to be stupid? I know that you are not a fool. They say goodbye to each other tonight. Are you trying to tell me that you think those two in that tent will ever meet again? I think you know in your heart that they are saying all that they will say to each other in this life. If Muna is to be believed, they will meet again – elsewhere.'

'But you, as a Muslim, do not believe in many lives?'

'I, as a Muslim from the Valley, believe many things. One thing I believe in is love – and you? Do you believe in love, green eyes?'

'I do not know. What do you mean by love – there are so many ways of loving.'

'Green eyes, come, let us sit together beside the fire, while the stars watch us, and talk to each other of love –'

191

'Eh! My honour will be in shreds – not only the stars will watch us!'

'Surely we can sit, three feet apart, and speak together, without your honour being tarnished! Green eyes, you will come, and you will sit, and we will talk of love – or I will talk, and you will listen. Come –'

It was full dark when Bella took a lantern and went to Goki's tent. Alan had already been asking irritably when Muna was coming to join him. When Bella lifted the tent flap and went in she found Muna sitting beside Goki, her face desolate, and wet with tears.

'Sahiba!'

Bella was horrified at the grief, totally uncontrolled, that Muna showed. How was she going to be able to help her so that she would join Alan without making him displeased? His jealousy of Muna and her love for her own people had not escaped Bella's sharp eyes. This would infuriate him, this complete collapse into sorrow for something that did not concern him.

Goki spoke, her voice firm and steady, 'Enough, Muna. I have to leave you, you knew that when we set out on this journey. Here is the one who will take my place – and you have a duty to your husband, who will not wish to see you thus. Bella, bathe her face – and then Muna, you must go. I do not wish to see you again. Live your life, my heart's joy, and bear all that you must. You are under protection. We meet again, when it is the will of the Gods. If you grieve like this, you cause me pain that I do not have the strength to bear.'

Muna, submitting like a child to Bella's ministrations with water and a cloth, sobbed aloud. 'Better if you had left me beside my mother's body. I cannot lose you – I who have nothing –'

'Muna! Be ashamed! Can you say that with truth?'

'Nay. I spoke evil. But forgive me – my heart breaks.'

'Hearts do not break so easily. Now. Let me see your face. Oh Rose of gold, child of my heart – go now. I shall be with you again, I shall see you attain happiness, somewhere in the passageways and through the doorways of another day. But for now – farewell, my gentle child.'

Muna looked at Goki for a long moment, and then left the tent. As Bella watched, Goki covered her face with her head cloth.

'I sleep now, for tomorrow I shall need all my strength. I do not need to tell you to take care of the Rose, for I know that you will.'

They left at dawn, Goki and her escort.

It did not take long for the carriage and the attendant riders to come to the place where the road turned off. Only the dust cloud of their going remained. The others turned from watching, and resumed their journey, Muna riding beside her husband, her veil pulled closely over her face.

Three days' journey brought them to a different climate, a changed countryside. They had been travelling along a road bordered with mango trees, and with wide, brown plains on each side so dry and infertile that saltpetre lay in patches, like frost on the English fields in the winter. Now they travelled between rice fields, as green as jade, each field edged by a raised ridge of earth where farmers walked between their labourers, who were mostly women, bent double, knee deep in mud and water, weeding, opening water channels, and standing to watch the party of northerners go by, like people watching a circus, with amazement and curiosity. The road was now bordered by banyan trees, strange and frightening to the eye, with their pendant swinging roots growing from their branches, reaching to anchor themselves in the earth, and forming a cage round the central trunks. Many of these trees had bits of bright rag tied amongst their branches, pledges of prayers that had been said beneath them, reminders to the deity that a boon had been asked. Holy men sat under these trees, in the caves formed by the hanging roots, their eyes glittering from ash-smeared faces, begging-bowls before them.

But some of the trees had no human inhabitant. A small earthenware dish of milk placed among the creeping roots would show what lived in the holes and twists of the trunks. Bella, riding beside Ayub, looked, and shuddered.

'Green eyes? You are afraid of something, or did a spirit breathe on your neck?'

'I had forgotten much about this part of India, but this I remember – the snake worship.'

'I did not know that you had been here before?'

'Yes. I was here with the man who married me when I was a girl.'

'A man of great fortune and happiness, to have possessed you in your youth.'

'That is as maybe. He did not have very much time in which to be happy and fortunate; he died of cholera, two years after our marriage.'

'He was indeed unlucky. And you, remembering him, have lived lonely ever since?'

'Ayub, let us not discuss my life. It is an old and dull story, put away now. But I hated this part of the country then, and I do not like it now. The heat, the people, and the snakes.'

'There are snakes in the north, too.'

'As you know, I have never been to your north. But here, the snakes have a special place. They are worshipped, holy. Those dishes of milk did not come there by themselves. They were placed there by worshippers, and kept well-filled. See, over there? The image of the God they are supposed to worship is made to look less than the snake in that shrine.'

They were passing a small shrine, little more than a plinth, on which a many-armed God stood, and rearing above him, forming a canopy over his head, was a stone cobra, its spread hood and forked tongue faithfully carved so that it was a life-like image of cold, watchful malevolence.

'Ugh, how horrible. It makes my blood cold, even in this heat.'

Ayub shrugged indifferently. 'These people are all idolators,' he said, and spat at the feet of the image. Then he put his hand out and gripped Bella's hands as they rested on her saddle. 'Do not be afraid, my leopardess. As long as I live, I will hold all your terrors away from you. As long as I live, and if Munabhen is right, I shall look for the fortune of guarding you in these other lives she speaks about. If she is wrong – well, I shall ask for you in Paradise, for without you it would be a desert. Green eyes, do not laugh at me! Why do you laugh?'

'I laugh at the thought of you in Paradise, surrounded by wonderful houris of great beauty, having any time even to think of me, let alone asking for my presence!'

'Laugh away, green eyes. I like to hear you laugh. But I am not laughing. I mean every word I say to you. Remember that.'

Muna, riding ahead beside Alan and Richard, heard Bella's laughter, and for a moment, envied her. She was oppressed by the heat and the strange dark trees, but Alan, deep in conversation with Richard, had not noticed, and did not try to soothe her fears.

Each day of their journey now, the climate grew worse. They left the rice fields behind, and the road ran through thick jungle, dark and tangled with creepers and thickets of bamboo. At night, when they made camp, they stayed close to the road, and lit large fires, in spite of the heat. The nights were loud with insect voices, and when they lay down to sleep they covered themselves from head to foot and lay stifling, because of the hordes of stinging pests that attacked them. They broke camp very early each day, and then rested through the hot humid afternoons, listening to the constant sounds that came from the dark thickets around them – strange birds shrieked, the cicadas kept up a steady, irritating buzz, and there were other stealthy sounds, rustlings and movements, as if unseen things were coming closer to look at them through the tangled creepers and the dark low sweeping branches of the jungle trees.

At last, two weeks after Goki had left them, they reached the coast. They crossed a wide sluggish river, as dark green as the trees that grew on its banks. They were ferried over in three boats, poled by men who did not speak to them, but who eyed them as if they had never seen anyone like them before. All the party felt relief when they were safely over the river, and were riding through a belt of trees, and it was difficult for Muna not to look over her shoulder to see if they were being followed. She saw Ayub speak to Faizulla and the other guards from Lambagh, and they rode with their swords loosened in their scabbards. But all was well, and they came out into open country, and there, grey and foam-flecked, was the sea, and the cool sea breeze.

They rode for two days along the rutted shore road, and saw few other travellers. Herd boys, perched on the grey backs of big horned water buffaloes, stared at them as the herd lumbered past, shouldering each other to get to the nearest green-slimed mud hole. There was an occasional bullock cart, rocking over the rutted road, the bullocks finding their own way while their drivers slept in the cart. Kites, wheeling and swooping, marked where a village was, even though there was no sign of it from the road. On the shore, men worked on strange boats, small slim vessels with sharply upturned prows, boats that floated so low in the water that the men who were standing in them, throwing their nets, appeared to be standing in the sea.

Suddenly Alan reined up, and turning to Muna, pointed with his whip.

'There – look, my dear, that white house on the shore. That is where we go. That is our house.'

'We are not to live in the cantonment area of Sagpur? That house looks to be a long way from the city.'

'It is about eight miles out. I asked for a house outside the city for you. The air will be better, and you do not want to be in a compound – this is much better.' He spoke with finality. There was no more to be said. They rode on, and the house came out of the distance and grew large and close, and they had arrived.

Domed, with wide verandas sheltered by elaborately carved marble screens, surrounded by casuarina trees and palms, the house stood on the shore, waiting to be made into a home.

Alan stayed long enough to see the baggage unloaded, and then took a hasty farewell from Muna and rode off to the Fort with Richard. The regiment he was to command, with Richard as his adjutant, was housed in old buildings that had been used by the army for over a hundred years. The barracks were low, white-washed blocks of rooms with arched doors and thick walls. They formed three sides of an expanse of trodden earth which was the parade ground. The stables completed the square, and the whole place was surrounded by a high wall. Alan and Richard were met by the two English officers they were relieving, and the white house and Muna, and all that he had left behind, faded from Alan's mind as he began the business of taking over the detachment of men who were to be his charge for his tour of duty in India.

In the white house on the edge of the sea Bella stood, hands on hips, looking round the high-ceilinged, empty rooms.

'Well – another Palace, it seems. And who would this one belong to? Some prince of this country, no doubt?'

Muna did not reply. This was a very different place from the little pink Palace in Bombay. Here were no fountains, and the air pressed down, damp and hot, so that every movement brought sweat prickling out on the skin. Muna wandered from one room to another, like a sleep-walker. Bella watched her, frowning. This was a Muna she did not know, this quiet, bewildered woman with sad eyes, whose beauty seemed veiled, like the moon hidden under clouds. It seemed that Goki, departing, had taken Muna's spirit with her.

Watching, Bella grew anxious. She went to Ayub Khan and, with his help, showed Kullunder Khan which packages and cases to open. Together they began to unpack and put the house in order. Bella chose the largest bedroom for Muna, and found, set in the wall of the room she chose, an arched niche, with a carved wooden shelf in front of it. The people who had built his house had honoured their household god with a shrine of his own, now empty and ready for a new occupant. Bella unpacked the figure of the Goddess, placed her in the niche, and put the little oil lamp on the wooden shelf. Then she went to find Muna, and taking her into the room, showed her what she had done.

'Is this to your liking, Sahiba? See, the niche could have been made for her. Now we will bring in what you need, if you will tell me where the things should go. This is a good room for you, these windows will give you the breeze from the sea at night – and there is a good big bathroom here, and a dressing room – also a bathroom and dressing room for the Colonel opening through that arch – presuming that he is going to

197

spend some of his time here.' But the last part of Bella's sentence was not spoken aloud.

Slowly, under Muna's directions, the room took shape, became familiar and comfortable, with her cushioned bed, and her low stools and carved screens. Presently Muna was left alone, to stand before the Goddess who had taken her life so long ago. She prayed for tranquillity of mind, and freedom from the grief of her longing for her son. But no voice answered her. She only heard the voice of the sea, beating on the shore below her windows. There was no break in the wall of silence that seemed to stand, once again, between her and the Goddess. Muna felt deserted and alone, in a very strange country. She was more lost and homesick than she had ever felt in England.

She did what she could to combat the homesickness. She worked to make the house beautiful. The empty white shell she had entered became a home. It was full of things that spoke of another place – the carved screens and chests, sweet with the smells of shisham and sandalwood, stood against the plain white walls. Carpets were used as wall hangings because the marble floors were cool to the feet; and as always there were piles of cushions, cotton-covered for comfort, heaped in the window alcoves, and on the low divans. All these furnishings had been sent from Lambagh, even the silver lamps, and the goblets from which Muna drank. Everywhere, worked into the carpets, carved on the chests and screens, engraved on the silver, was the peacock motif of the Rulers of Lambagh. It was as if she was being constantly reminded that she was one of the Lambagh family, as if she was being called back to the Valley. Muna's hands lingered on the beautiful things, touching them with love, and her eyes were bright – was it with pleasure, or tears? Her tears, however, if she shed any, were unseen. She went quietly about her house, making it look as she wished.

Outside, orange trees had been planted round the walls, sheltered from the sea winds, and grown in deep pots filled with special soil. They flowered and filled the air with reminiscent bitter-sweet scent. But they bore no fruit. The waxy, heavy flowers fell, and shrivelled, and lay in little heaps, blown here and there, rustling on the marble floor of the outside court. Muna had a pool made there, filling it from the sea with a complicated system of channels. It sparkled and shone and reflected back the sun by day, and the stars by night – unless it was the time of the full moon, and then the pool lay like a still, shining silver disc in the courtyard, and the sea fish that Muna put in it moved in its depths like stars, or like the secret thoughts that lurk beyond the rim of consciousness in the mind, the thoughts that only emerge in dreams.

Bella worked with Muna, and hoped to see her begin to look happier and more settled. Instead she saw with growing anxiety Muna grow thin, and in spite of all the interest she took in arranging her house, there was no peace in her face, and her eyes were haunted. She seemed always to be listening for something, expecting someone. Alan had not returned, although they had been in the house a full month, though there had been messages from him.

'What does she wait for?'

Ayub was standing with Bella one evening, watching the last of the big cases being unpacked. Ayub made no pretence that it could be Alan's return that Muna looked for when he replied,

'Allah knows. I have never seen Munabhen like this. She is a woman waiting for news that she is sure will never come –without hope. She misses the boy of course.'

'Yes. But – Ayub, there is something else. The spirit seems to have left her. I wonder –'

'What, green eyes?'

'I think I go for a walk along the shore this evening.'

'Then you do not go unattended. Alas, I have my duty here. But Faizulla will go with you. He knows I will kill him if any harm comes to you.'

In the cool of the evening, with the setting sun spreading purple and scarlet over the dark sea, Bella walked along the beach to the village of the fisher-folk. The village sprawled thatched roofs and cane walls among the palms and casuarina trees that grew between the house and the city. The fishers were shy, but as curious as children, and the women came out of their houses to stand staring at Bella, a little distance away at first, and then closer, until one put out a dark hand to see if she was real. Bella spoke to her, and the women's faces lit with pleasure. Urdu was not their tongue, but Bella could remember quite a lot of the language, and helped out by gestures, friendly relations were established. Bella sat on the sand and talked to the women, and Faizulla stood to one side and watched, and at lantern lighting time Bella got up to leave, burdened with fresh caught fish and coconuts and bananas – and the information that she wanted.

The next morning, while Muna was dressing, Bella told her of her visit to the village.

'There is a Temple on the shore, Sahiba. Between here and the village. It is set a little back, among the trees, and looks very old. I asked the village women about it, and they said it was the shrine of the Goddess who gave her name to the great city, Calcutta. Kali they call her. Would you like to see it?'

They went as soon as Muna was dressed, followed by Ayub Khan and Faizulla. Bella showed Muna where the Temple was, a tumbled pile of stones half swallowed by the jungle, creepers spreading bars over the entrance to the shrine itself. But there was still an entrance, carefully cut and cleared, and deep within the shrine, a light flickered. The Goddess was not neglected. Bella and the two men stood back, and Muna entered alone.

The shrine should have felt like home to Muna. Here stood the Goddess, illuminated by the flickering flame of an oil lamp. Here she stood – but how different from the other images Muna was used to. This was the figure of a girl, round breasted, beautiful, vulnerable, her face calm and contemplative. Black shadows were deep all round her, the only light came from the *chirag*. Muna found the shadows welcome, a respite from the sweating glare of the sun. There was coolness here, a familiar smell of incense and marigold flowers, and peaceful silence. Muna stood looking at this very human-appearing Goddess, expecting no more than the coolness of the shadows, the quietness, and the familiar surroundings. She made a reverence of hands, and said a ritual prayer, but it was said as a child says a lesson it has learned – recited without feeling.

Like the warning of a storm, a cold breath, colder than the

200

gentle coolness of the shadows, touched her, and the hair lifted on her nape. A feeling of fear, greater than anything she had ever experienced, forcing her down, first to her knees and then to a full length prostration. Muna lay, afraid to move, while a Presence filled the shrine, and a voice she had longed for spoke.

'So, my daughter, you have come to me at last – by a long road. Had you forgotten that this is my country, that I rule all here? I am the Giver of Death as well as Life, of desolation and sorrow as well as joy – I keep men's souls, or leave them to the demons as I please, accepting no questioning, I who am Kali – Kali the Destroyer. Fear me and worship me. Here is no one else to have dominion, only I.'

The cold travelled over Muna's body until she lay trembling, as one lying in ice. Then, under compulsion still, she rose, and began the old ritual dance, the dance as old as the worship itself, her body worshipping the Goddess with every muscle and bone, every beat of her heart, each breath she drew. The dance over, she fell again before the figure, and the flame on the altar stood straight and steady, like a sword. Slowly the Presence left, and the shadows were once more only shadows, and there was nothing but coolness and darkness, lit by the flame, wavering now in a sea breeze.

Thereafter, Muna went to the old shrine every morning just after dawn. The image in the niche still had a lamp burned before it, but it was to the shrine that Muna went to pray. She was always afraid there, but her feeling of total displacement had gone. She was, after all, still in the hand of the Goddess, and therefore her life had some meaning.

But she was lonely. She spent long evenings on the flat roof, looking over the sea, taking advantage of every cool breeze there was. She became fond of the sea, watching with pleasure the great breakers that rolled in to break in spray and noise on the sands below the house. From the roof she could see the Palace of Sagpur, and wondered what the inhabitants of that imposing white building would do if they knew who was living within sight of them. Perhaps they knew already. She decided on various precautions in case they began to take an interest in her household but discovered that, in fact, her safety was already guaranteed by the people Kassim had sent from Lambagh. Nothing she ate or drank came into her hands until it had been tested on some of the dogs that swarmed, starved and despised, round the outskirts of the fishers' village. Ayub Khan was in command of a strong guard of men. They were to be with her throughout her time in the south. Alan, she found, on questioning Ayub, was also guarded. 'He will never know this, Munabhen, but he goes nowhere without an armed guard close to him. There are several men from the Valley in his regiment.'

So Muna could look at the white Palace in the distance with no misgivings. Even within those walls, she had friends. Kullunder Khan came one day with a veiled girl, who threw off her veil to reveal a pretty, painted face, her eyes wide with awe and admiration as they looked up at Muna. She was the daughter of a woman who had worked for Muna in the house in Madore – she had been trained, and had done well, and had been sent south to the Palace by a man choosing dancers to please the family in the Palace of Sagpur. She was very young, only months out of her childhood, but the marks of her trade were already in her eyes. But to the Rose of Madore she would be as loyal as Muna herself was to the House of Lambagh. Muna had ice from the Nawab's ice pit, and fruit from his trees, and news of this and that whenever she wanted it.

Muna lived for her mother-in-law's letters. Each moment of her child's progress was charted for her; his growth, his ability at his lessons, and his extraordinary skills in riding and – 'Alas! Fighting. My dear, he is a fire-eater. He beat Lady Slater's son until he came yelling for help to the tea table. You may imagine my tea party broke up in disorder, and Sylvia Slater is very distant when I see her. Young Master Slater, however, does not appear to bear malice. He is Rob's greatest friend now. They ride all over the place together – I have given up trying to send a groom with them. Rob is a very headstrong little boy. How long do you think it will be before you come home? We miss you so very much.'

There were letters from Rob too. They spoke of riding, and

school, and holidays – and always asked the same question: 'When are you coming back? Will it be very long before you come?'

Ah, how long indeed! Muna sighed her heart out, looking over the sea towards the distant horizon, and longed to know. There had been no word from Alan for nearly ten days – perhaps it was because he was coming himself? But Richard was the first visitor from the Fort. He brought Muna yet another letter from Alan, and was a trifle shamefaced over it. 'He is working like twenty men, Mrs. Reid, and will come as soon as he can.'

'Of course, it is understood. Come, Captain Sunderland – let us have a drink together. Also I think it is full time that we, who have travelled so far together, begin to call each other by our names – Richard? Is the drink to your liking?'

'Very much to my liking – Muna. And thank you for the honour.'

'Now I should sweep a curtsey to you, and you should bow, and kiss my hand. But to curtsey in these clothes is ridiculous –'

'But I can kiss your hand –' said Richard quietly, and did so. He admired all that had been done in the house. 'I do not know how you have made this place so beautiful so quickly. When I first saw it, it was like a great white shell.'

'Well, it was not very difficult. There were many beautiful things to put in it.'

'Yes – yes indeed,' said Richard, and raised his glass to Muna in a silent salute.

He spent the day in the white house, but had to return to the Fort that night. Muna stood beside him in the courtyard to say goodbye, and he looked into the pool, saying, 'But this is a miracle – no lilies in your pool Muna, but instead you have stars.'

'On a moonlit night there is nothing in my pool but the moon,' said Muna, and Richard, looking at her, recited softly,

'You meaner beauties of the night
That poorly satisfy our eyes
More by your number than your light,

203

You common people of the skies –
Where are you when the moon shall rise?'

His eyes were eloquent, as he looked at her. Muna trailed one hand in the water, smiling at him. 'Richard – how beautiful are those words. Like a song! Did you make them?'

'No – they were written many years ago by a man to his lovely and beloved mistress. But if I could write such words, I would – now.'

'Now?'

'Yes, now. There has never been a reason before. Muna – listen – '

'Richard, I am listening, and I hear the horses growing restless. If you do not go now, you will be late. Go safely – and tell Alan I long to see him – will you?'

Richard held her gaze a moment longer, then he stepped back a pace, and said, 'I will tell him. Goodbye, Muna.'

'No Richard. Not goodbye. Good night. You will be coming back soon I hope, my dear friend.'

Richard did not reply. He bowed, and turned away, and presently she heard his horse, followed by his *syce*'s horse, going fast down the road. She stood, dabbling her hand in the salty water of the pool, but the taste of salt on her lips was the taste of tears.

When Alan came at last, he too admired all that Muna had done, but it was obvious that he had expected no less. He now took it for granted that Muna would always make a place both comfortable and beautiful. He was in a hurry to tell her all about the Fort, and his detachment of men. He was delighted with the men he commanded, men from the Punjab, and from the hill country beyond. 'Splendid fellows,' he told Muna, 'Absolutely splendid. The best troops I have ever seen. The Colonel sent a message to say they were handpicked, and I can see what he means. Great fellows, they make the men round here look like dwarfs.'

Muna did not dare to ask if he knew of the men from Lambagh among his troops, but she did ask if there were any men of Madore. Alan misinterpreted her question, taking the longing in her voice for anxiety.

'Yes, my dear, there are – also I believe there are some from the Valley, and I know the subahdar Major comes from Jindbagh. But do not distress yourself, my dear. You will not see them. There are no families, and you will therefore remain here, and I shall spend several nights each week in quarters. You need not fear that you will be recognised. I will make quite certain that you have no unfortunate encounters.'

So that accounted for the length of time Alan had stayed away from home! He was afraid that she would be treated with disrespect by the men of her own country. Once Muna would have tried to explain many things to Alan about her status among the people of the north, and about his troops' attitude to her as his wife, and as the mother of his son. But now it seemed to her that the time for explanations between them had gone. He would neither listen, nor understand if she told him that she had never been treated with anything but honour, and that now, a married woman with a son, she would be honoured still more. But she said nothing, and asked instead how long they would be staying away from England.

Alan had not expected this question so soon, and his answer was evasive. In fact, he did not know himself. But he had no intention of returning for some years. He had made that decision before they had left England. The longer Muna was away from her son, the more chance Rob had of being totally absorbed into the English way of life, and Alan felt this to be essential for his son, his only child – for Muna had never become pregnant again. Rob was Alan's heir, and he knew exactly how he wished him to grow up. He was sure that he was right in what he was doing, but found it hard to meet Muna's tragic, questioning eyes. So he answered her as well as he could, with half lies that she understood for what they were. He took her in his arms, and kissed her eyes, tasting the salt of her tears, and then carried her up to her room and the wide bed, where they lay together, and he tried to give her the comfort that he always found in her embraces. The sky was full of stars, and before he fell asleep he took her to the window and showed them to her.

'Look up, Muna – those stars are shining on Rob, as they shine on us. Do not fear or fret for the boy – you know how much he is loved, and how well he is cared for.'

Muna could have said that she missed her son with all her heart and mind, but she did not. She went back to bed with Alan, and lay against his shoulder, watching the stars blur before her eyes, and keeping her tears from waking him by turning her head so that they fell into her hair.

In the morning Alan said goodbye to her and rode off down the road to the Fort, and Muna returned to her lonely days and her evenings spent watching the sea and the surf-beaten sands.

19

The days turned to months, the months to years. The seasons changed little in the south, except for the Monsoon season. Then, before the rains came there would be a breathless, steaming heat, when even the wind from the sea failed to bring coolness. When the rains came, vision and sound of the outside world were lost behind a solid wall of water that drummed on the roof, making as much noise as the sea thundering on the shore. Everything felt damp, and green mould drew patterns on the white walls, and grew like moss on the carved chests and screens, and damp tarnished the silver goblets, and missed the glass of the lanterns. Bella complained that it was like living inside an enormous mushroom.

But when the rains were over the sea wind was cool again, and the marigolds and the jasmine bushes flourished. Muna had made a small garden on the roof, with flowers and bushes in large pots. She was glad when the skies cleared, and she was able to sit up there in the evenings again.

There was a rhythm in the passing days, in Muna's visits to the shrine; her walks along the edge of the sea, where the sea birds chased ahead of her, rising and flying and sinking down again like the waves themselves, her evenings on the roof, watching the sea, or the lights of the city; and then the nights in her big room, where the voice of the sea drowned out all other sounds, and she would lie, sending her mind out, trying to reach her son. Her letters from Rob, and her letters from Jane were her life-line, and she spent hours reading them over and over again, trying to picture her growing boy.

Bella's face grew less gaunt, and was coloured a little by the sun. Her hair was more silver than red, but her green eyes glowed and burned with their usual fire, and Ayub, when he was not guarding Muna, was never far from Bella. If he had succeeded in luring his hunting leopardess to his side, no one knew but the moon and the stars, and perhaps the shadows where the palms grew along the shore. There was no one who wished to ask questions.

Alan came and went, spending two or three days at a time, relaxing and enjoying the comfort of the big white house.

'They call this place the Gulabmahal, in the lines,' he told Muna one evening as they sat watching the sunset. 'The Gulabmahal – the Rose Palace. Pretty name, isn't it? I do not know why – you have had no success with your roses, have you? The climate seems bad for them here.'

'No – I could grow them; they grow them on the balconies in the city.'

'Muna! How do you know? You have not been going into Sagpur have you?'

'Oh only once or twice. I wanted kohl and some spices, and special oils. Do not worry, Alan, please. I went in a plain palanquin, and sent one of the servants in to do the buying. But I saw the pots of roses, and could have the same here, if you would like.'

'I do not care what you grow here, Muna – I want you to have everything you would like. But I am not happy with your visits to the town. Promise me you will not go again – it is foolishness.'

Alan's concern astonished Muna – she had thought he had no inkling of the dangers she ran, coming so close to the Nawab of Sagpur, the son of Hardyal. But Alan was thinking, it appeared, of quite another danger.

'If one of my men from the north should see you, and recognise you, it would be very difficult for me. Please Muna, remember my position – and yours.'

'I do not forget, lord.'

Muna's voice was very quiet as she looked at her husband.

208

How to tell him that the men from the north knew of her presence, that she had already had visitors, smiling giants who salaamed and greeted her with joy and respect, asking after her health, and the well-being of her son, and anxious to know if she had word from Lambagh about their Ruler, and their homes. Did he not understand why they called her house the Rose Palace? As well as being his wife she was still, to them, the famous Rose of Madore, the beautiful dancer. Muna could think of no way of telling Alan and so was silent, and Alan, feeling something was not quite right, took her hand and said, 'Ah Muna, do not be cross with me that I stop you going into the city. Is it so dull for you here? I thought you would be happy enough with your own things round you, and your own people. Can I do anything to make you happier?'

His words reminded him of the only thing he could have done to make her happier, and he looked anxiously at her to see if she would say anything. But Muna only smiled and shook her head at him. 'I am not angry, Alan – and of course I am happy. Let me give you some wine – Kullunder Khan bought quails in the market today, and the cook has dressed them as you like them best. We will eat soon.'

Alan heaved a silent sigh of relief. 'There,' he said to himself, 'there, I was quite right. She has settled down perfectly, and is not fretting any more. Everything is going well, and when we do go back she will be as happy to see Rob, grown and used to England, as I shall be. She is a good, sensible girl.' Content with his life, and his future, he held Muna's hand, and drank his wine, watching the last of the sunset colour the sea, while the good, sensible girl at his side thought of other things, and swallowed the tears she would not allow herself to shed.

Muna found other ways of alleviating the tedium of her days. She would walk to the rocks when the tide was out, and there, in a deep pool left by the sea, would strip and swim, her white body cutting through the water as easily as the fish that fled, startled at her approach. Bella, who always went with her, watched her with envy.

'I would like fine to be able to swim,' she said one day. 'It would be a wonderful thing to be able to sport in the water, and cool too. But I never learned. We were far from the sea when I was a child, and the only river was a burn, running fast over rocks.'

'Come then, now, and I will teach you. This water is so salt that it holds you up with no chance of you sinking. Have you a fear of the water?'

'None,' said Bella. 'None at all. But I'm not swimming mother naked. All very well for you, with your looks. But I look like the bone without the fish.'

'Ah Bella, do not be foolish! Are you thinking of asking anyone to come and watch you swim? You cannot come into the water in those pantaloons and a shirt! In any case, if you wet them, they will cling to your body, and you will be worse than naked.'

With no more argument, Bella, scarlet-faced, shed her clothes and slid into the pool. Muna held her chin and guided her movements, and in a very few days Bella was splashing and panting her way round the pool unaided. She never attained Muna's ability, but she could swim, and enjoyed it and was very proud of herself. The two women dried themselves sitting on the rocks, and when the tide began to thunder in, would walk back, wet haired and laughing, exercised and relaxed. Their bodies became tanned, Muna the colour of dark honey, Bella ivory-tinted to match her face. It became a daily habit for them to swim; the only days on which they missed their exercise were when Alan came home.

One evening, when the sea was calm and slapping lazily on the shore, Muna walked, bare-footed, on the sand below the house, stooping to pick up shells as small and as pink as a baby's finger nails. Birds ran ahead of her, at the edge of the sand where the sea broke into ripples, and behind her the leaning palms were silent; only the casuarina trees answered the sea's murmur with their eternal whispering.

She had just straightened from picking up one of the shells, when a voice spoke behind her.

'You bend with all your old grace – like a palm tree bending to the breeze.'

'Alan! You have become a poet! I am so happy to see you – I

was not expecting you until tomorrow.'

'Well, I came back because I had news. We go into camp tomorrow.'

'Camp? Where? Why? It is not the season is it? The rains will be on us soon, they are already late.'

Not the season? No indeed, thought Alan, not the season for manoeuvres. But because the rains were late, it had become the season for cholera. The men must be taken out – if it was not already too late. The sickness had started early in the close, crowded, foetid lanes of Sagpur, and the regimental doctor was shaking a grave head. There was no question of Alan not accompanying his men – but he was not going to tell Muna why he was going. Was he leaving her here in peril? Alan was beset with worry. It had been wonderful for him to come back to the big clean house, and then find his wife on the shore, picking up shells like a child, the silver grey sea merging with the sky to make a background for her. Surely she was in no danger here?

He parried her question by saying, 'Muna, dance for me? Here on the shore, let me see you dance again – '

The sea, idly slapping on the sands, the steady whispering rustle of the casuarina trees – to this music Muna raised her arms, and small feet keeping time, danced for her husband; his favourite dance, the dance she had first performed for him in the Begum Mumtaz's house in Lambagh. The seabirds were her flute players, her ears heard other music than the sea and the trees. Alan watched her as if it was the first time, and caught her up into his arms before she could sink into her final salutation.

'Come back with me Muna, into the house – '

'The shadows are deep under the trees – '

'No. I want you where I need fear no interruptions – '

The night was long, and they did not sleep. It was, to Muna, as if Alan could not get enough of her loving. She gave and took pleasure unstinting, and burned with his fire – and then it was morning, pale, with a yellow light on a grey sea, and Alan had to go. His farewells were prolonged, and after he had gone, Muna lay for a while thinking deeply, and then sent Bella for

211

Ayub Khan. He came and stood, head turned away from her as was fitting, and she asked him the questions that were troubling her. His answers troubled her still more.

'They go into camp near Bemari. It is a bad year. Munabhen. The cholera carts are out in the streets at night already. The change of wind is late, and the rains are late, and that always means cholera in these parts it seems. So the soldiers are always taken out into camp. No one is allowed into Bemari from the city. This is done, hoping to save the men from infection. But you know Munabhen, how it is. They are always late with their knowledge, these white Hakims. The cholera goes to camp with them, riding with the soldiers. Many will die before its burns itself out.'

Muna listened, tightening her lips. 'Is there an outbreak among the men yet?'

'Two men died three days ago – of fever, the Hakim said. Two more are sick. A cook's boy died two nights ago. It is there. Munabhen, but not yet in full strength.'

'So it rides with them, as you say. Tell me, who guards the Colonel Sahib?'

'Feroze Shah, and Phulana Khan. Do not fear the assassin's knife at that camp, Munabhen. No one will go to a cholera camp, even if he is offered his own weight in gold.'

'No, I know. It is another killer that I fear. Listen you to me, Ayub Khan. I go to the camp – No! Do not begin arguments with me. I am going. You know that I must. Can you get me past the guards?'

'At night, yes. You will wear Lambaghi dress, and look like a boy, and we will take a ration cart in. But Munabhen, you risk your life. I tell you, in three days the black flowers of cholera will be in full bloom there.'

'I know, but I must go. I can help. Not only the father of my son is there. There are also my own countrymen. I could not live if I did not go. Also, Bella comes with me.'

'No, Munabhen, that is very foolish indeed. She is not used to this country, she will be one of the first to fall –'

A sound behind him brought his head round. Bella stood in the doorway, glaring at him. 'And who are you to say where I go, or may not go? I would have you know, Ayub Khan, that where the Sahiba goes, I go. And furthermore, I have been close to cholera before. The black flowers, as you call them, made a garland for my husband.'

'Because you have been close to cholera before, and escaped, does not mean that you are safe now. I do not beg very much, or very often, but I am a beggar now. You will do no good there, either of you. I ask you to consider your son, Muna-bhen – '

'I have considered him. Do you think any son of mine would be content to know that his mother allowed his father to face death alone?'

'And who do you suggest I consider, Ayub Khan?' Bella's eyes glinted dangerously as she continued, 'Will you allow the Sahiba to go into the camp alone? No, I thought not. But I am to sit here by myself, twiddling my thumbs, and getting the funeral feast ready, no doubt?'

Muna smiled at them both. 'Wah! Such splendid fighters! What treasures are you trying to guard, Ayub? Nay, we be women, Bella and I, and we have work to do in that camp. Let us have no more argument, Ayub my friend.'

Ayub met Bella's glare full on, bowed his head, and said quietly, 'When do you wish to leave, Munabhen?'

'How many days' travelling is it? Three? Then we leave tonight. We will need pack horses, and – Ayub, send Kullunder Khan to Chunia. We shall require a daily supply of as much ice as he can get out to us.'

Ayub stood as if he had not done arguing, then shook his head and went out. Left alone, the two women began to make careful plans for all they would have to do. Bella remembered back to the sad days of her husband's death. He had been a strong man, and had fought his sickness, and was a long time dying.

'It was terrible to watch him sink, and struggle back, and sink again. But I learned some things then that will be of use now. There were some missionaries there. Scots folk they were, though not from my part of Scotland. But through long experience of fighting cholera among the towns and cities of that

213

province of the south, they had learned a great deal about the disease, and they helped me with my man – to no avail, but it was already too late when they found us. Now listen – for this is what we will have to do.'

Bella spoke with authority, and Muna listened, and asked for all the things Bella would need. The servants were sent running to buy the necessities, and the pack horses were laden, and a bullock bandy, as the carts were called in that part. No person was taken from the city. Muna's own people drove the cart, and led the pack horses. An hour before sunset, all was ready, and Muna and Bella, with Ayub and Kullunder Khan, set off with their little band.

20

Three nights later, as Alan sat outside the door of his tent looking at the lanterns that burned around the camp and the great stars in pale radiance in the dark sky, he heard a sound behind him. His hand went at once to the table where his gun lay. He had not been as unaware of the dangers that Sagpur represented for all of them as he had appeared.

As he watched, the tent flap moved, and opened, and he levelled the gun, and a voice he knew said quickly, 'Alan – you will not shoot me, surely?'

Alan gave a great sigh, as if all the breath had left his body. It was a few moments before he could speak, and then his voice was muffled, his face buried in Muna's long hair. Then he remembered where he was, and put her away from him, saying, 'How did you get in – what in the name of heaven are you doing here? If you have tampered with the guard to risk your own life, I must tell you that you have put the guard in danger too. He could be shot for neglect of duty.'

'Well, he will not be shot – because we did not come by the gates, and we saw no guards – so they are innocent.'

'We? In God's name how many of you are there? You must go back at once.'

'Has it started?'

'What do you mean?'

'Alan. Do not play with words. Has it started, the cholera?'

'How did you know? Oh, what does it matter. Yes, Muna, yes. My poor fellows.'

'How bad is it?'

'Bad enough. Twelve very sick, and five dead today. Almost half the battalion down with it. The Doctor and his orderlies are working like lunatics, but of course there is so little they can do for this disease. My love, you must go at once, whatever mad thought brought you here, I love and reverence you for it – but you must go now – Oh God, let it not be too late – you have been breathing this infected air for long enough – Go. I shall send Ayub back to Lambagh for this. He is useless.'

'Alan, please. You are talking nonsense.'

'No, Muna, you go, if I have to bind you and send you back as a prisoner –'

For answer Muna stepped to the back of the tent, and called quietly. Bella came at once, followed by Ayub Khan.

'Ayub, have them put up the tents we brought with us. Put a guard on them, who will let no one near. Now, Alan, you listen to me. Firstly, I will not return to the Gulabmahal, until this is finished, and you are with me. The second thing I have to say is this. Bella knows this disease well, and we will work to her orders. We have brought many things with us, to help us. You will eat nothing, and drink nothing but the food and drink we give you. There will always be clean clothes here in your tent. When you come in from the camp, take all your clothes off outside the tent, and bathe in the water you will find ready for you behind the tent. Then go in and put on the clean clothes that are in the tent, leaving the others where they lie, outside. You understand? This must be done each time you return from visiting the men. Bella – you are ready? Then let us go and find the Doctor. Please to show us, Alan –'

Alan was past argument. Muna and Bella had a sort of determined power coming from them, such as he had never felt before. To comfort himself, he told himself it was unnecessary for him to argue in any case. When the women saw what was waiting for them in the hospital tents, they would leave, and all he could do was pray that the evil infection had not already seized on them.

The hospital tents were set some distance from the rest of the camp. Alan led the way, the lanterns throwing a yellow light around them. Ayub walked, burdened by what seemed, in the dim light, to be a great sack of white stuff. Alan saw another man behind him carrying two more bundles. Muna and Bella carried cane baskets, which rattled and rang with the sound of glass, as they walked swiftly towards the hospital tents, clearly marked out from the rest of the camp by a low mud wall, which had been lately built and was whitewashed. Fires burned outside this wall, slow, heavily-smoking fires with evil smelling smoke.

'Sulphur,' said Alan briefly, as Bella sniffed and turned to him enquiringly. Bella turned away, and they walked on.

It did not need the wall to tell them they had come to the hospital tents. Long before they were close enough to hear the sounds of men in the throes of agony, they could smell death. Alan looked at Muna, but she was walking on, apparently unmoved. It was Bella who asked, 'How many men are sick in all?'

'More than half the battalion,' said Alan again, and it was a relief for him to speak. The façade that he had to keep up before his men, and even some of his officers, all the long days; the forced cheerfulness, the drilling and marching to try and keep the men from dwelling on these isolated tents and what was happening there, had placed a terrible strain on Alan. He had no longer the consolation of Richard Sutherland's strength – Richard had fallen sick the night before, Richard, the most popular of the young officers, and almost, it seemed, part of Alan's family. Richard, the beloved only son of his father, whose whole life had stretched ahead of him, joyous and easy. Now he lay groaning in his tent, nursed by his orderly, and Alan realised with horror that he was already thinking of him in the past tense.

They had reached the first tent. As they walked up to it, a man came out, staggered a few yards, and squatted, groaning. He was wearing only a shirt. Muna paid him no attention. She walked on and into the tent he had just left, stopping Ayub at the tent entrance. There he unloaded the sack he was carrying, and beside him stood his two companions. Alan saw two familiar faces, Kullunder Khan, who carried a bundle of raw cotton, and Faizulla with a heavy load of rolls of unbleached calico.

'When we call, Ayub, hand in the things we ask for. Kullunder, a big fire must be built in the centre of this camp. The firewood must be thrown over the wall. No one from outside must come in. Do not be slow – we need the fire at once.'

Muna's orders were instantly obeyed. As Kullunder Khan turned away and began to run for the wall, Alan followed Muna into the first tent.

The men lay on soiled cotton quilts, in their shirts, in two long lines, one on each side of the tent. There were twenty men in the tent, and they were all in varying stages of the terrible sickness that was one of the most dreaded killers in India.

Working calmly, without haste, Muna began to clean and comfort the first man in one line, while Bella started to work in the same way with the line of men on the other side of the tent. The extra lanterns brought in showed clearly the revolting sights and conditions that the two women had to deal with. Some of the men, still in the early stages of the disease, were embarrassed and distressed by their condition, and tried to cover their nakedness, pulling at their soiled shirts, in spite of the agonising spasms that seized them with dreadful regularity.

'This is not good, Colonel Sahib,' said one of the older subahdars, leaning up on one elbow as Muna stooped to clean him. 'Take your lady from this tent, and her woman. We be dead men anyway, and should die with dignity, not like children in the hands of their mothers. You put the lady of your house in great danger. Do you not know what cholera is like?'

Before Alan could answer, he heard Muna's clear voice replying, 'Oho Salwar Khan! And when did I become the lady, who is not to see you naked? You have forgotten much, or have changed, that you hide so carefully what once you boasted of – I have never seen you as a child, my old friend. Come, do not behave like one. You give up hope more easily than you give up your modesty. You are a strong man. Let us have no more talk of dead men – and let me take that shirt. If you wish, you may make believe that I have become your mother – though it seems a strange turn of fate to me – or have you forgotten?'

A slow, reluctant smile came to the subahdar's face. 'Oh Rose of Madore – if you are here, who amongst us would be dying men? I remember everything – and grow brave again at the very sight of you.'

In an agony of shame and anger, Alan turned away, unable to hear more – and on the other side of the tent, away from Muna, he went to stand beside Bella, and hand her the things she asked for. Here, too, the men were putting a better face on things, in spite of their pains – the presence of the women, and the extra lamps, and the laughter that Muna brought with her were working miracles. In spite of his shamed anger, it seemed to Alan only minutes before the tent was clean, and the men made as comfortable as possible, with clean calico covered quilts, and great wads of cotton under their hips. But death had not stepped back from everyone in the tent; some were already dead, and these were carried out at once. Others were no longer conscious, and these too were taken from the tent. The Doctor had appeared, his face grey and lined with fatigue. He helped to move the very sick from the tent, and brought in some from the other tents that were not so far gone in the disease, for whom there was still hope of recovery. It was decided that two of the tents would be kept for the men in the early stages, those that could perhaps be saved.

It was dawn when all the tents had been visited, and Muna and Bella had bathed and changed, and were sitting with the exhausted Doctor and several of the officers, and Alan. Alan, with the list that Muna had given him, gave the orders that Bella had said would be necessary for the maintenance of the camp. As soon as he had finished speaking, the meeting dispersed, and it was seen that new life and hope had come to every man there.

The camp became a hive of activity. Latrine trenches were dug, not only in the confines of the cholera camp, but also outside the camp that housed the men who were still uninfected. Muna had brought with her a cart loaded with quicklime. A layer of this was put down in every trench, and the men were told to cover their faeces with quicklime mixed with earth. Each trench was eight feet deep, and well outside the healthy

219

men's camp. All drinking water was boiled, and all milk. A detachment of men was set to do nothing but boil and cool the water for drinking and cooking. Bella, walking round the cook tents, saw a pile of the big green water melons, the kind with scarlet hearts and black seeds. They were popular with the men at this season, for they dripped with coolness when cut. 'These must go – they grow in manured ground and are watered with any water that comes to hand. Please to make it an order that they are taken away and buried. Indeed, no uncooked food is to be eaten at all, and all vegetables must be washed as well as cooked. Let there be someone in charge of the cooks and servers to be sure that they wash their hands before they handle the food.'

A graveyard had been set aside, and was a place of many comings and goings. Muna ordered that the graves be dug after dark by some of the camp followers, the untouchables, not by the troops.

'I do not understand why it is necessary that you bury all your men – some of them are Hindus, and would wish their ashes to go to the waters of the river. Fire carries all away, leaving nothing, which is especially good in the case of this disease, much better than this digging of holes and planting bodies to rot. But if you must have burials, then all I ask is that the digging be done out of sight of all. It does not help any of the men to know that these holes yawn for them.'

The days passed in a terrible nightmare procession, charting the progress of the disease by the gaps in the ranks of the men. It was on the third day that Muna asked for Richard, having been too busy to notice his absence when she had first arrived.

'He is sick, Muna.'

'Oh Alan – why did you not tell me? I have not seen him in any of the tents.'

'No – the officers are kept in their own tents when they sicken.'

'Within the camp – the camp of the healthy? This is madness. How many are there?'

'Only Richard, and one other – and we cannot move them

220

into the cholera camp. It frightens the men if they see one of their officers going into the camp of the sick. They lose heart.'

'Well, it will terrify them much more if they find all their officers dead, and that is what will happen if they are not nursed as they should be – also, it helps to spread the infection among those who are free of it. They must be moved in at once.'

'Muna, it is too late for Richard. He is dying – I went to see him this morning.'

Muna went off, grim-faced, with Bella, to Richard's tent. Skeleton thin, he lay as one dead already, in his disordered filthy bed. His servant had been taken sick the day before, and no one had done very much for him since. He opened his eyes when Muna bent over him, and feebly motioned her to go away. 'Get out of here, Muna – I am ill. Go – please.'

'I am going to take you where you will be more comfortable, and I will not leave you – so do not waste your strength, Richard.'

Richard was carried out on his bed, down to the camp, and put into an empty tent, where he was shortly joined by a young Scotsman, a cheerful red-haired youngster who lay quiet, biting his lips when the pains struck him. Muna left them to Bella to clean and make comfortable, as Richard showed such distress at her presence, but then she went in and sat with him, for it was obvious he was dying. The cholera had done its worst – now he lay quiet, the skull's grin already showing through the dragged skin on his face. Muna took the big bony hand that wandered helplessly over the sheets, and held it firmly.

'Richard,' she said, 'Richard – do you remember the verse you said to me, that evening in the courtyard? I have never forgotten it, and I never will. Whenever I see the moon and stars, I think of you saying those beautiful words. I did not thank you that night, because I was very sad – but I thank you now. It was like being given a beautiful present, a garland of flowers –'

She felt a faint dragging in the hand she held, and realised he was trying to take her hand to his lips, so she raised it and

221

rested it against his cheek. He could no longer see, his eyes were clouded, but his mouth smiled, and formed words she could only just hear. 'No, Muna – not flowers. A garland of stars. I will bring you a garland of stars –'

The words whispered into silence, and the clouding eyes closed. Presently Muna got up, and left the tent, and a short while after, the burial party came and carried Richard away.

Bella stayed with her countryman as often as she could, holding his head on her thin shoulder, whispering to him as if he were a child, singing as his mother must have sung when he was in his own country, and he died peacefully, early in the morning, and Bella wept for him. Ayub Khan, finding her in tears, took her close against his shoulder, saying, 'I never thought to envy a dead man – but I am jealous of those tears, green eyes,' which made Bella angry, and cured her weeping.

Bella and Muna had very little sleep. They called for brandy, opium, plenty of clean, boiled water, clean beds constantly to be changed, and all infected material burned – and the Doctor did as they did, and said he had never seen anything like the treatment that Muna and Bella had devised between them.

Slowly, very slowly, the fight was going their way. Three weeks after their arrival there were no fresh cases, and a great many of the sick were recovering. Those that came cured from the hospital tents brought hope to the others – this was not, after all, certain death. The cured also brought stories of the strength and kindness of the two women, and they were revered as if they were Goddesses made flesh.

One night, towards the end of the three weeks, Alan went with Muna and Bella on their rounds. There was still one tent where the sickness raged. The faces of the men round the sides of the tent were like ghosts in the darkness. The lantern light was concentrated where Muna and Bella knelt, working over pain-wracked figures. The heat and stench in the tent was terrible. Alan suddenly retched and hand to mouth rushed to the clean air outside, but the two women did not even look up. A man, newly washed, and lying on clean linen, thanked Muna weakly, and a few minutes later he wept, having fouled himself

222

again before she had finished cleaning the man on the next pallet. There was little sound, even when they vomited. Their weakness was so great that even groans became soundless. Only the monstrous eructations from their tormented bowels retained strength, and burst from their bodies in eruptions of vile gas.

From tent to tent went Muna and Bella, and now Ayub Khan, their lanterns like fireflies in the darkness. At last those still living were clean, and made as comfortable as possible, the dead had been taken out, and for a short time it was Muna's turn to rest, while Ayub and Bella remained on call.

Muna went to Alan's tent, and found it empty. She went round to the back of the tent, where an earthenware vessel of water stood ready. There in the darkness she removed all her clothing, and bathed herself scrupulously, including her hair, and then went in, naked, to the tent and put on a loose, clean muslin robe.

The camp was quiet. The night, past midnight, was emptied of the day's burning heat. Muna stood at the door of the tent, and looked over the darkened camp. Above, the stars shone, veiled in a mist. So they would be shining over the clean, sawtoothed peaks of Lambagh Valley. So they would shine, if it were a clear night, above Moxton Park, above her sleeping son. Muna had never thought that she would thank all her Gods because Alan had insisted on Rob staying in England.

A figure moved in the shadows.

'Muna, my love, why are you not in bed? You must be weary to death.' The words hung in the quiet air and Alan would have given much to recall them. Death was not a word to be spoken in this camp. But Muna moved easily into his arms, her own going up to encircle his neck.

'Why are *you* not in bed, you who are also weary? Come — take some wine with me, and we will share your bed and if we are too tired to sleep, we can at least talk.'

The silver goblets stood ready, the silver jug nested in ice.

'How you get this ice, I shall never know —'

'It comes every day, and is buried in sacking and straw.'

'But where does it come from?'

Muna laughed. 'From Sagpur. But not from the city – from the Palace itself! The Rani has it brought from the hills beyond Sanjur in winter, and buried in a great pit – and I have had all the ice I wished ever since we came to Sagpur, and the Palace people do not know!'

'Is this safe?'

'My lord, my life – would I endanger you? A girl, who is a Palace favourite, comes from Sunee. Her mother filled her with stories about me. Her mother was in the house in the Street of the Harlots and was my friend.'

'What – what was her name?' Alan's voice was odd – Muna peered at him through the darkness.

'The mother's name? Sita. But that has little to do with it. The girl is called Chunia, and is my friend. So I have ice. Enjoy it and do not worry.'

They sat close together, sharing a goblet. Muna sighed deeply, and putting her head on Alan's shoulder, said, 'Let the Gods hear me, knowing that I do not boast – but Alan, I think it is over. There will be perhaps eight now that we will not save, but there have been no fresh cases for over a week. I think Yama, who catches the souls of men in a noose, is satisfied. I will make a great *puja* to the Goddess when I get back to the Gulabmahal. She has fought on our side. This is not her way of taking a sacrifice. She does it cleanly, a swift death, not this lingering horror – '

'Why, Muna! You weep!'

'I am a woman, Alan. I have seen terrible suffering.'

'But you did not weep. Even when Richard died, you did not weep. Bella wept, but you shed no tears! Why now?'

Alan had, indeed, been startled by Muna's steady calm while she worked. Now she bent over her hands in a storm of tears.

'All those poor men – such a death – without dignity, without peace, they died. I could do so little, and I was so afraid for you, because you were in despair, and that is never good. One must always have hope that the Gods will hear, and save.'

Alan took her close into his arms. 'So,' he said, 'you are learning the meaning of love, I think, my beloved.'

'Fear for another – is that love?'

'Part of it. I was very afraid for *you*.'

'I told you not to fear for me. Alan, will you be able to return with us?'

'No. You know that, Muna. I must stay until this is finished, and I bring the men back. But you must go back.'

'I stay with you. So do not argue with me, time is so short. Let us speak of other things.' Her voice sounded weary, her body was cold in Alan's arms.

'Muna, you are cold –'

'Then, my lord, warm me –'

Alan forgot the memories he had been tormenting himself with, the knowledge that every man in the camp called his wife 'The Rose' or 'The Dancer'. It had been a heavy thing for him, even though their voices, speaking of her, had held nothing but adoration and reverence. Now, with her face raised to his, her pliant waist between his hands, he forgot. He bent and kissed her cold face, and her lips, and the round breast that lifted on a soundless sigh under his kisses. There was nothing to remember but this aching pleasure, this ever renewed passion that she brought him.

21

It rained suddenly that night. There were, without warning, heavy black clouds, and then floods of rushing, drumming water, beating on the tents, cutting gullies in the dry earth, turning the dust to mud, sticky, and as red as blood. Muna lay listening to it. At first it brought a feeling of relief. The coolness of the air made her skin prickle with goose-flesh, and Alan pulled up a cotton quilt to cover them both.

'Thank God,' he said, and she knew that he was thinking and hoping that the rain might bring health to his men, wash the cholera away for good. Devoutly she prayed to her Goddess that he was right.

When the rain stopped as suddenly as it began, and dawn came, and the sun rose over the camp, the heat was worse than it had ever been. Even before the rain it had been a damp heat, now it was steaming and horrible; the air smelled of mould, and by midday the men were beginning to scratch at the red rash of prickly heat that broke out in the folds of their bodies. But the cholera appeared to have been stayed. There were still no fresh outbreaks. The eight men who had died in the night were lowered into graves that gave back a splashing sound as the wet mud was shovelled in on top of the sheeted bodies. The mud clung to the spades and mattocks of the soldiers detailed for burial duties. Alan, watching the burials, felt he was consigning these bodies to the sea, not to the earth.

That night was terrible. Breathless, with a damp, penetrating heat that nothing seemed to relieve. Muna sat, naked, on their bed, both flaps of the tent turned back, and Alan did not chide her. He too was naked, and tried to find some coolness in pouring water over himself every half hour or so. But there was no breeze, and so he felt no cooler. Mosquitoes buzzed annoyingly around them, and no one in the camp got very much sleep that night. In the morning, Muna and Bella went as usual about their work, supervising, talking to cheer the men, and leaving calm and hopeful patients in every tent in the hospital camp; but out of sight of the men, they talked together, their faces anxious.

'If only they could move from here – I am afraid of the fever that this dampness could bring. Do you smell it, Bella?'

'Aye, it is here. Look there, the miasma lies like smoke above the ground. This is not a good place for them to stay now. Also I am afraid that the well is polluted – it lies too low, and this water is draining into it. Nothing is drying, in spite of the sun.'

Muna looked at the steaming mist that swirled and lay in drifts just above the ground. She felt exhausted suddenly, and longed for the sea breezes that would be blowing now on the roof of the Gulabmahal. Of the clean, clear air of the north she did not think at all. Those memories were safely in her heart, and were not thought of at such times as these. She looked a little longer at the mist and the red mud, while Bella watched her, and then she spoke, on a heavy sigh.

'The Colonel must move the men – now. They will have to be taken to the shore. It will be hot there too, but at least the sea wind blows at night, and there are none of these terrible mists. What is the name of that place on the other side of the creek – Durgapur. It is not much more than a day's march from here – Bella, tell Ayub. There must be carts for the sick, who will lie on mattresses, because of the jolting. Riding will do no harm to the others. But it is going to be hard to persuade the Colonel that he must make this move at once. Oh Bella, I am so tired – so very tired. I need all my strength, and the tongue of an angel for this next task, and I feel that I am without enough power to even whisper –'

Bella's face was very anxious as she hurried away to find

Ayub. Muna had looked utterly exhausted.

At first, when Muna spoke to him, Alan merely smiled, and shook his head. 'No, my love. I cannot break camp yet. I have sent a runner to Bagarat, to tell them of our plans. I cannot break camp until I hear from Headquarters there – and even then, I think we shall return to Sagpur. Not to the other side of the creek, there is no point in that – the Fort is near the sea in any case.'

Muna did not argue with him. She went to the Doctor, who was her willing slave. It took a great deal of talk to persuade Alan to go against all the regulations and army orders, but the Doctor's words about marsh fever finally made him move. The carts were ready, and by twilight, when the song of the mosquitoes was loud, and the mist was heavy, still lying about a foot above the ground, the battalion began to move out. The sick men lay in the padded bullock carts, and Muna and Bella rode close to them, holding their horses back to the slow pace of the bullocks. The healthy men sang as they rode, and were full of good spirits, glad to be leaving that haunted camp. Alan, riding at their head, and hearing the raucous, cheerful voices, began to feel less worried about the move. Behind him he left fifty men who had ridden from Sagpur with their companions. They, too, had then been singing, though not perhaps with so much vigour – for their destination had been the camp, and none of the men had been eager to go into the camp when they knew that it was to escape cholera. The Army had a long list of cholera camps in its history, up and down the garrison towns of India. Now those fifty men lay in graves marked only by planks of wood with their names scratched on them, and the red mud heaped over them was already turning green with weeds and creepers, as if the country was trying to obliterate all trace of the men who had died.

Alan turned his mind hurriedly from those fast-vanishing graves, and rode beside Muna for a little while. He did not like to see her looking so tired and pale. Her great eyes were sunken and circled with dark shadows, and she had grown very thin. He saw that Bella, although she had worked as hard as Muna, did not look nearly so exhausted. He became very anxious, and asked Muna why she had not ordered a palanquin for herself, but Muna laughed at him. 'Alan, I am not made of stone. Of course I am tired. But I shall be perfectly well again after a good sleep. I shall sleep all day tomorrow. All the long day, beside the sound of the sea, with the sea wind to keep me cool.'

Alan had to be content with this, and rode back to the head of his men with the feeling of worry still gnawing at the back of his mind.

By noon the next day, they were encamped, tents arranged under a cluster of palms, the hospital area a good hundred yards away from the rest of the camp. No men had died on the road – in fact the cholera cases appeared to be recovering in a remarkable fashion.

There was a small marble pavilion in a state of good repair, built close to the sea – some bygone Raja's pleasure place, now deserted. Muna took this for herself and Alan. Ayub Khan pitched a tent for Bella near it, and threw his own pallet down under the palm trees that leaned close by. Muna's pavilion had privacy as it had marble screens on all four sides, with an arched entrance on one wall, and a *chabutra* in the front facing the sea. At night the wind rose that blew until dawn, and there were few mosquitoes.

Alan now had only two British officers with him, young and inexperienced men, and had a great deal to do himself, without Richard's trained assistance. He had marked Richard's grave with a cross, and beside him lay the young Scotsman, Graham Morrison. Alan, going about the tents, giving orders and wrestling with endless amounts of paper work, missed the two men, and not only for their efficiency. They had been older than the others, and had been his friends. But he took pleasure in the fact that the men were cheerful and brisk – and the two young Englishmen would learn. His Risaldar Major was a splendid man, a big cheerful Punjabi Mussulman, with a voice like a bull and the experience of many campaigns behind him. He became Alan's right hand, and Alan himself was glad to learn from him.

The battalion settled into its new quarters with the minimum of trouble, a parade ground was chosen, and further down the beach, when they were off duty, the men would go to swim. Those who could not swim learned from those that could, and their voices came faintly back to the marble pavilion. Alan sat there, with Muna, feeling that one of the advantages of this move that he now felt he was entirely responsible for, was that he felt no guilt that she was still with him. She was as well here as she would have been alone in Sagpur. He sat with her, looking over the sands to the sea, seen only as the breakers came up the shore to turn white crests of foam in thunder on to the sands. It was a dark night, even the stars, usually so close and large in the Indian sky, seemed far away and cast no light. Muna was quiet. She sat at Alan's feet, leaning against his knees, and drank her wine slowly, while the sound of the sea grew loud, and louder yet as the tide came in. Alan, bending down to put his cheek against hers, was horrified to find her burning hot.

'Muna – oh God, you are fevered!'

'Yes, but it is nothing. Marsh fever, that is all. I have taken Bella's bitter remedies. It will break soon.'

But it did not break. Muna lay, burning, through three days and nights, the flesh falling away from her bones as the fever mounted. Bella nursed her, sponging the beautiful body that was getting so thin, forcing Muna to swallow bitter drafts of quinine, and then, when she vomited it up, forcing down more. By the third day, she was wrapping Muna in wet sheets, and then rubbing her until the honey coloured flesh flushed and grew scarlet under her hands. The bitter dosing went on. Muna's fever rose and fell. One day she would lie, drained, white and exhausted, but able to smile at Alan when he came in to sit with her. Then he would hope, and life would be safe again for him. But in the early hours of the morning, she would start to shiver, so violently that her teeth rattled together with a terrible sound – blankets and hot stones packed round her made no difference – the terrible cold seemed to be the chill of death. Then, slowly, the fever would rise, burning the wasting body – Muna would toss and speak in her own language, calling out sometimes, her forehead creased, her voice carrying an agony of longing. Only two or three times did she speak in

English. Once, deep in the night, she said questioningly, as if surprised, 'Love? I do not know love, do I?' and Alan took her hand and answered, 'Oh my dearest – you know love. We love each other – look, it is I, I love you –'

'Love?' said the faint haunting voice. 'Love?'

'Oh let her be, Sir,' said Bella, as Alan tried to make Muna look at him. 'Let her be. She wanders, she does not know what she is saying.'

But Alan went on calling to her. 'Muna!' he called desperately. 'Muna!' Muna, twisting out of his arms, spoke again, gently. 'Rob? Rob, where are you? I can hear your voice. Come out of the sun, my dearest child. Come in, it is too hot out there –'

Rob, miles away under a mild and gentle English sky. Alan went away, he could bear no more. As he went, he heard Muna speak again, 'I will have a garland of stars,' she said softly. 'A garland of stars, when the moon rises –' and wondered with dread if Muna would ever see another moon rise.

But when the new moon hung, a sickle low in the sky, Muna's fever had broken, and Muna lay on her bed, spent, bone thin, nothing but her eyes showing that she was alive.

The men of the regiment who had been watching and waiting, heard that she was recovering, and gave a great roaring cheer, until they were sharply ordered to be silent, lest they disturb Muna's first proper sleep. Then random little groups of two or three went out on raiding parties, and soon there was an enclosure where chickens pecked and scratched, and laid their eggs. A thin cow made an appearance, and was fed and cared for, and Muna had milk and eggs, and chicken stewed to rags and flavoured with coriander and turmeric. Slowly her wasted limbs began to gain flesh. She got up early every morning, before the sun, when the sea was pale green under a pale green sky, and swam, her now white body moving like foam on the water, and she grew strong again. She lay in the sun on the *chabutra*, and took back her honey-coloured tan. Bella brushed and oiled her long hair until it glowed with health again, and at last Muna was herself – full of energy and laughter – and Bella, surveying her one morning as they walked back from their swim, said, 'I could almost go and say a couple or three prayers to that Goddess of yours – I am so glad to see you like this. Indeed, Sahiba, I thought you were lost.'

'Bella, we should both go and make *puja* to the Goddess – and we will, as soon as we go to the Gulabmahal. But to you – what can I say? It was your care that kept my life in my body. You know how I feel, Bella, my dear friend and sister – I do not have to say any words to you.'

'No indeed you do not. What would you expect me to do – leave you to burn away and die?' Bella was gruff as always when her feelings were touched.

Muna laughed at her. 'Oh Bella – indeed, Ayub Khan is right when he calls you a leopardess – listen to you growling now. I am so glad you took no ill. You are a strong woman, Bella.'

'Aye. I come of fine strong race. As for Ayub, he is fortunate too. I thought once he was going to take the fever, so I gave him a great dose of quinine, and he had no more trouble. And not one of the men has taken it.'

'That is so wonderful to me – indeed, we will make a very big *puja* to the Goddess when we go back. We are so lucky.'

Bella, laughing in the rising sun, felt suddenly chilled at Muna's words. A shadow seemed to fall across their path, and she hurriedly made the sign against evil behind her back. She was astonished at Muna, usually so careful – to speak of being fortunate was never good. But the shadow passed as she watched Muna running lightly along the edge of the sea, her shadow chasing her. She looked like a girl again.

Alan treated Muna too as if she was made of egg shell. He kissed her as if he touched a moth's wings.

One night, when the moon was tossing silver prodigally over the white sand and the sea, and inside the pavilion the fretted marble screen drew diamonds and squares on the floor, Muna sat up and looked across at Alan's pallet on which he had slept since her illness. She saw him lying, not asleep, his eyes on the moonlight coming through the screens.

'Alan?'

'My dear – do you wish something? Water?'

'Water? No. Alan, do you remember the lake in Lambagh, and the moonlight in your room?'

'Yes. Very well.'

'I also. Do you want anything, Alan?'

'No, my love. Nothing.'

Muna got up, and moving into the centre of the room, so that the moonlight made its diamond patterns on her body, she began, very slowly, to dance. Her breasts, round and full again, her hips and thighs moved like silk in the silver light. She danced until she heard his breathing grow harsh, and saw his hand clench on the side of his pallet. Then she went over to him, and stood in timeless seduction before him.

'Alan – shall we not explore the nature of love?'

He did not speak. He took her, and the stars danced and the sea was full of the laughter of the waters of the world, until dawn came quietly to paint the pale sky scarlet, and found them asleep.

They lived in Durgapur for a month, and then broke camp to return to Sagpur. The cholera season was past, and it was safe to return. The troops went by a different road. Alan said goodbye to Muna in the pavilion, his mouth moving over her face and breast like a lover saying farewell to his beloved for the first time.

'I have enjoyed this place – I shall miss our evenings. But I shall try and come home more often, my love – are you sure you will be safe, travelling back alone?'

'But how not? I do not go near the city, and I have good guards. I too will miss this place, Alan. I grow lonely, waiting for you to come to the Gulabmahal. Do not stay away too long –'

They parted, and Alan thought of Muna's loneliness, and knew he had been unkind in the past. He made good resolutions, and plans.

The Gulabmahal was ready for their return, the pool flashed and glittered in the sun, and there were roses on the bushes that Muna had planted in pots on the roof. She slept deeply and well in her big bed, and wandered about her rooms, seeing each beautiful thing as if she greeted old friends. She sent to the city

233

for flowers, tuberoses, and big orange marigolds, and garlands of jasmine, heavy with scent – and took from her store of jewellery a fine gold chain, and a silver dish, engraved over every inch with figures of dancing Goddesses. Then she set off with Bella to the shrine. She took her offerings in alone. Bella waited outside.

'It would not be fitting for me to go in, Sahiba – am I not right?'

'You are right, Bella. She will take the thanks from your heart. She sees all things, wherever we hide them.'

Bella waited under the shade of the palm trees, and Ayub waited with her. She felt his eyes on her face, and looked up at the big man who stared at her, for once unsmiling. 'What – what is it, Ayub?'

'What is it? You tell me. I have no answer for this feeling that I have –'

'Ayub, I trust you are not going to speak in riddles.'

'It is a riddle. I told you, a riddle to which I have no answer. When I sleep at night, what do I see? Your eyes, your green eyes. I am a man, and there have been many women – and now, there is only one. I thought to snare a leopardess. Instead, she has set her claws in my heart.'

'As I said, you are talking in riddles, to which *I* have no answer.'

'Have you not, green eyes? I can remember a night when I saw an answer, and felt your tears – and then they were not for a stranger, they were for me.'

'Well, if you choose a time when I am already beside myself with worry, and then fall sick – that was an unfair advantage, that night –'

'Oho, was it so? Do I have to fall into a fever to get a reply from those eyes? I am fevered all the time, if you must know. Time moves fast, my leopardess, let us not waste the sweet days – we are not children.'

'Do not keep reminding me that I am an old woman.'

'Tsk, what lightning have I roused now? If you are an old woman, then I am fortunate not to be a boy, for I can equal you, and pass you, in age. I have time left, and strength. Must we waste this golden time?'

Bella turned to him, but what she would have said was left unknown to him, for Muna came out of the shrine, and it was time to return to the Gulabmahal. Ayub Khan stalked along behind them, and muttered to himself, but the sea drowned his words.

There were bowls and pots of flowers throughout the Gulabmahal, and Muna sat on the roof wearing her favourite emerald *sari*, so light a muslin that it blew round her in constant movement, waiting for Alan, who came as the sun was setting, and showed himself delighted to be back. They had their evening meal on the roof as well as their wine, and Alan was impatient for the food to be removed, so that they could be alone.

'Let us stay here, tonight – it is so cool and we can watch the stars – '

They stayed on the roof, but did not watch the stars for very long. Alan woke at dawn to find Muna still sleeping, her long hair tossed all about her, and dark shadows under her eyes, and reproached himself for his selfishness. But then he remembered the news he had not yet given her, and was comforted. She would be so happy when he told her his news! It would be all that she needed to make her really well again.

But when he told Muna that he had written to Bianca, asking her to pay them a visit, and that a runner had come back to say that she was coming, Muna confronted him, not with joy as he expected, but with a furious anger such as he had never seen her display.

'You have asked her to come *here* – to Sagpur, knowing the danger she will be in? Are you *mad*, Alan?'

'She comes of her own free will – she did not have to agree. In fact she comes because you will not go to her. You know that you should go to the hills Muna.'

'So, because I will not go to the hills like some puling white woman, you bring Bianca into danger! Oh Alan, should anything happen to her here – '

'Nothing will happen. There is only a boy, and that palace

235

woman that Hardyal married when she bore him the boy. They are not interested in us.'

'You speak of what you do not know,' said Muna rudely. 'Send a message at once to the Begum Bianca. I will meet her in Jauhati. I will go where I do not wish to go, to strange hills, to please you – and to keep the Begum from coming here. Does Sher Khan know that she comes?'

Alan stared at this fierce Muna whom he had never seen before. 'I do not know,' he said slowly. 'He must know. She comes with a retinue, no doubt.'

'You mean that you have not written to him? Perhaps he does not even know! What did you say in your letter?'

'I told her the truth – that you had been very ill, and were still weakly – '

'Still weakly! You did not find me weakly last night! Of course she comes, if she thinks I am ill. Alan, I am exceedingly angered with you. You have meddled in things that are nothing to do with you. You have acted like a fool.'

Alan drew a deep breath, and turned away. 'Muna, you will not speak like this to me. I think you have forgotten yourself. I am going back to the Fort now, and will return when you feel better. This anger is not at all becoming in my wife. I did not imagine you could ever behave like this. I shall come back in time to welcome Bianca – after all, she is my friend as well as yours. Goodbye Muna – I look to see you in better mind when I return.'

He walked off, moving very stiffly, and expecting to be called back by a repentant Muna. But she said nothing, and he rode away, his anger now almost as great as hers. He felt extremely badly done by, having only thought to please her.

Muna did not even turn to watch him leave. She sent for Ayub Khan.

'Ayub, you know that the Begum must not come here. You know the danger she would enter. You must ride hard – you should be able to intercept her at Orangapura. From there, take the road to Jauhati. I will meet her there, and we will go together to Sanjur. She must not come here – that is understood?'

236

'It is understood. But when you travel to Jauhati, who will guard you – will you bring Bella?'

'Ayub Khan, I will not put your leopardess in danger, do not fear. She will, of course come with me – and we will be guarded by Faizulla and Feroze Shah, and Kullunder Khan – is that enough to put your mind at rest?'

'Munabhen, I was told by the Ruler that if anything happened to you, my head would not stay on my shoulders. I will not hide from you that I think of the green-eyed one all the time – but it is you I guard, and I do not think that you can say I have failed in my duty.'

'Nay, Ayub, I did but jest. You have been a faithful friend always. But believe me, if anything should happen to the Begum Bianca, who is after all the stepmother of the Begum of Lambagh, your head will be very uneasy on your shoulders indeed. So I absolve you from your duty to me. She must be stopped, and you are the only man whom I can trust to guard her properly.'

Ayub stood back, salaaming, and left Muna crouching among her cushions, her eyes still flaming with anger and anxiety. Ayub went in search of Bella, and told her what he was going to do.

'Munabhen is as angry as a nest full of hornets.'

'Yes – I heard her speaking to the Colonel. Is there really danger here for the Begum?'

'Danger! Wah! If she comes here, she would walk with death every day. She killed Hardyal – or so it is rumoured. No one knows for certain, but having seen Munabhen today I think the rumour must be true. But never mind that now. I have to say farewell to my soul for a short time – my soul, and my heart. They are in your keeping, green eyes – guard them as you would guard yourself – or rather, as I would guard you if I could. Do I have to tell you that I love you, not with a boy's love, but with the love of all that is past, or all that my life has made of me? Have you an answer to my question yet?'

Bella looked away from him. 'I do not remember the question.'

'Ah green eyes – do you not? I think you lie, to make time.'

237

'Maybe I do. Because I do not know what this love you bring me means. I am not your kind of woman, Ayub. So, I could burn with a fire that would go out very quickly, and leave me charred beyond bearing –'

'The fire you have lit will not go out, green eyes. We will burn in it together, and then when it sinks a little, as it may do as time passes, we will still have a hearth fire with which to warm ourselves. Green eyes, do you weep?'

'Go away, Ayub Khan, with your sweet words. Yes, I weep. Why not?'

Ayub did not answer her question with words. He took her into his close embrace, and when at last she lifted her head, he kissed her until she broke away from him, gasping. He nodded, smiling at her and said quietly, 'So. Now you are sealed, and held. Have I answered any questions you might have had, my leopardess? I think I have. Now I go, and you will be careful as I said – yes?'

He rode away, turning in his saddle to see her watching him, and he was content. Bella dried her eyes, and went before he should be completely out of her sight – for it was unlucky to watch someone go away. So before the dust cloud he raised had totally hidden his broad back, and while she could still hear the sound of his horse's hooves, she went indoors, and looked for something to do.

Ayub Khan, riding hard, reached Orangapura in three days, and after enquiries, was relieved to find that no lady of any degree had passed that way. He went to the *serai*, dealt with his tired horse, and put it into the stable behind the room he rented. Then he wandered out into the square courtyard and had a quiet but thorough investigation of all the travellers present. With a calm mind, having found no one to worry about, he went to the cooked food stall and bought himself several large Mussulman chapattis and a bowl of beef stew spiced with red chillies, so heavily spiced in fact that it made his eyes water just to smell it. He took his food to his room and ate with appetite. Then, after a long drink of sour milk to cool his mouth, he strolled over to the gate of the *serai* and waited.

She came that night, riding, and attended only by an elderly woman servant and three men. Ayub Khan stepped forward, and salaaming, said, 'Khanum – my life for yours.'

Beneath her veil, he felt her scrutiny, then she leaned down to give him her hand, and he assisted her to dismount. She had a quarter already arranged, a man had been waiting, and at sight of her and her retinue had opened the door into a clean room, a little away from the others.

'Well, Ayub Khan. What has happened?' As always when Bianca unveiled, Ayub was silenced for a moment by her astonishing, ageless beauty. She did not seem to change – erect, slender, moving with grace, she walked over to the string bed in the corner and seated herself. Her veil slipped further back, and he saw then that above her unlined face her hair was pure white.

'Ayub Khan – speak! What is it?'

Ayub shook his head, like a man waking from a dream. 'Nothing, Khanum. But Muna sent to stop you here. She will meet you at Jauhati.'

'At Jauhati? Why?'

'She will take you to the hills of Sanjur. She needs the cool of the hills, Khanum. The fever tried her very hard.'

'Yes. No doubt. But now, Ayub Khan, tell me the truth – has there been trouble in Sagpur?'

Ayub made a wry face. It was no good trying to deceive the lady!

'No, Khanum. But she is afraid for you. It is, after all, Hardyal's State, and his principal town – and although he is dead, his widow and his son rule there. She is worried for you – she was very angered with the Colonel Sahib Bahadur when she found that he had asked you to come to Sagpur. She said he had called you into danger, and they parted in anger.'

Bianca nodded her head once or twice, her eyes looking far away.

'It is almost twenty years ago now – still, I suppose there are long memories – ' Bianca was speaking to herself. Ayub, who had an idea of where her thoughts had gone, was quiet, waiting until she remembered him. Then she said quietly, 'Very well, Ayub. We set off for Jauhati tomorrow. If Munabhen is late, we can order a boat, and be ready for her. The crossing of the river at Jauhati will take two days at least. Ayub, see to my men, and send my woman to me. She will prepare my food. We will leave here at dawn.'

Ayub salaamed and went, looking back to see her eyes once more staring into the past.

He found three men he knew well, from Lambagh's army, waiting for him. They exchanged news, and enjoyed long, remembering talk in his room, two at a time on guard outside Bianca's quarters. Kassim, the young ruler of Lambagh, was well – his son grew more like his grandfather Sher Khan, every day. Sher Khan was Kassim's Uncle, and the father of Sara, Kassim's wife. He had given the throne to Kassim soon after Kassim and Sara were married. He and his wife, the Begum Bianca now lived permanently in a small palace he had built just outside Madore. At present, they told Ayub, who was hungry for news of his old master, Sher Khan was with Kassim in Lambagh, for a hunting trip.

'He does not, I think, know that the Khanum has come on this journey. When she got the message from Sagpur, she left within a day. What ails Munabhen? Is she sick?'

'Nay – not any longer. Unless perhaps it is homesickness. She longs for the north as a man in the desert longs for water.'

'Is she as she was? They still speak of her in the cities of the north.'

'She is still the beautiful one – the Rose.'

'May Allah protect her,' said his friend, and got up to go out and take his turn at guard duty.

They left Orangapura at dawn, riding through the city gates before the guards of the city had finished opening them. Ayub sent one man ahead and took the rear guard himself, but there was no danger. They rode in peace for three days, down the long dusty road, branching off at Dariabakht for the river, and stopping at a rest house on the banks of the slow-moving oily looking water, near Jauhati. Muna was not there, but they did not worry, as they had made good time. They arranged for a long, flat-bottomed boat, with a reed roof, and two boatmen to be ready when Muna came. Then they waited.

After two days, Ayub Khan went to Bianca.

'Khanum, I am not easy. Let me ride back to Sagpur, and see what has happened – she was indeed very ill and it was marsh fever, which returns – it may be that she has fallen sick again.'

Bianca nodded. 'Yes. I also am worried. We will go.'

'Nay, Khanum – what use of all this detour if you now come where Muna thinks there is danger?'

'Ayub, my old friend. Do not let us argue. You and I will go, leaving my men and my woman here. We will travel fast – and Ayub Khan, I am coming. Let be. Take that look from your face. I speak as your Begum, as the wife of Sher Khan. If there is danger in Sagpur, it appears to me that it is danger for Muna. She would never keep us waiting here like this. You are of course ready to leave at once? Good. So am I.'

Fleet as shadows on the road they went, resting for the smallest possible time, and finally clattering up to Muna's Gulabmahal in the evening of the second day, while the sun was still making up its mind to set, and the tide was loud on the beach.

Bella came out to meet them with joy, her eyes going first to Ayub's face, before she turned to look at the other rider. Then a frown began to pucker her forehead.

'But – what has happened? Is the Sahiba taken ill again? Where is she?'

It was Bianca who answered. 'She did not come to meet us, so we came to find out what had happened.'

Bella's face grew pale under her tan, and her eyes were wide with the beginnings of fear. 'But she left here four days ago – Ayub – she went laughing, like a girl, suddenly so happy because she would see the Begum again – Ayub – '

Ayub was off his horse in a moment, and had taken her seeking hand. 'Softly, green eyes. See, here is the Begum. Take her inside, and we will hear your story. But be strong – she may have taken another road, and perhaps she did not travel as swiftly as we did.'

Over Bella's head he met Bianca's eyes, and her anxiety matched the fear in his own. There was no other road.

16

241

22

Bella had watched Ayub's figure grow small in the distance, then still shaken by their farewell, she went into the house. Muna was sitting in her favourite place, looking out at the sea.

'Bella, I have been foolish. I should have gone with Ayub. Then I could have been at Orangapura to welcome her, and we would have had the rest of the journey together. Also – I was wrong to be so angered with my husband. He thought to please me – and he could not know all the dangers that wait here for the Begum.'

'There are many dangers for her?'

Muna's eyes were full of memories as she nodded. 'Yes. There are. This is one place to which she must never come.'

She was quiet then, thinking deeply, and Bella wondered, as she often did, how much there was of this woman's life that she knew nothing about. They were so close, and yet Muna was a hidden person, and Bella felt, looking at her, that no one would ever really know her. Under her considering gaze, Muna moved, and looked up.

'When my husband comes back, Bella, will you tell him that I am distressed that I was unjust?'

'I? Why do you not tell him yourself? Sahiba! What are you going to do?'

'I am going to ride all night, and I am going to get to Jauhati in good time, and have a boat all ready so that we do not have to wait to cross the river. Bella, do this for me! Turn his anger, and when I get to Sanjur, I will send Ayub back to fetch you, and we will have a month in the cool of the hills. Please Bella, I must go. I shall go in any case, but it would be better if I knew that you would explain to my husband, and stop him coming after us to bring us back here, where the Begum must not come. Will you help me?'

'You know I will. But you must make proper preparations and not go running off like a madwoman. You will still get to Jauhati in good time if you leave at dawn tomorrow.' Bella folded her lips, and was adamant, and Muna had to agree.

'Very well. But I will not take a large retinue and thus advertise my departure. No Bella, I take Faizulla and two carrying coolies for the palanquin. I will ride Sandal.'

'And no woman?'

'Oh Bella, you sound like somebody's mother – "And no woman" – ' Muna's mimicry was perfect, even to the Scottish intonation that Bella had never lost.

'Sahiba, you may laugh, but you'll need to take a woman. You know fine no decent woman travels these roads without a woman servant.'

'Well, then, I will take Savriti.'

'But she is only a child!'

'Yes, but a clever child, and at fourteen, in fact, she is a woman grown, and protection enough for my virtue!' Muna was laughing at Bella, her tongue caught between white teeth, her eyes sparkling. Bella had not seen her look so young or so happy since they had said goodbye to Rob all those years before. Even as she smiled back at Muna, a feeling of disquiet fell on her, and her smile became a frown.

'Sahiba. Please be very careful.'

'Bella, do not spoil my journey by looking cross – you will ill wish me.'

'I would do no such thing. Just be careful. I wish I could come with you.'

'Of course you do. But you are a good kind friend, and will stay here, and dream about your great bear – ' and Muna went laughing from the room.

She left early in the morning. She rode, wearing the plain clothing of a good class serving woman. Savriti travelled in the palanquin, the curtains pulled close. The two carrying coolies were men of Lambagh. Faizulla rode in front of the palanquin, and Muna rode behind it, as a faithful servant attending her mistress. Savriti giggled delightedly within the palanquin, and amused herself by calling out ruderies to the carriers, one of whom was her brother. The whole party was in holiday mood, and all Bella's misgivings had left her as she watched them go, before turning to make her own preparations for the journey she had been promised, to which she was already looking forward.

The wind from the sea had been cool on Muna's party until they entered the narrow twisting streets of Sagpur. Then it was airless, the high houses kept all the wind away, and the streets were like furnaces. In the evenings it was the custom of the people of the town to take the breeze seated on their roofs. But now, in the early morning, the flat roofs were mostly empty, and the streets were busy. The little party drew closer together, and Savriti stopped calling to the coolies. Faizulla felt for his dagger and loosened his sword in its scabbard, his eyes busy among the narrow lanes and dark doorways that they had to pass. But no one paid them any attention. It was a feast day of some sort – the men were dressed in clean white loin cloths, the women carried garlands, and the streets were loud with laughter and high voices. As they passed one tall house, a rose fell from a window on to Muna's shoulder. She caught it, looking up, her *chadar* pulled close over her head. A woman's laughing face looked down at her from the window – the flower had fallen from a garland she was making, and was drenched with rose water. Muna smiled behind her veil, and took it for a good omen for their journey. A boy, standing nearby in a doorway, laughed, and called out a greeting to one of the carriers, who answered him, and the little cavalcade pressed on in an atmosphere of goodwill and festivity. Behind them the woman closed her shutter, the boy watched them go, and then turned and began to run lightly and fast, through the twisting lanes.

Muna's party left the city and the white Palace was before them, on the shore side of the road. They did not quicken their pace, but rode steadily, passing the high-domed entrance where sentries lounged before an iron spiked gate. In spite of herself, Muna held her breath – then they were safely by, and heading down the open road, the sea wind once more cool on their bodies, the green rice fields lying between them and the jungle on one side, the sea on the other. Savriti asked if she could put back the curtains of the palanquin and, given permission, tied them back, and dozed at her ease. Muna rode up beside Faizulla, and the feeling of excitement and pleasure in her journey mounted. It was wonderful for her to think that in less than two days she would see Bianca.

The soldiers came up with them an hour later. They did not come from behind the party. They rode out from a thicket of trees on the road, and Muna and her people were surrounded before they had time to do anything. Savriti was ignored. Faizulla had his sword half out of his scabbard when he was cut down. His blood spattered Muna's clothes as he fell. The carriers were ordered to turn the palanquin, and Muna's bridle was taken and her horse led down the road at a fast trot. Faizulla's body was flung across his horse, arms and legs dangling limply, his head almost severed from his body, a trail of blood following his horse's tracks in the dust of the road. In silence the party rode back towards the town, and turned when they came to the white Palace. Muna heard the gates thump shut behind her. She was told to dismount, and rather than be touched by anyone there, she did so without argument. She heard the thud of Faizulla's body as it was flung down from his horse, and then the two horses were led off.

Muna spoke for the first time. 'Hm – horse thieves as well as kidnappers of women – what a proud and honest place this is. Does your master know of your behaviour?'

The man she spoke to, the man who had been in charge of the party who had captured her, laughed. 'My master? I do not know what he knows. But I have carried out the orders I was given. You will do well to watch your tongue – Dancer!'

Muna nodded. 'Oh – so you know me? Strange – I do not remember you among those who used to come to watch me dance, and pay me much gold!'

'But that was many years ago, Dancer – ' the man's voice was silky, his eyes full of insolence.

Muna took off her veil, and stared him in the eyes until he looked aside, and then she pointed to Savriti and the carriers, standing together beside the palanquin, and said, 'These are my people. They have nothing to do with anything your Master may wish from me. Let them go.'

The man looked at the three indifferently, and nodded. 'Oh yes – they will go. I have orders about them. But you – come Dancer, there is one who waits for you, and is not very patient.'

Savriti watched her mistress turn to go into the dark shadowed door of the palace, and suddenly called out, her child's voice high and shrill in the silent courtyard, 'Go in safety, Rose of Madore – '

Her words were cut off sharply, as one of the guards slapped her, and Muna turned at once, but her guard pushed her on, so that all she could do was to call over her shoulder, 'Do not fear Savrita – we are in the hands of the Goddess.'

The child in the courtyard, with blood trickling from a cut lip, watched her go through the door, and saw the door closed behind her. Then, very afraid, she took her brother's hand and waited for what Fate held.

The woman sitting in the big, magnificently furnished room, was small and dark and hook-nosed. Her hair was dead straight, and black, and oiled so that it shone with the blue gleam of a raven's wing. It rested on her short neck in an enormous coil. She wore no ornaments, and her *sari* was plain white cotton, a widow's *sari*. She was not at all beautiful, but she had made the most of herself; her small eyes were artfully enlarged with kohl, and her bodice, low-cut, fitted her well. She lounged on a cushioned couch in the window, and turned her head as Muna was brought in, her gaze slowly moving from Muna's delicate feet, over her blood spattered clothing to her bare head. Muna looked back at her, and finally the woman spoke.

'And *this* is the famous Dancer? I had heard that you wore European dress, but it seems the tale was not a true one. You dress as a servant, instead. I see you have blood on your clothes, perhaps if you had given the Goddess blood, instead of flowers and gold, you would not be in this room today – perhaps she would have guarded you. The Goddess likes blood – she does not need gold and flowers – she needs the blood of a sacrifice to make her happy. Well – it does not matter. Dance for me, Muna. Let me see what you can do.'

'I do not dance to order – and certainly I do not dance when I have been taken prisoner, my man servant killed, and my journey to the hills so rudely interrupted by low caste servants. What do you want of me, Rani of Sagpur?'

'I have told you. I want you to dance.'

'You did not drag me here to see my dancing!'

'Did I not? Well, maybe. But now – Dance!'

Her voice cracked on the word. There was a feeling of terrible malevolence in the room, and the Rani was its centre. From her squat, crouching figure Muna felt power emanating, and it was very evil power. The two guards behind her moved closer. One of them held a round, lidded basket, shallow and closely woven. From within it came a stirring, a dry rasping movement.

'You had better dance, Muna – for if you do not, I shall leave the room, and go up to that balcony you see there – and my men will loose the cobras from that basket. Then I think we will see you dance, though perhaps not for very long – no?'

Muna, with that rasping, scratching basket held close to her, could refuse no longer. The woman would loose those poisonous coiling things without a thought, and enjoy the results. Deep in the black eyes that watched her, Muna saw a spark of hope. The woman wanted her to refuse.

Muna moved into the centre of the room, and raising her arms above her head, hands and wrists twining and weaving, she began her dance – and the Rani sat back with a sigh, and watched. Somewhere a flute and a hand drum began to play. Muna danced as she had never danced before, and forgot all her fears as she prayed to her Goddess, and danced her dance of worship. At the close of her dance she stood, hands palm to palm, head bowed. In her heart she heard clearly the words she waited for, 'That was well done my daughter. Do not fear. You are within my hand.' The words were as far and faint as always, and yet as clear as the sound of her own breathing. Muna stood proudly, and all her fears left her.

'Yes. Well, as they said, you are skilled. It is a pity you will not be able to amuse the court – or at least, not by dancing.'

'Oh why will she not, Mataji? She is better than any dancer I have seen, and also more beautiful.'

'Oho! Maharaj! Where are you? Who said you could watch?'

'No one tells me if I may or may not do anything!'

The boy who walked slowly down the staircase was tall, and perhaps sixteen or seventeen years old. He was dark-haired, pale-skinned, and handsome, with a proud insolent bearing. How well Muna recalled that walk, those eyes that, heavy-lidded, looked at her with an older man's experienced eye. How had this hideous woman produced such a son? But of course Hardyal had been a very handsome man. Muna looked to see the Rani melting with love, but instead the woman's face was like flint, though her voice dripped honey. She laughed, and said, 'So – you admire the dancer, my son. Well, that is their destiny – to be admired and arouse desire in men. But this one – well, she grows old, and it is time for her to leave now. We will find other dancers, worthy of your attention, if that is what you wish.'

'I think,' said the boy slowly, looking Muna up and down, 'I think I would like to see how old this one has grown.'

His mother was silent, watching him.

'Take off your clothes, Dancer,' said the boy.

Muna met the insolent eyes, and turned her head away, saying nothing. The flat basket in the hands of the man beside her was held towards her, and she heard again the dry rustling.

'Put that basket away,' said the boy suddenly. 'Take it away – at once. If I find such a thing in my presence again, the person responsible will die – of snake bite.'

So! He did have some authority! Muna watched while the man with the basket hurried out, his face grey with fear. The Rani moved sharply, her son turned his head, and the woman was silent, staring at him.

'Well – do you strip? Or shall I have you stripped? After

248

all – ' a note of coaxing came into his voice, 'after all, Dancer, I saved you from the snakes – '

Muna suddenly shrugged. She slowly undid the buttons of the loose shirt she wore, and took it off, baring her beautiful breasts. Then she loosed her skirt, and the blood-spattered cotton fell soundless to the floor. Naked, she raised her arms, and stood, perfect and as immobile as a statue, before the boy and his mother, and the remaining guard.

Moving towards her, the boy said, without taking his eyes from hers, 'This one is not old. This one I want.'

Muna widened her eyes at the tone of his voice, and lowered her arms. One perfect leg relaxed – her hip curved, and effort-lessly she stood as the images of the Goddesses stood, seduction in warm ivory, flesh instead of stone. The boy caught his breath, and the Rani spoke sharply, her voice as harsh as the cry of a jay.

'Do not be a fool, my son. This is a murderess. You look at the woman who killed your father!'

The boy stared, and Muna waited, her eyes on his. He spoke as if he dreamed, thickly, his voice muffled. 'Take her to my rooms – now!'

Muna, her clothes bundled round her, was led out, hearing the quarrel that broke out behind her, and wondering who would win.

When the boy came, she was standing, dressed in the silks that two frightened women had brought her. She had her hair done in the way of the women of Lambagh – coiled on top of her head. She was standing at the marble-screened window, looking out at the slow swell and dip of the sea. He stood just inside the door, and looked at her.

'You like the sea?'

'Yes. I like to watch it.'

'So do I – and to think that it covers half the world. I would like to see the world.'

'Why not?'

'Well – perhaps I will, one day. Did you indeed kill my father?'

Muna looked at him over her shoulder. 'Your mother says so.'

'My mother! She says anything she cares to. It is time she let me speak.'

'You seem to have spoken to some purpose this time.'

'What do you mean?'

'Well, you are here, and I am still here too. I expected the guards to come and take me at any moment. What are you going to do with me?'

He moved further into the room, closer to her. 'Will you talk to me? There are things that I wish to know.'

'*Talk* to you?' Muna spoke in astonishment.

'Yes. No one tells me anything. There are many things I do not know. The Palace girls, the girls my mother sends me – ugh, they are all hands and giggling.' He looked angry, and disgusted.

'And the boys?' Muna thought of the youths she had seen about Sagpur, richly dressed, beautiful, decadent. The Palace dancing boys, and the singers.

'And the boys?' she asked again.

For a moment his face was like theirs, beautiful and different, with a secret knowledge written on it. Then he shook his head. 'I do not wish to talk about boys. I wish to learn about women. Tell of the love of women. The girls are disgusting, they make me sick – but you are a woman, and beautiful. You will teach me about women.'

He paused, then said slowly, 'It is possible to love women. I know that. I would like to have a woman I loved. I am the Raja of Sagpur. I must have a son. I do not want to fail because I find women disgusting. You will help me?'

Muna felt great pity for this boy. She turned fully to face him, smiling. 'Maharaj – you will not have to be told anything about women. When the time is right, you will choose your own woman, and all will be well. You are a handsome man, a man to turn a woman's head. Never mind these Palace dancing girls; choose a girl of your own. I do not think you will find her reluctant. You will find that love of women is as enjoyable as love of boys. But leave the boys alone for a while.'

250

She saw his brows contract, and he looked away from her, and she said swiftly, 'Maharaj – you are the Raja. You do not have to have anyone about you whom you do not care for. If you dislike these boys and girls so much, banish them from court. Why not?'

'My mother sends them to me. Long ago, when I was very young, the older boys would come to me – to make me a man, *she* said. But they have not made me a man. They treat me as if I was a girl, and the girls now laugh at me, calling me little sister –'

The petulance in his voice, the look on his face – Muna had seen many youths like this, in her life. Almost spoiled beyond redemption, knowing the love of neither man nor woman, only lust in its crudest form. Her pity grew.

'Listen, Maharaj. Do not wait any longer. Have you any about you that you like, and know you can trust?'

The boy nodded. 'Yes. There are one or two. There was a girl who pleased me very much, but my mother took her away when she saw I was happy with her. Her name was Chunia. She was very young and sweet, Chunia. Like a bird, she was so small. But of course, my mother took her away at once. She sent more boys instead.'

What sort of a mother was this, that would debauch her own child? Muna shuddered, and said swiftly, 'But you do have some you can really trust?'

So Chunia pleased him, Chunia would be very good for him – she was young, younger than he was. The Raja was answering her question, speaking slowly.

'Yes. Not many. There are two of the singing boys, brothers, who are not like the others. And my old servant. There may be others also, for my mother is a cruel mistress, and they hate her, I know – but they are afraid of her, and so I have no way of discovering who is to be truly trusted.'

'Do you love your mother?' The loathing on his face was answer enough.

'Then, Maharaj, send her away. Do not look so surprised! Ask those you trust who else is of your mind, and get your men together secretly. Then send your mother away. You will find

251

that once you show your strength the whole court will come over to you. I cannot believe that she has all your people in her hand.'

'They never see me. She keeps me like a child, I have nothing to do with the governing of the State. *She* rules, as my Regent, saying I am still too young – and when the ministers come, she drugs me, so that I appear foolish, and they go away again, glad to have her quick mind and not my foolishness.'

'Then do not take the drugs! Oh, Maharaj, you are a man – throw off this evil thrall. I have heard tales in the city: your people will be behind you – you only have to make a show of strength. Look what happened today, you had your will, did you not? You are the Nawab, the Ruler!' Her eyes held his as she spoke, and she saw him straighten, and purpose grow on his face.

'You are right! Why did I not do this before! I shall be free of that conniving evil woman of no caste – and I will have a bodyguard of my own choosing, and a girl too – and later, a wife. But there is more you can teach me – you know all about the loves of men and women. Teach me how to love!'

'Nay, Maharaj.'

'Why?'

'Because I am old enough to be your mother – and you have had enough of age. Look for youth now, Maharaj. Send for your girl who was like a bird. I am sure she is still about the Palace. Let her learn about love with you. Young love is very sweet.'

For a moment he frowned, and she saw his father in his face and trembled. Then he nodded slowly. 'You are not old enough to be my mother. But you speak as a mother should – as my mother never has. I regret that you feel so old, but I hear that your words are right. One thing I ask – will you stay here with me, tonight? You see – ' he turned away, and spoke, looking out at the sea. 'You see, if you leave now, they will all laugh at me and say I have failed again.'

Muna put her hand on his arm. 'Prince, I will stay. I will dance for you, we will take wine and food together – believe me, they will not dare to say that you have failed.'

'My thanks, Dancer. Then tomorrow you will be returned to your house with all honour and ceremony.'

'And my servants?'

'What of your servants? I know nothing of them?'

'My guard they have killed. But my maid, only a child, was with me, and two carrying coolies from my house. I fear for their safety – '

'You are right to fear, if they are in the hands of my mother, cheated of you! I wish I had known – but I will do what I can. Oh to be Raja in deed, instead of only in name! It is hard to wait.'

'Not very much longer, Maharaj. You know the way.'

'Yes. And to you, my thanks. I hear you called the Rose – what is your name?'

'Muna. And yours, lord?'

'That title falls sweetly on my ears. I am Sagpurna, after my State. Now I shall send for wine and food. When will you dance?'

'While we drink our wine – and lord, do not forget to send for news of my servants.'

The man who brought the wine was old, and Sagpurna was at ease with him. They spoke together in their own southern tongue, and she saw the old man shake his head. Sagpurna turned to her, surprise on his face, and said, 'It seems that your servants are safe – the girl and the carrying coolies were sent away, with your palanquin.'

Muna felt a sharp disquiet. This was not in keeping with the malicious look she had seen on the guard's face when he had told her he had orders for them – but perhaps they had been sent away to avoid the kidnapping being traced to the Palace. Sagpurna saw the worry on her face, and said quickly, 'He is to be trusted. If he says they left here alive, be sure that they did. I have sent for musicians, for your dancing.'

There was a scratching at the door before he had finished speaking, and two boys came in, golden-skinned and beautiful, their slant eyes and long black hair reminding Muna of the dancing figure of the God Krishna in the temple frescos in the north. She looked with raised eyebrows at Sagpurna, who

253

nodded. 'They are my friends,' he said simply. 'They hate my mother. They play well, and I think they will please you.'

The flute music rose like bird song in the dusky room. The sun was setting over the sea, and the shadowed room was streaked with gold and scarlet light as Muna began to dance. The hand drum kept the rhythm, the flute played among the stars like a lark in flight, and Muna wove the music into a poem of movement that Sagpurna never forgot. He sat in a dream watching her, while his wine sparkled forgotten in his goblet.

When she finished her dance, and the flute and the drum were silent, Sagpurna poured her wine and gave it to her, and pulled a great ruby from his finger. 'For you – please – ' Muna took the ring and raised it to her forehead in her joined hands. 'I thank you – lord,' she said, and the boy smiled in pleasure.

They sat and drank their wine, talking as friends. The sun set, and darkness filled the sky. Lamps were carried in and set on stands, and the sea wind rose and blew the flames of the lamps sideways, so that shadows moved and flickered about the room. Muna felt the weariness of the long day falling on her, and the despair which she was trying to hold back – for had not the Goddess said that she was not to be afraid? Sagpurna saw the expression of her face, and ordered more wine, and said, 'For this one night only, Muna – we will not sleep. I know this is unkind in me, but this is my first night of freedom, and I long to share it with you. I know that no one like you will ever come my way again – so bear with me? We will talk, and listen to music, and talk again – we will talk the moon down the sky, and the sun up – and then I will send you safely home, as a Princess travels, because you have given me so much.'

'You are a Prince indeed, Sagpurna. Do not fear your future. It lies before you like a country in spring – beautiful, and growing.'

He raised his goblet, smiling, and drank deeply, then leaning forward, said, 'If my future lies so before me, it is because you have made me feel a man. Tell me, Muna – '

What he was going to say was never finished. His words ended in a gasp – an expression of desperate horror grew in his eyes – his lips moved, and then, as Muna sprang to her feet, he

254

fell forward, his head lying face down on the table. As he fell the door behind Muna opened, and three men hurried in. Muna's arms were seized, and a silk scarf was pulled over her mouth and tied cruelly tight, so tight indeed that Muna felt she would suffocate.

She choked, and heard the Rani's voice say, 'Not so tight, you fool – I want her alive. Yes, Muna the Dancer – I want you alive, so that I may send you home as a Princess travels.' Her voice cracked with rage as she quoted her son's words mockingly. 'Poor, foolish boy – and he thinks to rule! Hah – look at him. Sunder Singh, you know what to do?'

From the shadows behind her a tall man stepped into the light. Years of dissipation and danger and trickery had marked his face. He looked as Muna imagined a demon might look, masquerading as a handsome man. He looked down at the unconscious Sagpurna, and putting out one hand, ruffled his fingers lightly through the tumbled dark hair. He smiled, and said softly, 'Yes, Heavenborn. I know what to do. I know all that is necessary.' He did not look at Muna.

Her gag was a little loosened, and she was carried out into the dark corridor, her last sight of the room being the pool of light spilling over Sagpurna, and on the man's sinewy hand resting on the boy's unconscious head. The Rani closed the door, and in darkness Muna was hurried down the corridor, and then down a flight of steps, and along a stone passage that ended in a heavy door. Beside the door was an old man carrying a flaring torch, and Muna was put down on her feet before him. The Rani came up, and the man salaamed deeply, as she said, 'Guard of the door – open for me.' She held out a great key, and he took it from her hand, and unlocked the door. As it opened, a gust of dank, damp smelling air blew Muna's light silks about her, so that a fold of her *sari* lifted, and blinded her eyes. She felt the men who held her tighten their grip, and then the Rani said, 'Farewell, Princess – you go escorted to your home – well escorted. See –'

The men holding Muna let go of her. With a terrible feeling of dread, she pulled her *sari* from her eyes, and looked behind her, and saw the reed basket, the lid raised, and something like

255

a smooth shining brown rope begin to slide slowly over the side, the wicked flat head weaving from side to side, searching.

Muna forgot everything. Without thought, she turned and ran the only way she could go, along the sloping, twisting passage that led downwards, and turned and went steeply down again. It was quite light, and the light seemed to come from above. As she hurried, the whisper of her silks confused her – was that the sound of the pursuer, was that ghastly creature slipping quietly in pursuit? With a choked cry, Muna ran, and the light grew dimmer and dimmer, as the corridor twisted, and led her always in a downward direction. Presently she saw a different light ahead of her – torch light. Any human creature, however brutal, would be better than what was behind her. She hurried her steps, turned another corner, and the passage ended in a large cave, where there were torches set in iron sconces round the walls. She saw the silken shine of dark water, but there was no sight or sound of a human presence.

23

Half the underground chamber where Muna stood was a lake
– a natural pool. It stretched in front of her into darkness, still,
silent – so unmoving that it could have been frozen. There was
no other outlet that she could see, the passage ended in this
cave. The torches burned without movement in the still air.
Behind her, the mouth of the passage yawned – was that a
slithering sound? With a gasp Muna moved forward, and
found that she was standing on sand, so white and fine that it
was like powdered crystal. It sparkled in the flame of the
torches, sparkled like the snow in sunlight. The pool did not
sparkle. Like dull glass it stretched ahead of her, into total
blackness where the torchlight did not reach.

Muna looked about her. She saw a niche in the rock, close to
the pool, steps leading up to it. At least there she would be safer
from the horror in the passage. Perhaps it would not cross
sand? Her silks whispered in this quiet place, as she moved
swiftly over to the steps and climbed into the niche. There was
a plinth there – had there once been a God, or Goddess on it?
Muna climbed on to the plinth, and looked down into the cave.
From where she now stood, she could see the whole chamber –
the glistening sand, and the lake, jade-coloured and opaque.
There was a smell of damp and decay, and yet the sand under
her feet had been dry.

Slowly, like a tiger who has sighted his prey and creeps closer,
there came to Muna the thought that had been at the back of
her mind ever since she had come into the chamber and seen

the pool. There was no way out – only that passage, guarded by that slithering, twisting horror, and then a locked and guarded door. The torches – they would burn down. When they went out, there would be total darkness in this chamber. She looked at the torches measuring them with her eyes. They were large, long and thick, and burning slowly. Another two, or perhaps three days – or perhaps, for there were many of them, perhaps even four days. Then – a slow shiver shook her whole body. The dark water seemed to be waiting for something – what? She pushed further back into the niche, and – was that her silks, or was it a dry rustling from the passage? With a sudden violence she tore off her *sari* and threw it behind her. Now, at least, if she heard rustling, she would know what caused it.

It was then that the pool moved. Slowly, before her eyes could believe it, she saw a ripple start, grow, and widen until it lapped at the white sand. The water looked oily, no light reflected on its green surface. But another ripple came up, a bubble breaking at its heart – and then the water was still again. Muna felt her sight blur, and swayed, putting out one hand to support herself against the rough stone. Automatically she fell into the position she knew so well. In this strange chamber, in all her terror, Muna stood, an ivory figure, standing in the posture of the Goddess, graceful, balanced – and suddenly, no longer afraid. Death was here, there was no doubt in her mind about that. But death, she had been taught, was only the doorway into another life. She was sure that this niche had once held the Goddess. She began to repeat a prayer, and under the words of her prayer, she heard her answer. 'Peace,' said the voice that only spoke within her heart. 'Peace, my daughter. The sacrifice has been given willingly, and accepted. Wait.'

Muna did not understand the words, but she stood, the green water at her feet, the torchlight sparkling on the sand, and finished her prayer, and had hope.

In the Gulabmahal, Bella had finished telling her story, and Bianca's face was as pale and as worried as hers. She looked at

Ayub Khan, who had been questioning the other guards who had been left behind, and he shook his head.

'No one here knows anything. She left, in her own palan-quin –'

'No,' said Bella swiftly, 'she put the girl, Savriti into the palanquin. She rode Sandal, and she dressed as a servant.'

'So she knew there was danger – and still she left here – but what could have happened? You have had no news – and we have just come by the only road she could have taken.'

'Allah knows,' growled Ayub Khan. 'I go back now, to see if by chance she had pulled off the road, and we passed her. Bella, you have guards here for she only took Faizulla – who were the carriers?'

'One was Sethi, Savriti's brother, and the other was Dhana – both from the Valley.'

'And both beardless boys, with no knowledge of arms. Indeed, Munabhen did wrong to travel thus.'

Bianca had been listening to them, thinking deeply. 'Wait, Ayub Khan – did Muna have any dealing with the Palace of Sagpur?'

'Yes. She had ice from the Palace, and news from time to time. There is a dancer there, known to Muna. I think that Muna had known the girl's mother well in the old days, in the Street of the Harlots in Madore.'

'And you all knew of this?'

'Yes, Khanum. The girl is safe – she is of our race. I think the danger from the Palace is very slight. There is a son born to Hardyal, and there is his mother – she was a bazaar woman, and when she bore the boy, Hardyal made her his Rani. She is a woman of very low caste. The boy must be sixteen or perhaps seventeen, but the mother is still Regent. It is said in the bazaars that she keeps the boy down by drugs and – and other things, so that she holds the power. But she has shown no interest in our comings and goings. We have a guard on the Colonel Sahib, and the girl in the Palace tells Muna all that happens there. Kullunder Khan knows her – he knows her very well.'

259

Bianca was looking more and more anxious. 'Is Kullunder Khan here? Then bring him.'

Kullunder Khan did not need to be brought. Like all the other servants, when the rumour had gone round that there was trouble, he was outside the door. He came in at once, and Bianca began to question him, and listen carefully to his answers.

'The girl is called Chunia – her mother came from Muna's house in the Street of the Harlots in Madore. She is as true to Muna as we all are – we would die before harm came to the Rose. If it would please you, I will go at once, and find Chunia, and see if she knows anything. She has a quarter on the outside wall of the Palace, and has many visitors. She pleased the young Raja with her dancing, pleased him too much, so she was taken away from him, and used as an ordinary girl of the court-yard. She knows everything that goes on in the Palace.'

'Go,' said Bianca briefly, and Kullunder Khan hurried out, and presently, above the splash and drag of the waves on the sand they heard the sound of his horse riding hard towards the city.

Bella took Bianca up on to the roof garden, and she sat there, looking at the last glow of the sun on the sea. Everything here had been sent from Lambagh, but the arrangements spoke of Muna's taste and her ability to make a place beautiful and comfortable. The flowers growing in pots, sheltered from the salt wind by carved screens. The carpets and cushions, and the tables, inlaid with ivory. She saw the peacock motif on every-thing, and the colours, emerald and blue and purple – against the white walls, the colours blazed. Bianca, turning a silver goblet of wine in her hands, wondered how much happiness Muna had found in her strange new life, living away from her precious son, and away from her friends and her own part of the country – Muna, child of mixed blood, who loved the north where she had been brought up, where she had been famous and beloved. Poor beautiful Rose of Madore, thought Bianca, staring at the sea, and remembering the little girl that Goki had brought to Lambagh, the little, frightened girl who had loved her new family so much, and who had given everything up to save Sher Khan's daughter from the temple – little Muna, grown up into a beauty who became the talk of the cities of the north. 'Muna, Rose of Madore, I hope you found the love that you gave so unstintingly, I hope you found great love. And where are you now?'

In the great underground cave, the torches were beginning to burn low. As they burned down, the pool became clearly illuminated – it stretched green and still, right across the end of the cave. Muna could now see that there was a marble paving round part of it, between the sand and the water. The steps that went down from the niche where she stood were old, and carved out of natural rock, long before the paving had been put down. She could see that there were some steps down into the water from the marble, and also that there was a small lotus-shaped bowl let into the marble, and from the rocky wall above it a spring dripped a trickle of water, the noise of the falling water loud in that quiet place. There was a cup beside it. The cup was also flower shaped, and looked as if it was alabaster or jade. As time went by, Muna found her eyes turning more and more to that cup. She was very thirsty. The cave was cool and dry, and in spite of the strange smell, Muna had a strong desire to drink, and bathe in the water. But she still listened for the sound of the thing in the passage – she wished that she could remember if snakes crossed sand. They drank, she knew – but was there not some reason why the fisher-folk of the shore village slept in peace at night, and walked fearlessly in their huts on bare feet – *was* it because snakes would not cross sand? She was beginning to feel weak and light-headed. Several times she had sunk down and sat on the plinth, her head falling forward in sleep, and then wakened again in terror to search the niche, and stare down at the sparkling sand to see if there were any trails leading to the water. The pool, as far as she knew, had not moved again. It looked solid enough to walk on. It was so opaque that she could not see even an inch below the surface. The atmosphere of the cave, the feeling she had all the time, if she allowed her mind to go free, was one of terrible hopeless fear. It seemed that voices whispered, women's voices, desperate, pleading voices. She could always hear them when she first woke, and then, saving her reason, would come that inner voice saying, 'Peace, my daughter. Wait.' This voice kept her from going mad, and screaming her fear to the echoing, whispering walls. Muna clutched her courage round her, and recited her prayers, and slept when she could stand upright no longer.

Kullunder Khan was brought to Bianca where she sat in the sudden dark after the sunset. His voice, coming out of a face she could not see, sounded desperate.

'Muna was there. She was taken on the road somewhere. Faizulla is dead. But Muna is unhurt. She was taken to the Rani. She danced for the Rani, and the young Raja. She supped with the Raja, and then left again in her palanquin – '

'Did Chunia see her?'

'Nay, Khanum – but two of the girls bathed her, after she had danced, and robed her in silks, before she supped alone with the Raja. Chunia says that the Raja's own servants waited on them, an old man, and two boy musicians. She danced again for the Raja alone, and the musicians said he took great pleasure in her dancing, and she was at ease, and talked in friendship with the Raja. I could not stay longer, but Chunia saw the palanquin leaving, and it was carried by our two men, and two of the Rani's mounted escort went with her. Chunia is going to find out if there is anything hidden in this affair, and then she will slip out and come here. She will come at moonrise, Khanum.'

Bianca consulted with Bella and Ayub Khan as to whether they should send word to Alan, but they all three decided it would be better not to try and get word to him. He would immediately go to the Palace and try to find Muna, and it might be as well to let the Palace think that there were no suspicions roused. But Muna's fate began to trouble Bianca desperately, like a hand pulling at her. She sat, burning with impatience, watching for moonrise.

Late, behind clouds blown racing across the sky, a half moon appeared, a fitful, watery gleam. Bianca left the roof that spoke so eloquently of Muna, and went downstairs. She found that

262

Bella had prepared a room for her, and she had barely time to thank her, and sit on the low cushioned couch in the window, when Ayub Khan came in, with no ceremony, his face grim.

'I have news, Khanum. Very evil news. The palanquin has been found. In the brothel area of the city. It has been standing there for three days, outside one of the houses. No one paid any attention – it is not unusual for palanquins to wait thus in such places. But – today they stopped and looked, for there were many flies.'

The growing horror and grief on Bianca's face showed him what his words meant to her, and he said swiftly, 'Khanum – nay, do not think thus! Muna was not there. But the carriers were. Both dead.'

'Oh God! And Muna?'

'No sign of her. The men were our men – they had been garrotted.'

'And the girl? Muna's maid?'

'She was in the palanquin too. But you would not have known her for a girl – they had had much sport with her, poor child, before she died.'

Bianca felt, behind her rage, another rage, so fierce that it was terrifying. She felt as if someone was trying to speak to her, but she could not hear. It was then that Kullunder Khan came in, followed by a veiled girl, who sank in salutation at Bianca's feet, and began to speak at once. Her story was the same – there was no trace of Muna in the Palace. But the Raja's personal servant, who waited on him always, was dead.

'Two of the boys of the Palace have come with me. They played for Muna when she danced alone for the Raja. They would speak with you Khanum if you will –'

'Bring them!' Bianca's feeling of desperate haste, the sensation as of a hand pulling at her, was growing stronger. The boys, when they came in, did not fill her with confidence. She remembered the servants who had been about Hardyal, his favourites, and these boys reminded her of those others. But what they had to say held the room silent.

'The Rani went into the room, after the lady had danced. She took Sunder Singh in with her, and three of her bodyguard.

263

We did not see what happened, but Sunder Singh stayed in the room, and the lady was brought out we think her hands were bound. Jagoo here, says that he is sure her mouth was shut by a scarf. Later, we saw the palanquin leave the gates, and two of the Rani's guards went with it.'

Chunia chimed in, 'I swear she is not in the palace, Khanum. I have ways of finding out, and also I have searched. Also, these two boys have gone where I could not go. The Raja is drinking, and taking drugs again, and Sunder Singh never leaves him. The Raja had tried to break with him – I who speak to you, have reason to know this – but the Rani sent him back.'

'Yea – that Sunder Singh! He is a very evil man. He had the Raja dressed as a dancing girl, and the Raja was laughing like one run mad, and trying to dance as the girls do. He has not even asked for his servant all this last two days, and we think that the old man was murdered – by poisoning. Sunder Singh is the Rani's creature. Some say he is her lover, but with a man and a woman like that who can speak of love?' The boy spat disgustedly.

A voice spoke in Bianca's mind. 'Remember me!' said the voice. Bianca heard nothing more of what the boy was saying. All she could hear was the voice that she had last heard when she had been luring Hardyal, the father of the present Raja of Sagpur, to his death. This voice had first spoken to her in a ruined Temple hidden in a grove of mango trees. It had bolstered her courage throughout those terrifying hours, and now she heard it again, tolling like a bell, far away, tiny, but crystal clear in her mind. 'Remember Khanzada,' said the voice, 'Remember Khanzada –'

Bianca sat staring at the two dancing boys and at Chunia. 'Khanzada!' she said aloud, 'Khanzada – who was afraid. Chunia! Have you heard of the Pool of the Women?'

Chunia shook her head. 'No, Khanum – never.'

The elder of the two dancing boys stood forward. 'Begum Sahiba – I have heard. My mother was one of the Palace dancing girls, and I was brought up amongst them. I remember hearing the Pool of the Women spoken about when I was very small. It was a thing they used to frighten me with if I was

264

noisy – that they would take me there. But no queen has been that road for many years – it is all forgotten now. I do not think anyone knows where it is. I have heard that the present Raja's great-grandfather used it often.'

Bianca turned on him. 'Look you – can you get in to see the Raja?'

'Only if he sends for us, Begum Sahiba.'

'Oh, God – then, you Chunia, can you go in to see him?'

'Not without an order – and I have not seen him for many weeks now. The Rani took me from him. And when Sunder Singh is with him, no one sees him. No one has seen him for three days, since Sunder Singh first went into his room, and they took the Dancer out – except, you saw him, did you not, Jagoo?'

'Yes – as I told you – he was drunk, and trying to dance. His rooms are well guarded, Begum Sahiba, by the Rani's guards.'

'Are there none of the Raja's men that he trusted left?'

'We are three, Sahiba, and there are two grooms, and perhaps some of the guards – but we do not know for sure. One thing is certain – if we tried to get into his rooms we would be noticed, for we are known to be his friends.'

Bianca was filled with a terrible urgency. 'You say he was pleased with Muna, and that they spoke as friends? Then somehow, quickly, news must be taken to him to let him know that his mother has Muna – and has probably sent her to the Pool of the Women. Her life – if she still lives indeed – must be in terrible danger. I do not know what happens, but I know that the Pool is below the Palace. In the name of God, can you not think of some way of getting news to the Raja?'

The two boys looked at each other, and then Chunia broke into the conversation. 'Who guards the door tonight? There are some of the men who are easily distracted from guarding the Raja's door. After all, once he is with Sunder Singh, he does not receive anyone else, nor does he come out. He cannot – he is usually so full of *bhang*, and of drink – so the guards grow bored, and are not vigilant.'

'But even if you distract both the guards, Chunia, and we get in, can we make him listen, or understand?'

Bianca was listening to them, her eyes full of hope. Now she said, 'But how long has he been alone with Sunder Singh? Three days? Surely the drugs must be wearing off? They cannot keep him drugged too long, he will die.'

'The Raja is well used to drugs, Begum Sahiba. Not only *bhang*, either. There are other drugs that the Rani mixes. Still, if Chunia could hold the guard's attention for a little time – there are two girls who take food and drink in for Sunder Singh and the Raja – what thinkest thou, Niroo?'

The two boys conferred together, and turned back to Bianca. 'Heavenborn. We will try. We love the Raja. He is a good friend, and would be a good Ruler if his mother would let him. So we will try. The Pool of the Women – and it is beneath the Palace, you say? Then is it possible that you could have some men near the Palace, or better still, inside it? For even if we get the Raja to understand, and he knows where it is, we will need help. The place is sure to be guarded by the Rani's men.'

Kullunder Khan looked a question at Chunia, and she nodded. 'I can get you and any you bring, into my room. Come beneath my window, and you will find the cord. I will not be there, but if all goes well, I will return and lead you to the Raja's room. If all goes well.' Her words were chilling. So much could go wrong. The guards could be vigilant, too frightened of the Rani to be easily seduced from their duty. The Raja could be so deeply drugged that he would not understand, or he would be unconscious.

Suddenly Bianca turned to Ayub Khan.

'Ayub – where is Bella?'

'Bella? She cannot go, Khanum. She is known, the white servant of Muna. She would be going to her death if she entered that Palace.'

Bella, coming in, heard him. 'Ayub, will you let me speak for myself! You need me, Begum?'

'Yes, Bella – listen, the Raja is drugged, and may be also drunk. Do you have any kind of cure for this, something that could jerk him into sanity? Even if only for a short time?'

Bella thought for a minute, her face white and strained. Then she spoke to the dancing boys. 'What do they give him?'

'Opium sometimes – or *bhang* – it will be *bhang* this time, as Sunder Singh is with him. *Bhang*, and an aphrodisiac of great power that they make, and mix with wine.'

'Mixed with wine – very well, I will give you some powder. He *must* drink it, but how you will give it to him with that man watching you, I do not know. Wait – does the man drink too?'

'Very little. Usually brandy, and not much of that.'

'Never mind, that will help. I will give you a powder for him too – do you think you can give it to him?'

Niroo shrugged, and glanced wryly at his brother. 'Mem, we are going to try. If we succeed, we will see tomorrow's sunrise. You will know if we fail, for I think then, none of us, the Lady of Madore, Chunia, the men you send in, or my brother and myself, will ever be seen again.'

Bella nodded, and hurried out. Bianca surveyed the three who would attempt the rescue. She estimated that Chunia could be, at the most, fifteen. The two boys would be possibly a year or two older. To these children Muna's rescue had to be entrusted. And her husband? What of him? Bianca recalled the young Alan, charmingly diffident, enchanted by Sara, brave in time of danger, willing to fight for them although he obviously could not understand their peril, and patient under Kassim's lashingly sarcastic tongue, Kassim so jealous of Alan that he was willing to kill him. What could have happened to Alan that caused both Ayub and Bella, whose wisdom she trusted, to advise against sending for him in this present crisis – because he would only complicate it? Surely this was wrong, surely he should be sent for at once? Bianca opened her mouth to give the order, and then remembered how the young Alan had seemed to carry disorder and disaster with him – and how Kassim had blamed him, and him alone for the mischance that had caused Sara to be kidnapped by Hardyal. Kassim had neither forgotten this, nor had he ever trusted Alan again with anything important. There were men like Alan who, however well-intentioned, seemed to be unable to do anything as it should be done in time of danger. Bella and Ayub Khan had obviously seen this – and they knew the Alan of now, not the

Alan of her time. They must be right, and she must trust them. Bianca did not give any orders to send for Alan.

Ayub Khan, Kullunder Khan and Phulan Khan came to her, they were armed and ready. Three men, and three children – and then she remembered the voice she had heard, the voice which had reminded her of the underground pool.

Bella, her face creased into lines of fear and worry, was standing close to her, and Bianca took her hand suddenly. 'Bella, do not be so distressed. These children are under protection, and so are the men. I know it. You are a wise woman – do you not feel the power?'

Bella put a hand on Chunia's shoulder, resting it there for a moment, and nodded. 'There is power, Khanum. I do not know what power, and we would likely be afraid if we did, but it is very strong. Well, go then – you have the powders safely? The powder in the blue silk is for the Raja. That in the red bag is for the other. Whatever power that helps you, may it go with you, and keep you from harm.'

As she finished speaking, Bella's eyes were looking at Ayub. He gave a backward nod, and she followed him to the door. When they were alone he did not put his arms round her. He smiled at her, and said quietly, 'I am protected by our love, green eyes. Never fear. We have years ahead of us. Guard yourself well, as I cannot stay to do it.'

It was Bella, who, tall as she was, stood on tiptoe to put her arms around his neck, and kiss him, so that he folded her close, his arms going round her so tightly that she had the marks of the various weapons he carried on her body for hours afterwards. The others were noisy as they came out – Bella was already walking out to the courtyard before they came through the door. Bianca stood with her to watch the little party leave. Then Bianca turned and went back into the house, and followed by Bella, climbed to the roof garden.

'If we try to sleep, we will lie and imagine evil things. Come, Bella – tell me of Muna's life here – it is so long since I have seen her, and she does not write, and her husband's letters do not tell me very much. So you and I can perhaps forget our fears a little, while you tell me all that I do not know.'

So Bianca heard about the pink Palace in Bombay, and the journey down to Sagpur, and the loneliness that Muna suffered – and all about the cholera outbreak. Between the words that Bella spoke, Bianca learned a great deal about Bella, and was glad that Muna had such a faithful woman close to her. For her life did not appear to be a very happy life.

'So it was after the work in the cholera camp that she took the fever? Why did her husband not send her to us, in Madore? And you with her? I could have taken you both up to Lambagh. Although she was not born there, Lambagh became her country when she was a very small child and Goki brought her to us. She needs her own country, and her own hills, to heal her. I do not understand Alan –'

'He would have sent her – but she refused to go. I think that is why he asked you to come here. I think he hoped that you would be able to persuade her to go back with you. But Begum Sahiba, I have never seen her so angry as she was when she heard he had asked you to come here. She spoke to him as if he was a dog, and he left her without returning to say goodbye, and has not returned since.'

'Oh God,' thought Bianca desperately. 'How much more is this girl going to suffer through our family? It is as if we have thrown a terrible shadow over her life. It might have been better for her if we had tried to find some English people and sent her back to England, all those years ago –'

But if they had done that, and sent her back to England, what would her life have been then? Possibly an orphanage, and eventual service in some house – at least the life she had lived had been comfortable and luxurious, and Muna, in the north, before she had married, had appeared to be happy.

It was dawn, a fitful watery dawn, that turned the sea to a sullen yellow, and did not promise a good day.

'The rains are coming at last,' said Bella, hearing a distant rumble of thunder. 'They are too late for the crops, and so there will be famine this year, no doubt about it.'

Bianca looked round her in the pallid dawn light. This garden spoke so eloquently of Muna – the rich colours of the cushions and rugs, the screened plants, so lovingly tended –

jasmine and rose and marigolds – Muna must have been so homesick for the north. Not only England, but this part of India was utterly foreign to her. Bianca realised with a sudden shock that Muna had lived long years in England, and that she herself, born of Irish parents, had never seen Britain, nor had ever had any desire to visit the land of her parents' birth. India was the country of her heart, she felt she would die if she was taken from this lovely land where she had been born, brought up, married, and had lived for the whole of her thirty-eight years. How then had Muna felt, taken over the dark waters of the sea – and then, when she returned, brought to a part of India so far from her own country? Bianca felt a spasm of pain, as if she was within Muna's mind, as she looked about her. She said to Bella, speaking quickly, out of her pain, 'Bella – please – could I have some coffee?'

'I will make it now, and bring it up, Begum Sahiba.'

The two women drank their coffee together, sitting on a low divan. The yellow dawn had not brightened into a good day, but there was no rain. The sky was a strange leaden colour, which merged with the grey, heaving sea. The waves did not break in surf on the beach. They came up, and then sucked back again, almost soundlessly, unnaturally quiet. The casuarina trees kept up, as usual, their restless whispering, but the palm trees were still, their leaves silent. Bianca sniffed at the air, which smelt strange. Indeed, she thought, I am glad I do not live down here. A little ghost came back to haunt her: Khanzada, her husband's sister and her greatest friend, Khanzada who had married Hardyal, and had hated living in Sagpur, and had died, with her baby daughter in Madore, on the night when the Mutiny had begun to rage over India. She had not been killed by mutineers. There were still whispers that her death had been contrived. Bianca wondered, briefly, sadly knowing that there was no answer to that question now. There was no one left alive to answer it.

Bella had brought up the silver tray and the steaming coffee pot with the peacock motif engraved on its side – Sara's gift to Muna. Drinking the strong black brew, Bianca saw that Bella was looking at the sky and the sea.

'Strange – there are no birds.'

'Birds?'

'Yes – Muna feeds them up here, at this time. They are usually waiting for her. They must know that she is not here. There are gulls that come, and crows of course, and hoopoes, and the bird we call Willie Wagtail – I do not know what they call it here. But today – see, not a bird. And a horrible day. As if, like us, it was waiting for news, and feared it would be bad.'

It certainly appeared that the weather was waiting for something. The horizon was darkening from watery yellow to a threatening purple. The sea, grey and oily, heaved and thumped and sucked itself back as if it would avoid touching the shore at all. Both women turned and looked at the Palace. As they did, a wind rose, blowing sharply in their faces, then veering suddenly to blow from the land towards the sea, a fierce wind that tore at their hair, and pushed the sea back into oily rolls, higher and higher and higher, and then the wind dropped as suddenly as it had risen, and the sea surged back, but with no white surf on the oily ripple and waves.

'Ugh – what a horrible wind – it smelt.'

'Yes – it is a very strange day. You are right, Bella, there are no birds. I wish we could see into the Palace – what do you suppose happened there last night, and what is happening now. It seems so long already, and yet they have only been gone about four hours.'

Again they looked over to Sagpur Palace, bulking white against the grey, cloud-strewn sky.

24

The two sentries outside Sagpurna's door were bored. There were no enlivening noises from the other side of the door. No one came down the long passage, and although theirs was the morning watch, it was still dark, the oil lamps on the wall throwing a feeble glow that did not even catch a gleam from their drawn swords. It was so quiet that they could hear each other breathing – and then they also heard something else – the tinkle and clash of bracelets and anklets. It was a rejuvenating sound. Both men smiled as they lounged against the wall and, turning their heads, watched the figure of a girl slowly emerge from the shadows. She cast a demure, sideways glance at them as she passed – but boredom had made them bold. They did not care who heard them speak.

'Ho – Chunia! Wait, tell us what you have been doing – who has been fortunate this last night, to watch you dance? And did he – '

Chunia tossed her veil back from her face and stood, one curved hip forward, her face full in the dim light of the lamps. 'You ask too many questions, oh soldier – I, to dance for anyone but the Raja? What do you suggest?'

'You dance for anyone who pays you – and why not?'

'Why not, indeed?' said Chunia, then, lowering her voice and glancing at the door, 'Is *he* in there?'

One of the soldiers tried to look stern, 'We are not here to answer questions,' he said, and she pouted and turned away. His companion was of another mind.

'What are we here for? Yes, he is in there – and for all we know they are now both drunk and sleeping. No sound from them since we came on duty – and no one has been here, either to go in, or to bring us something to drink or our bread.'

Chunia turned back to them. 'Poor things. You starve for nothing – and I – what do I do? No one asks me to come and dance, I rot here in my youth, and I should be old and dead, if I did not keep myself alive one way or another. I would forget how to dance, and mayhap forget other things also, without practice. So – I practise.'

She smiled at them both impartially, and struck the pose that began the dance of love.

'Aiee – you have not forgotten how to dance! It is so long since I had enough money and enough free time to see a *nautch* – and finish it as I should. What do you say, Ram Sarn? Or are you only half a man, that you stand there glowering when this flower blooms so close to us?'

Chunia said swiftly, 'He is a whole man – and doing his duty as he should.' She smiled at Ram Sarn, her lips curving to show teeth like pearls, her eyes wide with admiration. 'What else should a soldier do but his duty?'

Ram Sarn unbent and nodded at his companion. 'He is not the only one who longs to see a *nautch*. I, too –'

Chunia smiled again, 'I have pity for you both, and for myself. Such beautiful young men to be wasted, endlessly standing outside a closed door!'

'And such a beautiful dancer, to remain unhonoured, and never sent for, because her master has another master – ' Even as he spoke, Ram Sarn looked sideways to search the shadows.

'There is no one there,' said Chunia, 'But I will tell you – why do you never visit me – you must have some time free? Come to my quarters, and I will have wine for you, and I will dance. What dances do you like? I can dance the dances of the north – thus – ' She swung into a dance and her skirts flew up to show her legs as far as her curved hips.

'Or, if you prefer, I can dance as the women do here – thus – ' Once again, she moved, her arms above her head, her body twisting slowly, and both men were staring. She stopped, and heard the infinitesimal sound that she had been waiting for, then she said, 'Your watch has been long – look, come here into the shadow. I have some wine in a flask and some almond cakes. I was taking them to – well, that is another story. He does not need them and you do. See – here. I will watch the door, but there is no need. This is the dead hour of the day, everyone sleeps.'

The men looked both ways and then moved swiftly towards her as she backed deeper into the shadows. As they began to pass the flask from one to another, she said, 'Watch – I show you a little of what you will see when you visit me.'

Her hands fluttering, her body curving, Chunia danced, and the wine flask was forgotten as the men watched. Two figures slipped from the shadows to the unguarded door; the soldiers did not see them, watching spellbound as Chunia's body curved and quivered. The door opened without a sound, closed again, and still Chunia danced and the sentries watched, crumbs of forgotten almond cake on their lips.

Inside the room, the lamps were lowered and the air was hot and stale. Sagpurna lay on the disordered bed, propped against pillows, his heavy eyes staring at nothing. He looked straight at the two figures that had come in, but it was obvious he did not see them. Sunder Singh was sitting in the window, and Niroo's heart sank when he saw him, for he was neither drugged nor drunk. His dress was disordered, he was tired – but his eyes were alert and he turned at once as the door opened and closed behind the two girlish figures in their gold-tissue robes, and he said, 'What do you here? I gave no order.'

'We were told, lord – to bring fresh fruit and wine, and the brandy for you; also cakes. We were told to come with clean raiment, and to make the room fit. But we can go, if you wish, lord, until you are ready.' Niroo did it well. He sounded like a frightened girl, addressing a man she admired but of whom she was afraid.

Sunder Singh looked round the chaotic room. 'Faugh – a sty fit for a pig. Yes, then, clean it swiftly little ones – and then – well, we will see.'

His caressing voice, his roving eye would have melted a girl who was already his slave. Niroo visibly melted. He lowered his eyelashes, he simpered, he stood like a helpless doe before a leopard. Jagoo, like a jealous sister, pushed him, and the two of them turned and began to straighten the room. It was important that the powder was given to the Raja quickly so that he would have time to come to his senses. Yet he must not come to them so quickly that he gave himself away to Sunder Singh. Niroo, pushing soiled clothes into a bundle and knotting a sheet round them, gave an imperceptible signal to Jagoo, and Jagoo, clean clothes in his hand, began to change the bed. The Raja inadvertently helped them by mumbling something, and Jagoo instantly filled a glass from the flask he had brought and, holding Sagpurna's head on his arm, forced him to drink.

Niroo was fluttering before Sunder Singh like a bird before a snake. 'Lord – I have almond cakes and brandy – will you?' The goblet shook in Niroo's hand, and it was not all acting, for the man he was trying to drug was as dangerous as a cobra. Sunder Singh turned back from the window and shook his head. Then, seeing Niroo's downcast face, he said, 'Why – you want me to drink? I have had enough. What I have had to do here these last few days has needed drink, by the Gods.'

'As my Lord says; but this is on ice – I thought – ' Sunder Singh leant forward lazily. 'Give me a cake then, little one.'

As he took the cake, his head and neck were free of any protection. With a cry of 'Jagoo!', Niroo whipped a wire from his clothing and wound it tightly round Sunder Singh's throat. Jagoo was there on the instant to take the other end; even so, it took their entire strength to hold the wire, and they were thrown about the room like puppets but, straining in opposite directions, desperate eyes on the door, they avoided the flailing arms and suddenly it was over, and Sunder Singh, his face black, his swollen tongue protruding, lay in his own excreta on the floor.

'Now,' gasped Niroo, and they heaved the man up and pushed him into a chair, so that he lay across the table, his face hidden in his arms, like a man asleep. Jagoo cleaned up the soiled carpets and straightened all had been set awry in their struggle. Niroo tightened the wire and tied it so that it sank deeply into Sunder Singh's flesh. The man was as strong as a tiger; who could tell if he would not recover if the wire went loose.

Then the boys turned to Sagpurna who was moving his head on his pillows like a man waking.

'Jagoo, put out the signal – that green scarf there – Ayub will be watching. Now, Maharaj – see, it is I, Niroo. Can you hear me?'

Sagpurna groped helplessly with his hands, and then vomited copiously, so copiously that Niroo was frightened.

'In the name of Kali – did you give him too much of that white woman's drug?'

'I gave what she said. Look, his eyes clear.'

'Lord?'

'Niroo? What do you here, dressed as a dancing girl, and Jagoo? I thought – ' His forehead creased like a boy about to weep.

'Do not fear, Maharaj, he will not trouble you. But can you help us? There is very much trouble, lord. Janki, your servant, is dead. And Muna, the Dancer – '

Sagpurna stared at him. 'What of her? Did I not send her home? I said, when we had spent the night talking, that I would send her home – but I cannot remember what happened – '

He rubbed fretfully at his eyes, and then seemed to realise what Niroo had said, 'Niroo, there is bad trouble – did you say Janki was dead? What happened, tell me quickly?'

Bella's drug had worked well. Sagpurna was at last sitting up, alert.

'Muna was taken by thy – by the Rani. Lord, we need your help. Muna is – if she is alive still, she is down in the cavern of the Pool.'

'Gods – the Pool of the Women? It is not possible! My mother – that woman knows nothing of the Pool of the Women. She was not – she is not of good blood.' Sagpurna's mouth was twisted with distaste as he spoke.

'Every woman who becomes the Rani of a Sagpur Ruler knows of the Pool of the Women, lord. Had you been a girl – who knows? Now, we need the key of the door – and we do not even know where the door is; but you know, lord. Can you tell us?'

'Tell you? Get me up! I will show you – but are there any loyal to me left?'

'A few, lord, and we have brought friends with us. Listen, lord – '

Through the heavy, closed door there were sounds. A clashing of steel that lasted only a minute or two, then a quiet knock on the door. Niroo opened it, and Sagpurna straightened himself as Ayub Khan hurried in.

'The Raja is recovered?' he said, speaking to Niroo.

Sagpurna answered, his voice cold, 'The Raja is recovered. How many men have you?'

'We are four, lord. I and one other are here. Chunia has taken Amin-Ud-Din to get the Rani.'

'But the Rani's quarters are guarded.'

'We killed the guard. The men who were outside your room are also dead. Have you any of your own you can trust?'

Sagpurna looked helplessly at Niroo, who nodded at him.

'Jagoo has gone to get three friends – so we are ten.'

'Ten,' said Ayub.

'Yes, ten, including myself. I can fight, and for the dancer, Muna, I would gladly die. I hope that death takes me in any case.' He took the sword that Niroo held out to him.

'The door is guarded night and day but only one man guards it, unless other orders have been given, for no one knows where it is. In any case, there is no one who desires to go down and meet the Guardian of the Pool, the white crocodile. A beast so old that no one knows how long he has been here. Years ago, he fed very well. But for the last twenty or so years, I think a priest takes him a goat every week. In the name of the Gods, we stand here talking – can we not go?'

As he spoke, he looked towards the window and then turned to look again. Niroo thought that it was Sunder Singh's body that had halted him, but Sagpurna passed the body without looking and leant out.

'What hour is it?' he asked.

'It is the fifth hour after sunrise, lord.'

Niroo, a boy from the north, could not imagine what made Sagpurna lean out, sniffing at the air and looking down at the sea. Then Sagpurna turned back, his face settling into lines of sudden maturity.

'There are many reasons for us to make haste – and one of them is that soon, very soon, the wind and the sea will strike us – and strike us very hard. None of you know this country do you? Then let us make haste. For once we have rescued the Dancer – if it pleases the Gods and she is there to be rescued – then we must leave here and go inland before the sea comes back to swallow us. I have never seen it thus, but I have heard stories. *Why* do we wait?'

The raw impatience in his voice was answered from the door. It was Chunia who spoke, 'We are now ready, lord. Your mother is waiting there – to assist us.'

Sagpurna gave her a wild, disbelieving look and then led the way out, and they hurried through the central hall of the Palace and down the staircase where Muna had been carried two days before. At the foot of the stairs, Kullunder Khan and three other men waited, and Kullunder Khan held the Rani, her arms twisted behind her, her face a contorted mask of hatred, which smoothed itself to a loving smile when she saw her son.

'Oh, Maharaj – my son. See how these barbarians have treated your mother! My guard is killed and myself dragged from my bed as if I was some woman of no account – '

'And what are you?' asked Sagpurna, and at his words and tone she was quiet, looking at him with little, hating eyes.

Ayub Khan stepped forward and unlocked the door, and would have walked straight into the dark passage, but Sagpurna saw the expression on his mother's face.

'Wait!'

He put his hand on Ayub's arm, 'Wait – search her.'

Roughly, Kullunder and Ayub searched the Rani's person, in spite of her struggles. A small, sharp-pointed knife, strapped high on the inner side of her thigh, was taken.

'Be careful – that will have poison on it,' warned Sagpurna. 'Now, you take that road, Mother – '

The Rani's eyes widened until the eyeballs stood out from her suddenly grey face. 'My son – '

'Each time you use those words, you make my heart more bitter.'

He stretched out his hand and snatched at her disordered *sari*, pulling until it unwound and she was naked in front of them, hideous, with fallen breasts and protruding stomach.

'Now, *Mother* – go, as a sacrifice prepared.'

He thrust her into the corridor and the closed door shut off her cries.

'But why – what are we waiting for? We must go.'

'We will not have long to wait. I think. Listen – '

He opened the door a very small crack and they all heard the sound of running feet, pattering away from them.

'She is a fool, after all,' said Sagpurna. 'She has forgotten that the Hunter will wait near the mouth of the corridor and that the Guardian will be there too, waiting, should she by a miracle escape the Hunter.'

Niroo, and Jagoo and Chunia stood beside Sagpurna and suddenly they heard what he was waiting to hear, a scream that rose and sounded back to them, magnified by the hollow echoes of the corridor. Sagpurna opened the door.

'Chunia,' he said, 'go you and get all the people of your race who do not know this country, and take them far inland, moving as quickly as you can, at once. For the wind and the sea are coming and I do not know how soon. The people of my own race will have already fled.'

'Leaving their prince behind?' said Ayub, his voice heavy with contempt.

'I have not, perhaps, filled the role of prince very successfully.'

But Ayub was not listening to him. 'Chunia,' he said, 'the Begum! Make sure she goes with you! The horses are there – '

'I know, Ayub Khan – do not fret. If I live, the Begum lives.'

Ayub turned away as Chunia spoke and the little group, led by Sagpurna, hurried down the passage-way, the route that Muna had run down in so much fear.

25

In the cavern, Muna had lost count of time. There were now only two torches burning, and shadows were gathering on the white sand. But the green pool was incandescent; even as the cavern grew darker, the water lay clear to the eye. Within it Muna thought she could see something move, come close to the surface and then vanish again. Staring, she could not be sure. The torches flared and flickered, and the shadows shifted and deceived her eyes.

She was tormented by thirst. The alabaster cup, beside the spring, was hidden in darkness now, but she knew it was there, she knew exactly its placing. She could hear the trickle of the water as it fell into the little marble basin, and did not know how to withstand the temptation of that cup. If she moved softly, quickly – even a swallow of water would be enough.

She was tensing her muscles for a run to the spring, when she heard the first scream. There was someone crying out in terror in that horrible passage that led to the cavern – and at the entrance to the cavern itself, coiled and waiting, Muna knew, was the snake.

She opened her mouth to cry a warning, and as if a hand was put over her lips, she could make no sound. She heard running feet; one of the torches flared, and a whisper, a dying sigh, filled the cavern.

The lake was moving again. Waves spread from a great central ripple, and this time they lapped very high on the sand, splashing Muna's feet with cold drops. She stared at the moving ripple in the middle of the lake, and saw a white snout rise, a long snout that had two large bumps in the flat head behind it. She could see eyes, as the creature came nearer, white-filmed eyes that turned blindly, this way and that, and the waves moved on the sand and splashed on the steps of the niche again, while Muna stood, staring, and frozen with fear.

The scream that sounded from the mouth of the passage took her by surprise, she had been so mesmerised by the sight of the creature in the pool. The scream grew in terror and ended in an ear-splitting shriek, as the naked figure of a woman fell forward on to the sand, her body convulsing and straightening again, twisting like the snake itself, the snake that was coiled about her body, its fangs sunk in her flesh.

One torch went out, and the water washed up on to the sand, higher and higher, and the blind white head began to move, the gross body behind it laying an arrowhead trail on the green water. The woman on the sand was quiet now, the snake coiled round her waist.

Light spilled from the passage, as men ran out on to the sand.

Sagpurna was one of the first. He ignored the body on the sand after one quick glance. He stared round the cavern, and saw the niche, and the plinth within it, where Muna stood, naked and silent. The light did not reach her, and he thought she was the figure of a Goddess and seeing the green *sari* crumpled on the steps, cried out in grief, thinking Muna already dead. But Niroo, seeing more clearly, said, 'Nay, she is there – that is the Dancer, in the niche, Heavenborn, she is alive and unhurt!'

Sagpurna ran to the niche and flinging his arms round Muna, leapt with her down the steps, snatching up her *sari* on his way. Ayub, on the sand, was slashing at the writhing coils of the snake. The Rani did not move. She was either unconscious or dead. Ayub turned his eyes from her terrible, contorted face.

'Leave her, Ayub Khan. She is the goat for this week. See, the Guardian of the Pool comes for his weekly dole – ' Jagoo pointed, and Ayub saw the white head, and long, tooth-snagged snout of a crocodile so old that it was snow white, and blind.

281

A wave lifted and washed over the Rani's body, moving it closer to the Pool.

Sagpurna was calling from the passage. 'Ayub, come! Would you jeopardise all we have done for that evil woman? Hurry – we have very little time to get to safety before the great wind strikes.'

Niroo walked over to the spring and the alabaster cup. He bent and lifted the cup, and as he did so, a bell clanged above his head, and the creature in the pool began to move fast towards the shore. Ayub looked at it, and shuddered, and with Niroo at his heels, hurried into the passage, leaving the Pool of the Women to its terrible Guardian.

On the roof of the Gulabmahal, Bella and Bianca felt the first gusts of a strange wind, a wind that blew strongly, bending the palm trees so that their leaves, rattling, almost swept the ground, and it seemed as if their trunks must snap; and then the wind would sigh into silence, leaving an eerie stillness. They looked at each other, the same fear in both their minds. Bella nodded, as if Bianca had spoken.

'Aye. Cyclone weather. I have heard about these winds. Khanum, if I show you where things are, could you put together what you think we will need in the way of food and drink and bedding? I will go down to the village on the shore, and bring back two men who will carry for us, for I think that whatever message comes from the Palace we will have to leave this place quickly. I am afraid of the sea.'

Bianca turned to look at the sea, following Bella's pointing finger. The wind was gusting again, and the tide was far out, leaving a great expanse of sand and slimy rocks.

'See those rocks?' said Bella grimly. 'Those rocks have not been uncovered while we have been here. Come with me and let me show you where everything is. I'll be back to help you as soon as I can.'

The village was deserted; only a few men remained, and they were dragging their log boats as far into the trees as they could. Two of them readily agreed to come and act as carriers. They had sent their families inland, and took it for granted that the people in the Gulabmahal would be fleeing before this

wind too. Bella hurried back with them, and found that Bianca
had already made one bundle of clothes and bedding. Working
quickly together, the two women gathered everything that they
thought would be of use, and finally had two large bundles tied
to a pole so that the men could carry their burden as easily as
possible. Then Bella and Bianca saddled the two horses that
were left to them, and were ready to leave. There was nothing
more for them to do except wait for news. The two carriers set
off, saying there was only one place to go to that was in reach
– a place on a small hill, inland, called Mokhandarai. They
were out of sight when Bella heard Bianca calling from the
roof.

'Bella, there is a rider coming from the direction of the
Palace.'

Chunia rode up, her gauzes and silks blowing about her, and
barely drew rein long enough to speak. She was breathless and
gasping, and told them to mount and ride, they could talk when
they had left the shore safely behind them.

'We must go to Mokhandarai, it is a place of safety. I can
tell you nothing of the Dancer, except that she was taken to the
Pool of the Women, and Sagpurna has been roused by the
drugs you sent and with the others has gone to find her. But his
orders to me were to take you from the shore at once. He will,
if the Gods are kind, join us at the Dome of the Winds at
Mokhandarai.'

There was no point in her trying to say more. The wind was
already blowing more strongly, and now it had a voice, a
strange high voice, a muffled, horrifying scream. They rode
inland, and their last sight of the Gulabmahal was veiled from
them by the tossing trees. The sea and the shore were left
behind, and they entered a place where the wind ruled so that
it was soon impossible to ride and they dismounted and began
to walk, moving slowly, dragging the frightened horses behind
them, forcing their bodies through what seemed to be a solid
wall, the wall of the wind.

But it was still a capricious wind. It turned suddenly and
blew from behind, pushing them forward so that they had to
run over the rough ground, and the horses snorted and tossed

their heads, their eyes stung by the blowing sand.

'Oh, this cursed wind,' said Bella, struggling with her horse, and her words fell into a sudden silence, for the wind had gone again, and there, ahead of them was a high wall, and a domed building with a ruined tower on one side of it, all built on a high mound. In the silence that had followed the wind, they could hear voices – there were people already in the Dome of the Winds. A great hope gave the three women extra strength. They struggled up the steep side of the mound, up a path marked by many feet, and went in through the opening in the wall. They left their horses in the courtyard, and entered the big domed room.

It was obviously a well-known place of refuge. It appeared that the entire population of the shore village, about twenty in all, were there, and various other people, who by their dress were from the city, and the Palace. But the three women stood forlornly in the doorway, their hopes unfulfilled. There was no sign of Muna, or Ayub Khan, nor of any of the band who had joined in the plan to rescue Muna.

Their carriers had made a place for them in a corner, and were waiting for them there. Bella paid them, and found hope in the fact that they tied the money into a corner of their loin cloths. They expected to come safely through the next few hours – or days, and that was a good thing, for they were people who knew the works of the wind and the seas. Bella opened the bundles and, helped by Bianca, spread out quilts, and they tried to make themselves comfortable as they settled down to wait. Chunia had gone over to the door, but the wind had risen and was blowing strongly from the land side, and the door had been pulled shut. There was a great deal of noise in the domed room, but Bella suddenly put her hand on Bianca's arm – 'Listen, Khanum!'

There were sounds outside, faint above the noise of the wind. Chunia was already struggling with the door, and Bella and Bianca ran to help her, pushing their way through the people round them. They got out into the wind-beaten courtyard in time to see Sagpurna sliding from his horse, with Muna in his arms.

Bianca had not seen Muna for many years. Now she saw no change in her, except the natural change that she thought death had caused. This she was unable to bear. She turned away, and covered her face with her hands. But Bella ran forward and took Muna's body from Sagpurna, lifting her as easily as she would have carried a child, and found her breathing.

'She lives! Khanum, help me!'

She carried Muna into the crowded, noise-ridden building, and while Bianca held Muna against her shoulder, Bella gave her wine, sip by sip, and they saw that she was drinking thirstily, although she appeared to have trouble swallowing.

'She should have water,' said Bella, and before she had finished speaking, Sagpurna was beside her, a brimming goblet in his hands. Muna would have drunk it all, but Bella prevented her, giving her only a little at a time. Muna's eyes were open, but very clouded, she did not seem to be able to focus them properly; it was as if she was looking beyond the others, at something they could not see.

Sagpurna leaned close, to look into her face. 'Is she conscious? She has neither moved nor spoken since we brought her from that terrible place.'

'Was she drugged?'

'I do not know. I was drugged, as I understand you were told. You sent me the potion that brought me to myself. I thank you – but now can you not help her? If they drugged her as they used to drug me, she may well die.'

'I can smell no drugs on her breath, Rajasahib.' As Bella spoke, the scream of the wind rose higher, and something crashed against the outer wall. 'Oh God – what a place to try and bring the Sahiba back to health! Is it safe? Will it stand?'

'This is the only place of safety we could reach in time. This is the place that all who live on the shore, or who are late in leaving the city come to. It has been used for generations at these times, when the wind and the sea take over the country. I would have taken her further inland if I could, but I had not time. Listen, I think the others have come.'

He got up and hurried to the door, and Bella was close behind him, leaving Muna in Bianca's arms. Ayub Khan came shouldering through the door, the rest of his band behind him, and then stopped, to stand and look at Bella as if he had never seen her before, and as if he could never look enough. Bella looked back at him, and smiled, and then with no word said between them they both went back to where Bianca was holding Muna, and speaking to her, her voice raised above the general noise.

'Muna! Muna, you are safe – Muna, my dear child – '

At last, from whatever place in which her spirit was wandering, away from the fear that Bianca could see on her face, Muna came back at the sound of that loved voice that she had not heard for so long, and looked straight at Bianca.

'Khanum! I can hear you, Khanum, but I would hear you better if you could ask those others to stop speaking.'

'It is the wind that you hear, Muna, and there are people all round us.'

'No. It is not the wind, and the people I hear are whispering.' Muna's voice was so low that it was almost impossible to hear what she was saying. Bianca bent close to her lips, and Muna said again, 'That terrible whisper – '

'What whisper, Muna? It is the sound of the wind.'

'No. It is the whispering, and the weeping of hundreds of women. I can hear it all the time. I know now what happened to them. They were thirsty as I was, and afraid, but their thirst was so strong that they picked up the alabaster cup to drink from the spring, and the lake moved, and they were taken. Night and day, in that cave they call for help, like bats crying high above sound. The Goddess did not help them as she helped me, and I do not know why. Perhaps she helped me to live until they were avenged. But for myself there is a terrible punishment. For the rest of my life I will hear those voices crying in my head, the voices of those frightened women.'

Her face was piteous, and Bianca did not know what to do. She looked for help to Bella, who went to one of the bundles, and came back with a cup into which she stirred with wine a pinch of grey powder.

'Sahiba, drink this, and sleep. The women have been avenged. Sleep and hear nothing.'

Muna drank, holding the cup as a person would hold a rope that would pull them to safety from a river in which they were drowning, and Bianca and Bella helped her to lie down, and Bianca took her hand and held it until she felt Muna's fingers relax, and knew that she slept at last.

From her seat beside the sleeping Muna, Bianca looked round the room of the dome, until she saw Sagpurna. He was with his Palace people, courtiers and servants. He appeared to be very much in command of them, his orders were being obeyed quickly. Bianca had found it easy to recognise him. He was Hardyal alive again, Hardyal as he had been when she had first seen him when he came to marry Khanzada. The same heavy-lidded eyes, the full curved mouth, as chiselled as the mouths on the faces of the Gods in these southern temples. He had Hardyal's arrogant bearing, his height and his voice. Bianca shuddered, watching and listening. Yet – he was not altogether like his terrible father. He was looking after Muna's comfort, and not only hers. He was also caring for his own people, including the fisher-folk. Hardyal would not have known that they existed. Hardyal would not have saved Muna and brought her back. He would have watched her die, for his own amusement. Bianca sat, holding Muna's hand, and decided, as she watched the tall young man in the tattered silks, that he was not, after all, so very like his monstrous father.

She was glad to have something with which to occupy her thoughts, something to watch, for the wind screamed outside, and it sounded to Bianca as if devils rode on the wind and surrounded this strange place where they had been brought to shelter. There was very little light. The people from the shore village had made a fire in one corner, and smoke coiled up into the domed roof and hung there, making a second ceiling of grey cloud that eddied and shifted with every gust of wind that shook the building. There were one or two makeshift torches in the old wall sconces, adding their smoke to the rest, and beside her Bella had put a hurricane lantern, but that was not to be lit except in extreme emergency, as the oil would not last long. Bianca wondered what in these conditions would be considered to be an extreme emergency, but there was no one to ask, so she continued to watch the scene around her.

Under Sagpurna's orders a guard had been put on the sacks of dried fish, and of rice, and the few vegetables that had been brought in by the fleeing people who had just picked up whatever was to hand. Some of the women were cooking, and Sagpurna's servants were setting up a bed of sorts, in a corner of the room, and hanging silk cloths up to give it privacy. The Raja must lie soft wherever he found himself, thought Bianca. The makeshift curtains in place, Sagpurna approved. She saw him nod his head, and then he came over to where she was sitting.

'You do not know me, Begum Sahiba; may I present myself? I am Sagpurna, the Raja of these parts. I ask your pardon for the conditions in which I entertain you. I hope one day to give you better hospitality.'

'Rajasahib, no one can blame you for an act of God.'

'An act of God, no – but there have been other things. I did not come to talk of them, however. I came to tell you that I think the Dancer would be more at peace in that bed of mine. I cannot think that she will be easy lying on the floor – not for many days to come, for her memories will torment her and she will be frightened.'

For the first time Bianca and Bella then heard from Sagpurna the story of Muna's ordeal, or as much of it as he knew. When he had finished his story they sat in horrified silence, looking down at Muna, wondering at the strength that had kept her alive. Ayub Khan had come up, and stood with them, and spoke to Sagpurna. 'Rajasahib, we owe you much. Without your courage we would not have got Muna away.'

Bella, her eyes as hard as green glass, opened her mouth to say something, but Sagpurna forestalled her. 'If it had not been for my mother, none of this would have happened – and who knows, you might have seen the weather changing, and got away before the wind struck. Do not thank me, Ayub Khan, for I am full of shame. Let be for now. Let us make the Dancer as comfortable as we can.'

He walked over to Muna and bent to take her up in his arms. Then he stopped, frowning. 'She is very fevered,' he said. 'See,

288

she is as wet as if she had been thrown in water.'

Bella stooped over Muna, and then straightened, shaking her head. 'She has no fever, but she is sweating very much. Look, it is the sweat of fear. She must be lost in a terrible dream – Sahiba!'

Sagpurna put his hand on Bella's arm. 'Hush – do not call her back too suddenly. It will harm her spirit, especially if you drugged her into sleep. I know of what I speak, indeed I know! Have you dry clothing for her? Then put it on her now, while she yet sleeps, and I will carry her to the bed. But be very careful. Let her sleep on if you can.'

Bella took Muna's sopping *sari* from her body, and Muna moaned and turned her head, but did not wake, and as Bella held her, Bianca took a dry *sari* and wrapped it about Muna's body, and then touched Sagpurna's arm. He turned at once and Bianca was astonished to see tears on his face. As he lifted Muna, he bent his head to rest it against hers as he carried her to the curtained bed. She watched him lay Muna down, and saw Muna turn to look up at him and say something, and then, leaving the curtains open, he came back to Bianca.

'Go to her,' he said, his voice rough, a boy's voice, a boy in pain. 'Go to her. A woman worth the price of a thousand years in eternal bliss, and she is in grief and fear. She spoke to me just now. She said "What is love, Alan, what is love?" And I – what could I say to her? I who had to be born into *this* part of her life! If I could but have been born soon enough to be her lover and her husband, I would have been a man to match her, and she would not have asked that question without an answer from me. But you go to her Begum Sahiba, she is awake and asks for you.'

Muna lay on the bed that Sagpurna's servants had prepared for her and tears ran down her cheeks and made dark stains on the silk cushion beneath her head. Bianca's heart ached to see her thus, remembering the girl who had gone so bravely and hopefully with her English husband to face her future in a strange land. Now, even in the dim light of the crowded room, Bianca could see that time had not taken from Muna's beauty, but that it was a different beauty now. She looked at the face of a woman who had suffered greatly, and seeing Muna's helpless tears, she could herself have wept. But she controlled her grief for this woman she loved so much, and spoke quickly, trying to keep her tone light. She felt that if she showed her own sorrow, and her fear, something terrible might happen, Muna might break completely, and lose the strength that had kept her alive so long.

'Muna – please do not weep! We meet after so many years –'

At the sound of her voice, Muna sat up, wiping her eyes with her hands. 'Khanum! I thought I had dreamed that you were here! We meet in a very strange place indeed, after so long!'

Bianca was relieved to see that Muna too was trying after a light touch, and was finding a little comfort in her presence.

'Then let us not weep together, Muna –'

'Ah Khanum, no. Let us not weep. I weep for the fears of long-dead queens, when I should be laughing with pleasure to see you again. But this is not an easy place in which to laugh, is it? Let us build another world for each other. Tell me everything about yourself, all the years I have missed. I do not need to be told that you have been happy, but tell how the years have passed, and how my dear Sher Khan Bahadur is.'

Sitting beside her, Bianca told Muna all that the years had held for her, all the changes, and the new way of life that she shared so happily with Sher Khan. 'We live outside the walls of Madore, not in the old Palace – Kassim still uses part of that when he comes for the yearly Durbars. But we live in the house that Sher Khan built for us beside the Rama Tank. You remember how like it was to the lake in Lambagh? Sometimes I forget, looking at the water, that I am not in the Valley.'

'Is Sher Khan happy, away from the Valley?'

'He is happy, yes. He is proud of his stables – the horses he breeds are among the best in Asia. The army come to us for their mounts, and now he is breeding race horses – and of course he is not long away from the Valley. We return very often. It is strange for me to hear Sher Khan called "The old Ruler".' Bianca paused, and then said quietly, 'I know that he handed over the power of Ruler to Kassim, and left Lambagh because of me. He was afraid that the Valley still held nightmares for me. Muna, I could live in hell with him, I love him so much – but after that long ten years when we were apart, when I was in my madness of fear, he cannot believe that I am completely cured. We are so happy together. I am not able to tell you how wonderful our life is. I am a fortunate woman, to have such a man, a man I can love, admire and adore.'

She saw Muna smiling at her; something in the quality of the smile struck her to the heart, and she said, 'Muna – come back with me. Come and live with us in Madore. You would be at home in our lives. All those beautiful horses to ride! And I have a garden of roses, and I sit in the evenings and watch the birds come flying in to nest among the reeds as I used to watch the birds in Lambagh. Come, my dearest Muna, come back to the north, where you belong.'

'Khanum, you could so easily persuade me. Ask me no more, for it is hard for me to say no to you. I have another life to live with a husband and a son – am I to abandon them? Ah no! You would not ask me to do that. I must live out this life of mine, and hope that in another life we will all be together again. I know that in your heart you understand. Now – let us talk of Sara, and her son. It is hard for me to think of Sara with a son, I see her still as she was when we were last together. She is happy?'

'She is very happy, and very well. Her son – I think he must be like his English grandfather, for he has bright blue eyes, and his hair is red when the sun strikes it. You can imagine how beloved he is – and how Sher Khan takes pride in him. He is a strong boy, and tall like his father and like Sher Khan – that at least he has taken from our family! Mumtaz, Kassim's mother, is bent on spoiling him, but Kassim is very firm. He goes to join an Indian Cavalry Regiment shortly – the regiment in which Kassim served.'

Bianca was talking of one thing, and thinking of another. From nowhere had come the thought that Sara had never asked why Muna did not return to the north, never once – and had not sent messages to beg her to come to Lambagh, and yet she was certain that Sara loved Muna as much as she had when they were children together. Suddenly Bianca found Muna's steady gaze difficult to meet, and then, without further thought, answered the one question that Muna had not asked.

'Kassim is well. He is happy, and contented. Sher Khan says he is a good Ruler, just and far-seeing. He has built his army into a very strong force – no one will try and breach our passes now! Kassim is also very interested in our horse breeding, and comes down more often than he did – and rides our best horses like a madman, as you may imagine.'

Muna nodded, saying nothing, and Bianca knew that she was remembering how Kassim had ridden, how he had looked on a horse. Bianca was astonished at her own blindness in the past. She was now beginning to understand many things.

'Muna – ' Something in her voice made Muna turn away, as if she was afraid of letting Bianca see her face. Bianca made a sudden decision. 'Listen Muna – Kassim has sent you something. He said to tell you to wear it, and remember the songs and dances of the long nights in Madore.'

A wave of beautiful colour flooded Muna's face, and the years seemed to drop away from her. Bianca saw Muna as she had been when she was sixteen. Youth had returned, and a girl's eyes looked up at Bianca, a young girl in the first flush of love. Bianca took a little packet from the pouch that hung at her waist, and put it into Muna's slim, reaching hands. Muna opened the packet, and a great round emerald, set in pearls on a gold ring, flashed green fire from her cupped hands.

'The Peacock Ring! He has sent me the ring he used to wear, look Khanum, from his own hand he has taken this ring, and had it made smaller for me! It is enough, life is kind, that I should have this pleasure – '

She bent her head over the ring, and Bianca went quietly away, pulling the curtains closed as she left. She wondered what she had done, but after seeing the joy on Muna's face, would not have changed anything. She would not cloud Muna's joy by telling her that the ring had been made smaller for Sara, and that she had pulled it from her finger, and sent it to Muna, with her love. She must have asked Kassim's permission first, because it was part of the Ruler's regalia – but apart from allowing her to send it to one so beloved by the whole family,

Kassim had nothing to do with it. Bianca shrugged off an uneasy thought that she was being disloyal to Sara. Muna deserved a little pleasure.

Leaving the curtained bed, it was as if she entered a different world. Talking to Muna, she had forgotten the wind. Now she realised that it was howling without pause, shrilling louder and louder, like an evil creature trying to get into the building where they sheltered. There were the homely smells of cooking, and there was a child crying, and two women arguing loudly together. Bianca was glad to hear such ordinary sounds, for the noise of the wind was terrifying. She found Bella pouring a cup of wine for Sagpurna, and asked for one for herself.

'What of the Dancer,' asked Sagpurna, 'Will she take some wine?'

'Later, I think. Now she is better alone. She rests.'

When Sagpurna called Muna 'the Dancer', it sounded like a title of respect, his voice held so much love and admiration when he said the words. Drinking her wine, Bianca looked about the room. Niroo and Jagoo were sitting a little to one side, with Chunia. The long day of struggle and fear showed in their faces, washed clean of all paint. They looked the children that they were – and these three had planned, and successfully carried through, Muna's rescue.

'Unbelievable!' Bianca murmured, and Sagpurna looked at them too, and nodded.

'Yes. How they were brave! They have always been my friends, the boys when we were all small, though I was older, they would often try to help me in any way they could. They will be important in my house always. I shall care for them as if they were my brothers. As for the girl – did you know that her mother came from the Dancer's town? She was trained in one of Muna's houses, and she trained her daughter. Chunia dances well, and is better in everything than any of the other girls that my mother had about the palace. She was virgin when she came to me, and I – well, I think she is still virgin. I think now, that I shall take her as my mistress. Then if she bears a son, well at least I shall know that the child was fathered by me, and I shall

293

marry her. I sometimes wonder who got me on my mother. There are not many sons in our family.'

'But Sagpurna – did you not know your father? No, of course you did not. You must have been a baby, or perhaps not even born, when he came to the north after his release from the British – ' Bianca stopped, embarrassed, but Sagpurna showed no distress.

'You mean after he was released from prison, where he was for nearly ten years after what he did during the troubles of '57? He was lucky to have his life. Yes, I was born after he died in the north.'

'Well, Rajasahib, I can assure you that you are his son. His eyes, his mouth, his very walk, and the way he turned his head – '

'You knew my father well?'

'Yes. I did. I knew him when he was a boy, and later when he came up to Madore to marry my dearest friend, she who died – and I met him again after his release from prison. Be thankful, Sagpurna that you have his looks, and not his nature.'

'Yes I see. You did not care for him.'

'No. In fact – ' Just in time, Bianca stopped herself. What good would it do to finish her sentence with the truth – 'I killed him. He was a monster of depravity, a devil in human form, the most evil man I have ever met.' What good? Nothing but disaster could come from that admission.

She turned away, and lifted her cup, and drank. Drinking himself, Sagpurna made a wry face. 'He appears to have been greatly hated by everyone, including the people of his own State. It is said that they mourned bitterly when my grandfather died, and Hardyal came to the gadi. But my mother must have felt something for him, even if it was only gratitude. She took the Dancer, because she said she knew that the Dancer had killed my father. Do you think that is true?'

'Oh *no*!' Bianca's cry was one of pure horror that Muna had borne the brunt of the Rani's vengeance for something that she herself had done, but Sagpurna only took it as a denial of Muna's involvement.

'I knew my mother was lying. But it would not have mattered. To kill my father, from all I hear, was a good and brave thing to have done.'

Bianca could only look at him in horror, because of what Muna had suffered on her behalf, and Bella quickly poured a cup of wine and gave it to Sagpurna, saying, 'Perhaps now the Raja would care to give the Sahiba some wine. She must be very thirsty still.'

Sagpurna took the wine eagerly, and walked over to the curtained bed. He spoke, received an answer, and parting the curtains went into the enclosed space around the bed, closing the curtains behind him. Bianca, shaking off the horror that his words had brought her, watched the curtains fall together behind him, and wondered in what state Muna would be. It would do her no harm to receive a little boyish adoration from Sagpurna. It could not be pleasant to lie alone with nothing but memories, while the wind screamed and tore at the walls of the room where you lay. What kind of a life could Muna have had with Alan, so that waking from a troubled dream she could ask that question about love? Had all the long years of her marriage never shown her what love was? Bianca tried to remember Alan, and recalled his shy diffidence, his courage – and the fact that in spite of jealousy, Kassim had liked Alan, had been his friend. In the middle of the roaring chaos of the room of the dome, Bianca sat wondering why Alan had not been able to expunge the memory of another man from his wife's mind – and knew in her heart that if she had not married Sher Khan, no other man would have truly filled her life – and asked herself no more questions.

26

Bella was sitting aside with Ayub Khan, sharing his cup of wine. Bianca, stepping round the many groups of people who sat together, each family keeping to their own little piece of floor, felt her own solitariness as she went over to join them. To be a woman alone at such a time; Bianca knew that half her terror came from the thought that she might never see Sher Khan again. Bella and Ayub Khan stood up as she came to them, but she sat on the floor, begging them to sit with her.

'Please, Bella, my cup is empty – forgive me for intruding, but I am not able to sit alone.'

Replenishing Bianca's cup, Bella nodded. 'This is not a time to be alone – what a fearsome thing that wind is!'

'Do not think of it Bella. Let us talk instead.'

Bianca lifted her cup and drank deeply, and then looked in surprise at the cup in Ayub Khan's hand. 'Wine, Ayub? I thought your beliefs were against the drinking of wine?'

Ayub smiled in answer to the half smile on Bianca's lips. 'Khanum, thou knowest. Like all of us in Lambagh, we have many habits that others, outside our Valley, do not share. It is our gain, that we live in such a place.'

Bianca smiled fully then, smiled with the affection that she felt for the big man showing on her face. He reminded her so much of his father, that brave man Shaibani Khan, who had died at the old Ruler's side. She realised, suddenly, that she was in fact sitting beside a member of the Lambagh family, for Shaibani Khan had been the old ruler's half-brother, the son of a Palace favourite, and Ayub Khan was therefore a blood relation of Sher Khan, and of Kassim. She felt less isolated at once, but sighed, thinking how far they were from their beautiful peaceful Valley. The wind was screaming like a thousand devils, and the building seemed to shake with each gust. Everyone had to shout to be heard, the noise inside and out was terrible.

Bianca looked at Bella and shrugged, then put her lips close to the other woman's ear and said, 'Will we come alive from this, Bella?'

'It seems impossible, but it is something that they all take for granted hereabouts. It happens every second or third year, so the people from the shore village tell me. There is one of their women over there, in labour with her fifth child. She says that only one of them was not born in a great wind.'

To have a child in such conditions! Bianca looked her horror at Bella who nodded.

'Aye. Terrible, is it not? But they have the village midwife here. The women think nothing of it, nor does the mother herself, but she will only have this one child, if it survives. Starvation or sickness took all the other four.'

Bianca looked at the villagers, and at the townspeople, and saw with clear eyes suddenly, saw what she had been too occupied to notice before. She saw skeleton thin bodies, hollow cheeks, deepset eyes in young faces. Hunger, long-accustomed hunger, looked at her. She thought of the people of the Valley with their firm-fleshed bodies and muscular arms and legs, their laughing, rosy-cheeked children, the filled granaries, the good strong cattle. Her heart burned with pride in her husband and his family, Rulers who had cared for their people, who built a fine race, and did not only think of making wealth for themselves. It was obvious that the people of Sagpur had not been guarded, or guided. They had been exploited by a degenerate Raja and his wife. She thanked the powers of heaven that Hardyal had never got a hold on Lambagh, in spite of all his efforts; and then remembered that from one of this family, Kurmilla, had come her own adored step-daughter Sara; and now, the present Raja, Sagpurna, did not appear to be all bad, although he was still so young that he could become anything.

She was roused from her thoughts by a cry. It was an unmistakable cry, the voice of a new-born child. Thin, wavering, disconsolate, the sound rose above all the other noise in the room, and even conquered the scream of the wind for a moment, as if the new soul voiced its defiance to the world. Even at this time of crisis and fear, women's faces softened, heads turned to the corner where the mother lay, and men muttered a blessing or a prayer.

Bella had been over to the birthing. 'It is a boy,' she said. 'God take care of him.'

Bianca nodded, thinking that she would try and ensure that at least this child grew up to manhood. She would speak to Sagpurna, tell him of the deaths of the woman's other children, give the parents some money – anything that would make it more possible for the child to live, out of all the hundreds that must die every month in this neglected part of the country. Just to save one child would be something.

But at present it did not look as if anyone would survive. Ayub Khan had brought their horses into the room of the dome. It seemed that the outside wall was going; above the scream of the wind came the sound of crashing masonry. The people in the room drew closer together and Bianca went over to Muna's bed, and joined Sagpurna. Slowly the rest of their party gathered round them. Chunia and the two boys, Niroo and Jagoo, Bella and Ayub Khan, and Kullunder Khan. Everyone was tense, waiting for something – what? The wind rose higher and ended its screaming. Instead, the air was full of the sound of a long, low moaning, a dreadful sound. Sagpurna looked towards the door, closed and barred, but bending inwards with the force of the wind.

'We must put everything we can against that door!'

People hurried to put bags and bundles against the door, until it was hidden behind a pile of their possessions. The moaning was loud, louder than the sound of the wind had been before. Bianca felt a terrible fear rising in her, a panic that brought sweat to shine on her skin. This would be a terrible place to die, far from her home in Madore and the loving safety

298

of Sher Khan's arms. She turned her head, and saw Muna looking at her, and felt ashamed. Muna too was far from everything she loved, and was showing no fear, and Bianca took hold of herself, and smiled at Muna.

'How much longer will this last, Rajasahib – or is this your first cyclone, as it is mine?' Bianca saw that Sagpurna appeared as unafraid as Muna, and his voice was steady as he answered.

'When that moaning sound begins, the wind is about to turn. There will be a very short, quiet period, which is the eye of the storm, then the wind will blow from another direction; let us hope that, as always in the past, this place will stand, and save those of us who are here.'

For the first time, Bianca realised that although the room was crowded, only a fraction of Sagpurna's people were here. Left behind, built close to the sea, was a whole city. She imagined what Sher Khan would feel if all his people were in danger, while he himself was safe, and her voice was sharper than she intended when she said, 'What of Sagpur – what will have happened to the people of the city?'

'Oh, they ran long before we did. They will be inland, in better places than this, watching the sea from towers. *This* place has always been the refuge of those who left last. There is a Palace built ten miles from here, inland. My family always went there when the warning came. I expect that during the four days when I was drugged, and my mother thought to take full power for ever, the warning came, and she was too busy to heed it.'

'What is the warning?'

'Always, old men – several of them – at this season go to certain points where it is possible to watch the weather and the tides. They are men who have lived through many such winds, and they know the signs to look for. They give warning when they see certain movements of the clouds and the waves and the birds – I do not know their lore, but they are never wrong. When they send a warning, the city empties, and the Palace. The people of the shore, the fisher-folk, seldom heed the warning; taking their living from the sea, they have no fear of it and they go last of all. The people of the city will be safe, and perhaps they will have saved most of their wealth too. But this time, nothing will have been saved from the Palace. We brought only one treasure with us, but that was worth all the rest.'

Bianca, who had been straining her ears to listen to him, found it was no longer necessary. She could hear him easily, the wind was dropping.

'Rajasahib – the wind! The wind has stopped. Perhaps we will be able to leave here.'

'No, there is no chance yet.' Sagpurna's face in the dim light was yellow, and glistened with sweat. Bianca knew that he must be feeling the effects of four days of drugging and debauchery, but he still spoke steadily. 'The wind will drop altogether, I told you it would. But we dare not go, for after the wind it will be the sea we must fear. Niroo, see if the tower still stands – the steps are there, under that arch.'

There was a low arch, and as Niroo went over to it, taking the precious lantern, Bianca could see that behind the arch there were stairs. Niroo came back to say that the tower was still complete, but that the stairs were very unsafe.

'Well, that tower is the oldest part of this building. It must be over two hundred years old, and was built by people who knew the country and the sea, and took refuge here when they had to. I want a man up in that tower to tell me what the sea does.'

As if they were islanded together in that sea of noise and disorder, while Bella brought water for Muna to sponge her face and clean herself a little, Bianca and Sagpurna talked to each other. She was astonished at the knowledge that he displayed, both about his State and about this extraordinary place where they were sheltering. Perhaps her voice had been condescending, but Sagpurna turned suddenly to look at her, and answered her with anger.

'I am despised. I am despised by all of you, I understand that. All of you except the Dancer. Do not imagine that tales of the Lambagh family have not been told to me. I have heard that they are arrogant and high-handed, and that my father was cheated of his right to Lambagh State by your husband, and his nephew. I can see that you think it is fortunate that none of my family can ever take Lambagh, and I can see that you are surprised that I am not screaming with fear in a corner, or drugged into insensibility.

'You have reason, no doubt, to feel all this, but you forget one person, whose blood I have in my veins. You have forgotten my grandfather, who was a man of honour and was a close friend of the old Ruler of Lambagh. I have always dreamed, when my mother had not drugged me to make me look a fool, I have always dreamed of being a Raja like my grandfather was — a man who cared for his people, a man beloved and admired, not a laughing stock, a dressed doll who spoke no words that were not put into his mouth — this was what my mother was making of me. But then the Dancer spoke with me, and I have changed. I will be like that good old man. I am not only my mother's son, I am the old man's grandson. I shall never forget that now — nor shall I ever cease to think of the Dancer with love.' His eyes were full of tears, and Bianca knew that he would never forgive himself or her if she noticed them. She spoke quickly.

'So, for that reason, because of your grandfather, you have learned so much about your State?'

Gratefully Sagpurna, his face turned away, took up the conversation again.

'Yes. Because I wanted to be like him, I learned everything I could. I know the strength of my army, and I also know what it could be if money had not been thrown away on other things by my mother. I know the farms, and the land laws, the property that has been unlawfully appropriated by creatures of the Rani. I know the city and its loyalties, its riches, the bankers and the moneylenders. I know the need for law and order, for men to be paid enough to keep them honest. I know the climate, and the weather, and I love my State, as Sher Khan Bahadur and Kassim Khan love Lambagh. You will hear of me, Begum Sahiba — wait, and you will hear good news of my State one day, you Rulers of the north. The south can be powerful too —'

'Powerful, and friendly too, I hope, Rajasahib?'

'Friendly? To the country that produced such a one as the Dancer? It should not be too hard for my State to be friendly to yours while I am alive at least! Begum Sahiba, you are very patient. At such a time, I have thrown words at you until you must be deaf. But at least you have not thought about the cyclone! Now I will see what my man in the tower has to say, and leave you in peace.'

To be in peace in the room of the dome seemed an impossible thought, but indeed, there was peace of a sort. There was complete silence outside, and it was eerie after all the noise that they had endured.

There was a sudden cry from the tower.

'The sea! The sea has drawn back very far, beyond the rocks. The rocks of Janta are showing clearly.'

The people, both the city dwellers, and the courtiers in their tattered silks, and the villagers, were tearing the bags and bundles away from the door. Once it was free, they opened it. Everyone moved towards it, and then they stood, out in the open, staring, stunned and disbelieving.

There was an extraordinary light in the sky, which was the colour of lead, and the air smelled of rotten meat.

'The smell of death,' said an old fisherman. 'This is the smell of all that has died in the deep sea, and now lies uncovered and rotting. When the sea comes back – '

'When the sea returns, are we high enough to be safe?' Sagpurna asked the question that was in all their minds. The old man who had spoken went over to three iron columns that, sunk in stone, still stood above the rubble of the outer wall. He stretched up to a mark on the central pillar.

'It was here, Heavenborn. This was the highest place that the water reached the last time the rocks of Janta were uncovered. I was a young man then, but I can remember. The room of the dome was safe then, but in those days the wall was sound. Now the place is not so strong. The outer wall has never fallen before, and the walls of the place were not repaired during the Rani's time. We are in the hands of the Gods, Heavenborn.'

Sagpurna, at the mention of the Rani, had turned away, his face bitter. He looked at Bianca, and then shrugged.

'You see? As I told you. Money that should have been used for things like this, was taken for other purposes. And now we face the dangers of the sea and the wind, in a place that was not kept sound.'

His eyes went beyond Bianca, and from the expression on his face she knew who was standing beside her. Muna. As if the sight of her had spurred him into action, Sagpurna turned and called to a group of his own men who were standing not far away.

'We must go and find another place of safety. This may continue for days. I need ten men to come with me.'

'Can we not all go from here now?' Muna, Bella and Bianca were all agreed that anywhere would be better than staying in the room of the dome.

'No. When the sea comes back – no, you *must* stay here. It is not very safe, but it is better than being in the open. I will try to reach Durgapur, where your husband is, Ayub tells me. If I get there, I will come back with him, and more men and fresh horses, and we will all get to a safer place. Until then, Dancer – '

He looked at Muna, and Bianca thought, 'But he does not expect to reach safety,' and on the thought heard the old fisherman say, 'Maharaj – do not go. The sea will come very fast. You do not ride to safety, Maharaj, you ride to certain death.'

'Only one thing is certain, old man: Have you a son?'

'Yea, lord. The man in the tower is my son.'

'Then listen carefully. If the waters broach the walls, the Dancer is to go up into the tower. If any harm comes to her, I will take your son and garrotte him in front of your eyes. It is understood?' The old man's face remained impassive.

'It is understood, lord.'

'Good.' Sagpurna turned again to Muna. 'Dancer, you heard? If, while I am gone, the waters enter this room, you are to go into the tower. There is only room for one person, but you will be safe there.' In a lower voice, leaning close to her he said, 'Let the whole world perish, Dancer, if you live.'

'I would be very lonely, Rajasahib – ' but Sagpurna had taken her hand and pressed it to his mouth, and turned away.

The old fisherman called to Sagpurna. 'Lord, if you wish to go, go now, go fast. The wind is sounding again.'

Indeed, they could hear the wind, far away like an echo inside a drum; they heard a deep sigh, and under it, very faint as yet, the terrible moaning. The old fisherman cocked his head, listening, and then began to shout directions to his people, and his raised voice was frightening with the strange sighing sound as a background to his shouts.

Bianca was watching Sagpurna. In spite of his height and his build which, although he was so young, promised to be as splendid as his father's, he looked haggard and unhealthy, his dissolute life already clearly marked on his face. But he was certainly no coward. Swiftly he chose from among his people ten men to come with him, picking them out with his eyes and a lift of his hand and being instantly obeyed. Jewels still gleaming on their torn, stained silks, they were slight, light-boned men, their eyes heavily outlined in kohl like the eyes of beautiful women; when Bianca looked into the painted eyes, she saw that they were calm and resolute. They handled their curved swords with ease and assurance. These were trained fighting men, who would give a good account of themselves in an emergency.

As the last man moved forward, Ayub Khan joined the group, his face grim. Sagpurna looked at him with raised eyebrows.

'I know the road to Durgapur. Let me go, Rajasahib. We owe you a life – '

'And what about us here? What happens to us?' Bella's voice, interrupting, was broken with fury. 'You go swaggering off to be killed somewhere, and leave us to die alone here? Where is your duty to the Begum Sahiba? And to the Sahiba?' She was shaking with what might have been anger, and her eyes, full of tears, burned like the eyes of a cat caught by lamplight in the dark.

Ayub Khan stood confounded, and Sagpurna put a hand on his arm.

'Ayub Khan, you and your people owe me nothing. I owe the Dancer my life and my kingdom. It is hard to stay with the women and children when there is action in the open, I know. But this is your duty – no?'

Ayub stepped back. 'Ay, Rajasahib. I forgot myself. As you say. And may Allah the all powerful protect you.'

'Lord – go *now*.' The old fisherman's voice was peremptory.

Sagpurna turned away without another word, or look, swung himself up into the saddle of the horse held ready for him, and with his men on foot behind him, rode away into the rubble and confusion beyond the broken wall.

The air outside was so foul that Bianca and Muna turned away from the toiling people, and went back into the room of the dome. The room was almost empty, as all who were strong enough were filling cloths with earth, to pile against the door and the walls, and the men were collecting rocks and carrying them in.

Bella was on the far side of the room, standing half turned away from Ayub, who was talking earnestly to her. Presently he shrugged, and went away to join the others who were strengthening the walls as well as they could. Bianca and Muna sank down together on to Sagpurna's bed, and looked at each other.

'Let us build pictures of words for each other again, Muna. I do not like this place.' The inadequacy of her words made them both laugh suddenly.

Then Bianca said, 'I have never thought of hell – Gehenna – but now I think I know what it is like. Let us try to forget it. Tell me of your life in England, Muna.'

'It is hard for me to tell you. It is as unreal as the moon. I do not seem to be awake there, I dream. I dream away the days.'

'And yet, your son was born there, and lives there. So far away from you, Muna! Why? You could have brought him with you.'

Muna shook her head. 'No, I could not. It is his father's wish that he grows up to be an Englishman in every way. He thinks I do not know, but I do. He keeps me away, hoping that if I am not there, his son will become completely English.'

'And your wishes?'

'I have no wishes. None that can be fulfilled, except that I wish for the continuing health of all those who are dear to me. Feel no pity for me, Khanum. I am very well as I am. I chose my life.'

'I sometimes feel that it would have been better for you if you had never seen our family, Muna.'

'Would you take the very heart out of my life, Khanum? My life was entangled with yours, who knows how many lives ago? And if the Goddess is kind, I shall be close to you and your family through many lives to come. Ah, Khanum, do not weep! I am content. No woman can ask for more than I have!'

Bianca, who had asked for much more, and who, deprived of children of her own, still had the whole love of her worshipped husband, and the love of a stepdaughter, could only shake her head.

'And love?'

'Love? I hear the word very often.'

'Sagpurna said that you asked "What is love?".'

'Yes. I was still half-dazed; I asked that question of the wrong man. But now you will give me a truthful answer, I know. Sarah and Kassim. Do they ask "What is love"?'

'No, Muna. They do not need to. They are completely content. Kassim loves Sara as he has always done.'

'Yes. I remember how he waited for her to grow, like a gardener guarding a rare flower. They are fortunate. So. Let us be done with questions. Unless we ask each other, and everyone else, how and when we leave this place – if ever!'

To Bianca's amazement she was laughing, and seeing her laughing face, Bianca saw the young Muna again, and was reminded of what it was that she had to say to her, news that she had pushed to the back of her mind, and was now afraid to mention to this Muna, who was laughing in the face of danger and death.

Bianca looked round her at the disorderly room, heard the hellish scream of the wind rising again, and wondered how she could phrase what she had to say. At such a time, in such a place, to hear someone of great importance in your life, someone you had loved deeply and tenderly – to be told that this person was dead could be a killing shock. There was no way to break bad news gently. Muna's eyes looked into hers, and slowly, Muna nodded her head.

'I know what you would tell me, Khanum. Goki is dead. She did not return to the Valley, did she? Tell me only one thing. Where did she die?'

'In Madore. She was burned on the shore of the Kanti river, but she asked before she died that her ashes should be taken to the Madoremahal. They are scattered there, under the big fig tree, a few steps from where the old Ruler, her Master, fell beneath the sword of Hardyal.'

'The old Ruler, her Master, and her lover. She was fortunate. Her ashes lie where she wished them to lie. Her spirit will already be living again, and no doubt searching for her beloved. May their meeting not be long delayed, let her not have to search through many lives.' Muna's voice was very low, and it was difficult to hear beneath the screaming of the wind. Before she could say anything more, Bella came up with Jagoo, and cups of wine, and some dry bread. The moaning sound outside was very loud, but there seemed less power in it. Muna, drinking her wine thirstily, asked for Niroo.

'At the last minute he went with the Raja. Also Chunia went.'

'Chunia! But she would not be allowed – what was Sagpurna thinking of, to take her with him?'

'He did not know. She went in my clothes.' Then Muna noticed that his loin cloth was a twist of bright silk, part of Chunia's *sari*.

'But that is not enough to disguise her – a girl!'

'It was easy. She bound her breasts, and wore a shirt, and cut her hair to her shoulders. One of the village women helped her. She makes a personable boy,' said Jagoo and smiled.

'But *why*?'

'Ho, she is mad for Sagpurna. Always she loved him, from the time she was first sent in to him. If he is going to die when the sea comes back, she will die with him.'

When the sea comes back! Said so casually, it sounded ordinary, but Bianca shivered involuntarily, and then looking at Muna, saw that she was deathly pale, her forehead beaded with sweat.

'Muna! Here, put your head low! Jagoo, call Bella Sahiba back, and tell her to bring more wine, Muna is faint.'

'No, Khanum. I am not faint. I am afraid.' Muna spoke with difficulty, and her grip on Bianca's hand was painful. 'Khanum, it was that green water. The dark depths of that water, that stirred and moved into circles. I was so afraid, that now even the thought of rising water makes my heart stop.'

She drank her wine, the cup shaking in her hand, and then, with a mockery of her beautiful smile twisting her mouth, thanked Bella, and gave back the cup. 'I should be ashamed. We are all in the same danger. Is there someone in the tower, Jagoo?'

'Yes, Dancer, the son of the old fisherman. They are taking all the care that they can.'

They were indeed. The door and some of the weaker parts of the walls were strengthened with stones brought in from the broken wall outside; there were makeshift bags filled with earth against the door, and these were reinforced by all the bundles and boxes that could be collected, stuffed and jammed into the crevices.

'If only we could see. It is so horrible not being able to see what is happening outside.'

Bianca hated being closed in, but as she looked about her, she too, like Muna, felt ashamed of her fear, for she saw that on every side people were behaving as if there was no danger. Those of Sagpurna's soldiers that he had left behind were talking and laughing, polishing swords and daggers and their belts while they talked, as if the enemy they were expecting could be driven back by physical battle. The women of the village were cooking food, and feeding their children. Bianca remarked on how few children there were to Bella.

'Yes. They do not rear many. It is difficult for them to get enough to eat. True, the children of the fisher village feed better than the poor children of the city, but still – the children are very precious to everyone, but to these people they are miracles.'

Bianca and Bella both had the same thought in their minds – the young man in the tower, the old fisherman's only son, raised to manhood, and condemned to death if anything happened to Muna.

Shaking her head, Bella started to walk over towards the horses, where Ayub was standing, and without a word, Muna got up and followed her. Bianca saw them speaking together, arguing in fact, for Bella looked angry and distressed, and so did Ayub. Then Muna said something, and Ayub put his hand on Bella's arm, and Bella stopped speaking and looked up at him, listening to what he was saying, and Muna left them, and sat down on Sagpurna's bed. She sat there, pensively turning the great emerald on her finger, the ring that Kassim and Sara had sent her. On her other hand was a ruby that almost matched the emerald in size. These were the only two jewels that she wore. There were plain gold studs in her ears, the kind that women wore to keep the holes in pierced ears open. Bianca remembered that Muna's ears had already been pierced when Goki brought her, a frightened child, to Lambagh. Sara had instantly demanded that her ears be pierced, so that she could wear earstuds too – Sara, when shall I see you again? Bianca's sad dreaming was interrupted by a shout from the tower.

'The sea – the sea returns – '

In fact, the cry was unnecessary. The moan of the wind had grown less, or the other sound was so loud that it deadened the sound of the wind. The roar was far away, and yet it was deafening. It was a noise too elemental to describe; no one in the room of the dome was able to stand alone and listen to it.

With no word said, the people of all castes and stations in life moved close together, standing touching one another, humanity confronting the eternal enemy, stretching out for human contact in the face of annihilation.

The roar grew, surmounted bearable level, and was upon them. Water gushed through the walls and the door – it seemed that part of the roof caved in, and the foaming, tearing current was swirling and sucking waist-high in seconds, and rising. It was so sudden, that for a breath people stood gripping each other. It was the terrified squealing of the horses, tied to one side of the walls, that roused everyone to action. Mothers held their children high, at arms' stretch above their heads, trying to clamber on top of anything that would give them extra height. Ayub and Kullunder struggled through the rising water to set the horses free, and cut their hobbles. The fisher-folk, remembering Sagpurna's command, set up a clamour even in this extremity.

'The Dancer must go to the tower – '

Ayub Khan and Bella were beckoned over by Muna. She was standing close to Bianca, and as they came up, she joined in the cry, saying almost in Bianca's ear, 'Yes, take the Dancer to safety in the tower!'

As Bianca turned to look at her in astonishment, she saw that Muna had thrown off her green *sari*, and was standing, wearing nothing but her *choli* and a twist of cloth round her waist. Still crying, 'Take the Dancer to the tower!' she flung her green *sari* over Bianca's head. Bianca felt herself seized and dragged through the water, her protests smothered and disregarded. The man in the tower dragged her up the narrow stairs, tearing the flesh on her knees and arms in his haste – then, still gasping denials, Bianca found herself firmly closed into the tiny room at the top of the tower. She heard the door shut and barred before she had got her hands free of the entangling *sari* that Muna had thrown over her – clever Muna, who had seen a way to save Bianca, and had taken it. Bianca, after banging ineffectually on the door, turned to the open windows, unshuttered and unbarred, looked out, and was silenced.

Around, all around, was the sea. Flecked with froth, rippling with waves, the ocean had taken possession and was coming in slowly, slipping between the trees, stopping and rising, and then moving gently on; so gently that it was deceptive. She could see that, in fact, it was flooding in. Only a very small part of the mound on which the dome and tower stood was left. Trying to measure with her eyes the depth of the water, Bianca reckoned that it would be between six and seven feet deep. The fisher-folk were short people – she shuddered at the thought of what must be happening down in the room below. But the water did not seem to be rising – that rush of water that had poured in must have been the crest of the wave. She turned to look inland, and saw the water sliding on wherever she looked – quiet, fast, pushing obstacles out of its way. The speed of its movement was brought home to her as a flat board, part of a roof, pushed past with two bodies on it. The current must have been very strong, for the board with its motionless burden was out of her sight before she had time to see if the two on top were alive or dead. The wind was still rising, and she was forced to lie flat on the floor, arms and legs spread wide, clinging like a limpet with her entire body, she was so afraid of being blown out of the tower. Up here, with no walls between her and the noise, it was unbelievable. Her ears ached with the high shrilling, it seemed to contain a million voices all screaming together. It was blowing from the sea and Bianca, beaten and bruised by its sheer power, wondered if it would whip up another monster wave. She lay, unable to move, and sent her mind to where her heart was – to her peaceful house on the edge of the great lake outside Madore, searching in her memory through each room, looking for the man in whose arms she had found peace and safety so often. She imagined that she could hear the waters of the lake lapping gently on the shore, and that she was sitting in the garden, waiting for Sher Khan to return from a ride. Drenched, shivering and terrified, Bianca sent her thoughts as far from her beaten body as she could, and closing her mind to everything else, she found within her a measure of strength and tranquillity, and slept.

27

In the room of the dome, below the tower, the water had risen.
Thick and vile smelling, it moved in slow surges, splashing up
into frightened eyes, filling mouths, so that men and women
choked and, gasping for breath, cried out in fear to their Gods.
The night had come it seemed, for it was growing very dark,
and the wind, free to enter through the broken wall, howled
and screamed like terror made vocal.

Muna had to find more courage than all the others. So lately
released from four days of captivity and lonely fear, her nerves
were raw. With Bianca placed in comparative safety, Muna
began to feel that this new ordeal need not be faced. Courage
was a coinage that she had spent so freely in her life that now,
for herself, she had no more left. Death was not something that
she feared. The doorway to another life would not be hard for
her to open. But to try to go on living in terror – she had no
courage for that. It was easier to let go, to sink, breathe no
more, fear no more.

It was a child's voice that saved her. A boy's voice, breaking
with fear. 'Mother!' said the voice. 'Mother – oh Mother,
where are you? It is so dark and I have fear.'

He was the child of one of the people of the shore, but to
Muna his voice spoke to her heart, like the voice of her own
son, Rob, afraid of the dark. She had courage again, spirit and
body joined, and she was no longer ready for the release of
death.

The people of the shore, and of the city, as Bianca had

thought, were small in stature. The northerners had little trouble in keeping their heads above the flood. In Ayub's case, the water only reached his chest, and Kullunder Khan was tall also. They took the children from their parents – there were only seven children in all, including the new baby – and put them on the steps that led up to the tower. Broken and ruined as those steps were, they were still a safer refuge for the children than the shoulders of their parents who were finding it difficult to keep their feet as the water washed against them with force.

Muna called out in the darkness, her clear voice rising above the sound of the wind. 'Oh people of the shore! You who fish in the deep water for your daily food – what do you fear? This is only water, dirty maybe, but still water. You can all swim. Swim, then, and stay alive until the sea calls its waters back again.'

As the child's voice had broken the spell of Muna's fear, so her voice helped the people of the shore. They swam, and called out to each other, and the familiar actions, and the sound of their own voices, answering each to each, pushed back panic.

Ayub Khan, with Bella close beside him, collected the people of the city who could not all swim, and made them link arms, forming a living chain, with himself at one end keeping them all afloat. Kullunder Khan stayed with the terrified horses, and Jagoo perched on the steps, holding the new baby.

Among all the other voices, a hoarse old voice made itself heard.

'The waters are going – they are returning whence they came –'

More voices took up the cry, and then everyone was shouting in triumph, and the noise of the wind was drowned.

A pale dawn came in through the broken walls, and the water was only knee deep and draining away fast. The wind was gusting, first from one quarter and then from another, but it had less force. In the sickly light the people looked at each other, grey with cold, plastered with evil-smelling mud, exhausted, but alive, survivors of disaster.

Someone had oil. There was nothing dry, and yet, like

magic, a fire was made, from the torches that had been set in the iron sconces round the walls. They had been drenched with oil for so many years, that with a little trouble they caught a spark from the flint and steel that the headman of the fisher village produced. He had kept the implements for making precious fire perfectly dry by knotting them up in his long hair on top of his head. The flame flickered, rose higher, and steadied, and there was fire, and a little warmth.

Ayub climbed to the top of the tower and opened the door, and looked down at the Begum Bianca, asleep in a tumble of cream-coloured, mud-spattered robes, with an emerald *sari* for a pillow. She woke at once, and at the moment of waking was immediately enraged. She demanded to know if Muna was alive, and her face was warm and vivid with her anger. Ayub, astounded, stumbled downstairs, lashed into haste by her stinging words, and saw her stalk slowly over to the half naked figure of Muna, still recognisable in spite of the mud that coated her body, and her tangled, soaking hair.

Ayub went quickly to Bella. 'I know not why, green eyes, but the Khanum is very angered with Muna. I think you should go. When women fight, be they high or low, there is no place for a man.'

'They are not going to fight. The Khanum owes her life to Muna.'

'Many times over. But she is one who does not like to owe anything.'

Bianca's voice was as cold as the water in which they were standing. The fire, built on a broken pillar, reflected in her furious eyes, and Muna, looking up, was astonished.

'Khanum?'

'I thank you, Muna, for putting myself and my family into your debt once again.'

'There is no debt between us, Khanum! Am I not your child? Would a loving daughter not try to save a beloved mother?'

'No child of mine would try to save her mother's life at the expense of another's. Had you forgotten what Sagpurna threatened before he left? That young man who gave us warning

314

from the tower would have been brutally killed before his father's eyes if you had drowned. My nights would have been very peaceful had you died in my stead, and the young man because of you. But again – I thank you.'

'I understand now, Khanum.' Exhausted, chilled, and covered with mud and slime, Muna turned away. 'I understand many things. I am no child of yours in truth. Out of kindness, you and Sher Khan took me into your family. Out of love, I wished to know that you would be safe. I was stupid. But you have forgotten one thing, Khanum. Although I am not your child, I have the right to try and save your life. I took the vow, "My life for yours, now and forever". So. I have the right to risk anything, take any life, to save yours. Ayub Khan too – we are your people.'

In the face of Muna's obvious exhaustion, Bianca's sudden rage died away. Unexpectedly, another voice joined into their conversation. The old fisherman, looking as old as Time itself, spoke to Bianca.

'Begum from the north. You would have found us all dead if the Dancer had drowned. We would have all drowned together. The Raja's threat was but empty words. If one died, we all died. Do not be angered with one who saved you, and with her courage gave us the spirit to stay alive. I am an old man, and I have seen many of these winds, but never one so bad. We are all fortunate to be alive. Let us not cloud this joyful hour with anger.'

This joyful hour – Bianca looked round at the broken walls, the mud-covered people, the terrible wash of slime and mud that reached high up on the walls – this joyful hour! Starving, cold, battered, and only just out of the shadow of fear, these people still gave thanks for life. She was ashamed, and could not understand herself. She turned, with remorse, to Muna, but Muna was gone.

Bella, her eyes furious, her voice as cutting as Bianca's had been a few minutes earlier, pointed to the broken wall.

'You have broken a brave heart, Begum, crumbled it as that wall is crumbled. If the Sahiba becomes ill, it will be because of your unkind words. Better that you try to heal the wounds

315

you have inflicted – for if anything happens to the Sahiba, you will be greatly hated, I think.'

'Where is Muna?' Bianca was so distressed that she did not even notice the rage and scorn in Bella's voice.

'She has gone out. You will find her alone in the court outside.'

Once over the rubble and slime of the broken walls, Bianca found Muna gazing at desolation with tears making channels through the dirt on her face. She drew Muna into her arms, and rested her cheek on the tangled hair.

'Muna, I do not know what was wrong with me – except that I was afraid you were dead. As a mother, tormented with fear for her dear child, will rage at the child in relief when it is found safe, so I scolded you. I ask your forgiveness.'

'I am not your child, Khanum.'

'I have no child of my body, Muna. But I have two daughters of my heart. What do you think Sara would say to me, if she knew that I had wounded you so? Give me forgiveness, or my heart will break.'

Muna, who seldom wept in public, gave a single, strangled sob, and then had command of herself again, and was able to smile at Bianca. 'It is forgotten, Khanum – gone like the wind – '

It was true, at least, of the wind. It had died away, and the people were coming out of the room of the dome, carrying whatever they considered was worth saving. Kullunder Khan and Ayub led out the horses.

'The old man says that we should go from here – when the sun comes this place will be like a steam bath, and the steam carries illness with it.'

Ayub had approached the two women with caution. He was followed by Bella, whose eyes were as hard as stones when she looked at Bianca. Bianca, loved by everyone all her life, had never seen such an expression on anyone's face, and was distressed, and Muna saw her distress, and understood the cause. But Bella was her own mistress – her opinions were her own, and nothing would change her until she was ready to change.

Indeed, thought Muna, it will be good to get away from this place – a place of safety it may be, but there was no feeling of peace in it. She mounted the horse that Ayub held for her, Bianca and Bella mounted their animals, and they set off, a little, tattered army of people picking their way through the fallen or leaning trees, and the thick mud that the retreating waters had left behind. It was difficult travelling. The mud in places was two or three feet deep, and beneath it the trunks of the fallen palm trees made terrible traps. The horses had to be led every step of the way. The woman who had borne the baby would not ride – she laughed, and said that she would die of fright if she climbed on to one of the animals, so Bella carried her child, and the mother walked at her stirrup.

It took a very long time, the whole day and part of the night before they heard the sea again – the ordinary swish and whisper of waves on a peaceful shore. Through all their journey the smell of disaster and decay, the terrible smell of death, had been with them. Now, at last, a fresh breeze blew on them, and they could fill their lungs and breathe properly.

Muna had been very quiet all the journey. Now, as they reined in their horses, Bella who had been watching her anxiously, suddenly handed the baby to his mother, and dismounted, calling to Ayub as she did so. They reached Muna in time to catch her as her head fell forward and she slid from her horse's back. Bianca hurried to join them.

'What?'

'What would you think? She is not made of stone. She spent a night in the water, before that she was a prisoner with no hope, as far as she knew, of rescue, and then, in her weakness, she was beaten with harsh words. She has the fever again, and I hope we can get her safely out of this second bout. The last one nearly killed her.'

Muna was shivering and muttering, and Bella turned away from Bianca as if she was not there.

'Ayub – where can we take her? The house will be impossible, for it will be filthy, so close to the sea, it cannot have escaped damage. If only we could *see* – if only the morning would come.'

317

'Wait you, green eyes. The dawn will break. Until then, let us not be afraid. I will see what I can do – all these people love the Dancer.'

He had no need to give any orders, make any suggestions. Already the people exhausted as they were, were gathering what driftwood they could from the slime and wrack on the beach, the precious dregs of oil were brought out, the headman knelt with his flint and steel, and a little dry tinder, and a fire was started. By its flickering light, they made a pallet bed for Muna, using all the dry clothes they had, the clothes from their own bodies, stripping themselves for her. She was put close to the fire; and still she shivered and moaned and tossed. Bianca lay down beside her on the bed of stinking rags and took her into her arms to try and warm her ice-cold body with her own warmth, and then from one minute to the next, Muna began to burn with fever. Bella mixed her special draught of quinine and herbs and a little wine, and forced it between Muna's teeth, and Muna vomited it all up, and then Bella made her swallow some more – and still the fever mounted. Bella found Bianca a willing and skilled helper, and forgot all her animosity when she saw Bianca's desperate anxiety. But nothing seemed to stop the fire that was now consuming Muna with more heat than the flickering flames of the fire they had lit on the sands.

The sky paled. Over the storm-beaten land, over the Gulabmahal, the dawn came flooding in, as peaceful as the reflecting sea. Muna's face was grey, and Bianca, in tears, was certain she was dying. Ayub had taken a team of men and women to the Gulabmahal, and by mid-morning one room was cleared and cleaned, and as dry as possible. The sun was burning from a clear blue sky, and it was a relief to carry Muna indoors.

Water was now a difficulty. The well in the courtyard that they had always used, once full of sweet water, now stank. Bella began to despair, but the fisher-people said that there was a spring behind the shrine – the shrine that Muna had been used to visit daily.

'Perhaps her Goddess will save her yet again,' said Bella.

Several of the fishermen went to the shrine, and brought

earthenware pots of water back, and Bella perforce had to use it, unboiled and unfiltered. There was nothing else – not even a drop of wine.

On the sandy spit beyond the town, Sagpurna's Palace stood, like a paper cut-out against the sky and the sea. The sea, now in its proper and appointed place, washed against the rocks on which the paper Palace stood, and birds hung and hovered above it in the clear sky.

'Strange – I do not recall that those rocks could be seen before. I think that the Palace is broken in some way.' Ayub was staring under his hand at the distant white glitter.

'No loss if it sank beneath the sea,' said Bella. 'Ayub – wait! I am wrong. Perhaps that accursed place can help us after all. Send some men there – it is possible that there is wine, or clean food still there – what do you think?'

The men sent to the Palace came back full of awe. The seaward side of the building was gone, they said, swept away; there was a great gaping cavern under the Palace, where the sea rushed in and out – and the Palace had been looted. There was nothing. So, thought Bianca, the Pool of the Women is no more. Never again would a Rani of Sagpur have to take that terrible journey.

She looked at the white froth of waves beating on the distant rocks, and then turned back to the room where Muna tossed and burned in a fever that seemed to be taking her life from her. To have survived so much, and to die in this cruel internal fire – Bianca found herself praying to the voice that had aided her on two occasions. 'Save her,' she prayed, 'she has suffered for us all and she belongs to you – you save her – ' Her words were silent, spoken in her mind, as she knelt to take Muna's hand, a burning hand that seemed to be all bones. Her prayer was forced from her, and left her weak, as if power had gone out of her, as if she had just completed some terrible, physical effort. She knelt, breathless beside Muna, and waited. But there was, this time, no answer. No voice spoke in her heart. Only the tumbling splashing waves, and the whispering of the casuarina trees. The image in the corner had been cleaned of the mud and filth that had covered it – but to Bianca, it remained only a block of stone. She held Muna's hand and wept, and Bella came, and took her out of the room, and told her to rest – 'For there is nothing we can do for her now but wait. If the fever is going to break, it will break tomorrow – and if it does not, then she will certainly die. But our tears and words will avail her nothing, Begum Bianca, and it will not help anyone if you become ill too. So rest.'

Bianca sat on the roof of the Gulabmahal, and stared at the sparkling, dancing waves with eyes that saw nothing but Muna's grey, emaciated face; to her the tossing waves were only a reminder of Muna, tossing in fever.

But in the morning Bella ran, like a girl, up the steps to call her, and she did not have to say anything, her news was carried in her smile, in her glowing eyes. Muna's fever had broken. She lay, white as bone, thin as bone, but alive and conscious.

It was thus that Alan found her, Alan riding up the road with a company of his men, and a palanquin, and clean dry clothes, and food and wine – and also angry enquiries as to why Muna had not been brought straight to Durgapur before the hurricane struck. Bianca, her voice trembling, told him that Muna had nearly died, and Alan walked into Muna's room without another word, while Sagpurna who had come with him, seized Bianca's arm and said, 'What has happened? What do you mean, she nearly died? What harm came to her? I *said* I would kill – '

'Oh be silent, you foolish boy! Kill who? The fever? You have such power – are you a God to talk of killing illness? Think a little. Are you the Ruler of your people, or a monster like your father, I wonder. Do you imagine that this is how the Rulers of Lambagh behave?'

'Always that comparison,' said Sagpurna, 'always I am to be compared with the perfection of the Rulers of Lambagh, who appear to have all been inhuman in their perfection. I grow weary of hearing of such unbelievably perfect men. No, I am sure they would die themselves before they would dream of killing a solitary untouchable. They have years of power and wisdom behind them. I on the other hand am just starting on the long road to becoming a good Ruler. I have little power, and must still learn to use it – or so the Colonel Sahib tells me. But I meant what I said. If harm had come to the Dancer through any negligence of my people, they would have paid. I have learned to be a man of my word at least. I was born too late to do anything for the Dancer but love her with all my heart – I would kill to save her life.'

'Killing does not help sickness, Maharaja.'

'No? We have a Goddess here, who delights in sacrifice – perhaps she would accept blood instead of Muna's life?'

'You speak wildly,' said Bianca, terrified suddenly of this strange young man, remembering all his background and his upbringing. Surely he would not carry out his threat of killing the shore people because Muna was ill? He saw the fear on her face, and it was as if he suddenly came to his senses.

'Forgive me Begum – you are right. I spoke like a madman, but only because I was in grief. Do not worry about the people of the shore, the fisher-folk. I know they would not wish harm to one who is in the hand of their Goddess. I give you my promise – I shall try with all my heart to be a good and just Ruler, because of Muna and her life.'

He looked around at the spoiled courtyard where Muna had left so much beauty; at the choked fountain, at the slime-encrusted white walls, the dying orange trees. 'This house is not going to be good for her for many days. Perhaps the Palace –'

'The Palace! You had better go and look at the Palace. The sea has not stayed out of your Palace, any more than it stayed away from here. Half your Palace is gone – on the ocean side. There will be no shelter for Muna there. In any case, Sagpurna, do you think that Muna would be happy to re-enter your Palace?'

'You are, of course, right. It can have nothing but horror for her – though I have memories of her there that I shall treasure all my life.'

He looked over at his white Palace, and his expression made him look old and tired – an old, tired man at seventeen – or was he even younger than that, wondered Bianca, watching him. She averted her eyes quickly from his face when he looked

21

down at her, for she was sure he did not want to let her see how uncertain and distressed he was.

'Well, as you say, the Palace is unsuitable. So is this house – but I can do nothing. She has a husband: no doubt he will have plans for her – in fact, some of them I have already been told, to my sorrow.'

Alan disclosed some of his plans to Bianca immediately, coming swiftly from Muna's room, and beginning to give orders before he was properly outside. They were all to return to Durgapur. This was the place on the other side of the spit of land that was Sagpur, and had been unaffected by the disaster. The little pavilion where Muna had lived after the cholera camp was clean, and swept by warm sea breezes. As soon as he had made sure that Muna would stand the journey, Alan carried her out himself, and put her in the palanquin he had brought, and gave orders that she was to be taken to the pavilion at once, accompanied by Bella and the soldiers he had brought with him. He would follow as soon as he had been into the city and examined the state of the Fort, if indeed it still stood. He would only need four men – the rest were to go with Muna.

Sagpurna, when he saw Muna carried out, stood staring, horrified at her looks. Pale, shrunken, she looked twenty years older, had turned, it seemed, into an old woman since he had last seen her. Even the ordeal by the Pool of Women had not changed her so much. He went over to the palanquin and knelt beside it, and he had tears on his face.

'My country has killed you, Dancer.'

'Not so, Maharaj. I am better. It is a fever, not your country. And your people were my saviours, do not forget that.'

'I have already been read a lecture by the Begum Bianca. Are you going to scold me too, when we have so little time?'

'So little time – ' repeated Muna softly, 'So little time – but time stretches, a long, endless cord.'

'May it be a cord of gold for you, Dancer. So you will not scold me – that is good. What will you say to me?'

'I shall thank you for saving my life. But how can I thank

322

you? There is nothing I can say, except that I will not forget – I owe you a life, Maharaj.'

'I owe you my manhood, and my kingdom, Dancer. The debt is paid, twice over. Remember me, keep me in your mind, that will be a reward richer than anything you can imagine. I will marry now, Dancer.'

'Marry?'

'Yes. I marry her – the girl who followed me into what she thought was death and she did it for love, not gain. It is good that she should be one of your people. Chunia – come.'

No one could have recognised the Palace dancer in the figure that came forward at Sagpurna's call. Chunia, her face bare of paint, her hair raggedly cut to her shoulders, was still dressed as a boy, and indeed, looked like one. But her eyes were full of love when she looked at Sagpurna, and Bianca heard Muna laugh for the first time since her fever.

'Ay, Chunia! Are you a boy, or a girl? I did not think you could ever look thus. What have you done with your breasts, and your gentle thighs? Maharaj, you have a figure here, like the figures on the old Temples – one who can pleasure both a lover of men, and a lover of women! Nay, child, do not hang your head. You are a brave girl, and should be proud. Lord, you gave me a rich gift in your Palace. Will you allow me to give it, with my love, to the one you will raise to be the mother of your sons? Let it be a pledge of friendship between us – I need no jewels to remind me of all that I owe to you – my life itself.'

Muna took the great ruby from her skeleton thin fingers and held it out to Chunia, who took it after a nod from Sagpurna. She put it to her lips, and then slipped it on to her finger where it burned in scarlet contrast to the green fire of the emerald ring that Muna wore. Chunia reached out and took Muna's hand, and raised it to her forehead. 'I say to you, Rose of Madore, the old words. My life for yours, now and forever.'

'Chunia! Hush! What do you say? That oath is for the Ruler and those of his blood only – thou knowest.'

'I know. But are you not of the blood?'

'I am not.'

'There were tales. I heard the women talking. The woman, your mother, came from Lambagh. It was said –'

Sagpurna was listening so intently that his concentration on her words halted Chunia in mid-speech; she looked frightened.

'Say on, Chunia – I listen. What said the women?'

'Lord – it was said by all, that the mother of the Dancer was a daughter under the rose of the Ruler – a daughter of his old age by one of the Palace women. I know not – but that was what I heard.'

Sagpurna raised his eyebrows at Muna. 'So – you are of the blood! Not only by adoption!'

'It is said. How many bazaar rumours have we heard, Sagpurna – or will have heard, when you are older. Forget this story; it means nothing but talk to fill an idle hour. I was taken by the Ruler as his daughter because he had a large heart, and his own daughter loved me. So – Chunia, forget all the stories. Yes?'

'Rose of Madore – I have forgotten. Go in health.'

'And you, Chuniabhen. Bear many sons for Sagpurna, and find great happiness. Do not be a boy too long. Grow your beautiful hair, and please your lord's eyes with the beauty and skills of womanhood.'

Chunia understood. She looked into Muna's smiling eyes, nodded, and stood back. As Muna's palanquin was raised, Niroo and Jagoo ran forward to say farewell. They are all behaving as if they will never see her again, thought Bianca, and felt a cold hand touch her heart. Sagpurna walked beside the palanquin for a little way – then he stood aside and Muna was carried out of his sight, Bella riding slowly beside her.

Bianca watched how he stared after their vanishing figures, and then went up to him. 'She is coming back – and Durgapur is not so far away. You can visit her there.'

'Are you blind, Begum Sahiba? I will never visit her there. I will never see the Dancer again.'

'What do you mean?' Cold fear was spreading through Bianca's mind.

'I mean that this country is not good for her. She will go from here, and she will never return. She will go to her husband's home, over the black water again.'

'How do you know?'

'Her husband told me. He is a man of such fortune, to have the Dancer as his close companion. We are the empty vessels, the people with whom she does not stay.'

Chunia had come up to stand beside him. She did not look at Bianca, but put out the hand that wore the ruby to touch Sagpurna's arm. He turned to her as a man waking from a dream turns to reality – not the lovely starlight of the dream, but the light of day, in which he must live.

'Come then, my girl,' he said, 'Come. We will go and see what is left of the Palace, and begin life together. Begum Sahiba, you are going to Durgapur. Remember, if there is anything I can do, send to me. I am your servant. If I were of the blood, I would say to you the oath, "My life for yours", but as it is, I say it only in my heart.'

While he was still speaking, Chunia walked away, saying no farewell to Bianca. Sagpurna looked after her in surprise. 'Forgive her manners, Begum Sahiba, she has much to learn. I go – do not forget. If you need me, send for me.'

Bianca saw him mount his horse, and ride away, his figure growing small in the distance as he cantered down the long curve of the sands towards the city.

When the servants had collected together the things that were saved from the wreck of the Gulabmahal, and had loaded them on to pack horses, Ayub Khan came to Bianca to ask if she was ready to leave.

'I am ready. But tell me something, Ayub, before I go. Why did Chunia walk away from me in that fashion, as if she could not bear to rest her eyes on me another minute – also the two boys, Niroo and Jagoo went the same way, with no farewell or salutation. Did you see this? Yes? Then tell me, why?'

'Khanum, they be people of the Temples, worshippers of Muna's Goddess, dancers and makers of music, and Muna is the greatest of them. They hold her very dear.'

'I see. They heard me speak to Muna – or Jagoo heard me, when I was so foolishly angered, and he told the others, and

325

they think I caused her to become ill?' Ayub bowed his head.

'And you, Ayub – do you blame me for her illness also?'

'There is nothing for me to blame, or praise, Khanum. I am your man. My life is yours, Heavenborn. I took the oath.'

'Could distress have caused that fever? If it is possible, then my debt is very great.'

'Munabhen would be sad to hear you speak of debt, Khanum. She looks on Lambagh as her country, and thought of you as part of her life, close to her heart. Our lives, she says, are forever intermingled. She feels no debt between you. She would give her life for any member of the Lambagh family as easily and willingly as any of us would. Do not vex yourself, Khanum. We have all looked death in the face. Let us now follow Munabhen to Durgapur, with no more delay, and forget these things that in the face of death are of no importance.'

Bianca, riding with her retinue of men and packhorses inland towards the other side of the bay, watched how Ayub rode, now dropping back, now riding fast ahead, and knew that he sensed danger. No doubt he feared that Chunia would tell the story, told to her by Jagoo, to Sagpurna, and Sagpurna would want vengeance on anyone who hurt the Dancer. Bianca, riding along the rough road, where the mud banks left by the retreating flood were still wet and squelching, knew that for her own sake she would never be able to return to Sagpur, as long as the head of the State and his Rani thought that she had harmed Muna. She rode on in a mood as bleak as her surroundings, while Ayub Khan kept ceaseless guard.

28

In the little marble pavilion, beside the sounding Indian Ocean, Muna recovered her strength slowly. Bianca was astonished at the care lavished on her by the regiment. Every day, fruit and vegetables were brought, and fresh eggs. Bella cooked everything that Muna ate or drank. She was strictly vegetarian, Bianca noticed. Had she always been so?

Questioned, Muna smiled, 'No, I ate as I chose. We be casteless, you know. But now I keep the laws of caste in gratitude to the Goddess for my rescue from that terrible place and for supporting me when I was there.'

'She did more than that.'

Muna turned a puzzled face, 'What do you mean?'

'She told me where you were.'

'What! She spoke to you?'

Bianca nodded, and told of the distant, chiming voice that had reminded her of the Pool of the Women. Muna looked at her in deep amazement, nodding when Bianca said, 'It was not speech – it was something that I felt – I cannot explain.'

'I know,' said Muna, 'She speaks to the spirit and the spirit hears. You are far on your journey, Khanum, if you, from a strange land, hear the Goddess's voice.'

'From no strange land, Muna! I am of this country, heart and soul, and have never wished for anything else – '

Muna nodded, 'That is true. And you gave her a sacrifice – yes, you are of her people, even though you do not know it.' She looked at Bianca and smiled suddenly.

327

'You are very beautiful, Khanum; had you entered my profession, you would have been very famous. I think they would have called you "the Silver Dancer". And Rajas would have put their jewels at your feet. But you have better things.'

'And you, Muna – you are not a dancer now! You are a wife and a mother.'

'A wife and a mother – ' said Muna, thoughtfully, her eyes looking over the sea. 'Yes – I am a wife and a mother, and a stranger – unlike you. I am a stranger everywhere now.'

There was nothing Bianca could think of saying, Muna had not seen her son for nearly ten years. Muna appeared to be a very lonely and a very sad woman.

But Bella said firmly, 'A stranger? What blether is this, Sahiba – when, wherever you go, you leave a memory, and men speak of you with kindness – from the north of India, all the way across the seas to England, you are known – and beloved.'

As if conjured up by her words, two young men were calling from the foot of the pavilion steps. They were the adjutant and a young ensign, and they came in carrying a big bunch of scarlet bougainvillaea and orange marigolds.

'Forgive the colour scheme, Mrs. Reid – it is a trifle bright, I fear,' said young James Morton, proffering the bouquet.

Mrs. Reid! To Bianca's ears, it sounded so extraordinary; but Muna received the flowers with exclamations of pleasure, asked the two young men to sit down, and gave the flowers to Bella to arrange for her, as to the manor born. In spite of her robes and the veil over her head, she became, in an instant, a complete English woman. Both young men treated Muna as if she were not only a great lady but also their dearest friend. The younger of the two was obviously in love with her. He could not keep his adoration from his eyes. Muna spoke to them both as if she had known them all her life. Bianca, listening, knew that English now came more easily to Muna's tongue than it did to her own. Bianca spoke to Sara in English always, but otherwise she seldom used her own language; and now she realised that it was not easy for her to speak it or to understand it.

Bella brought the flowers in, arranged with care in a bowl, and Muna had it placed on the flat top of the balustrade beside her. In the open air, with the sun streaking scarlet into sea and sky as it sank, the flowers were not garish. Muna was wearing one of her favourite colours, a brilliant emerald green silk skirt and *choli*, and her dark head was covered by a transparent green veil that fell below her shoulders, and lifted and drifted about her with every breeze. She looked beautiful but very frail. Presently, both young men took their leave, asking if they might visit her again on the following day.

Looking at Muna as she gazed reflectively at the flowers, Bianca asked, 'Are you feeling better, Munabhen? You look – '

'Yes. I know how I look. But fever always leaves me a little depleted. I will be better soon – you will see.'

'Come back with me, Muna, just to Madore. Think how much good it would do you.'

Muna's sigh had heartbreak in it. 'Do not ask me again, Khanum. I may not come. But remember me as you walk in your garden – and when you go again to Lambagh, and ride beside the lake, remember me then. The breath that lifts your hair as you look over the lake could be my envious sigh. So think of me when the wind whispers round you on a silver night when the moon is high.'

Bianca could not speak. She took Muna's hand and, looking into her face, felt her heart gripped in the pain that she saw in the beautiful eyes turned to hers.

Then Muna said quietly, 'A nightingale sings in the woods of Moxton Park in the early summer, on moonlit nights. It pours melody from its throat like the bulbuls do in Lambagh. I shall think of you with love then. Khanum, you must go home. I think you know that it is not safe for you to return to Sagpur. I do not think I shall be returning there in any case, but for you – you must go very soon although I think my heart will break to see you go.'

'Yes. I am only waiting to see you strong again.'

'Khanum, you cannot wait so long – I would like you to go soon. Ayub Khan and I think some of Alan's men will give you guard as far as Ratna – after that, you should be safe. Oh, Khanum, how will I bear to see you go! Do not let us speak of it. Bella – Bella, bring us wine and some salted nuts, and let us talk of other things until moonrise. Tell me – tell me of your grandson. Who is he like? I do not know what my son looks like – my beautiful Rob! He was only a little boy when I left him.'

Muna's smile, though fleeting, was unshadowed. They sat, talking and drinking wine, until the moon was high and the shadows of the palm trees moved, black on silver, on the sand. Muna raised her goblet and the moonlight shone on her white hand and gleamed back from the silver, and set the great emerald on her finger to burning with green fire.

'Listen!' she said, 'Listen.'

Bianca could hear nothing. 'What?' she said.

'Horses – two I think – Bella!'

Bella seemed to materialise from the shadows.

'Bella, I think your master and mine comes – let us have more wine and the food. They will be here in – how long, Ayub?'

Ayub, burly on the steps, said 'Half an hour, Munabhen, I think.'

'Yes, I think so too. Bella, there is hot water?'

'Sahiba, there is everything.'

'Good. Khanum, we shall have news – very soon.'

Alan, when he arrived, was tired, Bianca could see. But Muna built round him a wall of comfort. He was given wine, and then went off with Kullunder Khan; and returned, bathed and in clean linen, obviously already rested and refreshed. Their meal, taken by moonlight and by lanternlight, was leisurely. Kullunder Khan poured the wine, Ayub standing close by, and Muna led the conversation so that it touched on everything that Alan enjoyed – shooting, riding, his regiment. Bianca watched Muna spin her cocoon of relaxation round Alan. So she must have enchanted and rested her clients in the old days. There was not, thought Bianca wryly, very much difference between a good wife and a good courtesan. Then the only thing lacking came to her – the one great difference – love. The love that could exist between a man and a woman, could grow and last for a lifetime, so that passion and friendship walked hand in hand; lust was to be enjoyed as good food is

330

enjoyed – love crowned a life. Watching Muna, Bianca felt her eyes sting and her throat burn with tears she could not shed. This woman was a trained comforter of men – but for her, there could be no comfort.

Alan put down his goblet and stretched. 'Oh, this is good – I shall sleep tonight. The air in Sagpur is still foetid, the slime still clings about the streets and houses, smelling of a thousand deaths.'

He turned to Bianca, 'Bianca – my dear, you cannot go back there. I do not understand, but there seems to be some animosity towards your family still. They are strange people, the Sagpurna Royalty.'

Muna broke in – 'We will speak of all this tomorrow, Alan – now, as you say, let us sleep.'

Alan, as Bianca was sharing the pavilion, was spending the night with his men. He took a tender farewell of Muna and went, lighted on his way by Kullunder Khan with a lantern, glow-worming off towards the tents of the regiment. Then Bella came and helped the two ladies get ready for bed.

Later, the moon shifting, Bianca, lying on a bed on the other side of the pavilion from Muna, looked over and saw her bathed in moonlight, her hair a shadow round her face. She lay, like a figure carved on a tomb, still as stone – her face had a curious calm, a dreaming peace, but her eyes were open, outstaring the moon. Bianca watched her, and did not see her move – and then Bianca must have slept, for it was dawn, and Bella was there with tea and Muna was giving orders for Bianca's departure that day.

They did not say goodbye. Muna and Bianca stood apart, and then Muna took Bianca's hand and lifted it to her forehead.

'My life for yours, Khanum – go laughing through your life, with love.'

'Oh, Munabhen –'

Bianca said nothing more; but as she turned to go to her horse, Muna said suddenly, 'Khanum – I will send my son – remember me when you see him.' Then she went up the steps and into the pavilion, and Bianca saw her no more.

Alan helped her to mount, and she rode away with Ayub

Khan and six of Alan's men with her, and she could not see the path for anything, for her eyes were blinded by tears.

That night, Alan came back to the pavilion. They sat with their wine, watching the setting sun. They ate together, and when at last it was time to go to bed, Alan said, as he stretched out, 'Oh, this is good – I hate to sleep away from you. I am glad that we are together again.'

Muna said nothing, sitting propped against her pillows, her eyes on the road that Bianca had taken. In her mind's eye, she followed the road as it ran through India, followed Bianca's progress on her journey – here she would spend the night, here the road would turn off – leaving the Great Road, and becoming a small road, winding up; here Bianca would put on warmer clothes, and then, at a turn, the first sight of the foothills would be before her; and the day after, she would be climbing, and the air would be cold and fresh, and at the end of the day she would look up and see the ramparts of high peaks, gilded by sunset, ragged against the sky – the mountains that guarded Lambagh. Muna saw the peaks and felt a fresh wind blowing through her hair. Then, quietly, she lay down. Alan was asleep. He did not look over to see Muna lying wide awake all night, with one hand resting on her great emerald ring. He slept and woke, refreshed, when Bella brought them early tea.

But his wife's looks did not please him.

'Muna, you are not picking up as quickly as you did. Do not get up today – stay and rest, and I will come back in the evening. Bella, make sure that your mistress does as she is told, will you?'

So Muna rose and bathed and put on a fresh robe, and went back to dream the day down the sky into sunset.

When Alan came she had bathed again and was sitting up, wrapped in scarlet silk, her hair smoothly coiled, her lips and eyes smiling her welcome.

'You are rested, my love?'

'Yes – I am, thank you. Ayub Khan is back. Bianca's men were ready for her, and she is safely on her way.'

'Yes, I know – my fellows are back. They enjoyed their jaunt. There is so little for them to do, that they are very bored.

332

They do not like being down here in the south. I think they miss their families.'

'And they miss their hills,' said Muna, very low. Then she said, 'Why not set them to building huts – then there could be a permanent camp here that soldiers could come to when the bad season comes to Sagpur?'

'That is a most excellent idea. Huts and a mess hall. I will give orders tomorrow.'

The men worked hard, glad of useful occupation. Each hut accommodated six men, and had a window with a shutter to pull down. Muna sent for yards and yards of muslin from Pushti, the nearest small town, so that the huts could be made insect-proof against the singing, stinging mosquitoes and sand flies that were such a torment when the wind dropped. There was a cook house, and a big, open mess hall and, finally, a large hospital hut. When it was completed, it was like a village and the men were delighted.

Young Morton, paying his evening call on Muna, said, 'The men call it Munapur in your honour, Mrs. Reid, but they say there is only one thing wrong with it.'

'Oh? What is that?'

James Morton blushed, 'They miss their families, you know,' he said.

Muna laughed, 'Ah, yes. No women – yes, it is a terrible thing to be away from home for so long. Are you married, Mr. Morton?'

'No – no I am not. There is a girl –'

'Waiting for you? Poor girl, how long has she waited? You have been out here nearly four years, have you not? Will you marry when you return?'

Young Morton said that he probably would – but inwardly thought how pale and dull Chloe was going to seem after this gorgeous creature, with her supple body and great, dark eyes. He could not imagine what he had seen in blue eyes and golden hair. The blue eyes now seemed cold and fish-like to him, as he looked into Muna's eyes.

Alan, coming in, offered him a glass of wine, but James

thanked him and went away to dream. Alan shook his head at Muna, smiling.

'That young man is in the last stages of romantic love over you, Muna.'

'It is very hard for the men being away from their families for so long, Alan. Most of them have been out here with us for nearly ten years.'

'Yes – but it is not so bad for the Indian troops. It does not take them long to get home. The officers, true, it is very hard on them.'

'It is very hard on us. Rob is almost a man – and I will not recognise him. Do you wonder what he is like Alan?'

Alan looked and felt uncomfortable. He did not think very often of his son, and was ashamed of himself.

'It will not be much longer, Muna – we will be going home. My father wants me to return. He wants me to send in my papers – he feels he is getting old and needs me on the estate. You will like that?'

Muna did not know. To go back to the dream world again, leaving India behind. Even this India, still so strange to her, was part of her own country – or was it? Was it not as strange to her as England? While she was considering her feelings, Alan came and sat beside her, taking her hand to kiss it.

'I cannot bear to see you looking so frail, Muna. I hope my orders come soon. I would like to have you safely on the ship bound for home.'

Home! Home? The little pucker between Muna's brows grew deeper and took Alan's attention. He put his lips to it, smoothing it away with kisses.

'Do you not wish to return, Muna? To go home, and see your son?'

'Alan, how can you ask such a foolish question!'

'You often ask me questions as foolish.'

'I do?'

'You know that you do. What is the question you always ask me, Muna?'

'One that you have never answered,' said Muna, and turned her face away, and Alan had to put his hands on her shoulders and forcibly turn her to make her look at him.

'Tell me – do you not wish to return to Moxton Park?'

'Of course I do. I was only thinking – '

'Muna, my love! Stop thinking, and kiss me. Ah, Muna, I starve for you – '

Muna's lips were cool and sweet, Alan thought hazily, cool and as sweet and heady as iced wine. He took her into his arms, and entered his magic world, and Muna accepted and gave all that he wished, until he fell back at last, and holding her close to his heart, was asleep. As his grasp slackened, Muna slipped from his arms, and sat looking down at him. This wild turbulent world that she had shared with Alan, this world of the body, was this truly love that they had between them?

She could find no answer to this question, as she could find no answer to any of her questions. There was no one to answer her. She knew, in her heart, that Alan would have no answer – and it was not a question she would care to ask him.

The sea splashed, and dragged at the sand, and the palm trees rattled, and sent their familiar shadows over the floor. Muna lay back among her cushions, and listening to the tide coming in, glad that she was listening to it in such peace, fell asleep at last.

But in her sleep, it seemed one question still echoed down the pathways of her mind. A question she had asked so often.

What is love?

29

Three weeks later, Alan's orders came. The regiment was going home, back to the north of India. The men would have leave to return to their villages, but Alan was returning to England. The shouting that broke out from the barracks, and from the men on the hard-trodden parade ground that they had laboured so long to make, was like the roar of the incoming tide.

Bella came to Muna, where she sat on the *chabutra*.

'Do you hear the men, Sahiba? They've likely had news – good news, from the sound of it.'

'Yes. Those are hillmen rejoicing. They are going back to their mountains – and their homes.'

'Yes, I can hear the note in those voices. They are climbing the slopes already in their minds. But, Sahiba, you will be going home too – '

'I? Home? I shall be going back to my son.'

The two women, who had grown so close to each other, were silent, a sudden sorrow on both their faces, as the sounds of jubilation swelled from the barracks. Muna turned to face Bella.

'And you, Bella? What of you? You do not come with me, I know.'

Bella did not answer for a few minutes, her wide, green eyes looking past Muna at the sea. Then she went over to the couch where Muna sat.

'So – that makes it easy for me, Sahiba. You know already. Of course, you would know. You have the sight, as I have. I do not have to tell you that I shall never see the meadows and lanes of England again – nor the moors and mountains and rivers of my own country. Never again.'

'You say sad words, Bella, but your eyes sparkle like green water in sunlight, and your voice is the voice of a girl – a girl in love. Ah well – I did not need the sight, as you call it, to know this bit of news. Ayub Khan, come up here, and do not skulk there in the shadows, like the thief you are. What have you done, taking my dear friend from me?'

Ayub's great shoulders bulked behind Bella's tall slenderness, his teeth gleaming beneath his moustache. His smile was proud, though his voice was suitably humble.

'I have stolen her from you, Munabhen, because I could not help myself. It was a theft in self-defence. She has stolen my heart and my spirit, and so I am her prisoner. How should this happen to me, who have found love easy, and sweet, to pick up and eat like fruit, throwing away the rind? How should *I* become a prisoner to a woman – a red haired woman, as thin and as fierce as a hunting leopardess, with eyes of green fire? Think of me with sympathy, Munabhen, you who know the hearts and minds of men. Have pity on me!'

'Thou shameless one! I who know the hearts and minds of men, I have watched you. You wanted Bella from the moment you saw her; she was your coveted prize, the woman of your heart. There – I am not angry. I am glad. You will not miss your mountains, Bella. You have exchanged them for mine, and you will never be homesick.' Muna's eye glittered with tears. 'I am a fool, to weep in the face of happiness. Go you away, Ayub, you great bear, and leave Bella with me. We have much to say to each other in a short time, and you have all your life to sit and gloat over your prize – the hunting leopardess. Get you gone now – you take all my good wishes with you, my brave Ayub.'

After Ayub had left them, in spite of what Muna had said, they did not speak at first, Bella and she; they looked over the foam-flecked water in silence, Bella standing at the edge of the *chabutra*, one hand on the balustrade, and Muna sitting, leaning back against the piled cushions, her eyes also watching the tumble and roll of the sea. When she spoke, it was to ask Bella to come and sit near her. 'Bella – come, sit here with me. Time moves so fast. I am glad to think of you in my Valley, but I shall feel a great emptiness in my life.'

Bella moved to sit at the foot of Muna's couch. 'Aye. The empty place in my life will last a long time – for the rest of my days, Sahiba.'

She was silent then, looking at Muna, and Muna moved restlessly, and suddenly looked angry and rebellious. Then she glanced down at the green stone in the ring on her finger, and when she looked up again, there was no rebellion left in her face.

'I know what you have just told me, Bella. I have known in my heart for some months. Tell me, how long will it be?'

'Is it good for you to know? I cannot tell you as clearly as your own mind can tell you. But your time in this life is long enough, Sahiba. There are so many more lives.'

'So many lives. So many paths to wander, looking for those we love. These loves are so important that it seems that they will never be forgotten, that we will never lose them, that we will know exactly how to find them again. But it is not so. We do forget when we go through the gate of this life into the next. We forget. Why, Bella?'

'*You* ask *me*, Sahiba? Ask yourself. You know more than I do. But do we in truth forget? I think we remember in ways that we do not recognise. The beloved that was our life, the friends that were close to us – these are the souls we find again, the loved and the lost.'

'And the enemies?'

'Perhaps they still pursue us to our distress, hunting us down the ways of time – or perhaps they become friends and lovers, and hurt us in other ways. *I* do not know, if you do not.'

'I know as one who dreams in the night and remembers the dream faintly on waking. It was clearer to me when I was younger. Now, the mists of the many things I have done in this life obscure the light of reason and knowledge, and I lose my mind's sight. Bella – my son will come to Lambagh. Help him, should he need help.'

'Sahiba, he is the child I did not bear. I took him from your body into my heart. I shall never bear Ayub a son – so it is my life for his – and, indeed, Ayub's life for his, should he need us.'

'Bella – see, again, foolish tears. I am happy, and yet I weep. I wish you – with the knowledge that my wish will be granted – every happiness. Now, let us say no more. I see my lord coming, and he must not find me with red eyes at a time when he will be rejoicing. Bring wine, Bella, and ice – and he will tell me, with pleasure, the news I already know.'

Alan was bursting with news. He flung his words at Muna, like a boy throwing a ball in play, in a game he knew he was bound to win. Home – and the regiment, the joy of the men returning to the north, his release from the army, the delight it would give his parents; the voyage back, and how much good it would do Muna. As he spoke, his words sounded in his own ears like music to one who has been without the pleasure of sweet sounds for years.

Muna poured his wine for him, and listened to him, and her eyes were clear and smiling as she watched and listened to this man who ruled her life, and could answer none of her questions. There was no bitterness in the lovely eyes that watched Alan so faithfully. But Muna's hands were not still. Over and over, her slender fingers twisted the gold ring on her finger, the great, green emerald flashing in the sunlight, flashing like a green star would flash in darkness. Her silence went unnoticed by Alan. He had so much he wanted to say.

'And think, Muna! Rob – imagine, my dear, he will be fifteen, nearly sixteen. A great boy. We will not know him!'

'No – we will not know him. And we will be strangers to him too – ' Muna's voice was very soft.

'Oh, come, my love, you go too far! Not strangers – we are, after all, his father and mother. He will soon be happy and at ease with us. Children are unfeeling little beasts.'

'As you said to me, in different words, when we left England, all those years ago.'

'Well! Was it not true? He did not pine away. After all, I should know. I spent most of my boyhood alone in England, at school or staying with uncles and aunts, while my parents were out here. I do not think I suffered. I cannot remember feeling any great lack. But never mind that. We are not speaking of the past, but of the future. Ah, Muna! To be going home again! To take you away from this vile climate and back to gentle weather and safety. I am so happy.'

In a sudden transport of joy, he pulled her into his arms, covering her face with kisses, not caring who saw him.

'My darling wife – you *are* happy to be coming back? You will not mind leaving your country, will you?'

Muna opened her mouth to say, 'But this is *not* my country,' and closed it again, the words unsaid. The gap between her thoughts and Alan's thoughts seemed very great suddenly. Her eyes looked away from his face to the sea, and to the palm trees growing along the shore. She felt the moist, sticky air, the wind that at this time of day did not bring coolness. Alan had served with a native regiment in the north, he knew the mountains and valleys, and the burning, dry heat of the plains in the summer. Could he still think that this lush green country, where mould grew on clothes, and men constantly suffered from a skin irritation, called, suitably, prickly heat – *could* he imagine that this tropical, damp place reminded her in any way of the far north?

He was still talking; his words sounding in her ears made no sense. She sat, clasped in his arms, in a terrible mental solitude, looking at the sea, lost in a loneliness so frightening that she felt she could only see darkness, although the day was bright and the sun made diamonds where the spray broke on the sand, and her ring flashed and burned an ever brighter green, like the feathers on a peacock's neck in the sun.

When he bent his head over her face, she lifted her mouth to his kiss, and smiled, and held his hand, while her mind groped in darkness for some contact, something to strengthen her. Alan kissed her again, advised her to rest because of the coming turmoil of the journey, and rushed off, back to his celebrating men, leaving her sitting, quiet and still, while desolation crept over her as the waves crept up the shore.

They moved with the regiment as far as Madras. There the

340

men took farewell of Alan, and of the woman they all called 'Muna of Madore'. She stood on the veranda of the Dak Bungalow, watching them ride off, and her neck and shoulders were bowed under the weight of the garlands they had brought her. She watched the last tall, swinging figure vanish in the dust clouds raised by the horses, and could not tell if it was the dust that hid them from her, or her own tears.

Alan, standing beside her, garlanded as she was, was unashamedly wiping his eyes. 'Never has there been a finer regiment. Never. It has been an honour to serve with them.' He blew his nose vigorously, and took Muna's arm. 'My dear – come and sit. You look exhausted. Bella, come and take your Mistress's flowers, she is quite weighed down with them.'

Bella and Ayub were still there. They would stay till the last day. Bella came and lifted the wilting jasmine and marigold garlands from Muna's shoulders, and took her into the Dak Bungalow, and Muna bathed and refreshed herself; and, having refused food on the plea of being too tired to eat, she retired to bed and lay with closed eyes, once again following in her mind the twists and turns of the roads that led to the north, the roads she would never take in this life. It seemed that she could still hear the sound of the horses – or was it her heartbeat? She slept at last, and Bella closed the door of her room to Alan, begging him not to disturb Muna.

'She is exhausted, Sir – if you could just use another room tonight?'

'But of course. Quite right, Bella,' said Alan, and privately rejoiced that very soon this commanding, fierce-eyed woman would be left behind, and he would have his wife to himself.

They travelled by carriage to the Port of Calcutta, taking the journey easily, making many stops on the way. But no matter how often they stopped, how slowly they travelled, the day came in the end, when they arrived at the docks.

There, Bella and Muna parted.

They said their farewells with no words. For a moment, Bella clasped Muna in her arms, and felt she held a spirit, so light and small did Muna seem. Then Bella turned, and left. Ayub, for once with no smile on his face, took Muna's hand to

341

his forehead and said quietly, 'Go in peace, go laughing, oh Rose of Beauty. Our hearts go with you.'

Muna looked at him, bowed her head, and walked steadily away, to go down into the small boat that would take her, bucking over the rough water, to the ship.

They were three days in harbour, waiting for a favourable tide, and loading, and then, at night, the *Castalia* raised her anchors, and Muna, standing in the stern, watched the harbour lights prick out one by one like setting stars.

Dry-eyed, she turned away. There was nothing to which she could say farewell. She could not see across the country to the ranges of mountains that guarded her land. As the last light vanished, she went below, hearing the creak and whistle of the wind in the rigging, feeling the ship lift and heave beneath her feet. That part of her life was over. Now she must prepare herself for the next period and whatever waited in the future.

In the morning Alan came to her, where she sat on her berth, leaning against her pillows. He was proud of her ability to withstand rough weather. She never felt sea sick.

'We have some British troops on board, my love – the Royal Westchesters. The men are in a parlous condition, or most of them. It is a good thing we are not going into battle! Half the men are praying for a quick death, and that includes most of their officers.'

'They should stay in the fresh air.'

'No doubt. But their regimental surgeon will deal with them – if he has not succumbed himself. There are no families with them, and they are nothing to do with us. This is one time when you rest, and dream of going home. You have done enough, my love. Now I insist that you rest and gather your strength. I have arranged for the stewardess to attend to all your needs – there are no other ladies on board.'

Muna rested. At Alan's request, a shelter was rigged for her on the deck, and all day, and, when Alan would allow it, most of the night, she would sit, or recline there, on rugs and cushions, watching the limitless ocean. A fleet of flying fish, turning silver in the sun, was an event in the long emptiness of the days, each day melting into the next, with nothing to mark the change. There was a large gull that followed the ship for some time, hanging as effortlessly in the air as the fish eagles had done over the lake in the old days in Lambagh, lifting and swooping on unseen currents in a sky that came down to meet the sea in a curve, unbroken except for a paler line, the line of the horizon. Muna missed the gull when, one day, he was not there.

The weather was good. The ship moved through blue days, and nights that were full of stars. As darkness fell, the sea turned into silver flame as the ship's bows cut through the still water and phosphorescence glowed in the turn of each wave.

Muna lay, eating and drinking and sleeping, as Alan directed, and her thoughts were all that she had of her own. He watched her, at first pleased with her quiescence; then, later, it worried him. But to his anxious questions, she only said, 'Alan, I am doing exactly as you tell me – I rest, and grow stronger. Please do not distress yourself so much about me. I am well.'

But seeing her still face and dreaming eyes, Alan felt a distance between them. It was as if she had been left behind in India, as if only her beautiful simulacrum sat under the shelter. Her body welcomed him generously, as it always had, but he felt, lying in her arms, as if he lay with a stranger. It was his turn to ask questions in the darkness, lifting his mouth from hers to try and see her eyes.

'Where have you gone, Muna?'

'Nowhere, Alan – I am here, as always, as you want me.'

But she was not there. He grew importunate in his loving, looking for her, but more and more it seemed to him that he held only her body. Her spirit was elsewhere, and he did not know where she had gone.

The days and nights passed, fused into one long day and night; the ship came into the grey waters of Europe, and the air had a different smell, and the wind was cold, and even though Muna wrapped herself in her pushmina robes, so long unused, Alan did not allow her to sit on deck. She walked there, at least once a day, drifting on the wind like a dove's feather in her creamy robes. Rain splattered on the decks, sea gulls came screaming from nowhere, and the air smelled of the land again,

343

and the coastline of France was dark on the skyline.

Then, on a day of brilliant sunshine, Muna heard the sound of cheering break out, and went on deck to see, far ahead, gleaming white, the cliffs of England, saw tears in Alan's eyes, and wondered at the spell that a country can have on the heart. Alan was lost to dignity, he was cheering with the soldiers of the British regiment, and did not see her standing there, her robes blowing round her, her hair lifting, flying like a silk scarf in the cold channel wind. She watched the cliffs grow close, and closer, so that she could see the green grass growing on their crests. Then she went below to change into her tight-waisted velvet dress with its long sleeves and full, crimson skirts. She smoothed it over her body, and the emerald on her finger seemed to have red flame at its heart as her hands moved. Muna turned to her mirror, and coiled up her hair, high on her head, and a dark-eyed English woman with a great emerald ring on her hand looked back at her from the glass – all that was left outwardly of Muna. Within herself, Muna the Dancer, the Rose of Madore, listened to the winds of England thundering against the porthole, and felt, mutinously, the tight grip of alien clothes, and then heard beneath the wind the voice she had heard often before, 'My daughter, be still, and wait on life. Wait.'

Muna looked at her reflected figure for a moment, then turned and walked out of the cabin and up to the windy deck.

30

The family had not come to the ship to meet them, at Alan's special request. So Muna waited in her cabin until Alan came to get her – and there was Bates, smiling a welcome. His smile was warm and delighted, and he seemed well, but Muna, looking into his eyes, saw the sadness there, and remembered that the last time he had brought a carriage to meet them, Ratni had been with her, and he had been a young second coachman. Now he was head coachman, with white streaks in his hair, but there was no confused, bright-eyed young woman to catch his interest and be helped over her confusion in a strange country. Bates had, perhaps, learned what love was.

Alan was conscious of no shadow on anyone. As they turned in at the gates, he reminded Muna of their first arrival. But this time it was different. The whole family was out on the terrace to see them come.

Robert, grey and somehow shrunken, was the first to reach the carriage door. He took Muna into a warm embrace, his arm tight about her shoulders, and she could feel the fine tremble that ran through his arm.

'My dear Muna, my dearest girl – what a wonderful moment this is. Alan, my dear boy – '

Muna was caught into Jane's arms, felt tears on her cheek and knew they were not all her own. She looked into Jane's smiling, ageing face, ran her finger under the wet eyes that were still youthful, and said, 'Mother – you must not weep at my return,' and turned at last to the boy who was standing so quietly in the background. She closed her lips on an exclamation and stared at her son.

He was a reincarnation standing there, as if her heart, hidden so long, had defied her and formed a child to match her dreams. Tall, grey-eyed, black-haired, his every feature tore at her heart, reminding her of things long past.

But this is impossible, her brain told her. Impossible. This is *Alan's* son. I last saw Kassim two years before this child was conceived. I lay in Kassim's arms for the last time a full eight months before that lonely two years. From where does this boy then come?

In her heart, a voice she knew spoke, soundless, clear, the voice that had spoken to her all her life. 'You gave your heart to a man, and yet never altogether forsook me. See now, how I reward you. This is your son, born of your dreams. Your husband fathered him, your heart formed him.'

The boy stepped forward and took his mother into his arms. Muna's touch was as light, her kiss as gentle as if she was kissing a shadow, holding a ghost. Her son's clear grey eyes looked into hers, he smiled a little, and stood back, and Muna, too shaken to do anything but grasp at the rags of her poise, went up the terraced steps and into the house, hearing nothing that anyone said to her, hearing nothing but the chiming, crystal voice, the voice that had a laugh behind it, the voice that repeated, 'See, Muna, my daughter – Love is a strong power. As strong as death.'

*　　*　　*

Jane, lonely for Muna for so many years, felt as if her own daughter had returned. She was so jealous of Muna's company that she was glad that Caroline Addison would not be back from a trip to Venice until the end of the month. She did not wish to share this home-coming with anyone.

But as she watched Muna settling back into the routine of her life in England, she sensed a strangeness, and began to worry. They spent hours together, Muna hearing news of the years that had passed, news already so old that it seemed to

346

Muna like stories of another life. It was, of course, news for which she had longed – tales of Rob that she had looked forward to hearing – but now, nothing about the child she had left behind her seemed relevant to the boy who was her son.

Jane talked, told the stories she had saved in her memory to tell Muna, snippets of news, and watched Muna apparently listening with interest, and yet, in reality, not hearing a word she said.

When she spoke of Rob's boyhood, of his first days at school, and still saw no interest in Muna's eyes, she could not believe it.

'Muna! Listen to me – I am telling you about Rob! Where are your thoughts?'

'I am sorry, Mother – forgive me. I was watching – I was looking at Alan, riding up alone. His father did not go with him today?'

'No. He has grown very frail. I am so glad and grateful that Alan is back; Robert needs him, Muna. The winters try him very hard now, and his shoulder pains him greatly in the cold weather. He says that he – oh, Muna, he says he can feel his hand and fingers again as he could when he first lost his arm.' Tears stood in the eyes that had not altered in the face that time was beginning to mark.

'Muna – is Alan leaving army service?'

'I think it is so, Mother. He said he was going to send in his papers before we left India. I am certain that he will if he thinks his father needs him. But, Mother, Alan's father looks well – not so young, but who is young after ten more years of living?'

'You have not changed, Muna.'

'I? No, my race does not alter very much, unless we are poverty-stricken and in poverty bear too many children. Then our women look old at twenty.'

'Muna, you always speak as if you were entirely Indian. Have you forgotten your father was English?'

'It is hard for me to remember. I was so young.'

'Can you remember him at all?'

'Yes – a little. He was a big man with black hair and his eyes were very blue. He laughed a great deal – and he loved my mother. He used to call her "Sweetheart", I can remember that. He had a big moustache – but his face is not clear to me now. When I think "Mother" or "Father", I see you and Alan's father. You have become my parents.'

'Ah, Muna – you are so dear to me. We have lived all these years longing for your return. Tell me, are you happy to be back?'

'Of course I am happy, Mother! How not? Have I not come back to you, and to Rob?'

Muna's eyes were on a distant figure. A horseman coming closer, his powerful animal making nothing of various hedges and fences that were between the end of the garden where she sat with Jane and the open field beyond.

The rider magnified, and was, after one last breath-taking leap, before them, sitting his dancing horse easily, a smile crinkling his grey eyes.

'Rob! You are showing off – ' Muna's voice had laughter in it. Jane's tones were sterner.

'Yes – you could have broken your neck – right in front of your mother. That would have been a pretty sight, would it not?'

'She knew I was not going to break my neck – did you feel fear for me, oh my Mother?' The last part of the sentence was spoken in faultless Urdu. Muna laughed, and clapped her hands.

'My son – you have not forgotten your Urdu, then? How have you kept it so long with no one to speak it with you?'

'I speak nearly every day with a man from the north – General Mackintosh brought a retired subahdar back with him, and, Mother of my heart, he is from the hills; therefore, as you hear, I can speak Lambaghi too!'

Muna caught her breath. That voice! In Lambaghi. If she shut her eyes, it was Kassim speaking. Her hands clenched together, hidden in her skirt. Then she took command of herself, and was able to say, 'Well done, indeed,' in English. 'However, as your grandmother speaks neither Urdu nor Lambaghi, perhaps we should talk English; it seems more polite. Tell me;

that is a magnificent animal – where did you acquire him?'

'This is Samoonder, and indeed he is magnificent. He came as a gift to me from the Ruler – was it not generous of him? At the same time, he sent a black mare for you – she is very spirited, Mother, we will have wonderful rides. There is also a beautiful animal for my father, Falla, a chestnut. They arrived six months ago. We have here the beginnings of a stable that will be the envy of the country. I long to meet Kassim Khan Bahadur. He must be a wonderful man. I look forward to next year.'

'Next year?'

Muna looked a question at Jane, who shook her head. 'Rob, you are being ridiculous. I have already told you there is no question of your going anywhere next year! How do you imagine you might travel, when you will still be at school?'

'But, Grandmama, I shall be nearly seventeen!'

'You will be nothing of the sort. You are not yet sixteen. Please, Rob, do not be foolish.'

Muna broke into the conversation that appeared to be distressing both her mother-in-law and her son. 'Never mind all this talk now. We have days and days ahead of us in which to discuss plans. Mother, I would dearly love two things. A quiet cup of tea with you, and then, Rob, I want to see these wonderful horses. I think you should take Samoonder back to the stables – he is heated. Come to me when you have changed, and we will see our horses together.'

Rob, with a grateful glance, gave his horse rein and went off at a fast canter. The two women watched him go, Jane with anxiety, Muna with thoughts that she kept to herself.

Jane said in a dissatisfied voice she rarely used, 'Muna, you must speak to him – he rides too fast.'

'Mother, he rides well, and he will never ride any other way. It is in his blood.'

Jane looked affronted. 'Nonsense – Alan never rides in such a reckless fashion.'

She stopped speaking suddenly, remembering that Muna had been used to ride as wildly as Rob now did, and bit her lip. But Muna had not heard what Jane said. She was wondering at her own words, 'It is in his blood.' She had spoken nonsense. The man who rode as Rob rode was no relation of the boy's. So, the two women sat in silence, each regretting words the other had not heard.

Over their cups of tea, brought out by a plump, white-haired Daisy and Boots, now raised to the status of footman, Jane no longer told Muna of what had happened in her absence. She wished now to hear Muna's news. She asked about Bella first.

'I was very surprised not to see her with you.'

'There was no time to write and tell you. The letter would have come with us, in any case.'

'She really wished to stay? It was not just because of that old trouble? For that is all forgotten now. No one ever speaks of witches or witchcraft. The grass has grown over the ruins of Bella's house, and time has rubbed out all memory of those happenings.'

Muna shivered suddenly, as if a cold wind had touched her. 'The grass has grown over the ruins of Bella's house – '

She said, with no reference to what Jane was saying, 'The grave – Ratni's grave. I suppose the grass had covered that too?'

'What?'

Jane was confused by the sudden change of subject, then said, 'Ratni's grave? No, it is well tended. Poor Bates – he sees to his wife's grave with the most tender care. But, Muna, I was speaking of Bella – tell me of her. Is she happy? I would not like to think of her staying behind because she was afraid to come home.'

'No, Mother, she wished to stay.'

'And this man – what is his name? She has married him?'

Married? Muna smiled to herself. They would certainly marry, she imagined, in some fashion. But even if they did not have any form of ceremony that Jane would understand, Ayub Khan and his hunting leopardess with the green eyes would live together with pleasure and happiness all their lives. So she said to Jane, 'Yes, they are married, and very content. They love each other. His name is Ayub Khan, and he is as close to me as a brother would be.'

'So he is also a relative of the Ruler?'

Ayub Khan was the son of a bastard son of the old Ruler, Sher Khan's uncle. But how to explain this to Jane? Muna could think of no way. So, after some thought, she said, 'Ayub Khan is devoted to the Ruler. He would, if need be, give his life for any member of the Ruler's family.'

Jane did not altogether understand, but was too full of a desire for news to go on enquiring into Ayub Khan's exact status in this strange Royal household.

'So Bella remains in India, the country to which she did not wish to return. How odd life is! I shall miss her, and of course you will too. Now, tell me – that magnificent ring! I have never seen such an emerald. Is that a gift from Alan?'

'No, Mother. The Ruler and his wife sent me this ring. It is a famous jewel in the State of Lambagh. It is known as "The Peacock Ring" and I am honoured to have been given such a gift. It would normally pass to the Ruler's daughter. Now it will be worn, one day, by Rob's wife.'

'It is very beautiful. The Ruler must be a very generous man. Those horses that he sent – Robert says they are without peer in this country. Now, tell me – how is the Irish Rani, your friend – well, in fact, she is your adopted mother, is she not?'

'Say rather that I am her adopted daughter. She is very well. She came and stayed with me – ' Muna thought of the chaos and tragedy of the time of Bianca's visit, and stopped speaking. Blissfully unconscious of Muna's thoughts, Jane continued with her questions, inadvertently recalling to Muna all that she longed to forget, and then at last, noticed how shadowed and tired Muna's face was beginning to look.

'Ah, Muna – I am exhausting you. How thoughtless I am. Go and rest, my dearest child. We have, as you said to Rob, all the time in the world to talk. I do not think you should go to the stables today; let Daisy put you to bed until it is time to dress for dinner. You will have a full three hours' rest. I will tell Rob he must wait to take you to the stables until tomorrow.'

All the time in the world – Muna, going off obediently, felt the wind blow suddenly cold, as if the late summer's warmth was already turning to autumn.

In her room, she sent Daisy away, and after praying before the image in the corner, she lay quietly on her bed, waiting for what she knew would happen.

The tap on her door was very quiet; it was followed instantly by a conspiratorial Rob, who slid in, and closing the door, leaned against it and looked at his mother anxiously.

'Gran says that you are too tired to even look at the horses, that I am to leave you in peace – ' Fresh from his grandmother's presence, he spoke English. So strange, thought Muna, her heart caught into the sweet surprise that she felt each time she saw him – so strange to watch that familiar face, but younger than she had ever seen it. How could he look so like Kassim? It was not a resemblance – he was a duplicate. Everything, hands, stance, the way his grey eyes were set in a face that she knew from years of lonely longing. She knew the answer. Her mind and heart had been set in youth, and her thoughts had always been with Kassim. The power of love, as she had been told, was strong indeed. Her son's voice broke into her thoughts.

'Mother – you *are* tired. I regret that I disturbed you. I go now, and we will see the horses another day. After many years you have returned to me, and I do not think you will leave me again soon.'

Now it was beautiful, clear Urdu that he used. There was no broken accent. Muna only heard the last part of his sentence – 'I do not think you will leave me again soon.'

Oh, my son, she thought, grief flooding her, oh my wonderful son. Such a short time before I go again! Aloud, she asked, 'Were the years hard?'

'Very hard. At first, that is. When I went away to school. But I learned to make them easier.' He laughed, without mirth.

'How?'

Rob clenched his right hand into a fist, and lifted it, and she saw the old white scarring on his knuckles. 'I found these very useful, when they said things that I did not care for. Their hostility did not last very long. The English have one passion

352

– sport. I won my place first, by beating them in fights, and later, by becoming better than any of them at any game or sport in which they indulged. They soon forgot that I had a black mother!'

Muna's breath hissed between her teeth, and he moved swiftly to put his arm round her. 'Mother! I thought to make you laugh! Do you mind this, you who are made of honey and ivory, and more beautiful than any woman in the world? It is nothing, the talk of idiot minds, and it did me no harm. I could remember you. See, it is over – I beg of you, do not be distressed!'

Muna shook her head, trying to smile. 'I am not distressed for myself. If you are unharmed by such talk, why should I feel pain? But I think of your first years at school – the first years after I left you. You were such a little boy, Rob. Those years must have been very bad.'

'Yes. Bad. But they are over. I am no longer a little boy! Are you too tired to talk, my Mother?'

'Never!'

With a satisfied smile he settled himself on the floor beside her bed, squatting comfortably on his heels, and said, without further preamble, 'Mother, you must help me. It is of great importance. I am a man now –'

Muna looked at her son, sitting as no English boy could, and nodded. In India, at sixteen, he would indeed be considered to be a man.

'Yes, Rob, you are a man. I know that. But you are the son of an Englishman, and in his country, you are still a boy.'

'I am still a boy before my grandmother, that is true! She would keep me a child forever if she could! Mother, please, you can help me – and quickly, for if my grandmother gets the ear of my father, I shall be a prisoner here for another ten years at least. Listen, lie back and rest and listen while I tell you all the story.'

Rest, with this young tiger beside her! Muna lay back obediently, and admired her beautiful son while he spoke eagerly, his words falling one over the other in his haste, so that he was almost stammering. It seemed that Kassim had sent for him – and he wanted, more than life, to obey the summons.

'The letter came with the horses – a long letter. Mother, I am to be trained in his army – I shall live in the Valley you love, and be part of the Ruler's personal staff, when I have finished my training. Think of it, Mother, think of the life I will have!' His voice rose to a crescendo of excitement, and then dropped sadly.

'And my grandmother does not wish me to go. She says I must first finish at school, until I am eighteen, and then go to Oxford – and that I am only a child, and do not know what is good for me! I tell you Mother, I am a man. I have a beard – feel!' He seized her hand and rubbed it over his chin, and then kissed it.

Muna, half laughing, half inclined to tears, felt nothing but his lips in her palm, but she said, 'Indeed, my son, you are no beardless boy. That is agreed. But your grandmother has brought you up – you will break her heart if you leave her now. What does your grandfather say? Have you spoken with him?'

'Yes. He is wonderful. He would let me go. He knows I am a man, and he thinks – no, he is *sure* that I should become what I wish to be – a soldier in the State Forces of Lambagh. I am not English, Mother! How can I be? I am your son, your country is the land about which I dream, your language comes as easily to my tongue as English – indeed, more easily. I think of England as a place where I am visiting. India is my *home*.'

'But Rob! You were born here, of an English father, and you have never been to India – how can India be your home? That is foolishness.'

'Say you so, Mother, you who filled my mind with stories of India, so that when I slept, I dreamed of the Valley, of the lake, and the snows, the bears who walk upright like men, the jackals howling round the mud walls of the villages in the plains – all the colour and warmth of the world was in those dreams, and now you try to take my birthright from me? You, my own mother, who are yourself sick for home?' Muna ignored the last part of his sentence. She took a deep breath.

'What of your father? Does he not matter to you?'

'Of course! How not? He is my father. But he also loves

India and so long as my grandmother does not get his ear before you do, he will let me go – I know that he will. He cannot refuse you anything.'

Muna was perfectly certain that Alan would not agree to his son breaking off his education and going to Lambagh. As for her persuasion, it was, she feared, more likely to make Alan refuse point blank. He was already inclined to be jealous of his son. She looked at her son's eager, glowing face, and gathered her courage, calling on her Goddess to give her the strength to beat down the flame of determination she saw in the grey eyes gazing trustfully at her.

'When does your next term begin?'

'My next term? If I go, it begins next month, on the third. Why? Surely, Mother, you are not going to force me to go?'

'But yes. It is necessary that you finish the education your father wishes you to have. You owe him duty, my son. You are his only son, and his heir. The Ruler would not respect you if you did what he asks at the expense of being a bad son. His offer will still be open when you finish school.'

'But that is two years, Mother!' In his disappointed anger, Rob had spoken in English, and Muna smiled at him.

'You see? You speak your father's tongue as easily as you speak mine. Come, Rob, let us be sensible. Two years will pass like a long breath – and you will enjoy them, and be all the better for them. The Ruler does not want a half-educated boy.'

'And Oxford? Mother, please – Oxford I cannot face!'

'Well, Oxford is another story. I will speak with your grandfather. Then we will speak together to your father. If you do as you should, and go on and finish your schooling, he will be more inclined to listen to your desires. Rob, do not be angry, and make long eyes at me – I only tell you what is for your good. Would I, your mother, force you to do something that would harm you?'

'You might try to force me to do something to please my father – ' The boy's voice was resigned. He put out his hand, and fiddled with the great emerald on her finger. 'So I am to remain in prison to please you – and my father. Will you write to the Ruler, telling him that against my will I am held here?

355

And tell him also, that the moment I am free, I will go to him, if he still wants me.'

'Your father will write. Do not be sad, my son, Kassim Khan will think more of you for doing what you should. You will enjoy the next two years. Do you not love your grandparents, and this – your home, where you have everything you wish?'

'Of course I do. And now that you are here – but I had dreams that you would come with me, and that we would live in the Valley. As you said – how can one be homesick for a country one has never seen. It is my blood speaking to me, Mother.'

'Your blood, and because I was selfish, and built all my homesickness into you. What terrible harm have I done to you, my son,' thought Muna, 'in all my years of lonely dreaming?' She looked at the downcast face so close to hers, and Rob, seeing her look, smiled, and took her hand. 'Never mind, Mother. What I have to do, I will do. But *not* Oxford – you promise me?'

'I promise you.'

'That is enough for me. Now – are you rested? Can you come and see the horses?'

A single-minded young man. Muna, still bone weary, allowed herself to be persuaded. Like thieves they crept out of her room, and down the stairs in the afternoon stillness, and achieved the stables without anyone seeing them.

31

The horses were beautiful, and Muna praised them without stint, watching the grooms walk them round the stable yard.

'I knew you would be pleased with them, Mother. You know he breeds horses now?'

'He?'

'Yes, the Ruler – Kassim Khan Bahadur. His uncle, Sher Khan, began it, after he had given Kassim the throne, and then Kassim became interested, and now they have a wonderful stables in Madore – and from there Kassim chose these pearls of perfection. But Mother – wait! Wait until you see your mare, Chandni.'

'Chandni? She is named for the moon?' asked Muna softly, and from somewhere into her memory came a man's voice, saying, 'Where are you when the moon appears?'

The memory blurred like a dream on waking when they led out, one careful groom on each side of her head, the black Arab mare. Small, tapering head, arched neck, swift delicate movements – the lovely creature, perfection of her kind, looked about her, dancing sideways, trying to toss her bridle free.

Bates was suddenly beside them, his eyes glowing with as much enthusiasm as Rob was displaying.

'Is she not perfect? A real beauty. But wild still. None of us have exercised her properly yet, she needed so much gentling after the voyage. She took the journey badly. But she is back in condition now, and we will take her out every day – though I do not envy her first rider!'

'Was she unbroken?'

'No – only the voyage disturbed her. She has a mouth like silk, but she is very spirited. If only her own groom could have stayed with her – but he sickened here, hating the climate, and knowing no word of the language, so that only Master Rob here could speak with him. So Sir Robert took a passage for him and sent him back, and she still finds us strange. But she is getting used to us slowly.'

'*I* rode her, Mother –'

'Oh Rob!'

'Yes – I mounted, and rode her.'

'You mounted and rode her for exactly four minutes, Master Rob, and nearly broke your neck, and earned me the worst berating I have ever had from your grandmother. Her ladyship was so angry I feared she would turn me off – after all these years.' Bates was only half laughing; Jane had obviously been very angry.

Muna caught Rob's eye, meaning to scold, and he winked shamelessly – and again memory sharpened, and she saw another laughing face, another pair of fearless eyes, full of impudence and amusement. She turned away from those laughing eyes, and said, watching the mare sidle and toss her head, 'Rob. You know I cannot ride Chandni today,' and her voice was drowned in Bates's expostulations.

'Surely, Master Rob, you never suggested putting your mother up on the mare!'

Rob looked faintly surprised, and anxious. 'But Mother, you said you were not too tired –'

'I said that I was not too tired to see the animals. As for riding – Rob, I regret to disappoint you. But I cannot, I really cannot ride today. I am too newly off that ship. Like Chandni herself, I need to be broken in gently.'

The laughter in her voice satisfied Rob, who took her arm, saying, 'Then tomorrow morning –' but Bates looked narrowly at Muna, and his frown grew deeper.

'No, *not* tomorrow, Master Rob. If your mother wishes to ride in the morning, then she shall ride one of the other horses. Chandni is not ready, it would be like putting your mother up on a half-broken animal. It will be weeks before Chandni is ready.'

'You forget Bates – my mother can ride anything.'

Rob's voice was proud. Bates, watching, thought to himself, 'Yes, indeed, ten years ago she could ride the wind. But now? What did they do to her, out there? She has come back like the ghost of herself – can the family not see? Rob, who loves her so much, he should see the difference,' and then remembered that Rob had been a child when Muna had left for India. His memory would not be clear. Bates kept his thoughts to himself, but in the morning, when Muna and Rob came out at sunrise, there was a gentle cob waiting for Muna, and Rob was horrified.

'Mother! You will be asleep and fall off before you can get that – that rocking horse into movement. Or worse, he will fall asleep, and throw you. I shall go and find Bates, he has gone mad!'

'Rob, please. This horse is very well for me. I am still tired. Let me see you ride, and I will come slowly, as befits an old lady.'

'You! You are younger than any girl, younger than I am – oh, very well, if you wish to amble – ' He cupped his hands to mount her, and was surprised at how light she was. He looked up at her as she gathered the reins into small gloved hands, and suddenly unmindful and uncaring of the watching grooms, he buried his face against her skirt. 'Oh Mother – I have dreamed of this ride for so long! I love you so – I love you!'

Muna's eyes closed for a moment, then she smiled down into the grey eyes raised to hers. Of all the avowals of love that she had received in her life, this was the sweetest. To have her son's love, to hear it spoken – it was hard for her to control her feelings. But for his sake her voice was steady as she replied, 'I too, Rob – even if it is disappointing that I cannot ride as you and I would wish. I used to lead you. Now it is your turn to lead, and mine to follow. Let us go.'

Rob mounted, and was off. Muna's horse, feeling experienced hands and a firm seat, did no stumbling, and went well, but Muna did not attempt anything but a sedate canter. She came up with Rob where he waited at the other side of the second field, where a stone wall separated the meadows from the wood. He had jumped the wall, but he opened the gate for his mother, and they rode side by side down the woodland path, which had always been one of Rob's favourite rides. They had taken it together on the day, so long ago, when she had had to tell him that she was leaving him in England and going back to India. Now it seemed to him that riding with her again, in this place, would wipe out the memory of that day.

At a walk, they came to the great fallen tree that had once seemed such an obstacle to leap, when Rob had been a little boy on his first pony. Rob reined in his horse.

'Can we talk here for a little?'

'Why not?' Muna started to slide, unaided from her horse, but Rob reached up, and caught her in his arms, and set her gently on her feet.

'You are so light, Mother. There is nothing of you. I do not remember you being so small.'

'I do not remember you being so tall – perhaps that is why. Rob, you must be almost as tall as your father.'

'Not yet. But I have not finished growing, or so my grand-mother is always telling me. But never mind my height. Tell me everything that has happened to you. Over ten years, Mother, since you left me! A very long time.' But there was no reproach in his voice. Rob understood, it was plain, that his mother had no choice.

Seated on the fallen oak, their horses tethered, they talked. Muna told her stories of Sagpur, of the cholera camp, and the cyclone. Rob listened as a boy listens to an adventure story read from a book, his eyes on his mother's face. Time passed, un-noticed. The sound of a horse coming fast down the ride surprised them both.

It was Alan, and he was inclined to be angry. But their wel-come was so warm, he was pulled into their close communion, hearing Rob say, 'But this is perfect – we are all three together again at last,' that Alan, feeling their love include him, was mollified, and sat with them, only saying, 'Your grandmother was getting agitated – it is time for breakfast.'

Indeed, they saw that the sun was well up, the trees were

casting shadows on the side, and the birds were no longer singing dawn songs, but were busy foraging for the day's food. Alan looked around him as he sat with Muna, and sighed with contentment. 'It is very good to be home, is it not, my dear?'

Home! A word used so loosely, for so many places, it seemed. Now, for Muna, home was here, in the woods, with her son. There was nowhere else. As if all the paths of her life had led her to this one place, this one moment, she leaned her head back and looked up into the summer green of the trees and felt her body loosen and relax, as if after long toil she rested. She looked at the green, and the glimpse of blue sky above, and felt Rob leaning against her knees, one arm tossed across them, and on her other side, Alan, his hand on her hand to attract her attention as he told her of his plans for the day. Surely, here, at last there was peace. Muna listened to her husband, smiling – and all the time she could feel Rob's impatience, his longing to speak of his plans, and willed him to be quiet. Now was not the time. Who can say what message passed from her body to his – but he did not interrupt his father, and finally they all rode home together, looking so content that Jane's scolding died on her lips, and all she said was, 'Come – never mind about changing, come and have your breakfast as you are, we are starving. See, Muna, we have a peach for you, remembering how much you liked them.'

There were roses for Muna too, arranged in a great scented bouquet by Murphy, for this, Muna's first breakfast in Moxton Park, after so long; Murphy, a very bent old man now, but still, according to Robert, the best gardener in the county. Muna swept into breakfast, carrying her roses. Jane, watching her eating her peach with relish, forbore to criticise the strength of the coffee that Cook had made specially for Muna, remembering how she liked it. Cook was unchanged, the same round-faced, white-haired figure that Muna remembered.

After breakfast, when Muna had bathed and changed, she found Jane surrounded by patterns of materials, velvets, silks, sprigged muslins, and laces.

'I have the dressmaker coming this morning, my dear – you will find that fashions have changed greatly now. We must get you some new dresses before we start our entertaining.'

Indeed, it was plain to Muna that she was back in England again. She missed Bella greatly – but reminded herself of Bella's previously solitary life, and comforted herself with the thought that she had great happiness now.

The dressmaker duly arrived, and she and Jane conferred over fashion plates, and materials, and colours and trimmings, and Muna sat and listened, stepping deeper and deeper back into the old dream again. Listening to the dressmaker and Jane arguing over the merits of lace and braid, of velvet for winter dresses, of stiff satin or soft chiffon, it was impossible to believe that not so very long ago she had stood, almost naked, throat deep in dirty water, with Ayub and Bella beside her, while the cyclone raged outside the old crumbling walls of their precarious shelter. Of the cavern, the Pool of the Women, she would not think at all – even now she would wake in her big quiet room, and in the silence of the night, she would hear the desperate whispering voices that she had heard there – the voices of how many doomed queens, dying in terror and in the dark waters. Nothing seemed to take that memory away.

The new clothes arrived and were most becoming, even if Muna found them in many ways more constricting and uncomfortable than the previous fashions.

'You could, I believe, wear a sack, and look elegant, my dear,' said Jane, with pride in her daughter-in-law shining from her face.

A week later, Caroline Addison, now widowed, returned from Venice, bringing with her a niece, the daughter of her late husband's brother. She came to dine, two or three days after her return, bringing the girl with her. Lady Addison had not changed, except that her hair was quite white, which suited her. Her eyes sparkled as wickedly, her tongue was as quick as ever. She was delighted to see Muna, taking her into a warm embrace, and then saying, 'Well, at last beauty has returned to us. But my dearest Muna, what have you been doing? You are nothing but a handful of bones! Jane, we will have to feed this girl – like we feed geese for Christmas – however elegant the bones are, you must not be too thin. But even so, you will as usual take all eyes, beautiful Muna. I am so very glad to see you! Now, let me present to you my niece, Laura. She has been longing to meet you. She will be staying with me for some months.'

The girl was shy, and small, with hair as dark as Muna's own, and eyes like blue flowers when she raised them to Muna's face. She did not speak very much, but she watched Muna as if she was watching a dream made flesh, or a fairy tale Princess come alive in front of her. Muna drew her down, to sit beside her and talk; the girl lost her shy silence under Muna's skilful handling, and was at ease. She was a different person when she grew animated – the beauty to come showed from behind the childish gawkiness, as one can see the racehorse in the colt's unformed movements.

Alan and his son came in together. Alan, going straight to Caroline to kiss her, did not see his son stand dumbstruck in the door, staring over at his mother and the girl beside her.

For Rob, it was the thunderclap, the ultimate knowledge. It happens rarely; some people say it never happens at all. But that night, Rob saw his future there, beside his beloved mother, and was too young to school his face.

Muna saw him, and saved him by asking him to bring her a wrap from her room, and he was able to get himself out of the drawing-room, and have a little time to come to terms with himself. He was gone so long that Jane, who had overheard Muna's request, was all for ringing the bell for Symes; but Muna said it must have been a sudden chill, and had passed. When Rob came back, with a velvet cape which did not match Muna's dress, he was in command of himself. He kissed Caroline, and bowed over her niece's hand as if she was a grown-up young lady, which made her blush and lower her long lashes over her blue eyes. Rob stood, speaking of what, he never knew; his words meant nothing, even in his own ears, and Muna watched him, and thought, 'So – the moon has risen for you, my son,' and prayed for happiness for him. Caroline Addison watched her niece and Muna's son, without missing a word of what Robert was saying to her, and Jane and Robert were so glad to have their family and their dear friend all together again that they were incapable of noticing anything, they were so content.

It was Laura's first dinner party.

'She would not be here, of course, if this were not as much my family as her parents are – more my family than they can ever be, in fact,' Caroline confided to Jane. 'As you know, darling Jane, I do not agree with my brother-in-law at all, and as for that truly terrible wife of his – well! It is wonderful to think that they are to be in India for the next four years, and I shall have the company of my dear Laura. I venture to think that it is as pleasant for her as it is for me. She is a charming child – as unlike her parents as one could hope. Oh, that fearful snob of a mother – really, one would think she was a draper's daughter if one did not know differently. Where she produced this lovely child from, I cannot imagine. She herself – well – you remember what she looked like on her wedding day, Jane – a lizard in a creation of satin and laces that looked as if it had been tied round her.'

'Sh, Caro – her daughter may not care to hear her mother so described.'

'Her daughter cannot hear anything but Muna's silver voice. She is completely under the spell. Jane, what is wrong with Muna? She is too thin, and there is something – is she well?'

'She seems well enough, but very tired – the climate out there was trying, I believe.'

'She is still lovely – but what shadowed eyes! Alan kept her too long away from us.'

'Well, now they are back for good. Alan is leaving the army, and will help Robert with the estate, and the home farm. Muna will soon be her old self again and, darling Caro, I hope we will see a great deal of you. We must arrange some splendid parties – I feel like gaiety now that they are back with us.' Jane sounded like a girl, she was so happy. But Caroline, looking at Muna, felt the prick of an anxiety that she did not impart to Jane. Jane was worried enough about Robert's failing health, without having it pointed out to her that her beloved daughter-in-law looked far from well.

But Muna laughed at Caroline when they at last had the

opportunity to speak together. 'Dear Aunt Caroline, I am perfectly well. How not? Back here, with my son, and my family? You will see, two months if mother has her way, and I shall be as fat as one of the sacred cows in the temples.'

'I understand from travellers' tales that the sacred cows are frequently skin and bone!'

'Ah yes – poor things, those that wander in the streets, or work in the fields, drawing the plough. But in the Temples – they live better than those that serve the Gods.'

Alan, standing close by, came up, saying, 'Now, Muna – you are not still talking of India, I trust. You must forget all that now. We are safely home at last, and we shall stay. It does no good to dwell on past discomforts; better far to think of the future, do you not agree, Aunt Caroline?'

Caroline, turning to answer him, wondered why he had been in such a hurry to interrupt Muna – as if he was afraid of what she was going to say. She looked at Muna's quiet face, the schooled, controlled expression of one who has learned to hide her feelings, and remembered the girl with the wicked laughing eyes, who had danced to annoy and enchant her young husband. Involuntarily she looked over to the french windows, open to the summer night – and Muna followed her eyes, and smiled, and said quietly, 'Time passes, and brings wisdom.'

'Ah, Muna – not too much wisdom, I hope. I trust you have not forgotten your beautiful dancing.'

Muna's face contracted, and a terrible expression of fear showed in her eyes. Caroline could not know that she was recalling the last time she had danced, in the little room overlooking the sea in Sagpur's Palace, and what had come after. Caroline did not know what she had said to bring that look to Muna's face. But Muna had control of herself very quickly. She laughed and said, 'No – I have not forgotten. But in these clothes! The new fashions are, if anything, more restricting than the old.'

'But you will wear your own dress at home, surely, Muna? I had promised Laura that she would see you in your lovely Indian costumes.'

Muna glanced quickly at Alan, and said, 'Well, it will be as my lord pleases,' and Alan laughed.

'After the dressmaker's bills that I have just paid, I feel perhaps that you should give your new outfits a little use. They are very becoming. Your dress tonight looks well on you my dear.'

Indeed, Muna in cream lace and a pearl collar, a hand-span waist and a bustle that fell into a short train, did look beautiful. But Caroline saw in memory the floating silks, the rich brocade tunics, the soft yet brilliant colours of the muslins, lighter than air, that had drifted round the younger Muna. She looked at Alan and thought he had become, perhaps, a shade pompous, a little tyrannical. With a flash of waspish temper she thought, 'But what a bore the man will be soon!' while Laura said shyly, 'It is a lovely dress, Mrs. Reid, and so fashionable – but I would love to see your Indian dresses.'

'And so you shall, my love. We will come over one morning, very soon, and perhaps Muna will even dance?'

'For you, Aunt Caroline, anything,' said Muna, and Alan turned away, his face full of displeasure.

He heard Caroline Addison say, 'Now Muna, we know each other too well for me to be Aunt any longer. It is bad enough having this child address me as Aunt, thus constantly reminding me of my advanced age. Please call me Caroline, and let me feel that I still have a little youth.'

Alan did not hear Muna's reply, for they were going in to dinner. He took his mother in, Muna went in on his father's arm, and Caroline followed with Rob, her niece on his other side. The seating at the table seemed to please everyone. Rob and Laura did not speak very much, but appeared to be happy. Sir Robert talked to Muna about the new horses, and Jane and Caroline had all the latest happenings to discuss. The table was dressed with stephanotis and cream-coloured roses, roses the colour of Muna's dress, and only a shade paler than her lovely skin. The candlelight glowed and beautified all the women – but Muna needed no gloss from the soft light. Like a lamp herself, she sat, shedding the light of her personality on the whole party, holding Robert entranced, laughing over her wine glass, even catching Rob's attention away from Laura for a moment or two, helping him to relax, so that he turned back to the girl at his side and began to talk to her with ease.

Only Alan felt outside the circle, neglected and lonely. He listened when his mother or Caroline spoke to him, without really hearing anything they said. His eyes were watching his wife on the other side of the table. His wife: suddenly it seemed to him that he was looking at a beautiful stranger, that he did not know her at all. Her experiences in Sagpur had been terrible, but even so, he had not expected her to change so much. She never repulsed him, she was as loving, and as welcoming as always, looking to his comfort, trying to please him in every way; and yet, he felt as he had on the voyage – very far from her, as if she was only with him in the flesh, as if her spirit was somewhere else, listening to other voices, in some other place. His fixed gaze caught Muna's attention. She looked across the table at him – for a moment they gazed at each other, Alan's eyes searching, asking. Muna's eyes were shadowed, he could see no expression in them. But she smiled her lovely, practised smile, and lifted her glass to him – and he raised his in return, and tried to smile, and then Muna turned to answer something his father had said, and Alan was left to talk to Caroline, who was asking him when he would be free of the army, and what his plans were then.

The evening spun itself out – no one wanted it to end. They sat, afterwards, on the terrace, where the garden scents were sweet, their voices going out into the darkness in laughter and talk, until Caroline reluctantly asked what the hour was, and then rose, saying she must take Laura home, for it was after midnight. 'Come Cinderella – or I shall be in disgrace with your parents, if they hear that I am allowing you to stay up so late.'

All three men saw them off. Jane, watching Rob hand Laura into the carriage, said with satisfaction, 'His manners are beautiful,' and Muna laughed, and said, 'How not – with you to train him, and his grandfather's example before him?'

'And, of course, his school –'

'Ah, yes – school, no doubt helped. But his graceful manners come from you, Mother. Mother, I believe he has been worrying you to let him go to Lambagh; pray do not distress yourself about this. You are perfectly right. He must finish his education first. That is seen. But I think, once his schooling is finished, then it will do him no harm to have a period with the Ruler of Lambagh: the State Forces are becoming known. Please take the advice of his grandfather before any decision is reached.'

'Muna, I knew that you would understand. My dearest girl, do you know, he wanted to rush off immediately, as soon as the invitation came – said that he would visit you in Sagpur, and then go straight up to Lambagh, and join the Forces – and he is not yet seventeen. I did not know what to do with him. But now that you and his father are back, he will no doubt steady himself down to work.'

'No doubt –' said Muna, watching her son stand gazing after Lady Addison's carriage as it went round the corner of the drive, and out of sight. 'No doubt at all. I think you will find that Rob will be quite willing to stay here and will work very hard. Do not worry any more.' She thanked her mother-in-law for a delightful evening, kissed her, and was gone up to her room before the men returned. Rob followed her up, and kissing her goodnight, asked if she would be riding in the morning. His father coming in, vetoed this suggestion before Muna could reply. 'Tomorrow your mother rests. After such a late night she will need her sleep. Now off you go, Rob – your mother is exhausted.'

Rob was going at once, his brow clouded, but Muna pulled him back for another embrace, and close to his ear whispered, 'Like honey, like jasmine and roses, she is sweet –' and laughed into his eyes; and he blushed and smiled, and kissed her again, and went off happy.

Alan said, with dissatisfaction, 'It is time you stopped speaking Urdu to that boy – and also, it is obvious to me that you are going to ruin him.'

'Boy? Alan, in my country he is already a man.'

'And that is another thing, Muna, I wish you to stop this constant reference to "*My* country". India is *not* your home, this is your home, and this is your country – forever. Do you understand? We do not want all that old trouble starting again.'

'Old trouble?'

'Yes – all that nonsense about colour, and heaven knows what. It will only harm the boy. So no more about India, please. Do you understand?'

Alan spoke sharply, and with temper. Muna did not reply. She bowed her head, and began to remove her earrings, and her pearl collar, and then, lacking a maid's assistance, for she had sent Daisy off to bed because it was so late, she began the tedious process of unhooking and unlacing, and removing her clothing, and Alan, coming back from his dressing-room, made no effort to assist her, but lay in bed, with his eyes shut, looking remarkably sulky. So lying, he fell asleep, and much later, in the small cold hours of the morning, woke and found himself alone in the big bed. The memory of his speech to Muna, and of his subsequent churlish behaviour rushed into his mind. He started up, and in the dim light from the open window, saw her sitting, wrapped in a loose robe, her gaze on the night sky, and the quiet stars.

Alan got up and knelt beside her, and after a minute, when she did not look at him, he spoke, 'Muna – can you forgive me?'

She answered, her eyes still on the sky, 'I can. But I do not understand.'

'Muna, you have taken yourself away from me. I was angry and hurt because of this.'

'Why? I am here, and as far as I can see, I am as close to you as I have ever been.'

'That is not so. I feel – I feel that you are far away, gone from here, living in another country –'

'How can that be? I cannot be homesick, for this is my country – forever. You told me so, if you recall.'

'I did. I apologise for the manner in which I said it. But Muna – indeed, you cannot be homesick for Sagpur!'

'No? And yet you told me, when I first went there, that I was so fortunate to be back in my own country. Where is my home, Alan?'

'Surely, where your family is? Do you not feel you are at home here?'

'I expect I am. Sometimes it seems so. But home does not have chains, Alan. It is not a prison. One's thoughts must be free. You would, if you could, wipe all my memories away, both the good and the bad, thus taking from me everything that I am. What would you have left, do you think? Nothing but a body – and you complain that I am only that now. What do you want of me, Alan?'

'I want you to be happy and at home, and to love me.'

'Happiness – Home – Love –' The words ended in a broken whisper. Muna turned to look down at Alan. 'Alan, do you know what love is? I think you cannot answer my question, because you do not know the answer yourself – or you do know the answer, but have never been able to give it –'

But Alan could stand no more. He took her into his arms, and back to their bed, and did not feel the tears that ran down the face he kissed, for he was lost in the only kind of love that he could understand.

32

Muna did not ride the next morning. She had a late breakfast, and afterwards strolled with her father-in-law down the sun-dappled pathways between the last of the summer roses. She spoke of Rob, and his future, and Robert listened to her quietly, and when she had finished, and was waiting for his answers to her questions and suggestions, he stopped beside a rose bush, still laden with blooms, and taking out his pocket knife, cut a perfect bud, creamy white in its green calyx, and heavy with perfume.

'There, my dear – I have longed for the time when I could see you among my roses again. Hold that in your hand, and it will open in that gentle warmth. Now – you want to hear what I think about Rob's future? Well, I agree with all you have said. Rob is a soldier in his heart, already, and I do not think that a sojourn in a university will be of any help to him. He has not got an academic brain. Next year he will be seventeen, and in my opinion he should then go to Lambagh. But I suggest that he only goes there for a year, and then returns here and does a period of training in the Military Academy. If this is put to his father, I think it will help to persuade him to allow Rob to go. And the Ruler himself should approve of this too. After all, not only was the Ruler born in England, but he did all his schooling here. What do you think of that suggestion, my dear?'

'As always, Father, you are wise – and I think that plan is good.'

'The hardest part of this is going to be persuading Alan to agree to any of it.'

'Yes. I know. I was – I *am* trusting you to do that. In fact, when the time comes, I do not think that you will find it too hard to persuade Alan to let Rob go, Father.' Muna spoke quietly, looking down at the rose in her hand.

'What do you mean, *I* will have no difficulty? My dear girl, you are not going to leave it all to me? I shall need your gentle persuasion as well!'

'Oh, you will have it, Father, I promise you that. Very strong persuasion.' Something in her voice made Robert turn to her attentively, but before he could say anything, she took his pocket knife from him and, cutting a small crimson rose, placed it in his button-hole, smiling up into his eyes as she patted the flower into place.

'Ah, Muna, what a charmer you are. I can see you when you are an old lady, still as lovely as an evening star – that is, I could, if it were not ridiculous to think of age in connection with you. You have another favour to ask, I know it. I grant it to you now, before I even hear the request.'

'Father, *what* a dangerous thing to do! But I do have a favour. I need your advice. Father, you know that I have very much money – not only in jewels and gold, but also in property?'

'Yes, my dear, I know.'

'You know also where it comes from – how I earned it?'

'Yes, Muna.'

'And you do not mind?'

'Muna, you ask very strange questions. Your money, and the life you lived while you earned that money, are not my business, except that they are part of your life. I only know you as you are – the wife of my son, the mother of my grandson, and a most beloved member of my family. Need I say more? Muna, do not weep. Come, sit here with me on this seat, and look over the park, and smell the rose in your hand. Rest your heart and your mind for a little while. Then tell me what you want me to do for you.'

They sat in silence together, and then Muna, her eyes dried

372

of their sudden tears, gave him a grateful glance.

'I need your help. I wish to make a will, and I have to be sure it will be honoured. In my country – I mean, in India – I would tell my oldest male relative, and my wishes would be carried out. But here in England, how is it done?'

'I shall have to find out about that, Muna. But I can promise you that any will you make will be honoured. You cannot suppose that Alan would not accede to your wishes? He is an honourable man, and in any case, he will be rich enough in his own right to have no need to interfere with the disposition of your wealth. In heaven's name, Muna, on a beautiful morning like this, why are we speaking of wills? I shall be sleeping in the churchyard long before your will is read!'

Muna's brows contracted, and then smoothed again as she smiled. 'Never mind speaking of this time or that time. I like to know that all is in order – for my desire is one that will seem very strange. I want everything I possess to be left to my first granddaughter.'

'Your first granddaughter – Muna, what on earth?'

'Yes, I know. I told you it would seem strange to you but it is my firm wish. Everything I possess is to go to Rob's first daughter. Rob's son will have no need of money, there is much for him to inherit. But my granddaughter could be a free and happy woman with the aid of my riches. If he does not have a daughter, then it is all to be made over to the family of Lambagh, and they may do as they wish. They have no more need of my wealth than you do, but if I am unlucky enough never to have a granddaughter, that is where my property is to go. It is understood? I will make a writing, if at some time you could take me to a man of the law – yes?'

'Yes, my dearest Muna. I will take you to a man of the law. You will probably cause his death from shock, but nevertheless, I will take you to him. Have you thought of what will happen if Rob has several daughters? Think of the resulting strife! Still, I daresay his inheritance from our side of the family will assist. For heaven's sake, let us now speak of other things – let us go and see the horses, and forget wills, and all other depressing things.' But before they turned to go to the stables, he felt

Muna looking at him, and met her grave eyes, and nodded to her. 'Do not be afraid, Muna. All will be arranged as you wish.' He saw her smile with such radiance as he spoke that it was as if he had given her a rich and longed-for gift. He shook his head in bewilderment, tucked her hand under his arm, and they went together into the stableyard.

Robert said nothing of his conversation with Muna to Jane. He worried about it himself, was distressed by the implications of her remarks about disposing of her property, but saw no reason for telling Jane something that he knew would frighten and worry her very much. He tried to comfort himself by remembering that she had just returned from a long stay in a very trying climate, and that during her years in India she had been under great strain, and had also been ill. Surely this was enough to depress her, and to turn her mind to the uncertainty of life. However hard he tried, he still worried, and finally talked to Caroline Addison, knowing her for a woman of good hard sense. He came away from his talk with her a little soothed – and when, on a suitable day, he took Muna on what was ostensibly a pleasure trip in a new phaeton he had lately bought, they called and collected Caroline, before going on to the real reason for the journey – a visit to the family solicitors. There, the will was duly written, witnessed, and signed – and when they came out of the musty, dust-smelling office, with its rows of leather boxes which, each embossed with a name, reminded Robert unpleasantly of coffins, he was delighted to fall in with Caroline's suggestion that they should stay and drink a glass of champagne with her, before they went home.

Sitting in the green shade of Caroline's lawn beneath her rose arbour, with Laura leaning forward to listen to every word Muna said, her eyes bright with interest, he saw his relief at an unpleasant task finished mirrored on Muna's face, and was content. Caroline was remarkably quiet for her, watching Muna and Laura together, twirling the stem of her glass between her fingers, and finally drawing Robert to one side to speak to him on the pretext of arranging for Murphy to come and advise her own gardener on the trimming of the arbour.

374

When they had got out of earshot, Caroline said, 'Robert, I am worried about Muna. I have been ever since she returned. She has a look – Robert, she appears very frail. Can you, without alarming Jane, suggest that she insists on extra nourishment, and extra rest? Alan should do it, but he has not your tact; he will frighten poor Jane out of her wits.' Robert said he too was worried, as she knew, and he would do his best.

But Muna, from that day on, seemed better, both in spirits and in health. She appeared to have begun to put on a little weight, and she started her morning rides again, sometimes alone with Rob, sometimes with Alan and Rob together. But she still did not attempt to ride Chandni, though she spent a great deal of time in the stables, making much of the mare, and Chandni now looked for her coming, and was as quiet as a lamb under her hand.

The summer was over. September brought evening mists, and blowing leaves, making the patterns that Muna remembered on the lawns and paths. Jane had fires lit every evening, in case Muna, so newly returned from the east, should feel the chill of the coming winter. Rob returned reluctantly to school, giving his mother meaning glances as he kissed her a prolonged farewell. If she missed him, she refrained from letting the family know.

Now she frequently rode alone, sometimes riding over to Adcombe Manor, the Addison estate, where Laura would welcome her rapturously. There was much coming and going between the two houses, and Laura had her wish and saw Muna's magnificent robes, and said that beautiful as they all were, she preferred the soft pushmina hill dress, because, 'You look more beautiful dressed in that than you do in anything else, however rich the other clothes are – you do not need anything to make you beautiful.'

Laura flushed crimson as she said this, afraid of ridicule, but no one laughed at her. Caroline said she showed remarkable good sense, because what she said was perfectly true – and Muna took them up to her bedroom to show Laura some of the fabulous jewellery that she so seldom wore. Laura gasped at the blaze of rubies and diamonds and emeralds spread out on the big bed. 'But it is like a queen's jewellery!'

'Some of it was worn by queens: that neck-piece for instance, belonged to the Rani of Suddra, and those earrings were worn by the famous Rani of Jhansi.'

Laura did not like to ask too many questions, though she longed to know how the jewels had come into Muna's hands. She watched Muna putting the things away, pushing them into a big chest as if they were so many beads. The room smelt faintly and pleasantly of sandalwood. Looking round her, as Muna and Jane and Caroline talked, Laura saw the little lamp that burned before the image in the corner of the room, and saw flowers on the stone. Shocked in spite of herself, she turned away, and later, driving back, she was full of questions.

'Is – is Mrs. Reid a Christian, Aunt Caro?'

'I think not, my dear. She has her own religion. Are you going to tell me that you like her less because she worships God in another way?'

'No – oh no! I love her. But it must be difficult for Rob?'

'Why? I see no reason. She has not interfered with his religion in any way. Rob is certainly a Christian, by both training, and baptism. *I* am his Godmother.'

'Oh – I did not know.' Laura settled back into her seat, looking happier. Caroline watched her face.

'Does it matter so much to you, Laura?'

'What, Aunt Caro?'

'That Rob should be a Christian?'

The girl flushed to the roots of her hair. 'No – no not really. It is just – I *like* them all so much, and Rob's mother is so wonderful – such a magical person – but it was that stone *thing* in the corner of her room. It was rather a shock. It was such a *horrid* thing. So old, and somehow malevolent.'

'But if Muna was a Catholic, with a *prie dieu* and a figure of the Virgin Mary with a lamp burning before it, that would have been all right?'

'Oh yes – well, after all, that is different – isn't it?' asked Laura, suddenly uncertain.

'I am sure I do not know, my dear. We all have our own beliefs, and for myself, I do not think that anyone is entitled to interfere with another person's worship, or faith.'

'But – but they send missionaries to India, and China, and Africa. You remember Aunt Adelaide? She went out to India as a missionary.'

'Your Aunt Adelaide went out to India as a missionary because she could not stand living with your Grandmother Addison any longer, and that is the truth. She came back swiftly enough when she met and married that young chaplain – though what on earth she saw in him, I could never discover.' Come, Laura, stop worrying your head about Muna's beliefs, she is what she is – Muna. It seems impossible to call her anything else. To call such an exotic "Mrs. Reid" seems impossible to me. You love and admire her, I can see that. Do not think of anything else.' She took the girl's hand, and Laura leaned against her shoulder with a sigh of content.

Looking down at the dark head resting so confidingly against her arm, Caroline wondered ruefully what her sister-in-law would have said to the conversation. She had this child for four years – would it be enough time in which to bring her up as a human being, teach her to go entirely against everything her mother thought right? Time enough to give her courage, and the ability to live life fully, and not throw her years away on some loveless marriage, suitable in every word but the way that mattered – the meeting of mind and body, instead of a young spirit sold to the highest bidder? Caroline was not even very sure that it would be either right or kind. The girl was speaking, quietly, dreamily – speaking of Rob.

'He rides so well, Aunt Caro – as if he and the horse had an understanding. He seems to love all animals – not a bit like the Warren boys, who want to do nothing but hunt and shoot.'

'Are you falling in love with Rob, Laura?'

Laura flushed, a splendid, ripe crimson flowed up from her neck to her forehead. She looked away, and Caroline put her arm round her.

'What a wonderful sight – a blush like a crimson rose! My dearest child, never be ashamed of love. Be proud to be able to feel so much. And Laura – ' The girl turned back to face her, and under that clear expectant gaze, Caroline's words died away. She had been about to say, 'This is your first love – there will be many more – ' but to that gaze, so straight, so happy, she could not say anything. She smiled instead, and drew the girl closer. 'We will have to buy you some pretty dresses, my love. You are growing out of everything, and there are bound to be parties. Oh, not grown-up parties – but still, clothes will be necessary.'

She was rewarded by a smile of such happiness that she felt her eyes stinging. Memories of her own youth sprang to her mind, remembrance of the days when she too had felt that unalloyed joy, and that complete trust in the future. 'Oh, Laura, Laura, how can I take that look from your eyes? Time will do it soon enough,' she thought sadly.

The carriage slowed for the turn into her drive; they were home, and Caroline put her thoughts away, unwilling to face them. In her heart she knew that by allowing Laura freedom, both of thought and of movement, she would be laying up unhappiness for the girl in the future – and yet, it was not in her nature to fetter a young and ardent spirit. She had seen the girl turn from a subdued and withdrawn child into what she was now: a girl beginning to enjoy her life as she should, making her own decisions, forming opinions, finding laughter and beauty in life. But Caroline remembered the narrow, tight mouth of her sister-in-law, speaking to her of Laura's future. A finishing school in Switzerland, and then a great marriage – and she recalled her brother-in-law's only remark about his child: 'Well – she's not a son, which I needed, so she will have to marry well, and get me a suitable heir that way.' As if Laura was some animal to be mated for breeding.

If only Laura could have been born to her! Be her own dear daughter! Well – Caroline swallowed a bitter sigh. These next four years were a gift. Caroline put all doubts away. She would use them to give Laura the strength and courage she was going to need to face her life.

33

Autumn passed in a blaze of glory, the coloured leaves that matched the first bonfires in the garden fell, and were swept away. The roses were almost over. Muna rode alone now, and one morning, very much against Bates's wishes, she took out Chandni. Bates spent a terrible hour, and was about to take out a horse and go after her when she came back, glowing, full of praise for the mare. Thereafter she exercised Chandni every day, and was soon riding as she had been used to in the old days before she went back to India. Jane went out to see her return one morning, and watched her leap a fence and a hedge, and then read her a lecture that lasted all through breakfast. But later she admitted to Robert that it was good to have the old Muna back, to see her putting on a little flesh, to see the drawn look leave her face, and hear her laughing again.

When Caroline came over to ask if Laura could ride sometimes with Muna, Jane was delighted. 'But how excellent – that will force Muna to be careful, for the child cannot ride as Muna does, and she will slow down herself, in order not to let Laura come to harm.'

But this was not what happened. Laura come over every morning, rising before sun-up in order to be at Moxton Park at sunrise, which was when Muna liked to start out. They rode in the meadow near Ballnet Woods, and Muna taught Laura all that she knew herself about riding – and there was very little that Muna did not know. She broke Laura of many bad habits. Laura had good hands and a natural seat. Soon she was riding with as much pleasure and abandon as Muna, though Muna was careful and did not allow her any foolishness. Caroline came over one day towards the end of the second month, to take breakfast with the family and fetch Laura, and stood on the terrace laughing, while Jane, aghast, said, 'Oh *no* – !' and Muna and Laura, their animals taking the hedge as if they were birds flying over, came up, flushed and laughing, and delighted with themselves, Muna looking as young as her pupil. Jane looked at Caroline – after all, Laura was Caroline's responsibility, and all that lady said was, 'Bravo – that was magnificent. It was worth coming out at this horrible hour just to see that.'

Jane frowned at Muna, and Muna, dismounting, came up the steps and said, 'Do not be angered with me, Mother. We took no risks, I promise you,' speaking like a coaxing girl, so that Jane could not hold her displeasure, but was forced to laugh and accept Muna's kiss of peace.

However, she spoke later to Alan, and thereafter he rode with his wife and Laura as often as he could, and the rides became more sedate. Laura practised at home, in a field behind the stables in Adcombe Manor, and Caroline did not discourage her, until she found her niece riding astride bareback, in an old pair of breeches borrowed from a stable boy who had been making big eyes at Laura for some time. Riding thus Caroline, her eyes snapping, forbade, and Laura, never having seen her Aunt angry before, was horrified.

'I'm sorry, Aunt Caro – terribly sorry! I did not mean to annoy you. Muna rides astride very often, wearing her own hill dress, and I wanted to see if I could too. *She* says it is much safer – you fall more frequently, perhaps, but the falls are not so dangerous as they are when you are riding side-saddle.'

'That may be. What Muna does is her own business. I am certainly not criticising her way of riding. I am telling you that you will *not* ride astride – and certainly you will *never* borrow Jack's breeches again.

Laura was suitably contrite. In the privacy of her own room, Caroline laughed herself into hiccoughs, and decided that the stableboy, Jack, suffering from a dreadful attack of calf love, would have to be sent up to her house in the north until he had recovered. As for Laura, she decided that she had probably frightened her into taking care not to ride astride again. At her age – Caroline's mind ran on various medical facts she had gleaned during the years, and the next time she was alone with Muna, she spoke of the episode to her and, without mincing her words, of her reasons for not wishing Laura to ride astride, and bareback. Muna sat listening to her with interest, one of the last of the autumn roses twirling in her fingers. 'So – this is very interesting. Do you also display the sheets in England?'

'The sheets?'

'Yes – the sheets from the marriage bed, to prove that the girl was virgin.'

'Great God,' said Caroline, startled into profanity. 'Certainly not! But nonetheless – ' she paused, uncomfortably aware that Muna was laughing at her.

'Ah, Caroline, do not distress yourself. I know the importance of virginity for a girl who is marriageable! But I do not altogether believe that the hymen is punctured so easily, just by riding. However, I will ensure, without saying anything that could alarm Laura, that she will ride as she should. But I will never understand the terrible ignorance in which you keep your young girls. We train our girls for marriage, from the time they can walk – and they know everything that is necessary for their husband's happiness and their own, before marriage. The English habit of keeping all hidden until the moment of bedding the couple is to me a terrible thing – one imagines that a girl could be frightened into total frigidity for the rest of her life. Is this what an Englishman desires from his wife?'

Caroline shook her head. 'Muna, I beg of you, do not speak like this to your mother-in-law – she would be so shocked.'

'You are wrong, Caroline. We have often spoken of these things. She thinks that it is cruel to keep a girl in ignorance, and she speaks of her good fortune in having married a man who was kind and loving.'

'Good heavens – what wonders you have worked! I have never discussed this with dear Jane. But she is right. On the marriage night is not the best time to discover – '

'That we are also animals as well as spirits? No. Not the best time. It would be better to know that the spirit and the flesh can meet and be something greater than one ever dreamed – *that* is how it should be.'

'Muna – like Sheba, you have wisdom and beauty.'

'Sheba? Who is this Sheba?'

'She was a queen – you can read about her in the Bible.'

But Jane came in then, followed by Daisy with the coffee pot, and the conversation changed.

A week or two later, one of the Moxton Park grooms rode over with a note, inviting Caroline and her niece to a small party. The invitation was received with rapture by Laura.

'Look, Aunt Caro – a dance! A real dance!'

'What your parents would say to me, I dread to think. You are supposed to be cloistered in the schoolroom with Miss Grey, learning French verbs and conversation, preparatory to going to Geneva to Madame L'Abri's establishment for the daughters of gentlemen. But never mind. What is this entertainment in honour of?' Laura's beautiful blush gave her the answer. 'Oh, of course – how stupid I am. Rob is coming home for his mid-term exeunt. Well, this will have to be known as a children's party – and kindly do not say anything else when you write to your Mamma, Laura, or she will remove you from my evil influence.'

'Oh I won't say anything – nothing at all! May I put my hair up, Aunt Caro? Dearest Aunt Caro, say yes –'

'Put your hair up at fifteen? My dear child, nothing could be more unsuitable. In any case, your hair is so beautiful you should be glad to wear it down as long as possible. But you shall have a new dress, my love, so stop looking sad. I shall enjoy choosing you a new dress.'

With the promise of a new dress, Laura had to be content – and indeed she was, although in the privacy of her own room, she tried her hair this way and that, coiled high, as Muna sometimes wore hers, and longed for the day when she could put it up, and come out in public as a fully-fledged grown-up young woman.

On the great day, the carriage was ordered for seven.

Caroline was *en grande tenue*. She still wore black, but covered her frock with a great cape of sables, and with diamonds in her ears and at her throat, and her white hair dressed high, she was very elegant. Caroline had never been a beauty, but she had an attraction that enabled her to give the impression of beauty, and that had outlasted the years. Her niece thought she looked lovely, and told her so, and Caroline laughed gently, and thanked her.

'Never forget, my child – not that you will need to remember – but furs, scent, and diamonds will help the plainest woman to deceive most people into imagining they look at beauty. But, as I say, you will not have to remember that.' Laura was far too excited to ask her Aunt what she meant – and Caroline smiled to herself; vanity was obviously not one of her niece's faults.

The carriage rolled up to the front of Moxton Park, where Rob waited with his father to welcome them. While his father was greeting Caroline, Rob seized his opportunity, and whispered to Laura, 'I ask for the first dance Laura – and the supper dance – and the last dance. And as many of the other dances as I can have – ' and then turned back to let Alan lead Caroline in, following with Laura.

At the back of the house, beyond the bricked path that led from the stables, there was a great bonfire. It was growing dark, and the young people, sons and daughters of the Reids' friends, boys and girls who had known Rob most of his life, still in their cloaks and capes, congregated round the flames, and presently their elders came out to watch also. Chairs and cushions were then brought out. Rob took his mother's arm as soon as she appeared, and took her over to a pile of cushions, and she sank down amongst them with boneless grace, and thanking him, said, 'Off you go, Rob, and enjoy yourself. This is your evening, so make every minute of it perfection.'

'But I have barely spoken with you, Mother – '

'No – but what need for speech? Do we need so much speech, my son?'

'I wanted to say thank you.'

'Thanks – between us?'

383

'For a great gift. My grandfather told me how you spoke to him of Lambagh – and that you and he together will persuade my father.'

'That is nothing but what I should do for my son. But Rob – do not speak with your father yet. This is not the time. Enjoy yourself tonight, I wish to see you very happy.'

'I am happy. To have you here, and to have found – '

'I know what you would say, my son. You do not have to tell me. Go. She is looking round for you, the flower-face.'

'You like her, Mother?'

'I love her, Rob. I am glad to have met her. But you have a long road ahead of you, and not all of it easy, I think.'

'Well, Aunt Caro likes me – and with you to help me when the time comes, perhaps her parents will not be too difficult. If only we were not so young!'

'Rob! Never say that! Do not wish your life away. Live every second of it. Life is a gift from the Gods.'

'But I have to wait so long! In our country, Mother, we would be married.'

'Rob, do not say that in front of your father! Laura is English, and I think you had better remember that you are also. Go now Rob. You are wasting precious time.' Rob glanced over his shoulder to where Laura stood, and went without another word.

Muna sat in a pool of radiance. The flames of the bonfire caught sparks from her rings and the jewels in her ears. She sat, smiling, her face serene, but she was afraid. The flames and the crackling branches brought her no pleasure. She felt utterly alone and bereft. The sound of the burning branches and the sight of the leaping flames caught her out of her surroundings, and the noise that she heard was not only the dry tinder catching fire, it was the beginning of the breaking of her dream. The dream she had lived in, the protective bubble that had held her away from the realities of her strange life, was cracking at last. The ground under her seemed to shift and change – no longer thick turf, but rocks and the tough grass of another country. The wind that moved in her furs and whispered in her ears blew from the lake – but not the quiet lake of

Moxton Park. The wind was fresh, and tasted of snow. The colours of the bonfire, the voices and the laughter round her, blurred and were gone. Muna sat on the edge of the lake in Lambagh, and saw the ridges of snow-capped mountains in the distance, and the only sound that she heard was the voice of the wind that came from the mountains to clear the clouds from the moon, and rustle among the pine trees that grew down to the edge of that remembered water.

Alan's hand on her arm brought her back with a start, to the present.

'Muna! What dream do you see in the fire? We are going in now, before we all get chilled. You will want to re-arrange your hair and your dress, no doubt, before going in to start the evening.'

Muna, looking about her, saw Rob standing, leaning on a long rake, gazing into the flames. Laura must have already gone in to the house, for he was alone. He looked like some splendid young warrior standing guard over the pyre of a great prince. Indeed, it was like a pyre, this great leaping fire – the burning of the body of summer, summer dead and gone for another year.

Muna took Alan's outstretched hand and rose, and went into the bright lights and the laughter and happiness of the warm house. Her inward eyes were still full of the stars and snows of a distant beloved place. The dream was going, but like all dreams, fragments lingered, like the twists of smoke outside in the late autumn evening. Muna went upstairs, removed her furs, allowed Daisy to re-coil her hair, and went down to her family and friends below.

Laura had been upstairs too, had gazed trembling with excitement at her image in the mirror in Jane's bedroom, while Daisy and Jane's maid had twitched and patted her hair into place, and had brushed her hair. Her dress was a poem of white muslin and lace, perfect in its simplicity. Caroline did not approve of jewellery on the very young, so Laura's pretty throat was encircled with a thin, black velvet ribbon, and her hair, brushed and smoothed, fell below her waist, thick and shining like heavy silk. With a last look into the mirror she went downstairs, while the two women who had been attending to her, watched her go, and whispered together. Laura had caught beauty for this one night – no longer the promise of what was to come, but the glory itself, fugitive perhaps, but there to be seen. Like the young moon she stood, looking through the open door at the people gathered in the room – all known to her, all her friends, and yet, as she paused, they turned and stared as if she was a stranger. She was immediately too shy to go in, and half turned away to leave, and then Jane hurried forward.

'Why Laura! My *dear* child, you are in such looks that we did not see who you were. Come in, there are no strangers here, no one to fear! You look as if you are confronting a lion!'

'And so she is,' said her Aunt, coming up. 'The lion of the public eye; something she will have to face all her life. But not yet. As your Aunt Jane says, my darling child, you are among friends, or you would not be here at all at your age. What your mother would say, could she see you –'

But Rob had come up, asking if he could take Laura over to his mother, who wanted to speak to her. Laura moved forward into the room with Rob beside her, and Caroline, watching her go, thought she looked beautiful indeed.

'She is going to be a beauty – a great beauty –'

'Yes, my dear Caro – and as you once said of Muna, she is going to be a great nuisance too. Do you recall? The first time you saw Muna you said that.'

'Indeed I do. But this one will never have that incredible heart-stopping beauty that Muna had – and still has. Muna belongs amongst the beauties of history. Laura – well, she will be a beauty of her time, which is bad enough. Look at her sailing over the floor like a newly-launched ship, with no more idea of the voyage on which she is bound than the ship itself has. Well. I have four years – let me make what I can of her, so that she may find her way through life with the minimum of trouble. She will get no help from that truly fearful mother of hers, I can tell you *that*. All her mother can think of for her is a title, and money – and never mind what goes with it.'

'Well –' said Jane, with a significant glance. Laura was sitting, laughing, beside Muna. At her side stood Rob, his face telling stories that were plain to read.

Caroline looked, and nodded, and said sadly, 'Yes – and oh Jane! What trouble lies ahead. You must realise that?'

Jane was at first inclined to look affronted. Then, under Caroline's steady gaze, she said slowly, but with determination, 'Well – the money and the title, you said – and never mind anything else. So? She can have little enough to say against what is obviously going to be offered. There is plenty of money, since we must be common and speak of that. And she can scarcely turn up her nose at a title as old as ours – that lizard!'

'*Jane!* And you scolded me the last time I said that!'

'*Well* – ' said Jane, and met her old friend's eyes defiantly, and both ladies laughed suddenly.

That laughter, full of genuine, understanding mirth, set the tone for the whole evening. It was a magic evening for both the young people, and their elders. Jane had used a drawing-room that opened into her conservatory, and also on to the terrace. The walls of the room were banked with flowers and potted plants, and the musicians, a pianist and two violins, played their instruments on a balcony above, so that the music sounded soft and muted, like music from another age. The floor was never empty when the dances were played. Jane danced with her husband, and her son, and her grandson, light-footed as a girl. Caroline led the quadrille in style with Robert. Muna, waltzing once with her son, surprised him.

'Mother! You dance like an angel – I did not know that you danced.'

'You did not know that I danced! Come, Rob, let us not be stupid!'

'No, Mother, I know you dance – but not this kind of dancing.'

'You mean that you thought I could only be a dancing girl – ' For a moment Muna, in the midst of the whirling figures round her, struck the dancing girl's pose, her hip rounded out, her head shifting like a pendulum on her neck, her hands posturing. Rob gasped, and caught her back into the waltz. 'Mother! If my father saw!'

'How do you know that he does not like me to dance?'

'I do not know anything. It is just that somehow, these days, the very mention of India seems to annoy him – and it is important not to make him angry just now.'

'I know. You do not want him annoyed because you hope to charm him into letting you go next year. Rob, are you sure you still want to go?'

Rob's eyes turned to where Laura, a white swan, drifted over the floor. 'It will be very hard – but I know that I must go.'

Muna tightened her hand on his. 'You are right, my son. And for your comfort, I will tell you something. She will wait for you.'

'You think – ?'

'I know. Rob – remember this, when things become difficult for you. There is your girl. She will wait. You are fortunate – you have found your heart's desire together. Nothing will part you. Remember that.'

'Oh Mother – if that is true! But you speak to me as if you were never going to discuss this matter with me again – which is not so. I have so much I want to ask you. There is not enough time now, but when I come back next holidays –'

Muna did not reply. The room had gone dark around her, it was as if she had become translated into some other place, where there were no lights or music, only silence and a chill wind. Rob noticed nothing. He whirled her round in a final circle, and then led her back to her seat beside a great bowl of Murphy's precious hothouse roses. 'There, Mother. You sit among flowers as you always should. It is the supper dance next, and I am taking Laura in – will you forgive me if I leave you?'

Muna, from the darkness in which her spirit groped, found words to send him away, smiling. Then, very shortly, Alan came to claim her for the supper dance – and she was back in the land of voices and music and laughter. Like someone returning from a long journey to find loved friends, she became one of the happiest people in the room, her eyes outshining the candles, her beauty catching fire so that she looked as young as when Alan had first seen her. Everyone remarked on her looks, and Alan was proud, and whispered to her as he used to when they were first together, saying that he wished the evening would end so that they could be alone. Muna laughed at him, and after supper was taken away to dance again, drifting about the floor as if she was made of air.

There was no end to the night; it was impossible to imagine the end of such enjoyment. They were all caught out of themselves, the older people re-living their youth as if it had never passed. Robert and Jane moved in as much of a dream as did Rob and Laura. The years since Jane's girlhood, and all her tragedies were forgotten. She danced, laughed and sat close with the man she had loved from the first moment they had met. Caroline sat, watching – her memories appeared to have no gall in them, she was as quietly amused by her surroundings as she had always been. Muna and Alan danced and talked together, Alan looking and speaking to his wife as if she was the first girl he had ever met. The whole company were full of enjoyment. But the light of the evening shone from the two youngest people there – Rob and Laura moved within their own flame like young phoenixes, renewing their pleasure every time they looked at each other.

There was a lull in the dancing while the musicians refreshed themselves. Jane and Robert, seeing Caroline sitting alone, went over and joined her. Together, they watched Rob and Laura – and smiled and sighed as they watched.

'They will possibly grow out of it?' Jane did not sound very sure as she spoke.

Robert said quietly, 'Jane – how old were you when we met?'

Jane's soft eyes smiled. 'I was fifteen –'

'And did you grow out of it?'

'Oh, Robert – how can you ask?'

Caroline laughed. 'Dearest Jane – then why should you suppose that Rob and Laura are any less smitten? In fact, I think Laura does not yet know – her happiness is untouched by any thought deeper than the fact that she enjoys Rob's company. But Rob – Rob, I think, is stricken –'

'Yes,' said Robert. 'It was the same with us. I was stricken at sight. Jane – well, Jane, you were very young –'

'Robert, you know that I fell in love with you at once.'

'No, my love – not at once. But in the end, thank God, you did – and I have been the happiest of men ever since. Now Jane, for heaven's sake, no tears. Come, we are selfish, we speak only of ourselves. Caro, you must have many memories.'

Caroline's laughing eyes did not change. 'Yes – many. I cannot match your tales of instant love and constant romance. My dear old Harry – well, we got along famously; if there were no heights, well, there were no depths either. We had friendship and laughter – when I could get him to see the joke. Usually he laughed with me, but some of the things I laughed at he was inclined to disapprove. But it was a good marriage, and I miss him.'

'Ah – but wait Caroline. I remember that summer – it must have been about two years before you met Harry. *What* was that young man's name Caro, the one that went out to the Crimea and got himself killed? He was made for you, and I seem to remember –'

'Well, my dear Jane, that was a great many years ago. Enough of memories. Let us watch the young, and drink a toast to their future, because it is their world now.'

Muna and Alan had joined them, and the five sat together, with Muna bringing her own form of lightness and gaiety to their company. Robert was glad of her brilliant wit and her kind laughter. For a moment he had seen pain on Caroline's face. His dearest Jane was so secure in her own happiness that she did not always see that there were hidden places in other people's lives, places where it did not do to probe.

It was the last dance. Everyone took the floor, and as if held by some enchantment, no one spoke. They circled the floor in silence, while the music fell in gentle cadences, as if mourning the end of a perfect evening. As the last notes died into silence, Rob whirled Laura out through the open door, and on to the terrace.

Dawn was close. Under the paling stars, the whole world seemed clear and refreshed. The sweet air of early morning, mild as spring, moved about them as they stood, looking down into the garden only half seen in the dim light. Behind them, one of the musicians, putting his violin away, first played a few bars, gentle, nostalgic.

'Oh, what a beautiful finish to a lovely evening!'

Laura laughed and sighed together, putting up her hands to lift her heavy hair from her neck. The boy beside her stirred, moved closer, but did not speak. She sighed again, with contentment.

'It was *perfect*. I am so grateful to my Aunt for letting me stay for the whole night. My mother would never have said yes. Rob! You say nothing! Did you not enjoy our dances?' She turned to look into the face so close to hers, and as she turned, Rob bent his head and easily, gently, kissed her. The kiss on her mouth was as light as a sigh – but she gasped and drew back, feeling, in spite of her youth, the power of his controlled passion.

'Rob – ?' It was as if she asked for reassurance that it was he, and not a stranger – and he answered at once.

'Yes. I am here. And it was a perfect evening – one I shall never forget. There is something that I want you to remember, Laura. Are you listening?'

'Yes.' Her voice was a whisper.

'Remember this. I love you with all that I am, and I always will. Go home, now Laura – they will be calling for you in a moment. But remember what I said. I shall come later, this morning, and perhaps we will ride together. Good-night, my dear love – '

She heard her Aunt call her from within. The light was strengthening round them. A moment longer she stood there, looking at him, and then, leaving him in the dimness of the terrace, she walked into the ballroom, and was gone from his sight.

34

The beautiful evening was over. The company dispersed, yawning and laughing and reluctant, to their carriages. One by one, the rooms darkened, and the voices died away.

The fire in Muna's bedroom was still burning brightly. Alan, coming in from his dressing room, found her undressing alone.

'Let me be your maid – as so often before, my love – ' He bit his lip remembering an earlier evening, when he had allowed her to struggle out of her clothes alone. But Muna's face, as he looked into it, had not changed. She held no bitter thoughts. His hands shook as he undid the clasp of her necklace, and saw the firelight gleaming on her shoulders and breasts. His voice rough, he said, 'As usual, there was no one in the room to touch my beautiful wife – you stood alone, there is never anyone as beautiful as you.'

The eyes she raised to his were shadowed with fatigue, but she returned his kisses with her usual warmth, and when he said suddenly, 'Dance for me, Muna – here in the firelight? Everyone has seen your beauty tonight – now dance for me alone; it seems a long time since you danced for me,' her hesitation was so slight as to be unnoticeable.

She danced, naked and beautiful, her eyes closed, her expression attentive and distant, as if she was listening to music she could barely hear. She danced the dance of worship, not one of the dances of love – but Alan did not know the difference. Before the dance was finished, her detached expression had made him angry – he took her to bed, and his loving was as burning and consuming as the fire.

The sky was light, and the fire had died when he fell asleep, his last murmuring, 'I love you – you are mine forever – mine – ' sounding like the ashes settling in the grate. Muna lay listening to his deep, peaceful breathing for a little while. Then she slid from under his arm, and put on her velvet robe, pulling it closely round her, for she felt cold. Winter was only a breath away.

She went to the window, hearing a familiar sound, and was in time to see Rob riding off as if pursued by time itself. It was not hard to imagine where he was going. She turned back, and saw Alan sleeping deeply in the tumbled bed. A sudden longing to be out in the air, to feel the power and freedom of movement that riding gave her, seized her, making her forget her aching weariness. She went out quietly and bathed, and dressed in her Lambaghi riding dress she went back to the bedroom lest Alan should have wakened. But he still slept in the quiet room, he did not stir as she came in. She stood for a moment before the image in the corner, saw that the little lamp burned well, and then went out, closing the door behind her.

Quiet as a spirit she went down the stairs. No one moved in the house, she felt that it was full of sleep, busy with dreams. Rob had left the door a little ajar – it opened silently to her touch. She went out into the fresh, stinging air, and round to the stables, where she found a sleepy groom. She asked him to saddle Chandni. 'Not a side-saddle, Jim – you know the saddle I wish.' Chandni had never really grown used to a side-saddle.

Jim was very young, only lately raised to the status of groom, having worked his time as a stable boy while he was trained. He gathered his courage, and said, 'Excuse me, Ma'am – you know you haven't ridden her for three days – and no one else takes her out. She'll likely be very fresh – ' He spoke because Muna looked bone weary, her face drawn, her eyes darkly shaded. But she smiled at him, and told him to bring the mare out.

'Do not worry, Jim. She knows me. We understand each other.'

Jim, seeing there was no help for him, went into Chandni's stable, and presently brought her out, sleek and beautiful, ears twitching forward and back, her head tossing. She whickered gently when she saw Muna, and as Muna came forward, the mare lowered her lovely head to lip Muna's palm, and blew gently into the front of her tunic. Jim was reassured. Chandni did seem to have an understanding with her Mistress; he had never seen her behave so with anyone else. Muna gathered the reins in a capable grip, and mounted before Jim could get round to help her. It was always an amazement to the grooms when Muna rode astride, mounting and riding as easily as a boy. Chandni began to dance, but only for her own amusement. Muna took a firm hold on her, and they left the stable yard at a controlled walk. Once on the grass path leading to the fields, Muna let her go a little, and felt her mettle. She was indeed fresh! Muna set herself to keeping her under control, and soon Chandni was answering to her rider, and Muna could relax. She took the mare over the fields towards Warren Woods, knowing that Rob would take Laura on his favourite ride – the ride to Ballnet Woods – and not wishing to break in on their privacy.

It was easy going, the ride she had chosen. She did not have to worry about Chandni, and could look about her and enjoy her ride. The sky was misty, and here, in the open fields, there was a wind, cold and fresh, tasting of winter. When she entered Warren Woods, though the trees were leafless, it was sheltered and there was no wind, and the mist was lower, clinging about the dark branches. As she rode under the violet-misted branches of these bare, black trees, shadows seemed to gather about her. Chandni pricked her ears, and her stride grew choppy and nervous. But Muna rode on, her face bright, like a girl going to meet her lover. Riding through the wood, in this strange misty light, she felt suddenly that somewhere, round one of these mist-filled corners, someone was waiting for her, and leaned a little forward in her saddle, excited, expectant.

The path was thick with fallen leaves – Chandni's hooves made no sound. As soundless as the mare, ahead of her Muna saw a rider, tall and supple, a horseman on a magnificent horse.

394

She recognised both horse and rider. With a glad cry, she kicked Chandni into a fast canter, but the rider ahead, without increasing his speed, seemed impossible to catch. Now she was galloping, Chandni going like the wind, and as if there was a wind, Muna's long hair escaped from its coils and fell round her shoulders; and still she leaned forward, urging Chandni on – and still the man in front was out of reach.

Then, like a woman waking from a dream at last, Muna knew what it was that she was pursuing. This was her long love, her never to be realised hope. Her dream had broken indeed, her foolish dream that had seemed to have no ending.

Kassim! Never for her. She had always known it, yet never accepted it. Now she took the knowledge into her heart like a knife. There was nothing in front of her – nothing but the shadows of a winter morning, in an English wood. Blinded by tears, Muna reined Chandni in. But Chandni did not wish to stop. She tucked her chin in, ignored Muna's firm hand, and went on.

The lake gleamed ahead, and the low stone wall that straddled the path, the gate closed. In spite of her headlong gallop, Muna was not afraid. She had jumped that gate with Chandni many times. She put her hand up to wipe tears from her eyes, and a rabbit darted from the bracken on one side of the path, and scudded over in front of Chandni, just as they came up to the gate.

Chandni took the jump at an angle, and Muna, unprepared, was thrown. She fell soft, on damp grass, unhurt, and rising on her elbow was kicked on the side of her head by Chandni's nearside hind leg.

The pain was sharp, but gone, it seemed, in a second. Muna barely had time to feel it.

The voice that she had heard so often in her life sounded, for the first time as if the words were being spoken clearly, by another woman, someone kneeling close to her. 'My daughter, hear my words now. There is no bridge which love cannot cross. There is no world in which love cannot live. Love is more powerful than death. See now Muna, how one life leads into another. Know you now, that down the long roads of your lives to come, you will meet your love again, and possess all that you have lost. Sleep, and waken to a new life.'

A kind of still, radiant happiness rose in Muna, a certainty and a knowledge of truth, and love. Now, at last, there were no questions in her mind. She knew the answers to everything. She knew what love was. Muna turned her head, and as if she laid her cheek on a known and well-loved shoulder, she closed her eyes, smiling.

They found her quite soon, because they came searching, and saw Chandni standing with drooping head beside her still figure.

Muna lay as if on her bed. Her face was unmarked, her long hair spread all about her, and her closed eyelids were like violets in the pallor of her face. She still smiled in her quiet sleep, and none of the others realised that she was dead. But Alan, kneeling beside his wife where she lay in her tossed cream robes, knew she had gone.

'Gone where I shall never find her,' he thought, looking at the smile that lay so happily on her lovely mouth. 'She has gone where she longed to be – and I never took the trouble to find out where that was.'

He had never been able to answer her question either. He thought he could hear her voice. 'What is love?' the voice asked, wistfully. Now and forever, he could give Muna no answer. He heard the voice again, but it was only a bird crying, deep in the woods.

They had brought a hurdle, but he waved it away. He took Muna up into his arms, and started the long walk back to his home, where the morning had barely begun.

KATHARINE GORDON

THE EMERALD PEACOCK

The Emerald Peacock is the story of a great and dangerous love between a beautiful Irish girl and an Indian prince. Amidst the turmoil of the Indian mutiny, Sher Kahn – ruler of Lambagh and heir to the Peacock Throne – flees with Bianca O'Neil to his remote hill state.

But as enemies pursue the Emerald Peacock, symbol of Sher Kahn's power, Bianca is caught in a whirlpool of bloodshed and betrayal. Years of sacrifice will pass before she can even glimpse the possibility of lasting happiness.

Post·A·Book

A Royal Mail service in association with the Book Marketing Council & The Booksellers Association.

Post-A-Book is a Post Office trademark.

KATHARINE GORDON

THE PEACOCK RING

THE PEACOCK RING is the story of Robert Reid, son of Muna the temple dancer and Rose of Madore. Devastated by his separation from the woman of his dreams Robert returns to his mother's homeland in the remote state of Lambagh, to claim his birthright and seek out his destiny.

In England, the exquisite Laura also pines for her love and eventually follows him to India where the couple are blissfully reunited. But their happiness is unjustly brief: ruthless enemies surround the rulers of Lambagh, threatening not only their love, but possibly their lives . . .

CORONET BOOKS

KATHARINE GORDON

PEACOCK IN JEOPARDY

PEACOCK IN JEOPARDY tells the story of Sarah, grand-daughter of temple-dancer Muna, who returns to India in 1946 to save her disastrous marriage to Richard Longman. In her plight she captures the hearts of two men, one of whom is the influential Nawab, Sher Khan. He instals her in Ranighar, a beautiful house facing the palace and offers further protection when she and her children must flee from Richard's brutality and sordid political involvement. To her horror, Sarah discovers that her husband is prepared to go to any lengths – even murder – to gain possession of the famous emerald Peacock, the prized symbol of the Rulers of the State of Lambagh . . .

CORONET BOOKS

ALSO AVAILABLE FROM CORONET BOOKS